Savage Girl

Also by Jean Zimmerman

The Orphanmaster

Love, Fiercely: A Gilded Age Romance

The Women of the House: How a Colonial She-Merchant Built
a Mansion, a Fortune, and a Dynasty

Made from Scratch: Reclaiming the Pleasures of the American Hearth

Raising Our Athletic Daughters: How Sports Can Build Self-Esteem
and Save Girls' Lives (with Gil Reavill)

Tailspin: Women at War in the Wake of Tailhook

Jean Zimmerman

Savage Girl

VIKING

VIKING
Published by the Penguin Group
Penguin Group (USA) LLC
375 Hudson Street
New York, New York 10014

USA | Canada | UK | Ireland | Australia | New Zealand | India | South Africa | China
penguin.com
A Penguin Random House Company
First published by Viking Penguin,
a member of Penguin Group (USA) LLC, 2014

LIBRARY OF CONGRESS CATALOGING-IN-PUBLICATION DATA
Zimmerman, Jean.
Savage girl / Jean Zimmerman.
pages cm
ISBN 978-0-670-01485-9
1. Orphans—Fiction. 2. Adoption—Fiction. 3. New York—Fiction. I.Title.
PS3626.I493S29 2013
813'.6—dc23
2013018408
Printed in the United States of America
1   3   5   7   9   10   8   6   4   2

Set in Dante MT Std
Designed by Francesca Belanger

This one is for Betsy Lerner

Sweet as the first wild violet, she,
To her wild self. But what to me?

—Charlotte Mew

Savage Girl

✠ Prologue ✠

Manhattan. May 19, 1876

I wait for the police in the study overlooking Gramercy Park, the body prone on the floor a few feet away. Outside, rain has cooled the green spring evening. In here the heat is stifling.

Midnight. I've been in this room before, many times in the course of my twenty-two years. The Turkish rug on the floor, the Empire chairs, the shelves of uncracked books, all familiar to me. A massive mahogany partners desk, from England, in the William IV style, installed as proof of the late victim's diligence, a rich boy's insistence that he is, after all, engaged in honest work.

Of the dead man, a schoolmate of mine, I feature two possibilities. She killed him, in which case they will surely hang her. Either that or I killed him, in a fit of madness the specifics of which I have no memory.

This last is not as unlikely as it sounds. I have taken the rest cure for neurasthenia several times and every so often suffer faints, waking to find a small swath of my life gone. Peculiarities of the recent past, a series of strange incidents and dark coincidences, force me at least to entertain the idea that I am a monster.

The fact that in recent months I developed a passionate hatred for the dead man increases the possibility of my involvement in his demise.

On the other hand, if she is indeed the murderer, I can prevent her day of reckoning only by taking the burden of guilt upon myself.

So you see, either way, if I must assume her guilt or confess my own, it works out much the same, demanding identical action on my part. My path is clear. I need to be caught red-handed. I have to wait in this room until discovery, alarm, arrest.

I summon up the mental image of a stern-faced detective with a fat, unkempt mustache. *Mr. Hugo Delegate*—for that is my name—*you must accompany us to the Tombs.* Will he place me in restraints? Will it be that bad?

But they will come, rest assured. There are numerous lawmen who would be highly interested in what has occurred on Gramercy Park this evening. From where I sit, I can almost sense them drawing near, having journeyed from all over the country—from Nevada, from Chicago, from Massachusetts and New York—their disparate paths converging at a millionaire's mansion off a private park in Manhattan.

Not only the constabulary either but the gentlemen of the press, rabid dogs all, will no doubt descend upon the scene of the crime. The pack will be in full howl. From my experience, newsmen are even more relentless than police, profit being superior to justice as a great motivator of human beings.

The witness is a participant, or so my mother once told me. I followed the girl murderess here to this house. It is never difficult to track her. She is oddly without guile, so possessed of a naïve faith that no one would suspect her of crime.

I feel . . . what do I feel? Paralyzed. A sense of impending doom hovers over me like psychosis. Another brief shower patters at the windows. I think of the gentle rain that droppeth in Shakespeare.

The body. My longtime acquaintance and sometime friend, Beverly Ralston Willets, twenty-four years old, or perhaps twenty-three—young anyway. His corpse, in a suit of brown serge.

He has been done as the others have been done. A slashing stab to the femoral artery in the groin, meaning exsanguination within two or three minutes. A blood pool the size of a bathtub stains the twill of the carpet. The killer mutilates the corpus after death.

I position myself so I do not have to directly confront the victim. Close up, death has an arrogant smell. Should I dab some of the gore on my hands, stain the seas scarlet, impress the detectives?

There are a couple of jeroboams of blood in the human body. Six quarts, more or less. This I know because in my classes at Harvard I

pursue the study of medicine and practice as an anatomist. I dissect
the dead, who do not bleed.

Could not my anatomical work serve as a reason for the authorities
to suspect me of this killing? As well as for me to suspect myself?

The prosecutor, in court: *Gentlemen of the jury, I submit that Hugo
Delegate is a habitual plunderer of men.*

I am alone. I am already dead. Perhaps she will murder me in this
exact same manner. If not, I'll almost certainly go away to spend the
rest of my life behind bars.

The body emits a horrible, gaseous sigh, startling me out of my
musings.

Cocking my right leg over my left, I sit, waiting for them to come.
On my way here through the city, I got caught in a spring shower. I
occupy my time watching the rain dry on the leather upper of my
boot.

Then, later that night, the Tombs, south two miles from the murder
scene, on Centre Street in Lower Manhattan. The Halls of Justice. The
majority of mortals rightly fear a trip to the prison; it is such a forbidding brick heap, a cold, ugly, heavy-pillared structure as gloomy as its
nickname. Where the city's criminal miscreants (that's me) languish,
and where justice languishes as well.

Not that I know it intimately, but I have been to the Tombs before,
too, a couple of times, as an observer. The law grinds on, night and
day, pulverizing its victims to dust while elevating others, attorneys
and jurists, to heights of wealth and power.

For the Tombs is not just a prison but an all-in-one buttress of justice, with busy courts, jury rooms, clerkdoms, offices for judges and
prosecutors, smoky hallways, and deal-making alcoves. A palace of
diligence or, if you happen to be wearing police bracelets, a hive of
evil.

The building rests upon the site of a former swamp, and it began
sinking into the ground immediately upon being erected. Vapors rise
continually from its foundations, resembling the fingers of demons,

pulling all occupants, willing or not, toward the stinking pits of Lake Avernus.

As I did in the little Gramercy Park study, I wait, having been brought here, yes, in bracelets.

I delight to imagine my lawyers, William Howe and Abraham Hummel, two lords of the Tombs, hurrying to my prison lair.

In the still of the night! At four A.M., the deserted hour, the hour that no one wants!

Such are the benefits of wealth. I am the son of Friedrich Delegate, nephew of Sonny Delegate, grandson of August Delegate, so lawyers hurry through the dark.

The surrounding neighborhood represents the foulest that Manhattan has to offer. The streets are deserted of all honest men at this time of night and the nearby financial district wholly abandoned of its scrivener ants and predatory beetles. In my mind's eye, I see my attorneys, two figures, one tall and plump, one short and bony, proceed through empty streets.

At the portal of the prison, a uniformed officer of the city sleeps at his post. He wakes, alarmed, at the creak of the massive brass door. "Attorney Howe, sir! Attorney Hummel!" A common enough sight, these two, even in the wee hours, but somehow their arrival is forever unsettling.

Howe is resplendent in dozens of diamonds, which he wears even to bed. Hummel all in black like a crow, observing perpetual mourning, they say, for the death of his conscience.

Deeper and downward they come, closer to where I wait, into the prison's fetid lower levels, the cramped cell block designated "Murderer's Row" because it lodges killers. Finally to arrive at an end-of-the-line passageway.

Where I sit, calmly passive, on a rude pallet in a filthy cell, the confessed assassin.

Hugo, Mr. Howe says, wringing his hands and rushing to my side as if I were his dying mother. The man is always a shade histrionic. Abe Hummel a silent shadow beside the talkative Bill Howe.

Howe rails at the turnkey about my accommodations, the scandal of it, treating an eminent scion of Manhattan this way, it is totally outrageous, did he, the turnkey, know who I, meaning me, was, if he, Howe, and his esteemed partner in the law, Hummel, have anything to say about it, the turnkey will soon find himself transferred to outdoor duty at potter's field on Blackwell's Island, et cetera, et cetera.

So the three of us, myself and my attorneys, move to more comfortable quarters for our talk.

Upstairs, we pass through dark, echoing halls.

On the way they explain (Howe, that is; Hummel remains mum), that because I had been arrested on a Friday night, they will likely not be able to arrange my bail until Monday.

Three nights in the Tombs. Perhaps a sympathetic judge, and they know many, will see his way clear to hold a special arraignment hearing. If not, they will endeavor to make me as comfortable as they can. Stay by my side through thick and thin. It is best not to be caught in the commission of a crime on the weekend, Howe counsels me.

Four flights up, more empty hallways. A right turn into the offices of the director of the jail. Unoccupied. Howe and Hummel make us at home.

Say nothing to no one except us, Howe says, admonishing. But to us, Hugo, you must tell everything.

Hummel silent as a snake, as usual.

I don't know where to begin, I say.

It is traditional, in these situations, Howe says, fluttering his hands expansively, to begin at the beginning.

I take a deep breath. There was a cabin in the wilderness of the Washoe, I say, where a headless body was discovered.

Another body, Howe says, a mournful expression on his face.

Yes.

Not the one discovered this night in Gramercy.

No. This is outside Virginia City, Nevada, in the Comstock.

We must interrupt you, Attorney Howe says, twisting his face in little moues of apology. At times I think he has taken Hummel on as partner only so that it might appear natural for him to speak in the royal "we."

We must ask, Hugo. Did you yourself discover this alleged body?

Well, no, I say.

He asks, Then were you present when the discovery occurred?

Again I say no.

So we must stop you at the outset, Howe says, directing you, in your best interest, not to speculate, not to fabricate, not to re-create scenarios from whole cloth but to stick to the hard fact of what you yourself saw, heard, and experienced, and refrain from flying off halfway across the country to a cabin in the wilderness.

Yet that is where— I start to say, but Howe interrupts.

No, Hugo, no. We must insist. Only that of which you yourself have firsthand knowledge. The truth and only the truth. Out of that we, your duly engaged attorneys, will pick and choose.

I recall a directive of my father's, coaching me in business practices. It is a good idea, he said, to tell your lawyers everything.

Why do I have to tell it at all? To these men who will never understand, who represent the wider world, that also will never understand?

I begin again, saying, *In June of 1875, we made our way down Virginia City's "A" Street* . . .

Part One

In the Drone Cage

In June of 1875, we made our way down Virginia City's "A" Street, proceeding south from the center of town toward the mountains.

Inwardly I had to smile at the picture rendered by our little group. Two women, one earthly, one Celestial. My mother, Anna Maria Delegate, and her lady's maid from China, Song Tu-Li.

My mother swaddled herself in vast amounts of white satin. Tu-Li wore the blue silk smock of her countrymen, hers rendered in rich brocade, so that at first you might mistake her for a peasant while on closer inspection you would conclude she was a princess.

Then, wandering behind milady and her maid, adding the zest of oddity, the berdache, the Zuni man-woman, Tahktoo. Anatomically male, garmented as a female, an indigene from the deserts of the Arizona Territory.

And me, along on this tour of the American West with my mother and my father, to be shown the family business and be removed from the unhealthy vapors of a New York City warm season. I had been in a sanatorium, down with a woeful bout of disturbed thoughts, restlessness and depression of spirits. Having barely seen the inside of Harvard Hall all spring, I wound up taking a leave from school.

The funny thing, the striking fact of the matter, was that amid the numberless crowds on "A" Street that afternoon, our company elicited not a wayward glance or comment. A Celestial, a man-woman, and two terrestrials, one of them a nutter. Few among the busy rabble noticed us.

In the High Sierra, a brisk, springlike Nevada summer. The crowded, unpaved thoroughfare rang with shouts of teamsters and the noisy leather-and-wood creak of their rigs, the snorting of mules, the excited bellow of commerce. Wide pedestrian walks ran alongside the street in both directions, packed shoulder to shoulder with people.

It astonished me that my mother and Tu-Li were the only women among the multitudes, the only ones on "A" Street, "B" Street or "C" Street either, the only ones in the whole of Virginia City (except, perhaps, those in the very specific red-lit neighborhood down on "D" Street).

Out and about in the mining town, sometimes it seemed that Anna Maria Delegate and her maid were the only females in the newly minted state of Nevada, for that matter the only ones on the whole planet.

My own private musing, of course. I knew that the governor himself had a wife somewhere. And there was "The Mencken," a performer who strapped herself to the back of a horse in a nude body stocking and did tricks on the stage of Maguire's Theater.

Still, the unbolted street hordes were entirely male. Prospectors slathered in dried muck. Drunks pickled in tarantula juice. Assorted dips, tossers and clips. Mountain men carrying their Navies on their belts, ready for a quarrel. Mexicans hawking corn flatcakes. Paiutes in rags and fringes. Potbellied nabobs in cutaways.

And Chinese laborers, universally called coolies or, more poetically, Celestials, since they hailed from the Celestial Kingdom.

Any farther from the States, locals said, and you'd fall into the Bay.

We were following Tu-Li to a spectacle of some sort, one that she had discovered but would not describe, keeping us in suspense.

"Where is it?" asked Anna Maria.

"Just ahead, madam," Tu-Li said.

I have never called my mother "Mother" nor my father "Father" since I was a child. This was at their insistence. Mother was Anna or, more properly, Anna Maria. Father was "Freddy."

We were "equals, equals!" Freddy informed me, over and over. My parents were much under the sway of Dr. Froebel and the other new child-raising experts. Freddy's real name was Friedrich-August-Heinrich, too much of a mouthful for anybody.

"My God, what a place this is," Anna Maria said.

Virginia City was most definitely a "my God" kind of place. Like a riot at a carnival. The north-south avenues in the town were so infernally busy that a buggy could wait a full half hour to cross them. New arrivals and Comstock veterans alike trotted along pushing wheelbarrows piled high with their belongings, weaving in and out amid the wagon traffic.

I amused myself, for a time, by dropping back and walking a few feet behind the cross-dressing berdache, Tahktoo. Passersby, those not too boiled to focus, allowed a look of confusion to pass over their features before they walked on. Was that . . . ? Man? Woman? The berdache existed in the crowd like a question mark.

Just then a wild-eyed creature ran pell-mell past us down "A" Street toward the iron-fronted, vaultlike headquarters of Wells Fargo, a handful of blue dirt gripped in his fist, screaming out, "The assay! the assay!"

No one else paid the yowling fellow any mind, but my mother turned her head to follow his progress. He dodged wagons and drays until he disappeared. The assay, the assay. Would he be trampled by mules? Swindled at the government assay office when he attempted to place a valuation on his scrap of ore? Or would he be the newest entry in the swelling ranks of Washoe millionaires?

Virginia—locals dropped the "City"—was a town that drove men mad. *There is a hole in the human heart,* Anna Maria once informed me, part of her effort to school her son in the ways of the world. *It is deep and cold,* she said solemnly, *and can never be filled.*

Except by gold.

From beneath our feet as we walked came the muffled *whump-thump* of explosions, repeating every few minutes. I could feel the force rise through my ankles. They were blowing apart veins of silver in the mines below the town.

If gold could not be found to fill the hole, then silver might do.

My mother had clearly worn the wrong clothes. Dressing Anna Maria this morning, Tu-Li told her, "You will be the only woman in fashion west of the Mississippi." Her trailing silk overskirt with its ruffles, pleated frills and ruching, her bonnet, a parasol! All in white. She looked like an angel, a stern angel, the kind that might knock you on your behind.

But here in the Washoe Valley, white was redundant.

The street, the mountain that rose over the town, the canvas wall tents and saloons and banking establishments, and especially the men—all were covered in alkali grit, plaster white, fine as flour, taken up off the ground by the constant, hellish wind, swirling out of the myriad man-made holes in the earth, stinging the eyes, burning the lips, sweeping everywhere before settling on everything like thick cream on a spoon.

Until the whole place resembled a whited sepulcher.

Dust and wind, dust and wind. You went to Virginia and what did you find? Dust and wind.

It hadn't mattered what my mother wore. She could have been in mourning black and she would have wound up in white. Dust freckled Tu-Li's blouse of deep indigo blue. A Negro, walking those streets, magically became a white man. Dust lay ankle deep on the porches and walks.

"A" Street, the first thoroughfare settled in Virginia City, was no longer the busiest in town. By 1875 it had been fifteen years since miners carted the first "blue stuff" out of the earth.

Blue stuff.

Wet, mucky cobalt gravel, at first carelessly discarded, considered only as a waste by-product of the tiny bits of gold-flecked ore it carried within.

Some genius finally bothered to look at the blue stuff closely, and the detritus revealed itself to be silver ore of the highest grade. Silver ore can be made to pay at six-percent purity. This was sixty-eight percent.

Bonanza!

A dismal wagon-track crossroads in the middle of the Nevada nowhere saw itself instantly transformed into a silver-rush boomtown. Within a week after the discovery, "A" Street was packed thick with tents, plain-board shanties, and had wooden-framed storefronts going up.

Virginia. Or the Comstock, for the man who gave his name to the first famous mine. Or the Washoe, for the valley it faced. The Silver-land. The residents called it by every name except its own. They cursed it when it came up dry, and worshipped it when it came in blue.

The assay! The assay!

Above the town, silver seekers had carved the slope into numerous narrow ledges, dotted with rictuslike wildcat mines, the face of the mountain eaten away and pitted as if with a wasting disease.

Overhead, the turquoise reaches of the sky flooded with the spar-kling sunlight omnipresent in the West. So different from our home in New York City, with its dull cloudscapes in every season, even summer.

But what amplitude Virginia had in sunlight it made up for with a total lack of vegetation. No trees, no shrubbery, no green grass. Only sparse sagebrush, its pungent, earthy scent floating on the ever-present Washoe winds.

"Give way!" came a shout.

We all jumped back, nearly run over by a dray muscling past, its flatbed stacked with gleaming silver bricks under a loose sheet of flap-ping canvas. The slouch-hatted bullwhacker managed to hold the reins loosely in one hand and a bottle tightly in the other, while his cargo's guards, two stone-faced men propping scatterguns against their thighs, sat stoically suffering every jolt.

Late afternoon, near the end of the second shift in the mines. The work at extracting wealth from the earth ran on around the clock, day and night, every day of the year. Capitalism, as my political-economy professor at Harvard said, was a perpetual-motion machine.

My mother brushed off the mud that clung to her snow-white hem after the near collision. She stepped forth under the balconies of the flat-fronted buildings, an intrepid schooner navigating between Scylla and Charybdis.

My father styled himself a social scientist, but I considered Anna Maria to be the more discerning observer of the family. The raucous Nevada settlement offered much in the way of spectacle: mansions, parades, cockfights, bear and bull baiting, duels, bicycles, nitroglyc-erin, wild Indians.

Whiskey over all. Virginia City averaged a booze-soaked murder a day.

We proceeded past the Nevada House, inviting diners to take meals at fifty cents but with a smell of rancid grease wafting from inside that repelled all appetite.

Next door a bounty stockade, stinking also, stack after stack of ill-cured wolf pelts, bearskins, immense piles of mountain lion hides, the maculate coat of a jaguar nailed to the pine-log wall, eagle and hawk carcasses collected in heaps.

A bounty officer lounged at the portal of the place. Hunters got paid in government money (fifteen dollars for a wolf skin, ten dollars for bear or cougar) for their exterminating efforts. Coyote, fox, lynx, bobcat, wolverines. Man the predator clearing out competing predators, claiming his territory.

What really distinguished Virginia was its saloons. We had only recently arrived in town and were staying not more than a week, but I most wanted to investigate these popular gambling-and-drinking venues, the site of so much rascality.

Enter and lose your shirt. Leave and win a kick in the pants.

"I am interested merely as a witness," I told Anna Maria. "Not as a participant."

"A witness is a participant," she said.

The Red Dog. The Old Globe. Bucket of Blood. The Silver Queen. The Suicide Table.

And now, at the far south end of "A," my personal favorite so far, a dangerous hybrid establishment, Costello's Saloon and Shooting Gallery. The threshold of the front doorway, I noticed, had been set with dice.

Through the saloon's single window shone an amber whiskey gleam. A peppering bang of gunshots could be heard from the interior.

"Just ahead, madam," Tu-Li said, motioning my mother forward. Tu-Li had been out at dawn to bring our garments to the Chinese district to be laundered. There she heard of a place to visit that might attract the curious of mind.

"Just ahead where?" Anna Maria said, halting and holding on to my arm. "There is nowhere else to go."

"A" Street stopped just past the saloon, dead-ending at the steep rise of the mountain. Above, the ledges and mucked-out mine holes. The men working them appeared, in the slanting afternoon light, like scarabs crawling over the raggy surface of an Egyptian mummy.

Garish billboards punctuated the slope directly above town. Carter's Livery. Balthazar Bier-Keller. The Melodeon Hall of Dance. A large freshly painted sign for the International, the town's respectable hotel, in which we had taken a floor.

"Where?" I said.

Tu-Li bowed imperceptibly and motioned with her open palm, a maître d' showing diners to their table.

An alley ran alongside the saloon. Lined on both sides with carts, booths, tents and hovels, the pathetic offerings of peddlers, hawkers and cheapjacks of the type that crowded the whole town, ancillary commerce to the mines.

At the mouth of the alley, a hand-painted sign.

SAVAGE GIRL, it read.

Or rather the sign had originally spelled out SAVIJ GIRL, and then someone with more orthographic sophistication had come along and corrected it.

"Here?" my mother said.

Tu-Li nodded. "You will see," she said.

The sign, the misspelling and the subsequent rectification somehow struck me as particularly dispiriting. I could read a whole history in it. The entire alleyway stank of poverty, failure and claims that hadn't proved out. I was ready to pop over to Costello's for a glass of beer and some target practice.

Upon the apparition of three tourists and a Zuni hermaphrodite approaching the mouth of their little hell, the vendors in the alleyway of broken dreams woke up and began to beckon Anna forward. She was, in her European finery, clearly the mark.

Come buy my patched-together mule harness, come buy my rusty Ames shovel, my mended socks, my rags, my nightmare.

No, no, no. I witnessed my mother at the moment of decision. She would definitely not venture into the little alley.

Tu-Li had led us on a goose chase.

Anna Maria would turn around, push her way down "A" Street, retreat to her hotel suite or, further, to our family's private railcars, parked on a siding of the Virginia & Truckee line, waiting to whisk her across the endless plains to the East, out of the tiresome, ever-present alkali wind, back to civilization and happiness and our clean, dustfree, sparkling existence in Manhattan.

"No, no, thank you," Anna said.

"I think you will like it," said Tu-Li. "It is what you look for."

"Absolument pas," Anna said.

But I had a different idea.

Beside the words, the weathered wood of the Savage Girl sign had a smudge upon it. I leaned forward. The sign maker had drawn a picture, very crude, a hairy animal countenance with oversize, oddly human eyes and a woman's mouth painted in lurid, now-faded red.

The hand of the wind stirred the dust in the little lane. I shivered, feeling a frisson of . . . of exactly what? Fear? Attraction? I couldn't say.

Anna Maria had planned a rendezvous with my father at the Brilliant Mine just before sunset. We had arranged to meet Freddy after completing our walkabout through town. By the slant of the sun, Anna Maria could see that it was getting close to the agreed-upon time, and she wanted to hustle us along.

"I think I will go down for a peek," I said. The dirt of the alleyway had been laid with muddy duckboards.

"We must join your father, Hugo," she said. "Tu-Li, Tahktoo."

"Come along with me," I said to Anna Maria. "You who have forced open so many closed doors in your life."

"Flatterer," she said.

"Just a brief look," I said. "Unless you're fearful."

She hesitated. Then she took my arm and we headed into the alley. My mother could never resist a challenge.

Avoiding the peddlers tugging at our sleeves, we followed Tu-Li along the little lane. There the alley ended at a tongue-and-groove façade with a plain pine door, two blacked-out and boarded-over windows on either side. A barn of some sort, constructed of exhausted, peeling wood.

The building stood at the bottom of the slope, but the ground behind it fell away into a gulch before rising, so that which we stood before actually represented the building's second story. My mother looked over to me, on her face a bride-at-the-altar mix of anticipation and disquiet.

The portal's homely plank boards had a peephole. As I stepped forward, the door cracked open.

Blocking the threshold appeared one of the oddest-looking beings I have ever encountered. A human toad of sorts. His slits were like eyes. A white-coated tongue emerged from a lipless mouth, and behold, he spoke.

"We don't allow no women."

Addressing my mother, who from my experience was easily up to the task of dealing with wart-giving creatures of all stripes.

"Young man," she said, giving his humanity the benefit of the doubt, "you must let us in."

"No women and no Celestials," the Toad said. He looked at Tu-Li, who stared back at him evenly.

"No women?" Anna said. She pulled the berdache forward. "What about my friend?"

The doorkeeper could not wrap his mind around Tahktoo. I witnessed the tiny engine of the man's brain seize up and begin to smoke.

We had gotten this far, and we weren't about to turn back.

Anna Maria said, "I'm entering."

"We don't allow no women."

"Not allowing," my mother said, "is not allowed."

More brain sizzle from the doorkeeper. He couldn't handle that one either.

Then, as if he had been jerked up to heaven by an abrupt act of rapture, the Toad suddenly disappeared with a yelp.

In his place stood a huckster in dundrearies and a blue-checkered suit, smiling, bowing, gesturing us forward. His nostrils flared. He had the look of a man who smelled money.

The Toad might not recognize a three-hundred-dollar silk gown, imported by Anna Maria this year from Worth in Paris, but the huckster most certainly did.

"Madam, madam, please, you are most welcome," he said, correctly assessing my mother as the true power in the group. "My name is Professor Dr. Calef Scott. I will assure your safety and comfort."

"Thank you," Anna Maria said.

"My assistant, Mr. R. T. Flenniken, has his marching orders but, like so many individuals of limited capacities, is burdened by a pronounced inability to modify his instructions with good judgment. In short, he is a fool."

During this speech he ushered us into his establishment. If his assistant resembled a toad, Scott himself was a stuffed duck.

I waited for my eyes to adjust to the interior but then understood that the barn was not just dim, it was wholly dark. Canvas tent cloth had been stapled to the walls, obstructing the late-afternoon light coming through the gaps in the planking and also, I realized, keeping out the peering eyes of the nonpaying public.

"We ask a small token, madam." Dr. Scott winked, and my mother pushed a gold eagle into his hand.

It was too much. The dollar entrance fee for each of the four of us, times five. Scott smiled like a happy child.

"This way, if you please," he said. "I will place you in complete segregation from the hoi polloi."

We had entered upon a gallery or balcony of some sort, a narrow platform that ran the length of the barn, with a sagging railing marking its far edge.

The gallery gave out onto the two-storied barn proper. We stared down from our second level to the rectangular floor below, thirty by fifty feet, an unswept dirt surface scattered with straw. In one corner stood a large cage, its door haphazardly shut, a soiled blanket tossed over it that obscured its interior, barely visible in the gloom anyway.

On the opposite side of the space from the cage, an odd edifice, a tall, circular galvanized tub, perhaps five feet high and almost the same in diameter, its lip spilling over with water. A stock-dipping tank or some such.

A slim pipe angled down from high on the far side of the barn, eye level with we who stood in the gallery, positioned so that it dribbled an uneven stream of scalding water into the tub. The pipe, and the surface of the bath itself, threw off wisps of steam into the murky shadows of the interior.

Tapping into no doubt one of the myriad local hot springs. The overflow from the tub drained away down a gutter cut into the dirt floor.

"Where is she?" called out a greasy workman among the audience. The five-o'clock show, the second of six performances daily.

The ragged company of spectators packed close to the rail. I counted seventeen of them, with more coming every minute. The dude beside me casually tossed the lit stub of his cheroot to the floor of the gallery, not bothering to stamp it out. I stepped on the burning fag, thinking of the firetrap barn we were crowded into, and the fellow glared at me as though I had somehow trespassed.

Whiskey vapor, tobacco smoke, sweat, exhalations of eggy bad breath. The foul human stink engulfed us more as the audience grew in size.

Far from being made nervous by the hurly-burly around her, my mother assumed an expression of intelligent intellectual engagement, as though she were observing some indigenous foreign tribe, that she might one day lecture upon it.

Dr. Scott maneuvered us to a corner of the gallery, where a chastened R. T. Flenniken, whom it amused the doctor to dress in livery, quickly positioned four rickety wooden chairs, fawning and smiling all the while.

Scott made as if to withdraw but addressed Anna. "Madam, I discern you may be a woman of some parts. If you wish to discuss the natural phenomenon you are about to witness, I will make myself available after the spectacle."

He backed away, bowing.

Then, at the last moment, his glance fell on me. With the practiced eye of a showman assessing his audience, he gave a secret smile and tugged at my arm. Pulling me away from my mother, he physically positioned me in the absolute far corner of the balcony, right up at the front, shoving aside a drover dressed in chaps to put me there.

"Keep a sharp lookout and you'll see something," Scott whispered. Then he left.

A long, restless beat.

"Where the hell is she?" the workman repeated. "I paid my dollar!"

"Shut up," someone else said.

By this I understood that the crowd was made up of an uneasy mix of first-timers and regulars.

Directly below us, on the floor of the barn, a torch blazed up in the darkness, wielded by Dr. Scott. He began to speak.

"Gentlemen!" he shouted. Then, with a bow toward my mother, "Ladies."

He waved his torch in a circle as though it were a baton. The pine-pitch flame traced loops and flowery arcs in the darkness.

"Cast your minds into the blank and trackless emptiness of the Sierra wilderness. Savage, wild, forsaken by God and man. Thronged with ferocious packs of bloodthirsty beasts!"

A high, keening howl tore through the darkness of the barn, and I nearly jumped out of my skin.

❧ 2 ❧

Two hours later my groin tightened and my stomach fluttered as I felt
myself dropping down, down, down, a thousand feet deep into the
earth, riding in a sweltering wrought-iron hoist.

My mother, Tu-Li and the berdache remained above, seated comfortably inside the clapboard office of the Brilliant Mining and Milling
Company. I had volunteered to go down and fetch my father for them.

I was assigned Colm Cullen, security chieftain at the Brilliant
Mine, a guide to the underworld for the stripling son of the firm's
owner. I met him up top, at the mouth of the mine, where he seized
my hand with a grip that could mangle steel.

"I'd like to see my father," I said, sounding, to my dismay, like a
child wanting his daddy. "Will you take me to him?"

Stepping into the lift, I craned my head up to the purple sky above
me, with just a dusting of stars emerging. Below, the blacker pit.

We rode down in the "Elephant," the mine's number-one steam
hoist, which hurtled fully as fast as a train. The heat rose up to greet
us like a fist.

"Gives the impression of warmth, don't it?" Colm said. False bon-
homie with the owner's son.

It did for sure give that exact impression. Other mines I had ventured into—just a cautious step into one here and there, never beyond
where I could safely see the light of day, being afflicted with a bit of
physical impatience in tight places, "claustrophobia," my physiology
professor labeled it—were cold and clammy. This one a steam bath. As
wet as the tropics, but dirtier.

"Can I take a look at your iron?" I asked.

Colm Cullen had a big LeMat pistol strapped to his thigh, and when he unholstered it for me, I reached out, and it, too, was hot to the touch.

Sharp-jawed, red-haired Colm wore a navy flannel shirt and navy work pants tucked into his knee-high boots. All miners preferred dark blue clothing, he explained, since it showed the dirt less. He had a bit of a squint and an almost invisible scar that ran along his cheekbone. He appeared coolly unaffected by heat or vertigo.

I must have looked a little dazed, still in recovery from my recent encounter with Savage Girl in the barn.

A breast, as white as any moon . . .

I was not helped by the uniform that the Brilliant Mining and Milling Company had given me to wear: heavy rubberized shoes, thick cotton shirt and trousers, a felt hat and, for this swift trip down into the mine, a coarse woolen coat.

The car did not ease into the mine. It dropped. The grille to the side of me—the hoist remained open on two sides—scorched my fingertips when I brushed it by mistake. Another cage passed us, rising up with a full load of ore that looked like a heap of blue-black sand. Steam rose from the pile.

"Do you know what the body of a man sounds like when it falls a thousand feet?" asked Colm.

A thousand feet was how deep we were going.

Below, when the cage crashed to a stop, I stumbled forward into a finished-off gallery. I was aware of almost nothing but heat and closeness. The rock walls glistened with water, and drifts of vapor obscured the timbered reaches above me. I saw no one but could hear human voices. The acrid smell of nitroglycerin.

A tremendous bang sounded somewhere close, its echo feeding off itself until the reverberation engulfed the whole space.

"This is level one!" shouted Colm. "We got two more below, a thousand feet then another thousand feet more."

Pumps and pipes pulled steaming water out of the walls and ran it up to the surface. Otherwise, Colm told me, scalding floods would spout from the cavern's sides. In the early days of the Comstock, untold numbers of mine workers had been boiled alive.

"Do you have an egg?"

"What?" I said.

"Most of the tourists bring an egg," Colm said. The water down here, he said, had boiled its share of souvenir eggs. Someone once brought a big one from an ostrich, and the waters had cooked it fine. Hadn't I got one?

"I'm not a tourist," I said, although in my ill-fitting rig I am sure I looked the part. "I'm just here to find my father."

We crossed into the first chamber, a square space barely taller than a man and about the same distance wide. Then into a larger gallery. Rough-hewn timber stock and plank ladders stood propped up from one end to the other.

Deeper and deeper we penetrated into the mine. Workers stripped to the waist, their shoulders and biceps gleaming like marble, wielding sledgehammers and drill bits, jamming charges into seams in the quartzite rock. The pick handles burned so hot that the job required gloves.

I suffocated. From the heat or the fear of small spaces, I wasn't sure, but I felt a fountain of panic bubbling within my chest. *Get me out of here!*

Thousands of candles illuminated the gallery, flickering faintly, their tiny warmth swallowed within the larger furnace, like puffs of breath in a cyclone. The candle boxes affixed along the crumbly walls, Colm said, doubled as receptacles for human excrement.

Bowels of the earth indeed.

Staggering, I extended my arm and grabbed for Colm's shoulder. It felt hard, like a seam of rock itself. I would faint.

"Hugo!"

"Father," I said, half swallowing the word.

Freddy made his way into the chamber, pink-faced, his graying walrus mustache drooping, spangled with tiny droplets of water. He had shed his coat, and his cotton shirt stuck to his torso, having been wet through and through.

With Freddy were a half dozen men, his engineers, mine foremen, surveyors.

"What are you doing down here, son? It's dangerous for you to come!" Meaning I had been sick and was too weak for such exertions. I had been down, over the past year, not only with emotional illness but physical ones: erysipelas, infections of the eye, then bronchitis resolving into pneumonia.

"I'm fine," I lied. I was always the weakling in the family. My younger brother, Nicholas, who wasn't along on this Western trip, was the strong and sturdy one, more like my father.

I had seen Freddy just that morning, but it was different encountering him in the mine he owned, catered to and cosseted by his minions.

"Isn't it a marvel?" Tom Colfax, Freddy's construction supervisor, said, gesticulating so broadly that his arm swept the cavern's wall. "Every day we bless the name of Philip Deidesheimer. All these timbers."

A honeycomb of wood framed up the soaked, sludgy walls of the mine. The famous German engineer Deidesheimer had invented the structural design, enabling the further disemboweling of the earth, keeping the death toll among miners down to an acceptable number.

"Square-set timbering," said Colfax. "Six hundred million feet of timbers, buried now in Virginia's mines."

"That's an amount of wood enough to build a town of thirty thousand two-story frame houses," said one of the vaguer underlings.

Freddy reached over and gripped my arm, seeing what none of the others saw, that the heat was about to overcome me.

"We send down ninety-five pounds of ice each day for every man working," he said, propping me up. "And if you'll accompany me, you can have a lemonade up top."

Cullen and Colfax stayed below while Father and I took the Elephant upward. Rising slower than it had dropped, but still fast enough to make my stomach heave.

Do not vomit on Father, I told myself.

"Why'd you come down, son? I told you not to."

"Anna Maria and I have something to show you," I said. "Tu-Li found it."

He went silent, the hoist cranking upward. Do you know how the body of a man sounds, I asked him, when it drops a thousand feet? I provided the answer as well as the question.

"Like the whistle of a cannonball," I said. "Just exactly like the whistle of a cannonball."

Freddy did not respond. Unlike Colm Cullen, he had probably never heard a cannonball scream past him, having not attended the War of the Rebellion. Freddy had in fact paid substitutes to serve in his place, a common enough practice for the wealthy.

I couldn't read my father. As I often did, I felt as though I were disappointing him. Going into a swoon on a mine visit.

Back on the surface, I immediately recovered my equilibrium, my nausea vanishing to leave behind only a faint sense of embarrassment.

My mother came to us across the equipment-cluttered yard.

"Friedrich," she said to my father by way of greeting. "You are going to want to see this."

An Indian drumbeat, hollow and repetitive.

The deep-voiced tones of Dr. Calef Scott sounding in the dim barn.

"In a draw in a rock-choked valley, John Trent and his pregnant wife, Dollie Bertles Trent, both from Georgia, had built themselves a sagebrush hut. The lowest habitation, just above a coyote hole. The valley being the site of a Paiute-Pawnee massacree, the newcomers all ignorant of its evil reputation, its hauntings by the ghosts of the dead, Trent and his wife toiled to establish a mining claim."

Freddy stood with Anna at the balcony railing. Tu-Li and the berdache had not returned to the Savage Girl show with us, but though I had seen the whole spectacle that afternoon, I judged myself eager to witness it again.

Scott continued with his tale. "Espantosa, the Spanish call the little valley where John Trent unknowingly sited his humble domicile, a name that means 'frightful or menacing.' Americans have a different name for it. 'Satan's Vale.'

"There, on a black night in 1860 marred by a thunderous storm,

Dollie Trent, large with child, enters labor. The birth went to compli-
cations. The agonized prospective father leaps aboard his mule and
rides to seek help—a doctor, a midwife, anyone who can aid his wife,
wholly maddened by the pangs of birth."

The same script as this afternoon exactly, identical cadences, Dr.
Scott applying matching theatrical emphasis to the phrases.

I left my father's side to claim my former place at the far corner of
the gallery but found a lanky, clean-shaven cowboy occupying it. He
stared intently at the cage on the floor of the barn. He knew what was
about to happen. He had been here before. I attempted to move in on
him. Without looking, he shouldered me backward.

"As Trent rides on his heroic quest"—I braced myself, and there
was a tremendous crash—"a thunderous bolt of lightning strikes him
from his mount, and he falls dead."

The "thunder," an immense sheet of tin, manipulated by Scott's
toady down below, died to silence. Into which rose an eerie sound, a
newborn baby weeping (a kid goat, squeezed and poked by R. T. Flenniken). Then assorted yelps and growls (a trained dog) overcame the
weeping and also died to silence.

"When neighbors arrive at the little brush hut the next morning,
they find Dollie Trent lying dead. There is no sign of the infant. The
baby, it is surmised, had been dragged off and eaten by the rabid beasts
of the wild. Fang marks showed on the woman's breast. A pack of
wolves left tracks in blood upon the scene."

Scott pronounced this last in perfect Shakespearean iambics. "A
pack of *wolves* left *tracks* in *blood* upon the *scene*." I could only imagine
what my father must think of all this. But I was more intent on claiming my former vantage point at the rail. I nudged the cowboy. He
turned to look at me, surly.

I held up five fingers.

Understanding immediately, he shook his head.

I used both my hands, spread out ten fingers. He nodded, I gave
him a ten-dollar silver piece, and, grudgingly, he moved aside.

Freshly ensconced, looking down into the gulf of the barn, I silently mouthed the words: *Our story has only begun.*

"Our story has only begun!" Scott shouted. "Ten years later a lowly shepherd is confronted in sheer panic by a pack of lobo wolves ravaging his herd. But that is not the true terror. Running alongside the wild beasts, dashing about manically on all fours, is the apparition of a human girl, naked as the wind!"

The door of the cage on the barn floor clanged open, the crowd in the gallery above surged forward, the balcony rail groaning with their weight, and two forms appeared down below at once.

A bleating sheep.

And the quicksilver outline of an adolescent female, indifferently clothed, crossing the darkened space with amazing speed, slamming into the poor animal and knocking it senseless.

A collective gasp from the audience in the gallery. The sight of a human being running about on all fours asserts an almost mystical sway upon the modern sensibility. It is difficult to describe. It possesses the ghostly power of a long-suppressed memory.

Another burst of inexplicable speed and she was gone. Fled beneath the rickety gallery. The crowd craned over the railing but could not see.

Down below, the Toad dragged away the dazed sheep.

The shepherd's tale is doubted, I said to myself.

"The shepherd's tale is doubted," Dr. Scott said, taking up his tale. *But other reports begin to come in, fantastic tales . . .* "But other reports begin to come in, fantastic tales, a cowboy alone in the high chaparral, confronted by a witch, half human, half wolf, a sheepfold ripped through and human footprints found, a stakeholder's wife, frightened mute, witness to a piglet-stealing creature she cannot even describe."

The gallery was wholly silenced. Dr. Scott had his audience mesmerized. Even I felt swept up.

This is where I myself enter the story. . . .

"This is where I myself enter the story," Dr. Scott said. "Hearing these reports, my curiosity was excited, my interest piqued as an esteemed natural scientist with several degrees from highly prestigious universities in the East."

He bowed modestly.

"I organized a search party. By means of a simple subterfuge"—below, R. T. Flenniken tossed a raw beefsteak into the center of the barn floor—"I managed to take hold of the savage girl of Satan's Vale."

The figure crept from below the balcony, snatching up the piece of meat, and Scott pounced on her. She screamed like a monkey, biting, clawing and kicking.

It appeared a real battle, entirely unchoreographed. The two grappled and rolled about the floor, banging into the walls of the barn, shaking the whole structure.

We saw that Savage Girl had been equipped with a ridiculous extension of her hands, a set of six-inch talons that acted as claws. Ridiculous yes, to the rational mind, but in the dim murk of the barn, terrible and horrifying.

Another full-throated shriek, half sob, half howl.

Savage Girl straddled the supine form of her erstwhile captor. She raised the hand talons above her head. With a look of fury, she drove them downward.

"Watch out!" shouted one of the spectators.

Scott rolled to one side, and the claws barely missed him but embedded themselves instead in the dirt of the floor. Thus immobilized, Savage Girl was easy prey for the triumphant Dr. Calef Scott. He roped her with a lariat and hog-tied her limbs, capturing the creature who only moments before had been on the verge of murdering him.

The crowd erupted with hoots, catcalls and applause.

Dr. Scott bounced to his feet. "Gentlemen!" he called out, forgetting, for the moment, my mother in the gallery. "I give you the Savage Girl of Satan's Vale!"

Clapping, shouting, stomping, the audience members sought to collapse the very balcony upon which they stood.

Below, Savage Girl revealed.

Bound, she remained ungagged and snarled pathetically. The thin muslin garb she wore might as well have been transparent. The stimulating display continued as Dr. Scott trod victoriously in a circle around her, the dominant, strutting male who had tamed the rebellious female.

He peeled off her hand scissors and tossed them dismissively aside.

From my post I could gaze directly down at her. Flashing amber eyes. Jet-black, thickly matted hair, tangled to the degree it resembled a swatch of carpet, not locks, more like a mane. I had expected her to be filthy, yet instead she gave off an air of catlike cleanliness.

She was nothing but a child. Seeing her thus a second time, I felt the hand of pity brush against my heart. It passed in a moment. In that moment, though, I swore she looked directly up at me. Not supplicating. Not pleading.

Challenging.

With Savage Girl's capture, some of the vitality went out of the presentation. But Dr. Scott was not finished.

"By painstaking degree I have pieced together the story of this low creature, the Savage Girl. For years she had lived alone in the wilderness, accompanied only occasionally by her pack of lobos. How did she survive our terrible winters? She found a cave, and within that cave she found a hot springs."

Dr. Scott knelt down and began to untie his captive.

Shouts of "No! No!" came from the audience. The spectators feared for his safety.

"And with that knowledge I found the key to pacify my wild quarry. Because you see, gentlemen—and if there are those among you affronted by female nudity, avert your eyes—yes, gentlemen, there is nothing Savage Girl enjoys more"—pausing for effect—"than to take a bath."

Wild cheers, whistles, throaty, guttural catcalls.

"She became accustomed to daily, sometimes hourly, lavations in her cavern redoubt. Would you wish to witness her tamed and domesticated, no longer savage but rendered meek and unresisting by her enthusiasm for hydrotherapy?"

"Yes! Yes!" cried the spectators.

"Show me!" Scott roared. "How strong is your desire? Is it a weak thing? Demonstrate your approval!"

They showered coins down upon him.

The figure of R. T. Flenniken appeared below to erect a chaste curtain in front of the tub.

Audience members booed and hissed this process. They chucked projectiles at the offending factotum, balled-up handkerchiefs, wads of tobacco, spent bullet cartridges. The Toad endured the rain of scorn.

But I, positioned at the far corner of the balcony, possessed a secret view. The erected curtain failed to extend wholly across the tub. For the second time in a day, I caught a fleeting glimpse of an unclothed Savage Girl as she stepped daintily into the bath.

A breast as white as any moon . . .

The Toad took away the curtain. The spectacle of her nakedness was somewhat obscured by the water and steam, just enough to further tantalize the male gaze. Only her shoulders showed.

Then, and this was perhaps the most bizarre element to the show, Flenniken inserted a pole into a pair of U-shaped metal clamps affixed to the side of the tub. Setting his feeble-looking shoulders to the pole, he managed to turn the tub, with Savage Girl in it. The bath apparently rested on some hidden roller apparatus, exhibiting all aspects to the spectators above.

In his action turning the tub, the Toad resembled a trudging mule, in harness on a circular track, powering a pump, perhaps, or grinding meal. He gazed worshipfully up at the girl as he plodded round and round, round and round.

But none of us upstairs marked the Toad at all. We were, to a man, transfixed. Peering down, praying for the steam to lift, the water to part as Moses did the Red Sea.

"See her bathing there," Dr. Scott intoned, "her naked shoulders, a breast as white as any moon. . . ."

In a splendid touch, Savage Girl fished a hand mirror from beneath the surface of the water in the tub, gazing at her own face as she turned round and round, round and round.

You possess a rather remarkable memory, says my lawyer, Mr. Howe. And we can see where this is going. An incredible tale, wouldn't you say, Hummel?

Hummel coughs.

But it is daylight already, Howe says, we have a long way to go, and I am ravenous.

He summons a police officer and orders up the most enormous breakfast I have ever seen a human being tuck into, delivered there to him in the prison director's office—table, plate, silverware and all brought in from Howe's second home, Delmonico's restaurant.

Caviar and oysters, shirred eggs, pancakes, a pair of immense pork chops, applesauce, a whole trout, cornbread, scalloped potatoes, hominy, muffins and a sirloin. Pots of coffee and a gallon of orange juice to wash it down.

A condemned man might lose his appetite, forgoing, out of terror, a last meal before hanging, but if he retains counsel, he can count on his hungry attorney to take up the slack.

Continue, Howe says, his mouth full. Go ahead, young Hugo.

3

"His show," Freddy said. "The little drama Dr. Scott plays out. He has forgotten the third act. The resolution."

Breakfast the next morning. My mother wasn't down yet. The dining hall of the International Hotel had nearly filled when I stepped in at eight o'clock to meet my father. I took the "rising room" elevator down from the sixth floor, an impressive experience despite its resemblance to the Elephant of the previous evening.

I had slept only fitfully. Wolves prowled my dreams.

We used the club dining room on the mezzanine, white tablecloths, less public than the busy restaurant off the lobby down below. As an alternative, we took meals privately in our rooms.

In the presence of wealth, every man transforms into a tout. A public appearance by my father, widely recognizable in town, often brought out hordes of faceless supplicants, each proposing some transfer of funds from his pockets to theirs. Pity the miseries of the rich.

The very air of the Comstock provoked money hunger. Even at eight in the morning, we could hear the steam whistles and the brisance of nitro from out in the hills, the stamp of the presses from the mills.

"A third act. Scott has the protasis, the epitasis, but he lacks the catastrophe. Don't you think?" Freddy asked, helping himself to fried potatoes.

Aristotle. Greek drama.

"A third act. How would you say it goes?" I asked.

"Well, it's very clear, isn't it?" He peeled off a slice from his rasher of bacon.

"Is it?"

"She completes her bath."

Me, chewing. "Yes."

"Dresses. End of epitasis."

"All right." Swallowing toast.

"Am I embarrassing you?"

"No." A gulp of coffee.

"You look a little flushed," my father said. "Pink about the ears."

"That's just the java," I said. He enjoyed teasing me. "And then?"

And then Tom Colfax entered to interrupt us, accompanied by Michael Hart-Bentley, another of my father's business intimates, a few steps up the ladder from Tom. We were joined in quick order by the silver magnates Oliver Stringfist, Stanley Beales and Dixon Kelly. Suddenly I found myself at the richest table in the room.

The servers arrived instantly, toting well-singed beefsteak, pickled salmon, mutton pie and heaps more fried potatoes. Two immense steaming pots of coffee.

I was boxed in. The magnates seated themselves in a semicircle beside my father, leaving me alone on the side of the table against the window.

I said, "I'm sorry, gentlemen, I rather feel in this arrangement as though I am facing a panel of jurists."

Hart-Bentley said, "Why, have you done something that requires judgment?"

The fabled Ollie Stringfist had a wealth of sensational whiskers, which he wore parted and tied snugly under his chin. "What do you think of our Virginia, my boy?" he asked.

"A Babel of noise and a Cologne of stinks."

Stringfist laughed. "It is at that."

"You are at school," accused Dix Kelly, the only one of them who did not wear a waistcoat, a fob and a tie.

"Yes, Mr. Kelly." It is indicative of our set that I did not need to mention which college. Harvard was assumed.

"Never saw the use of it myself," said Stringfist. He used his belly as a table for his coffee cup.

Stan Beales waved his arm vaguely at the mountain that domi-nated the town. "Out here," he said, tearing a biscuit in two and swal-lowing half of it. "Greatest university in the known world. There's profit to be made, son, profit like lightning."

"Medicine, is it, that what you're studying?" Stringfist said. "Doc-tors, a dose of humbug and a great big bill."

I was beginning to get the drift. These millionaires had been sum-moned not for business but for a Stern Talk with the Young Delegate Boy. Freddy's friends glared at me but gazed at him with fond affec-tion. And why shouldn't they? He had helped to enrich them all. Men love you if you make yourself a benefit to them.

"Marvelous time in the Comstock," said Hart-Bentley. He spoke in a clipped, hurried manner. "New opportunities every day. Deep, deep, how we dig now. The deeper, the higher our returns. Big Bonanza discovered in '73. We all learned, dig deep, manipulate the soil, then comes a sulfuret. Not magic, no, science. Your father knows about that. Best science mind of his generation. Only a chemical, silver chlo-ride, though it drives men to lunacy."

"We tore this town out of the wild," said Stringfist, the whisker knot bobbing below his chin. "Wasn't so long ago that men bunked in shelters made of blankets or potato sacks or old shirts. That's the way it was."

What guff. I happened to know that Oliver Stringfist hired other men to do his tearing of towns out of the wild. He had never slept under a potato sack in his life, or even ridden down in the Elephant, being afflicted with the same kind of coffin panic as I was.

A second course materialized. Not only were there griddle cakes and syrup, we had, somehow, chervil and lettuce salad. And boiled eggs—I had a doleful thought they might have been cooked down in the Brilliant Mine.

I found myself distracted by the entry into the clubroom of a tall, rangy fellow, his face weathered to a sheen of high-polished leather.

A *real western character,* the easterner in me thought instantly. A lawman, or a desperado. No one wore a hat in the dining room except for him, and his white-gray Stetson Boss was a monument to all headgear. The red of his shirt blended with the red of his bandanna and the red of his sunburn.

As he progressed across the room, his boot spurs dragged over the wooden floor, clanking rhythmically. He was one of those men who managed to appear even bigger than he was. He took in everyone, and it seemed he had a special, hard look reserved just for me. I felt a slight chill.

"Now, young Delegate here," I heard Stringfist say, "we could take him in hand, teach him the business from the ground down. Eh, fellows? From the ground down?"

General laughter. Jokes are much funnier, I've noticed, if the teller has a few million in the bank.

The lawman-desperado stopped at the tableside of a heavyset, dark-blond man with a full beard and mustache, seated at the opposite end of the room from us.

"The crucial thing now is milling," Hart-Bentley said. "Roasting the ores brings in five thousand dollars a ton. Hear the stamps outside? That's the tattoo of money."

Something was happening across the room. The blond man attempted to rise, and the lawman shoved him back into his seat. Their raised voices were audible from our table, but I couldn't quite make out what was being said.

A group of gentlemen tourists entered the clubroom, admiring the sizable aquarium beside the doorway.

A server came across to us with a plate of oranges.

The Comstock booster committee still talked at me, oblivious. Someone said, "Twenty-five thousand souls in the Washoe, and more coming every day."

The tall, weathered gent in the spurs drew his six-gun from its holster and shot the blond man in the chest. The victim slumped backward in his chair, a scarlet stain broadening on the white silk brocade of his vest, a gasping, clenched look on his face.

The stain, I remember as my first thought at the time, was surprisingly small.

"We have more gas lamps in this town," Stringfist said, "than in Main Line Philadelphia."

·   ·   ·   ·   ·

The event, Freddy told me later, should best be characterized as a ho-micide, not a murder.

"A finding of murder can only be determined in a court of law, by a jury," he said. We had left the International Hotel and proceeded over to "A" Street. " 'Homicide' is the more neutral term."

All right. A homicide. Victim, a freight-service owner named Hank Monk. Shooter, a former lawman (my guess had been right) from Reno named Butler Fince. Affirmed by all at the scene to be "a rough customer." So perhaps lawman-desperado had indeed been an accu-rate assessment.

I was surprised by the casual reception the killing had received. The diners, including the men with my father and me, appeared un-perturbed. Butler Fince was allowed egress from the premises with-out hindrance. The tourists at the aquarium scattered, but table service proceeded uninterrupted. Crowds of men poured up from the first-floor dining hall to gawk, though they dispersed when the body of Hank Monk was taken away.

The consensus seemed to be that this sort of thing was so very ordinary. Folks evinced a wondering pride as they quoted the "murder-a-day" statistic. Bad men made their reputations on the number of good men they had killed.

The particulars of the murder—who shot whom, what it was all about—ran like lightning around the clubroom within minutes of the shooting itself.

"Fince maintained that Monk had killed his brother," Tom Colfax said, having garnered the intelligence from the waiters, reporting back a little too breathlessly for the phlegmatic magnates around our table, who did not enjoy having their morning cigars disturbed.

I could not take the shooting with the same level of equanimity as the others. I had seen animals die, but never a human being.

As an anatomy student, I had, in the previous year, dealt with hu-man cadavers on the dissecting table. "The breathless dead," as Ho-mer calls them. At times I wondered at my ability to tolerate my future career. Even with a hunted whitetail, shot in the wilds of the Adirondacks, say, the moment of passing from life into death seemed to me a gut-wrenching, incredible, numinous event.

Animated flesh, then, abruptly, clay.

Walking south, Father and I passed Costello's Saloon and Shooting Gallery, quiet at this time in the morning, and turned in to the little alleyway that led to Dr. Scott's barn.

Freddy posed a familiar question. Why did I think he and my mother were so interested in instances of the feral-child phenomenon? They previously journeyed, just a few years before, to France, in order to investigate the home ground of Marie-Angélique Memmie Le Blanc, 1731's Wild Girl of Songi, as well as that of Victor of Aveyron, the celebrated wild boy of 1800.

Freddy felt himself fascinated to the degree that he bought at high expense a few tooth relics dating from the Songi girl, which had fallen out of her mouth when she left the forest and began to eat a European diet. Eighteenth-century thinkers worried over the question of whether wild children could be said to have a soul. They seemed to exist in a no-man's-land, neither rational being nor instinctual animal.

I knew, or thought I knew, why such bizarre creatures fascinated my parents. Freddy occupied himself as an independent natural scientist—independent, that is, not associated with any university or institute. The question roiling the world was, of course, Darwin's idea of natural selection. His book threw a monkey wrench into everyone's works.

Freddy became an instant proponent.

The wild child is a blank slate. He (or she) is perfect for investigations of whether our physical inheritance influences us more than do the circumstances of our raising, or whether it might be the other way around. Nature or nurture? Can a proper, caring environment make a silk purse of a sow's ear, in other words, or must that ear remain what its nature made it, the auricular flap of a swine?

Freddy and Anna Maria always hoped to acquire a feral child of their own, which they planned to include in their household, somewhat like King George I's keeping a court pet, Peter the Wild Boy.

Or perhaps it was more than that. My father saw himself turning science on its head with his research. He collected people. The naturalist John Burroughs studied beetles. Darwin himself did barnacles. Friedrich-August-Heinrich Delegate, on the other hand, would be satisfied with nothing less than the hominid in whole.

He collected within his net Tu-Li and the Zuni berdache, both of them specimens prized for their exotic bearing, from whom he hoped to learn the secrets of the self. And those two were not the first, only the most recent.

My mother had a more personal interest in the affair, seeking a surrogate replacement for my late sister, a treasured daughter lost in toddlerhood.

"They're always fakes," Freddy said as we approached the barn at the end of the little alley. "Any wild child we have ever been presented with has always proved out totally bogus. This one here, for example. We will walk in and catch the girl reading her Bible."

He swung open the door to the barn, failing to knock, perhaps as a strategy of surprise.

But rather I was the one surprised, for upon entering to the balcony gallery of the place we found Dr. Scott waiting as if he expected us.

"The Messieurs Delegate, *père et fils*," he said, opening his arms to embrace my father. Freddy headed him off with a hearty handshake.

My father had evidently made an appointment with Scott. He constantly put me off my guard in this fashion, showing himself to be a step ahead, working in secretive ways.

"We are sorry to be late," Freddy said. "We were held up by a killing in town."

"Poor Hank Monk," Dr. Scott said, bowing his head for a full half second before brightening again. Monk, he indicated, had been a Savage Girl enthusiast.

With Scott was a welcoming committee of sorts, made up of two remarkable-looking individuals, one whom the doctor introduced as Jake Woodworth—an ancient, entirely white-haired mountain man dressed head to foot in elkskin—the other a round-bodied woman of middle years whom he called the "Sage Hen."

"The Sage Hen?" Freddy asked.

"The Sage Hen, Your Honor," the woman in question said, performing a curtsy.

Not quite believing my ears about that last, I left the group to venture to the railing.

Savage Girl was indeed below in the barn, but not at the Gospels. Instead, with one of Dr. Scott's extinguished torches in her hand, she used the snuffed-out charcoal at the tip to draw idly on the canvas-covered walls in front of her.

Off to the side, seated atop Savage Girl's cage, R. T. Flenniken, watching her while trying to appear not to.

Even in the brightness of a sunny day, the interior of the barn remained dim. But it wasn't as dark as it had been the evening before, and I appreciated Dr. Scott's strategy of running the Savage Girl show only as the light waned in the afternoon, or in the full darkness of evening. Murk helped along the mystery.

Seeing the spectacle's leading lady this morning disappointed me somewhat. She looked more simply a real girl. Petite, narrow-shouldered (I considered perhaps she had been malnourished by her years in the wilderness), thin of face, the cheekbones pronounced, the ugly mat of hair hanging limp at the back of her delicate, elongated neck.

If anything surprised me, it was that she was entirely unconstrained. Her cage door hung open. She made odd clicking sounds as she worked at her drawing.

I had not noticed it before, but the far wall of the barn was covered with many lines, figures and small sooty renderings, pictograms of some sort, done to the height of a person. It was impossible for me to understand their meaning. Whether Savage Girl had drawn every one or whether Dr. Scott saw this as some sort of enhancement of the dramatic effect he reached for, I could not know.

She suddenly turned her head away from her drawing and looked up at me. The eyes that I saw the evening before as amber now appeared an ordinary hazel. Her expression contained, amid its wildness, an uncanny glint of intelligence.

Did she recognize me? A member of her public who had now come to see her spectacle twice in a row?

She obviously had many such adherents. I felt myself, under her stare, diminish. I wanted to turn away, but she had me fixed. She dropped her gaze before I could drop mine.

R. T. Flenniken climbed the ladder from below and approached me. "You are Hugo, right? The son?"

"Yes?"

"You might want to take a try at these." He held out the pair of claw devices that Savage Girl wielded to such great effect during the show. "Sure, put 'em on," he said. He spoke in a wheezing stridor, passing his words through his nose.

I expected the claw hands to be somehow fabricated out of gray-painted wood, false as the act itself, but taking them, hefting them, I realized just how lethal they were.

A pair, identical, one for each hand, three blades on each, like triple stilettos. All six razors measured a half foot long in honed steel and were attached to a metal rig that was similar to the guard on a fencing foil. This guard had an iron peg running crosswise through the middle of it. The whole device came off as well smithed and ingenious.

"I had 'em made up myself," Flenniken said.

It so happened I liked knives. I slipped my hand inside one of the vicious claws, folding my grip around the crosswise peg. Then the other.

"We first tried giving her fangs," the mouth breather said, "but a girl with fangs just looks silly, and besides, they wouldn't fit right and made her gums bleed. These here were just the ticket. A man feels reborn with a set of knives on his fists."

Reborn, yes. Unassailable. I waved my *bayonetas* in the air and instantly gashed the back of my left hand with a blade of the right.

"First blood," the Toad said, smiling, and retrieved the nasty things from me.

"You neglect the third act," I heard Freddy saying to Dr. Scott. "Your show needs a turn."

"It is poor theater, you are right," Dr. Scott said. "The huge crowds it attracts are unsophisticated in the extreme."

"My darling has followers," spoke up the Sage Hen, "who come here night after night." Her voice resembled a deep-seated squeaking.

"Let her bathe, then let her be dressed again," Freddy said, gesticulating with his hands, framing the imaginary scene below. "The spectators believe that the show is over. They shuffle and mill, unsure if they should leave."

"I always told 'im we should be selling waffles to the audience," interjected Jake Woodworth.

My father would not be deterred. "But it is a false ending. From outside the barn, a wolf howl is heard, then another, and soon a whole chorus. They crowd all about, surrounding us in the darkness, yowling."

Freddy threw his head back and let loose a full-throated howl. I had to laugh. Like many confident men of wealth, he had mastered a trick, one I had not yet gotten hold of myself, that of not caring what other men think.

I glanced over my shoulder at Savage Girl, considering whether she might answer my father's wolf call. But after looking mildly up at us, she returned to her drawing.

"It is her wolf pack, returned to collect their own!" said my father, effectively imitating Dr. Scott's theatrical delivery. "Chaos! Trembling! Abrupt banging sounds against the building walls!"

"I shout out, 'They have come for her!'" said Dr. Scott, getting swept up in the moment.

"Your torch somehow snuffs itself out," Freddy said. "Darkness. Forms move down below."

"I could get the dogs to do it," Scott said.

"And when the torch is finally relit . . ." Freddy said.

"She is vanished," Scott said.

"She is vanished," my father said, nodding.

"Oh, my," said the Sage Hen.

"That'll do," pronounced Jake Woodworth. He let go a black stream of liquefied tobacco down onto the barn floor below.

Dr. Scott was silent for a beat, his face straining with contained excitement. "Yes, that's very good. I might use that."

He bowed to my father. "I yield to a dramaturge of superior abilities."

"But don't you realize, Dr. Scott—or Calef, may I call you Calef?"

Dr. Scott bowed again, preening.

"You know, Cal, this is no life for a young girl."

Freddy said it gently, bringing us all back down to earth after the extravagance of his previous presentation. It was another marked characteristic I noticed in my father's dealings among people, the ability to switch moods completely and abruptly. It made his interlocutors strain to follow him and thus put them in his power.

He walked over to the railing. "No life for a young girl at all," he repeated softly, looking down at Savage Girl.

My father is an autodidact. A self-taught dabbler with a lot of time on his hands, and there can be nothing more annoying than that. At various times in his life, he studied Sanskrit, Swahili and the Occitan dialect of the Languedoc. Still, it surprised me a little to hear my father call out in a language I had never heard.

"*Kimaru, nai-bi,*" he said.

The effect upon Savage Girl was immediate. It was as though she had touched the leads of a galvanic battery. She jerked her head around and stared at my father, a look of pure excitement seizing her features.

"*Kimaru, nai-bi,*" Freddy said again.

Savage Girl let out a screech, a sound I had never before or since heard a human voice make.

She rose to her feet, bounded across the barn, leaped up one of the pillars that held the balcony in place and, before any of us could react, had scrambled to the other side of the railing opposite my father, to where her face was inches away from his. She stood balancing there for a long moment, grinning, a wild-haired banshee.

Then—my heart stopped—she back-flipped down to the floor of the barn with a resounding thump. Racing around the space like a madwoman, running on two feet and occasionally on four, she finished up by zipping suddenly into her cage and slamming the door shut.

She did not come out for the remainder of our visit.

4

I remember thinking green, green, *g* in "green," *g* in "gin," and marveling at how the whiskey went in the green bottles and the gin went in the brown.

Well, no, that didn't much make sense. It was the other way around. The first sign I wasn't myself. I had drunk gin and whiskey both, since returning to Costello's after dinner that night, chasing a chimera, drawn to a creature I could barely believe existed.

Gin the rising favorite, newly fashionable, a gin drunk seen to be more sophisticated, less likely to result in one's stomach emptying upon one's shoes.

"We tried to buy her," I informed the muttonchopped stranger next to me, an excellent gent I had only just met, matching me drink for drink and keeping up.

"Tried to buy her?" Muttonchops asked, unfocusedly. Unfocusedly?

"We tried to buy her, and they would not sell."

"Offer 'em more," he suggested.

"We did," I said.

"'D' Street?" he asked. "The Barbary?"

"'A' Street," I said. "Right next door."

This caused Muttonchops to erupt in drooling chuckles. "Sheee?" he said. "Shee-hee-heeee!"

We had indeed tried to buy Savage Girl. Or rather Freddy had. Before I quite knew what was happening, earlier that morning at the barn, my father had become engaged in a spirited bidding war. Although "war" might not be the word for it, since he was bidding against himself.

"I think five hundred would be fair to take her off your hands," he had said to Dr. Scott.

I felt myself confused. Why was my father offering to buy a creature he had labeled a fraud? And hadn't we fought a nationwide war just a decade earlier, whereby human flesh could not be bought or sold by other humans?

"Five hundred!" Dr. Scott crowed. "Five hundred gold? Why, that's most generous!"

"Do we have a deal?"

"Yes!" Scott said, seizing my father's hand. Then, abruptly, pulling back.

"What am I doing?" Scott said. "I have partners in this concern."

"I own half of her," Jake Woodworth said. "I found her near dead up in the hills, and she's half mine."

"Then the Sage Hen here, she is owed a great deal," Dr. Scott said. "She nursed her back to health."

The Sage Hen nodded, well, sagely. "Yarrow smoke, mesquite oil, orange water."

"And laudanum," Dr. Scott added.

"A scant dram," Sage Hen said.

"Six hundred, then," my father had said.

"Deal!" Dr. Scott had pronounced again.

Only not. A pattern emerged, recognizable from my time the previous summer working under the speculator Jay Gould on Wall Street.

A price, agreed upon, then jacked up, agreed upon, then jacked again.

As Mr. Gould would say, *By God, I have him well cooked!*

In our case at the barn that morning, Dr. Scott had been the one who had managed to fricassee us.

"She needs my constant minding," the Sage Hen said. "Without me I believe she is like to perish from sadness."

Whatever is not nailed down is mine, Mr. Gould used to say. *Whatever I can pry up is not nailed down.*

Only we couldn't pry her up.

After I spent untold hours that night drinking in Costello's Saloon and Shooting Gallery, the room went cockeyed. The ceiling seemed to be somehow dropping, drumming its stamped-surface designs upon my cranium. My sadness abided. I needed the Sage Hen to come take care of me.

"I have lost her forever," I said.

"Let's have another drink," Muttonchops said. "Are we on gin or whiskey this time around?"

I had already fallen once, when I slipped on a brass cartridge casing. I saw dozens of rimfire .22 shells scattered across the linoleum, all of which, the shells and the linoleum, looked to me as if they wanted to come up and hit me in the face.

Good to stay put. Whiskey. I had never consumed so much even on the loosest night at college.

I felt light, high, and then down and heavy. My head was one with the bar. All true drunks, Bev Willets used to tell me, consider the floor their best friend.

At some point in the evening, I felt myself assaulted by Muttonchops and a confederate, who put me in a corner and began an aggressive search of my pockets. There seemed to be some disagreement about paying for drinks, but that was no reason for them to steal my shoes. No other patron noticed or cared that I was being robbed right there in the establishment.

Colm Cullen came through Costello's dice-set doorway just about that time. My hero. He muscled the assailants away, regained my footwear and returned a jackknife that had been stripped from me. I decided it might be wise to move back to gin from whiskey.

"You'll need to keep a good lookout while you're in Virginia," Colm said, shaking some of the drunkenness out of me. He wore his hair slicked back with brilliantine and his mustache well waxed. "It wouldn't do for us to lose Mr. Hugo Delegate."

Two men stood behind him, dressed in the local uniform of blue flannel shirt, blue pants and tall leather boots. I *believed* them to be two anyway but was unsure.

"My associates," Colm said. "Grainger and Markham."

Good. They were two.

"Would you take a drink, gentlemen?"

My soft, pink hand went out to grasp their rough ones, and then the same hand returned to me.

"Chew?" offered Colm.

I shook my head. Chew had always been sick-making for me.

"Smoke, then," said Colm. He removed some shreds of tobacco from a pouch and wrapped one tightly in paper.

I didn't smoke either. Yet now I did.

The lamps down the bar threw a flickering light over Colm's Irish countenance as Grainger and Markham concentrated on their drinks.

"Your finest tarantula juice!" commanded Markham.

"Another whiskey!" I echoed, even though I had switched to gin.

"Hugo's in deep with the Brilliant," said Colm. "Took him down the throat of it yesterday."

We tossed ours back. My vision went temporarily missing. When it returned to me, the boys were swaying, while I was perfectly still.

I decided I would rather be perfectly still outside Costello's. I rose from the barstool and found myself transported at a staggering trot out the back door of the saloon, on a little trip to the porch, taking deep, shuddering breaths, winding up leaning heavily against a shaky wooden column.

Gunfire, crisp in the night air of the Washoe. Next to me a half dozen shooters with puny .22 rifles, blasting away at the mountain.

The obsidian western dark. Nose smarting from the alkali dust. The moon had come out white and then went lopsided. I glanced up at the flank of Sun Mountain, where the big billboards glowed vaguely like a deck of cards that had been scattered there. Everything looked hollowed out.

I could see Scott's barn beyond the shooting gallery, the front of the place drenched in shadow. I bowed my head, hoping my dinner would stay where it was supposed to be. It didn't. I staggered to the railing of the porch and retched down into the gulch.

Always puke from an upper story if you can. Much more entertaining.

When I lifted my eyes, I saw a vendor put away his wares in the little alley that ran up to Scott's barn, setting goods in sacks and laying the sacks on a low barrow.

It was time to go.

At the shallow ditch in the back of the barn, where the structure met the rise of the slope, a small figure moved hurriedly in the darkness. Wrapped in an oversize coat, clutching at a blanket.

With bare feet.

I stood still. I couldn't hear my breathing. I had stopped breathing.

She moved toward me, right beneath the blaze of the shooting gallery guns, slipping past us all, past the puffs of dust sent up as the slugs tore into the slope.

"What did you say to her?" I had asked my father, earlier in the day, wondering about what possible incantation he'd used to bring Savage Girl running, racing, leaping up to him like a puppet on a string.

"I said, 'Come here, young woman.'"

I was beside myself. "In what language, for heaven's sakes?"

"Comanche," Freddy said.

"Comanche? Comanche?" A tongue I was entirely unaware my father knew.

"I've picked up a few phrases here and there, and some grammar," he said. "It's the common language of the Plains, you know." Freddy had done a couple tours of the West already and for all I knew had spent time camping out in a tepee.

"Whyever on God's green earth did you think Comanche would work on her?"

"There's no need to bring God into it," Freddy said. "The pictograms she was drawing on the wall were Comanche."

There on the porch of Costello's Saloon and Shooting Gallery, I paddled through the inland seas of alcohol sloshing in my brain, trying in vain to remember the magic words my father had used to summon Savage Girl.

"Ka-ka-ka-roo," I stuttered, before giving up. Instead I was reduced to saying softly, almost to myself, "Come here, young woman," in the useless language of my mother tongue. She couldn't hear me over the bang of the sharpshooters on the firing range and passed out of sight down the little gully behind Costello's.

But first, I swear, her eyes caught mine. If you told me this creature had come fresh from heaven or had been flung out from hell, it wouldn't have mattered.

I would still have wanted to run from her, or save her.

The next morning, feeling like the opposite of a million dollars, I cleaned the throw-up off myself and ventured forth once again from my befouled nest at the International.

Whole body throbbing, my head ringing like a dinner bell (though the thought of food revolted me), I went to find my father, only to be told he had left the hotel early. I made a wild guess where Freddy had gone and followed him there.

On the streets of Virginia, the normal chaos reigned, the noise and stench a fulsome challenge to my delicate, gin-bruised sensibilities. At the intersection of "A" Street and Summit Avenue, an altercation. Some fool had brought a salt-laden camel into town, and the sight of the strange beast frightened a team of horses, which had run up the sidewalk and mangled a passing Celestial.

Both teamsters bellowed at each other, the horses screamed, and the stubborn dromedary looked stupidly around for some victim out of which to take a piece. A camel's bite, I had heard, was vicious, so I kept my distance.

"You see the wild in collision with the domesticated," said my father's voice, Freddy suddenly appearing at my side. "The domesticated is alarmed by the recrudescence of the wild into its peaceable kingdom."

A false metaphor, I thought, since both camel and horse had long been tamed by man. But I let it go.

Freddy went accompanied that morning by a man in a fresh black derby hat and dark pin-striped suit, whom he did not introduce, and had Colm Cullen along with him as well. Both men appeared sober, Colm magically so after the excesses of the previous evening, and both wore expressions of grim determination.

Something was up.

Wordlessly, Freddy led the way past the raucous crash scene to the end of "A" Street. The sound of screaming horses faded. Costello's, the scene of my floor-crawling drunk the night before, lay fallow and silent.

We turned, like a platoon in march step, into the little duckboarded alleyway.

My father and I left Colm and the derby-wearing stranger waiting in the lane and proceeded on to Dr. Scott's barn.

"Friedrich," I said formally, "I want to employ Colm Cullen."

"Sure," he said. "We'll take him on at Mill Valley."

"No," I said.

"In the city? At the office?" Blandly agreeable.

"No, I mean I want to employ him. Me, personally."

Off his look I said, "I require a bodyguard, and it can't be your man, it has to be mine. I can't have you always snooping into my life. I need to have privacy, somewhere you can't go."

The minor squabble with Muttonchops of the evening before had reawakened my need for protection. During my here and there nocturnal ramblings, I felt at times that I was getting in over my head. I wanted a second man to back me up should I encounter fellows I couldn't handle alone. Yes, I required a praetorian and wanted to make sure he would be someone who wouldn't report back to my father.

"Colm Cullen?" Freddy asked.

"What do you think would be a fair price to hire him?"

We were at the barn by then, where inside the same trio of blackguards greeted us, Woodworth, the Sage Hen, the oleaginous Scott himself.

"Delegate!" Scott called out. "I have good news."

He thrust himself forward and grabbed my father's hand.

I looked below, locating Savage Girl in the gloom. She slept, or appeared to sleep, curled up like a tabby in a corner next to her cage, watched over by an equally sleepy Toad.

"Very good news," Dr. Scott repeated. "The three principals here—myself, my friend Jacob Woodworth, and the Sage Hen—you may congratulate us on our hard work, we have agreed upon a proper level of remuneration."

"Ah," Freddy said. "I thought we had determined that formerly."

"Changed. Negated! Those negotiations we cancel, withdraw, obviate and declare void. Instead of an outright sale, and after laborious give-and-take between the three of us that became quite heated at times—"

"You must grasp the degree of our sacrifice, losing the dear creature," interjected the Sage Hen.

"We have come to a magnificent compromise," Scott announced, sounding as though he had reconciled God and Lucifer. "It involves, and I know you will be as excited by this concept as we are, a lease arrangement rather than a complete transfer of ownership."

"See, we would be losing her forever if we didn't keep a hold of her somehow," Jake Woodworth put in.

"That is correct," Dr. Scott said. "I must say it was the Sage Hen who broke the jam. It is she for whom we must all be grateful."

"Por nada," said the Sage Hen.

Scott raised himself on his tiptoes in a show of ecstasy. "A woman of most surprising capabilities, I have to say, as is evident by her multilingual phraseology."

"So . . ." my father said. "One thousand, or was it two when we broke off yesterday?"

"Oh, no, no, these new terms require a complete reorganization of payment. We have mutually agreed upon a sum of five thousand dollars for a yearlong indenture."

"Six months," said the Sage Hen and Woodworth simultaneously.

"Yes, yes, I apologize, we went back and forth on this also, and such a flurry of numbers and terms always work to dizzy me. The contract is for five thousand dollars for six months, such contract renewed at end of term by mutual agreement of the parties, with a concomitant adjustment in payment."

"Upwards," said the Sage Hen. "Of course."

"Of course," my father echoed.

On the barn floor, R. T. Flenniken had dropped his somnolent posture and stood directly below us, staring up at the group on the balcony.

"I have taken the liberty of employing my attorney"—Scott snapped his fingers imperiously, summoning an officious little man in a gray frock coat from the shadows at the end of the gallery—"Rodney Estes, to draw up a contract, embedding said terms within legalistic constructs."

"Rodney Estes, Esquire," the gray frock coat said, pushing forward a sheaf of papers.

Scott said, "I would rather this be done on a handshake, but the Sage Hen insisted we formalize—"

"May I make a counteroffer?" my father said, interrupting.

"It will not be heard, sir!" Scott said shrilly. "It will not be heard!"

Flenniken had begun making small sounds of distress down below, pulling at his sparse, dirt-colored hair and walking in circles, muttering to himself.

"I'm sorry, I'm sorry for my tone," Dr. Scott said to Freddy, regaining his composure. "If you knew what an arduous process it was to arrive at this agreement, you would not ask, sir, you would instead express your eternal thanks for the generosity of the Sage Hen here, and of Woodworth."

He abruptly left us, strode to the balcony railing, and screamed, "R.T., will you please strangle yourself!"

I looked at my father, feeling sorry for him. It appeared as though they had him boxed in.

Scott returned, smoothing his hair and face.

Freddy said, addressing the whole group, "Begging your pardon for any discomfiture it might cause, but I would like to express an answering offer to you all."

His bearing silenced them. My father could be almost regal sometimes.

The trio of handlers, a quartet now with the addition of Estes, waited on him, expectant.

"My offer is . . . nothing."

They had leaned forward a few inches to hear him, and now they fell back as a group, nonplussed.

"Nothing," Scott said softly.

"Not a penny," Freddy said.

Scott managed to conquer his surprise by going into high dudgeon. "An outrage, sir, you waste our time, we come to you in good faith," he said, sputtering out the phrases.

"I tol' you we was pushing him too far!" Jake Woodworth shouted.

Scott was not quite through working himself into a paroxysm of wounded indignation. "That is all, Mr. Delegate, we do not have to endure your abuse. Leave this place at once."

"I will, but I will take Savage Girl with me."

New squeals of rage from the quartet. "You shall not, Delegate, you shall not! Mr. Woodworth, I must tell you, is an expert in all forms of fisticuffs, a man mountain who flattened the Truckee Giant with a single blow!"

"You will meet me in court!" shrieked Estes, stepping on Scott's last words.

"Thief! Thief!" called out the Sage Hen, as though raising an alarm.

Freddy merely turned away from them, opened the door, and summoned in from the alleyway outside Colm Cullen and the stranger in the derby hat.

"Gentlemen, the Sage Hen," he said, "this is Marshal Jack Pite, duly empowered authority of the Second Judicial District, State of Nevada. He is here to remind you, although it really does not need to be said, that to hold human beings in any form of peonage, slavery or illegal indenture, or in any way against their will, can under the Thirteenth Amendment to the U.S. Constitution draw federal felony charges down upon the perpetrator."

Pite did not look big, but he had an air of calm authority to him. And Cullen appeared able to handle anything that might be put forth by the eighty-year-old, white-haired man-mountain vanquisher of the Truckee Giant.

Hurrah! I thought. Lincoln freed the slaves!

Many things happened at once.

"I tol' you, I tol' you and tol' you!" Woodworth shouted.

The Sage Hen withdrew an evil-looking twin-barreled derringer from her person and pointed it at Marshal Pite.

My father leaned over the railing and summoned Savage Girl. As if under the spell of a djinn, she rose immediately and padded across the barn.

The Toad tried to block her, but with an effortless fake move Savage Girl made him trip over himself and fall. She walked around the man and went below the balcony to appear, only a second later, at the top of a ladder at the far end of the gallery.

Marshal Pite stepped over to the Sage Hen and took the derringer from her. Somehow frozen by his gaze, she did not resist. He tossed the little pistol back over his shoulder, and it clattered to the barn floor behind him.

"I've got a bigger one," he said, extracting an enormous Colt from beneath his suit jacket.

And that was that.

I had never been so proud of my father. Foxing the con artist and endorsing the rights of man in the bargain. Life, liberty and the pursuit of et cetera.

Freddy threw open the door to the alley and motioned Savage Girl to accompany him outside, as if into the heady atmosphere of freedom.

She hesitated.

Did she not want to go? Was she terrified of Scott? Or was the responsibility of independence too much for her?

Colm Cullen and Jack Pite had the quartet of her former masters backed off down the gallery from the rest of us. The marshal holstered his sidearm in a casual way that I could never have imitated had I worked for years at practicing it.

Savage Girl suddenly slid over the balcony rail, shinnied down one of the support pillars as if it were a sidewalk she were walking along, crossed to the enormous bathtub and reached inside.

The hand mirror. Her arm streaming with water, she retrieved it, reversed her course up the ladder and headed through the door beside my father.

Mewling out the mournful toad cry of his species, R. T. Flenniken emerged from the dark end of the balcony and charged toward Freddy.

"You shan't have her!" he cried. "She's mine!"

Marshal Pite put him low with a single fist blow to the temple, and the five of us—Colm, the lawman, myself, my father and Savage Girl—stepped out of the sideshow barn into the alleyway, trusting never to return.

✵ 5 ✵

We lost her.

My parents had made ready for a fast getaway. At the end of the alley, Anna Maria waited in a closed coach driven by a swarthy *pistolero* with a reckless gleam in his eye.

Savage Girl came willingly. We piled in, Freddy handing off his new protégée to Anna Maria, then climbing inside himself with me behind. Colm Cullen mounted up to sit beside the driver in the cab.

Leaving Marshal Pite to guard the alley's entrance onto "A" Street and cut off all pursuit, we jolted away in haste.

It was the closest I had ever been to Savage Girl, and it allowed me the opportunity to examine her closely. She sat hunched at our feet, seats and benches and erect posture seemingly foreign to her.

Again I was impressed by her slightness. She looked waiflike, or rather urchinish. I had the uncanny sense that we, as a family, had acquired a new pet. She smelled rather nice, though, not like a dog. Her remarkable hazel eyes, the left one marked by a tiny rectangular fleck of black.

I wanted her to display excitement, pleasure, a wild gratitude, but she embodied none of those emotions. She looked not at us but mainly at the floor of the coach. She reminded me of the shyness displayed by the local Paiute Indians I had met in the Washoe. I always got the sense they were embarrassed for me. As if I were behaving in a mawkish or inappropriate manner.

The female at my feet seemed vital enough. Savage Girl's diminutive size appeared to come from having all excess somehow burned away, so what remained was a skeletal rigor. I remember thinking that

I would not like to face off with her in a wrestling match. Too much caged energy.

"Dear one," Anna Maria said, reaching out. Savage Girl did not react to her touch. But at least, I thought, she did not snarl and bite off one of my mother's fingers.

"How old do you think she is?" Anna Maria said.

Neither my father nor I answered, lost in contemplation of the being we had suddenly invited into our lives. Creature or beast or human or ghost, we didn't know. Her presence filled the coach with a palpable sense of oddity.

"Say some Comanche to her," I urged.

"Is she a Comanche child, then?" Anna Maria asked.

My father remained silent, fidgeting with his hands, inscrutable. Anna began to pet Savage Girl's black, tangled mane.

"Virginia," she said. "That will be her name."

Freddy and I both knew what that meant. I had lost my little sister to scarlet fever, when I was seven and she four, our darling, named Virginia, after, in fact, Virginia City, where my father's mines produced millions a year. We had all doted on her and felt the deep wound of her death. She had been replaced, two years later, by my brother, Nicholas, but it was not the same.

A hole in the human heart, my mother had said, referring to the gulf that gold was meant to fill. But Anna Maria possessed an inner void of her own, created by the death of my sister and bored deep by longing.

Thus I suddenly understood my father's need to bring Savage Girl with us, not out of any special idea to study her as a feral child—because he believed, at that point in time, that she was a fraud—but quietly to put her forward as some sort of replacement for my lost sister.

Virginia, my mother wanted to call her. The transubstantiation of this child for the one vanished into death had already commenced. Savage Girl would be around the same age as my late sibling, had little Virginia lived.

My father poked the trap window open to the driver. "Stop at the International," he said, "and then we go on to the train."

Why did we make that fateful detour to our hotel? My father never explained. Halting in front of the busy hostelry, he leaped out and vanished within. My mother made a move to leave the coach also, and there was a moment of confusion.

I definitely did not want to be alone with Savage Girl, and neither did I think she should be left without a watchful eye trained upon her. Climbing out to accompany my mother, I thought to ask Colm Cullen to transfer himself from the driver's bench to a post inside the coach.

Doing so, I left her alone but for an instant. When Colm moved past me, he suddenly stopped. "Where is she?"

Startled, I looked back. The coach's interior was empty.

"Mother," I said sharply.

We had her, and then we lost her.

On the seat, left behind when she vanished, her precious hand mirror.

"Oh, no," groaned Anna Maria.

I was forlorn after our panicked search turned up nothing, not from a sense of losing Savage Girl herself but because I knew that her disappearance would disappoint my mother.

I had failed my parents once more. In a cruel replay of her earlier grief, Anna Maria would see an already beloved daughter taken from her.

We reunited with Freddy. Colm and I scanned the crowded street to no avail. I kept assuring Anna Maria that Savage Girl would be found but finally agreed with Freddy. We had lost her.

As of that moment, my parents and I were seized with the same feeling, a sense of unhappiness with the International Hotel, the scene of bad luck and misfortune, up to and including murder in the club dining room. It was agreed: We would move back into our private train, which was parked on a siding at the northern end of "C" Street in the lower part of town.

I was sure Freddy would be totally crestfallen, but I was mistaken. My father took the news of Savage Girl's disappearance with disturbing composure.

"No doubt she returned to Scott," he said. "The devil she knew being preferable to the gods she did not."

I don't often feel this way, but at that moment I wanted to sock my father. Such an incredible masterstroke, extricating her from Scott's clutches, and then to be so blasé about losing her!

"If she does not want to stay with us, Hugo, we can't attempt to imprison her," he said wearily, covering his eyes with his hand. "If we did, we would be exactly like Dr. Scott."

"We can snatch her back again," I said. Thinking of my poor mother, who had the look of someone bearing up under hardship.

Freddy remained silent.

We continued, without speaking, to our cars on the Virginia & Truckee siding.

Two days on, I sat in the second-to-last car on our train, the parlor car, brooding, staring out at a bleak landscape of mill piles, smokestacks and tailing dumps that represented the effluvia from the Virginia silver mines.

Sandobar, Freddy had named the twelve-car consist, with sleepers, a galley, parlors, a shooting car and a six-man crew to keep it running. But a train car at rest, I discovered, resembled a coffin. We remained stranded on the siding, provisioning for the epic trip across the continent, Freddy commissioning some work on the interiors. He was always remodeling.

Virginia City was right there, clearly within view, the town boundary fifty yards away, but after losing Savage Girl we shut ourselves off from it.

Tahktoo joined me that afternoon, entering the parlor car silently, easing cross-legged to the floor to work on his knitting.

Melancholy, I gazed out the window some more. "You know, Henry Comstock wound up committing suicide," I said, to myself rather than to the berdache (he didn't converse much). Comstock, the early miner who had swindled a couple of others out of what turned into the biggest claim ever in the history of the country. Then lost it all.

"They named the whole sixty-million-dollar lode after him, and he put a bullet in his head in a nickel-a-night flop."

The alkali wind swept through the chock-a-block town jumbled at the foot of the mountain. The berdache did not seem contaminated with the same mood of mournfulness.

Wait, wait, Bill Howe says.

Tahktoo had upon first meeting struck me—

Wait, wait. The rotund attorney waves his hands. Your father had a twelve-car private train?

Sandobar, I say. Named after Grandfather's estate on Long Island.

By that time, late morning Saturday, the warden's quarters where we speak are a little more lively, busy with a half dozen clerks, factotums and secretaries, all summoned from the law offices of Howe & Hummel. Actual personnel from the Tombs—turnkeys, bailiffs and such—visit only occasionally.

Out the window, across Centre Street, the firm's immodest billboard-size sign dominates the area, in enormous block letters that are illuminated by night (HOWE & HUMMEL'S LAW OFFICE), looming over the Tombs as if to declare that the prison is a mere annex to the illustrious partnership.

Imagine an arraigned criminal, bonded out of the Tombs, wavering in his conviction of what to do next. Whiskey always foremost in his mind. But then the huge blazing billboard. Perhaps, before a drink, an attorney. It sometimes happens that way.

The firm's clients include the most celebrated citizens of New York City, the highest of the high. Bankers. Brokers. The actor Edwin Booth. P. T. Barnum. And the lowest of the low. When seventy-four brothel madams were rounded up during a purity drive, every one of them named Howe & Hummel as counsel.

With all my talking, I am perhaps overtired, since I don't feel like sleeping but rather exist in a sort of in-between twilight of mind and memory. I still have blood on my clothes, random spatters from the corpse in the Gramercy Park mansion.

One of the cars wasn't our own, I say. We were transporting Lincoln's car back to the East as a favor to Huntington.

Huntington, Howe says. That would be the Central Pacific man.
Yes.

Lincoln's car. Of the martyred president.

One made for his use, I say. Unfortunately, he only ever occupied it in death. It carried his casket from Washington, D.C., to Springfield.

Howe asks, This car was in your train on the siding at Virginia City?

I didn't wonder at his special interest. The Lincoln car holds great significance for many people. Stories, myths and tall tales are linked with it in the popular mind.

Do you mark it, Mr. Hummel?

Hummel nods and produces a soft sound such as "Uh-hmmn." His first verbal communication of the morning, I believe, although he is a furious note taker.

I see the thought wheels turning in their massive brains. A possible defense strategy. On his trip across the country, the Delegate boy becomes inhabited by the ghost that haunts the Lincoln car. He (that is, me) is driven mad. The late murders are to be assigned not to me, not to her, but to some disembodied ectoplasm. The spook of John Wilkes Booth himself, perhaps.

I am found innocent by reason of demonic possession.

A ludicrous strategy, but William Howe is known for putting over all sorts of ludicrousness to juries.

An anecdote they tell of him: When Howe was once rehearsing his dramatic closing speech to the jury in a capital case, his partner, Hummel, suggested that at a precise climactic moment in the oration some sign of emotion might be appropriate.

A tear, perhaps, said Hummel.

Howe considered, then asked, From which eye?

Had he been on the boards, Bill Howe could have been the greatest actor of the day.

I will order lunch, he says now. But pray continue on.

Tahktoo had upon first meeting struck me as an incredible grotesque, either laughable or sneerable, his craggy form appearing ridiculous, draped in a dress. But the longer I associated with him, the more I came to recognize his beauty.

Lhamana, the Zuni called them. The twin-spirited ones. Members of the tribe, both women and men, who crossed boundaries to take up the costume, behavior and activities of the opposite sex. "Berdache" was a name the Spanish saddled them with, meaning "slave."

Eventually I came to realize that Tahktoo had a greater aura of personal dignity than anyone I had ever known. His appearance tended to trigger instant fury on the part of outsiders. But somehow he kept himself (she kept herself? pronouns went funny around him) immune to ridicule, raillery, intimidation, insinuation, humiliation and the other sundry slings and arrows with which we humans sometimes assault each other.

Freddy had collected him in San Francisco. He had been abandoned there by an Office of Indian Affairs Quaker who with the best intentions had lured the berdache away from his homeland in the mountain desert of the Southwest. In order to show him the superiority of the white man's habits.

When Tahktoo failed to be sufficiently impressed by our national culture, the Quaker became miffed and sailed home to Washington, D.C.

The berdache wandered, bereft. Almost everyone he met heaped abuse upon him, some of it violent. But he didn't seem at all wounded by the experience.

When I asked him, or when Freddy did, what it was like, those days he spent alone in the hugger-mugger of the Bay, he pronounced the Zuni word *"Uhepono."*

The ruler of what his tribe called "the fourth world." Hell.

I sometimes tried to see our American world through Tahktoo's eyes. Something out of Bosch or Bruegel. One nightmare after another, rolling through the misty red night. He contained within herself both Aeneas and Dido. Or Tiresias, the perfect witness, who although blind is able to see all sides.

What are those demons up to now? Tahktoo would wonder, gazing at one drunk hammering at another as they both tumbled down

Telegraph Hill. How long will you rape one another's lives? It doesn't matter to me, but I'm just curious. The berdache had seen in his lifetime Zuni babies impaled alive on Navajo lances. So the sins of San Francisco didn't impress him much.

His homeland in the Arizona and New Mexico territories was, to Tahktoo, the true paradise. His people gardened diligently, producing a surplus every year. All our American virtues, all ambition, all endeavor, all thrusting oneself forward—were looked upon as negatives in Zuni culture. The community worked by a relaxed consensus.

In San Francisco my father had discovered the berdache at a meeting of railroad men, a huge social affair, cigars and brandy and backslapping. Later, the girls. During coffee, after the meal, Tahktoo was brought forward and introduced as entertainment, displayed as a freak.

The sight of him, a male dressed as a female, elicited the usual reaction of robust disgust from the men. The eminences at the party began to toss wadded-up bits of dinner roll at him. They shouted phrases, meaningless, of course, to Tahktoo himself: "invert," "homogene," "fairy."

The scene turned more and more unpleasant. The railroad men began to demand that Tahktoo undress. They wished to ascertain his sex physically.

Show it! they shouted.

Freddy should have tried to stop it there. But he was aghast at the sheer ugliness of it, the howls of the American businessman when an unfamiliar element entered his world.

Show it! the men began to chant, stamping their feet rhythmically. They were ready to rip the berdache's clothes off themselves.

What's she got under there? Show it!

So Tahktoo did.

She lifted the flap of her dress and peeled down his underclothes. Stunning the room to silence.

The man-woman had an organ the size of a blacksmith's forearm.

One of the drunken railroaders, John Beese, stared, and stared, and then vomited all over himself.

Freddy departed the gathering when Tahktoo did, tracking him down and proposing a retainer relationship, something between a ward, a servant and a long-term guest.

The berdache joined our family. I had known him since I was eighteen. He was my teacher, and her unsoothing lessons stung my soul.

That afternoon, as I sat alone with him in Sandobar's parlor car, Tahktoo gestured out the window. There had come another one of them, Savage Girl's faithful followers, heaving rocks at our train. A ginger-bearded drunk.

Where is she? the man cried. *You won't take her!*

A few such fools had come out to confront us at the siding, a couple every day or so. At first we thought they had been put up to it by Dr. Scott, but this was not the case. The whole town had heard about the kidnapping of Savage Girl and considered it an uncharitable act of betrayal by rank outsiders. We had robbed Virginia of a local treasure.

Although in fact we had not. The story of the Delegates' taking the girl made the rounds, but the sequel of her vanishing failed to keep pace.

One of the dejected drunk's rocks banged into the side of the train. "Oh, for pity's sake," I said.

I went up front to ask Dowler, our steward, to chase the idiot away. The poor tortured soul outside had progressed to where he leaned his cheek against the varnished wood of the galley car, weeping and muttering. He knew what love was.

A couple days before, a trio of cowboys had shot up our engine tender a bit, demanding the release of Savage Girl into their care. And though I had been asleep for this incident, Freddy told me that the Sage Hen had been nabbed trying to slip inside the engineer's cab with a hammer, intending to spike the boiler.

"That lady's a devil," Freddy said. "Bit Dowler good as he escorted her off."

While I was at the front of the train seeking out the steward, I stumbled into something peculiar. Third back from the locomotive was the baggage car, *Black Diamond,* stuffed to the ceiling with our impedimenta.

It had been partitioned off. In one corner our hired carpenters made a small room. In that space, still in the process of being installed, was a gigantic bathtub that resembled the one in Dr. Scott's sideshow.

I would have to ask Freddy what was going on.

When I returned back to the parlor car, Tahktoo had begun a game with Tu-Li, employing the ivory gambling tiles from China with pictures of animals on them. The two of them played it incessantly. Another dreary day on the tracks.

By that time I just wanted to get the hell out of there, out of the dust and wind and away from the whiskey-bitten, lovelorn fools, back to New York and civilization.

⚜ 6 ⚜

A night later, while I slept, Sandobar left the Washoe forever. She traveled south to Carson City, north to Reno, and joined the Central Pacific tracks east toward the States. During this I was all unknowing, locked within a dreamless sleep.

No doubt the rhythm of the train soothed me, and also perhaps some deep interior awareness that we were leaving behind the dust and upsets of the Washoe Valley.

I have never been particularly well or healthy. My unsettled mind was beset by delusions and fancies of the most vile sort. For a period in my youth, I dwelled repeatedly and uncontrollably upon self-murder, developing an elaborate fantasy of plunging a knife into my own heart. I found myself locked in a recurring thought loop, in which suicide appeared to me to be the only true expression of human free will.

My dreams took me into violence against others, too. When I was sixteen and at St. Paul's School, headmaster Henry Coit expelled me after I was discovered, during one particular four A.M. bout of sleepwalking, standing over a sleeping freshman boy with a ball-peen hammer in my hand. I had to take Coit's word for it, since I had no memory of the incident myself. I dodged a sanatorium only by pleading amnesia, but I had secured my reputation as a thoroughly demented soul.

Even now, years later, I had my tics. I was a quiet man, but one dogged by a fascination with knives, bayonets, blades of any sort. Search among my pockets and you would turn up some kind of cutter. My compulsion helped draw me to the anatomical profession, with its well-honed scalpels and lancets, alongside an innate curiosity about what lay beneath the human skin.

Also, in any room I entered, I had the habit of casting about with my gaze until I located every bit of the color red—rugs, paintings, chinaware, anything. Red, the color of blood. I didn't wish myself to be so beset, but the obsession had gripped me ever since my teenage years.

"What is your connection to these specks of red you force yourself to catalog?" asked my physiology professor at Harvard, posing an obvious question. "Isn't the relation simply between an observer and the observed, nothing more diabolical than that?"

Such calming words helped but did not cure.

So I probably should not have been exposed to Virginia City, a town steeped in murderous red as the earth below gave up its silver blue. I needed peace, not savagery. Even Harvard at times proved too much in the way of contention and competition. The groves of academe, red in tooth and claw.

At any rate, I remained asleep as we left the Washoe and stayed that way until we were well into the great flat wastes of the Humboldt Basin. I remember waking, realizing we were moving and putting up my shade. Four A.M., by the watch on my bedside table. The deserted hour.

Outside, the landscape gleamed with unearthly light. Well, of course it was unearthly—it was the moon! Bright as the sun that night, as though we inhabited a different reality, spectral white instead of daylight yellow.

In the reflection in my window, I saw my own face, haggard and drawn. The effects of my recent illness had not, perhaps, totally receded. Our adventures in the Comstock exhausted me.

And then, just for an instant, beside my own, I saw the face of Savage Girl. A fierce and feral apparition. Teeth bared, eyes raging, brows arched. She looked as though she would eat me. Frightened, I gave a cry of alarm and turned to look.

Nothing there.

After that, when I tried to return to sleep, I found myself restless, shaken by my vision. I dressed and walked back past the servants' car, past the master sleeper and the parlor car, into what Freddy termed the shooting car, which everyone else called the den. The last in the consist, it had an open deck hanging off its back and racks of shotguns and rifles arranged along its bulkheads.

I rang for tea and felt peckish by the time it came, served by a sleepy-eyed Petey, our waiter.

While the light came up over what's marked on maps as the Great American Desert, some of the most unhappy landscape in the world, I sat alone, musing. Meanwhile, the somnolent Sandobar slowly woke.

A private train represents a mansion on wheels, a small community, a mobile caravansary, population twenty. "Drone cages," the railroad workers called luxury carriages such as ours, a laborer's sneer, or "private varnish," in tribute to the naval-like finish on the exteriors. Privileged worlds, rolling past the track layers as they sweated and heaved. They were the worker bees, we were the drones.

I remember being introduced to railroading in general and Sandobar in particular by a locomotive engineer named Walter Siemonds, a boyhood hero of mine. I was a child of ten and enamored of all things mechanical. An earlier version of Sandobar idled in the West Side yards, a six-car consist back then, Freddy's brand-new toy. All around us were trains of different lengths and sizes, some of them having just come in and still belching smoke.

Our locomotive in those days was a 4-0-0 hog in the American style, a behemoth to my young eyes. Walter Siemonds brought me up onto the engineer's deck, where I swooned over the boiler and the red-hot firebox, the blast pipe that caused the engine's *chuff-chuffing* sounds.

Is there anything a man can do more to please a boy than to let him blow the whistle on a train? With a V-shaped cowcatcher, a massive headlight, an elegant diamond stack with a screen that destroyed sparks by pulverizing them, the steam locomotive was an amazing machine.

"The smokestack has a thing that kills sparks by pulverizing them!" I shouted to Freddy, my ten-year-old voice lost in the whoosh of the boiler as Walter got up steam.

I fell in love with the microcosmic world of it, not only the power plant but the whole train. "Consist" came into my vocabulary, which meant the order of the cars, along with phrases like "jerk a lung" (to disconnect an air hose) and "gandy dancer" (a track worker). I remember thinking of Sandobar as a kind of human body, with a locomotive head, a galley belly and parlor-car arms and legs.

Walter ran me up along the Hudson River to Tappan Reach and back. The main fact about a locomotive (that particular one, *Mercury*, was decorated with a painted brass cartouche of winged sandals) is that a child can drive it, or at least be safely allowed to pretend to drive it. While I might run a buggy off a road, I would have to err pretty badly to derail *Mercury*.

"Pound her out!" I'd scream, and Walter would help me notch up the throttle, the Palisades flashing by across the river like stone sentinels.

Over the years Freddy had added to the original until our train was a full dozen cars long, all "bogies," eighty-foot monster steam cars fitted with Westinghouse air brakes. They all had names, too: *Anna Maria, Black Diamond, Evening Star, The Brave, Topaz, Nighthawk, Porpoise, United States, Fury, The Bruce, Crucible* and *The Globe*.

Sandobar had come a long way from her beginnings at the West Side yards. She was now crossing the pan-flat Nevada wastelands, aimed directly at the dawn.

Sitting alone in the shooting car (*The Globe*), I thought that the first servants had to be waking by now, up front in the galley, Cookie Lewis and her two Irish girl helpers, Rose Devlin and Annie Heffernan. I imagined them firing the stoves, rooting in the ice closets for breakfast supplies, bickering amiably.

Always, on a long journey, the early days are taken up with settling in, getting straight on schedules, activities and duties, the bustle of leave-taking before the lapse into routine.

I suppose I could have gone up front and participated in some of that lively commotion, but I preferred solitude. It is usually as difficult to be alone on a train as it is on a ship. Even on Sandobar, where I had my own sleeping compartment.

Everything irritated me—the splendid desolation of the landscape, the *clickety-clacking* of the carriage, the steady, nauseating rock of the train. Like a child, I wished to sulk by myself and at the same time wondered peevishly why I was being ignored.

I picked up a two-day-old newspaper from Virginia City, reading without interest until I came to this:

GOLD HILL NEWS, JUNE 12, 1875

The most cruel, outrageous and revolting murder ever committed in this city was that of Hank Monk on Friday morning last. At breakfast in the club dining room of International Hotel, he found himself surprised by the scoundrel Butler Fince, a disgraced Reno lawman, recently of Deadwood, in the Dakota Territory. Monk, a stage coach dispatcher esteemed by all, sat at repast when Fince stalked into his presence, and the two had words.

Fince pulled iron and summarily assassinated Hank Monk, found with his head lying on the dining table at which he so late had et, a napkin over his head and face, the tablecloth beneath his head being saturated with blood. There was a single wound in his chest, and the back of his left hand was somewhat lacerated in his struggle to free himself from the grasp of the fiend who had him in his power. The murderer took himself off and even today walks free on the streets of Virginia, seemingly immune to prosecution.

From the testimony of witnesses, including Bay financier Hon. Oliver Stringfist, Fince accused Monk of perpetrating the cowardly murder of his brother, Peter, a wildcatter, in a cabin in the Washoe, whose mutilated and headless corpse was found 27th last, cold and stiff with death. Sheriff Dick Tolle and a board of coroners inquiry found Peter Fince's death to be the work of wild beasts, as plentiful animal sign was found at scene.

Monk's is the third murder at the International Hotel in the past month.

It certainly is to be hoped that the murderous villain,

a Democrat, may eventually adorn the end of a rope.
His victim was a native of London, England, whence he
emigrated, when quite young, to New Orleans. . . .

The newspaper fallen across my lap, I dozed.

Finally, when the day had fully come on, Anna Maria stuck her head
into the car.

"Oh, Hugo, we all wondered where you were," she said. "Do you
have everything you need?" Not waiting for my answer, she turned
around and left.

I was somewhat baffled by her composure in the wake of Savage
Girl's disappearance. Freddy, too, maintained his equilibrium. I wondered if they knew something I didn't, that the creature had turned
out to be too dangerous, too wild to be safely adopted, and therefore
good riddance.

A little later my father, like my mother distracted and preoccupied,
came through the car. He carried a shotgun, went the whole length of
the den to the gun cases, broke the breech and placed the piece in a
rack, locked the rack, and then took care to check the locks on the
other cases, the ammunition drawers, the trigger locks on the pistols.
An efficient, military-like procedure.

Only when he finished did he notice me, sitting in a satin-brocaded
club chair off to the side.

"Shining time, Hugo, old boy," he said. Freddy could be madden-
ingly banal when he wanted to be. "We're on our way."

Then he, too, left me alone, placing his hand on my shoulder
briefly as he passed.

Since my predawn tea, no one had bothered to see about my breakfast. They had all forgotten me. The service bell was a handbreadth
away, but I could not conquer my ennui to ring it.

At last, after an hour of this, I felt sufficiently sickened by my own
moodiness to rise and head toward the parlor car. I met my father
heading back to fetch me.

"Hugo!" he said heartily. "Come along."

"I was going to anyway," I mumbled.

"A surprise," he said.

I followed him forward to the parlor car and found the whole population of the train gathered there.

The staff in a stiff rank. Dowler, the steward; Cookie and her girls; Anna Maria's housekeeper, Mrs. Mary Kate; Freddy's valet, Gilbert Gates; Petey and Brownie Laughton and a brute named Cheevil, known collectively as "the boys"; B. C. Coyle, pipefitter; Tu-Li and the berdache, of course, thick as cousins; and finally our new addition, whom I hired on in Virginia, paying him with my own allowance money, Colm Cullen.

Almost everyone present and accounted for, except for Anna Maria and the engineer, Bob Cratchit (his name wasn't Bob Cratchit, but we called him that), and perhaps the random parlor brakeman and a cook's boy or two.

"I wanted to speak to you all," Freddy said.

"Should you wait for Anna Maria?" I asked.

"She'll be along," he said. He looked annoyed at me for interrupting him. This was to be his Big Speech to the Staff.

Freddy cleared his throat and launched in. "Something like ten or fifteen days from now, depending on the track traffic, we will be in New York City. The modern miracle of this I know will impress you all.

"If you but gaze to the side of the tracks today, you will notice the skeletons of horses, mules and oxen, the rusted and decrepit remains of abandoned wagons, and if you look sharp, you'll see the grave markers of those who traveled these lands before us.

"They took five months to complete a trip which we will accomplish in two weeks. Many of them did not survive the journey at all, while we travel in safety and comfort. We honor their effort as we marvel at our advancement.

"We will make an excursion at the Great Salt Lake. We'll stop over two or three nights in Chicago. I want you all to consider this a grand adventure, enjoy your time aboard, and come to me with any difficulties or concerns."

Gilbert Gates spoke up. "I think I speak for all the staff, sir, in thanking you for the opportunity to cross this magnificent country."

It would be the first transcontinental journey for most of those present, myself included. We had come from New York not on Sandobar, which was being refitted in Sacramento, but with Freddy and Anna Maria by sea to Central America, across the miserable heat-struck and mosquito-infested isthmus, then north to the Bay. It had been, all told, a dreadful voyage.

I turned to go back to the shooting car.

"Hugo?" Freddy said, interrupting his civilities with the staff.

"I didn't think I needed to stay," I said. "I know all this." I couldn't understand why I was behaving this way.

"Hold on a bit," Freddy said. "There's just one other thing."

Just one other thing. I had underestimated the showman in my father. He loved extracting rabbits from hats. I remained with the others in the parlor car, sullen, pretending I had pressing business elsewhere, putting off the flirts of Rose and Annie and the conversational sallies of Colm Cullen and Mrs. Kate.

"It will be a few moments," my father said.

The door at the far end of the car opened. Anna Maria entered.

"Ah, here you are," Freddy said.

With my mother, who held a protective arm around her, came Savage Girl.

Freddy smiled widely as he presented us with his new protégée. Leaving me to wonder, the ignorant rube in the audience, how on earth she had materialized. Had she been on Sandobar all along? The new bathtub in the baggage car stood explained.

In a cowed posture beside my mother, the girl herself appeared wretched. She wore a plain drop-waisted dress of white silk, shapeless as a nightgown, and approached the small crowd of staff at the back end of the car with hunched shoulders and a guarded, unreadable mien. Her atrocious head of hair!

"I'd like to introduce to you the newest member of our entourage, this young lady, Virginia," Freddy said. "Some of you have met her already."

He walked over and stood near her, and just at that moment the train lurched and threw him against her, so that he wound up at her immediate side, like my mother. They resembled twin pillars supporting a tremble-kneed prospect, two proud parents of a bouncing not-quite-baby girl.

She stood shivering between them.

"Virginia has had something of a difficult time in life," Freddy said. "She may behave in ways with which you are unfamiliar. She is highly intelligent, though she does not speak—not English, not yet anyway. She will sleep in the sixth"—*Nighthawk,* the servants' car, where Tahk-too, Tu-Li, Dowler and Gates had their private compartments—"and take her meals with the family. I want you all to look out for her, care for her, extend her every courtesy."

Anna Maria spoke. "She is our guest. I know you will come to feel for her as we do, with warmth and affection."

The staff, not knowing quite how to react, broke into a polite patter of applause.

I seethed. *Some of you have met her already?* What was this, a gigantic secret? Had she been aboard even in Virginia City, while her suitors fired their six-guns and pelted us with dirt clods?

I held the suspicion that far from being a pitiful pawn of Dr. Calef Scott, Savage Girl was fully in league with him. We would see ourselves robbed, murdered in our sleep. The Sage Hen, Jake Woodworth, R. T. Flenniken and a whole crew of desperadoes waited to waylay us, on up the line.

Swarms of other questions occurred to me. Was she dangerous? Verminous? Diseased? What did we really know about her? Had my parents invited a viper into our midst? And what of her escape from us? Could it have been engineered by Freddy? If she hadn't been hidden on the train, where had the girl been during that time?

A memory floated to the surface of my thoughts, dim and well marinated in tarantula juice. The night before we freed her. Savage Girl, furtively leaving Dr. Scott's barn, slipping past Costello's Shooting Gallery and disappearing into the night. Where was she going? Why had she been allowed to leave?

A certainty stole upon me: Whatever she was, wherever she might find herself, this creature was never a captive of anyone.

7

I hesitate to report that our rail trip across the continent, such a prized and in fact almost required experience for anyone wishing to qualify nowadays as a fashionable American traveler, was in our case largely inconsequential. A few notable incidents obtrude. But for the most part, the journey had the charm of banality, the miles rolling out, the days slipping by, a certain Lotos Land flavor characterizing the whole.

At times this was literally the case. Thrust into tight quarters (although not too tight, as I had the whole of an eighty-foot sleeper car to myself), individual quirks of passenger behavior became apparent.

Every Sunday, Tu Li's day off, the door of her sleeping compartment stayed shut and front to rear Sandobar stank of opium, the slender coolie maid's recuperatory drug. Lotos Land indeed. Mondays were a little dreamy for her, but by Tuesday she was back to her solemn, ironic, dewy-eyed self.

Similarly, the berdache's bowel movements were fulsome events noted by the whole company. Sandobar's water closets were of the very latest design, and a steam hose ran the whole length of the train, so we had running hot and cold water in every car. But Tahktoo insisted on using the old-fashioned jakes in *Black Diamond,* where you could hear, in fact feel, the carriage's *clickety-clack* as you strained at stool, and your offerings were deposited directly onto the track bed.

Of Savage Girl there are only a few things to report. She remained on the whole docile, attached to my mother or, increasingly, to Tu-Li. And she loved the berdache. That first day, at the end of Freddy's introductory speech, came an incident that entertained the whole company.

Savage Girl (the name Virginia never seemed to stick for me, even shortened to Ginny or, worse still, to Gin, a syllable I could not even pronounce without queasiness) stood in a thoroughly deflated posture between my parents but suddenly brightened upon spying Tahktoo.

She strode purposefully forward, stuck her face into his, pulled herself back and examined the man-woman head to toe, and laughed delightedly. Then she performed an acrobatic pas de chat straight up into the air, seemingly as an expression of her overbrimming pleasure, before leaning forward to him again and grinning.

The maneuver was decidedly odd but somehow entirely charming, and several members of the staff burst out laughing.

Through this the berdache maintained his usual tranquil demeanor, but I detected a tiny smile playing at the corners of his meaty lips.

Anna Maria came forward to retrieve Savage Girl, and the moment passed. But Tahktoo and she became great friends.

I wondered what she made of me. No acrobatics for the eldest son of the family. In fact she seemed not to notice young Hugo at all. Her attitude didn't overly concern me, but I was slightly baffled by it. We were both young, she perhaps a bit younger, and I had enough experience with the weaker sex to expect some degree of attention, triflings, self-conscious posing. Something anyway. With her, nothing.

Her age was indeed a minor puzzle.

The morning after her introduction, as Sandobar nosed toward the dark line of the Wasatch Mountains, ahead of us to the east, Freddy and Anna and I sat together at tea in the parlor car.

Tahktoo, Tu-Li and the Savage Girl formed another trio a little distance away, gathered around an upholstered sofa. Tu-Li attempted to untangle the ugly mat of black hair that rode on our new friend's head like some sort of particularly unfashionable snood. Virginia—Ginny—Gin stole wondering glances at Tahktoo, peaceably at work knitting a shawl.

"How old do you think she is?" I asked, repeating my mother's question of a few days before.

"Who?" said my father. I pulled a long look at him, and he laughed.

"She says she doesn't know," he replied.

"'She says'? What do you mean? She doesn't speak!"

"Your father communicates with her," Anna Maria said. I noticed that her eyes never strayed for long from the group across the car.

"In Comanche?"

They both were putting a calm front upon a thoroughly unsettling situation, and it infuriated me.

"Sign language, dear," Anna Maria said. "The lingua franca of the Plains."

Freddy passed his right hand laterally across his chest, then waved it significantly in a circular motion.

"Oh, for pity's sake," I said. I didn't believe a word of it, or in this case a hand twirl of it.

But it was true, Freddy said. And it was the answer to Savage Girl's abrupt disappearance in the Washoe.

While she crouched at my feet in the coach after her rescue from the sideshow, I had been absorbed by the mere presence of her, but somehow I'd failed to notice that Freddy and she were having a conversation. An entirely nonverbal conversation, conducted in hand signs.

Where? she'd asked. Meaning where are you taking me?

Home, far, east, Freddy had signed.

They had been engaged in a discussion, there in the coach! And me not knowing!

"I don't know whether to believe you or not," I said.

"That's uncharitable, Hugo," Anna Maria said. She called over to her maid. "Tu-Li, don't tug at Virginia's hair so!"

"Believe me or don't," Freddy said, shrugging. "She did leave, and she did return."

I felt totally flummoxed. Whole worlds of activity going on, a rendezvous arranged, baths being built, all beyond my ken.

"The tub in the baggage car," I said. "I suppose she asked you to do that? With sign language? What's the hand sign for 'bathtub'?"

"That was my idea, dear," Anna Maria said. "I wanted her to feel at home. Really, I don't know why you are getting upset."

"I'm not upset!" I cried.

Freddy summoned Dowler over and requested a sheet of paper, an inkwell and a pen.

"I think we should catalog what we know about her," he said.

"Who?" I said acidly. "You aren't considering doing a study on her, are you? You said yourself she is clearly a fraud, not a feral child at all."

Anna Maria left us and sat down next to Tu-Li. She and the berdache both joined in on the impossible task of untangling Virginia's hair.

"One," my father said, writing on the sheet of foolscap that Dowler had provided. "She is of European heritage."

I looked over at her. Her sideshow pallor was underlaid by a nutbrown burn from the sun, but yes, she clearly came not of native blood.

"All right," I said.

"Two, she has spent time with a Comanche tribe."

"I'll have to take your word for that," I said. "I've seen you fake knowledge of a language before. What did you say to her again? In the barn."

"I invited her to come over to me," Freddy said.

"Do it once more."

"*Kimaru, nai-bi,*" he pronounced.

Savage Girl immediately swiveled her head, causing some difficulty with the hair-untangling process. She rose and came over to us, standing before Freddy.

He gave her a hand sign that evidently meant, *Thanks for coming over, but I really don't need you.* She returned to her trio of hairdressers.

"Why don't you just cut the damn stuff off?" I called over.

The three beautifiers looked at me pityingly, as though I didn't understand some basic fact of the universe.

"All right," I said, turning back to Freddy. "She had some sort of connection with the Comanche."

"She has a rudimentary grasp of English, probably from exposure at a young age," Freddy said.

"Oh, I don't think so," I said.

"If you monitor her closely, you'll see her respond to certain words."

"She doesn't respond to me at all," I said. "If she understands how to speak, why would she remain silent?"

"Elective mutism," Freddy said. "It's a recognized phenomenon. There was that Philadelphia woman, a survivor from a fire—"

"Pish," I interrupted him. "This girl doesn't talk."

"Do something sometime," Freddy said. "Catch her gaze and hold it. You will see, when you look into her eyes, a hint of a ruined, frightened child. Of course she doesn't speak. The cat of fear has gotten hold of her tongue. It will take some while. But I am confident that with enough care, when she feels secure, she will speak. And then our real work can begin."

"So your theory is simple and optimistic," I said, feigning a nonchalance that I didn't feel. "She spoke English as a settler child, she was taken by Indians, you don't know how young, she was raised up as a captive."

Even as I said it, I thought of my earlier insight. *Never a captive of anyone, always where she was by choice.*

"Yes, that's about it," Freddy said.

"But in any case, she's not a feral child at all and thus not a suitable subject for research," I said. "Too bad for your purposes."

"Don't neglect a fourth thing we know about her," Freddy said.

"Which is what?"

"Her independence. She is able to operate wholly on her own. She demonstrates agency. Look at her."

I did, I was, I had been.

"Self-contained, not other-directed. Which implies that she has spent a good deal of time alone."

"Being raised by wolves," I suggested, not seriously.

"Or raising herself," Freddy responded.

Day passed into night.

Depots, punctuation in a run-on sentence. Humboldt, Mill City,

Winnemucca, Golconda. Some of them little more than a single wood-framed station shack, a water tank, a stock pen, huddled in the dust. Others able to summon drummers, hunters, townspeople, trade.

We left the wastes of Nevada and entered the wastes of Utah. Coin, Bovine, Terraco, Matlin, Ombey.

No other landscape I had ever experienced more proved the point that beauty and terror are sisters. I stared out at the desert and felt its challenge. Sandobar, so mighty and impressive, seemed dwarfed by the country, dwindling to a puny, uncertain sanctum, huffing and puffing but making small headway.

Anna Maria had directed the furnishings and ornamentation of the cars, rich carvings of oiled walnut, plush upholstery, a Brussels carpet in one, Turkish in another. There were great expanses of mirrors in gilt frames. From home she brought a tiger pelt, with its large, proud head, its striped fur still untattered, sleek and glossy years after Friedrich's late brother, Sonny, my uncle, brought it back from India.

We spent most of our time on our trip in the big, unpartitioned parlor car, second to last in the consist, called *Crucible*. It was here that we drowsed in the overstuffed chairs by the windows, sometimes catching a lucky break to witness a bald eagle soaring alongside, flying with us as though it were one of our party.

The berdache and Tu-Li played at the game of Chinese tiles or at cards, dealing hands of vingt-et-un while Savage Girl knelt beside them on the carpet, watching their faces as they managed the play. She had been entirely mild these few days, wholly unsavage, as a matter of fact.

Late morning on our second day out from the Comstock, the quartet of ladies gathered in a tight grouping in the corner of the parlor car: Tu-Li and the berdache working at Virginia's hair, Ginny herself with eyes closed, leaning back on a red satin fainting couch, Anna Maria reading to them from *David Copperfield*.

> My new life had lasted for more than a week, and I was stronger than ever in those tremendous practical resolutions that I felt the crisis required. . . .

I crossed the parlor to witness the detangling process, a futile one, I thought, doomed to fail. And unnecessary. I didn't understand why Savage Girl warranted all the attention.

One single hair separated laboriously from a strand, teased out to the length of its tangle, traced back to its knot, picked at, freed. Tu-Li employed the paired sticks the heathen Chinese use in place of eating utensils. Tahktoo worked only with his fingers, which were thick but surprisingly deft. All that knitting and weaving he did.

> As yet, Little Dora was quite unconscious of my desperate firmness, otherwise than as my letters darkly shadowed it forth. . . .

Watching them work, staring down at her closed, expressionless face, I thought I might go mad from impatience right on the spot. They had been at it for a day and a half and had completed a portion but three inches in length.

How many individual hairs on a human head? As an anatomist I was distressed that I didn't know. Thousands. I turned and left the parlor, finding my own refuge at my drawing table. Shave her bald, for all I would care.

My car, *Fury,* divided itself into four generous compartments. First my sleeping quarters, with water closet. Next was supposed to be my brother Nicky's room, but I had taken it over for anatomical specimens. My glass specimen jars ranged in serial ranks, inside a cabinet I kept locked, more to prevent surprises to the staff than over any worry about theft.

Adjacent to this, what I called my office, with the custom-made drawing table that Anna Maria had installed in front of an expanse of windows. Finally my parlor, in which I entertained guests, of which there were never any.

I sat down and lost myself in my drawing.

After a light supper at noon, which we took in the main parlor car (omelets, kippered salmon, Cookie's fresh-baked rolls), Anna Maria, ever the ringleader, announced that we would perform tableaux vivants.

"We will simply get out whatever old costumes we have, and all the spare sheets and blankets," she said. "I will assign the roles."

Having always abjured taking part in a tableau, I had nevertheless observed, in the last few years at dinner dances, charity balls and coming-out parties, most of the girls I knew throw themselves whole-heartedly into their performances.

Dowler, Mrs. Kate and B. C. Coyle rigged sheets in the parlor car into something near resembling a framed space in which to perform.

My mother was an inveterate raffle rigger. She only pretended to draw names of participants from a hat.

"Freddy?" she said. "Hugo?"

Tu-Li laughed and clapped her hands.

My father looked game, so I could not very well refuse, though I felt unaccountably shy. Colm Cullen joined in, that we might further dilute the humiliation among three of us.

We rooted through the costume trunk and awaited our instructions. But a simple representational painting or a biblical scene was not the particular hoop through which my mother intended us to jump.

She made a show of drawing another slip of paper from the "subject" hat. "Woman's rights!" she announced.

What an assignment! I looked at my father, Colm looked at me, and we shook our heads helplessly. However might we represent such an abstract concept?

But we did what we could, and as Dowler drew back the theatrical "curtain," we appeared motionless, figures in a still life.

Me, adorned with a mophead for hair, Anna Maria's paisley shawl around my shoulders, a look of the fierce crusader on my features (or what I thought was such a look, though I am afraid I only managed to appear to be suffering an attack of gas), I stood, eyes trained on the far horizon of equality.

Freddy and Colm, vanquished and humbled males, lay sprawled at my feet, doing their best to look like wounded animals. I had my foot athwart my father's neck. Lightly, of course.

Anna Maria and the girl sat on the divan in front of us, Mother gleefully laughing and holding Virginia's hand in hers. Tu-Li and the berdache stood behind the divan, clapping politely and smiling.

We were a success.

That afternoon I worked at my drawings, and when I returned to the parlor, they were still seated in a tight grouping. Savage Girl retained the exact same position as when I had left her, curled on the divan, as lazy as a cat.

"Hugo," Anna Maria said, rising from her chair, "read to them. I have to go up front and speak to Cookie."

"All right," I said. "But not *David Copperfield*."

For whatever reason, I had brought my own novel along to the parlor, Mary Shelley's *Modern Prometheus*. I wasn't even reading it at the time and had no thought of doing so. I sat down, opened the volume randomly, and began.

> A flash of lightning illuminated the object, and discovered its shape plainly to me; its gigantic stature, and the deformity of its aspect, more hideous than belongs to humanity, instantly informed me that it was the wretch, the filthy daemon, to whom I had given life.

So far during her time with us, Savage Girl had remained absolutely docile, with no inclination to run off. Why would she? Enthroned in opulence, the center of all attention, with plenty of meat on the table. In fact, she usually seemed sleepy and passive.

Can one think without words? Observers of feral children endlessly tugged at the issue of language. Of all the wild ones—raised by bears, by wolves, by wild goats, even, in one reported case, by rats—most were unable to learn to speak and thus were deemed idiots.

After innumerable lessons by the kindly Dr. Itard, Victor of Aveyron managed only two words, *eau,* for "water," and *Dieu,* for "God." He mainly sat and rocked. King George's Wild Peter could play for hours with a watch or a glove. He was an expert pickpocket but never spoke.

Such creatures lived in the *nunc stans,* the Eternal Now. Gusts of identifiably human emotion blew through savage children, and Napoleon once described Victor with an inimitable phrase, remarking on "the boy's sad pleasure in the natural world." He loved snowfall and could lapse into melancholy looking into a pool of water.

Sad pleasure. I understood that.

Against such historical evidence, what did we have in the girl Virginia? Wordless yes, but somehow, we were all convinced, very smart.

That afternoon a singular incident struck me during my reading from the *Frankenstein* epic. As I spoke the words, I glanced occasionally at Virginia. She sat expressionless as before. But once or twice a sadness crossed her face, and something else, a sense that I could not readily admit.

Understanding.

The mute, language-bereft creature was somehow following the tale.

I pause, lost in memory. One of Howe's minions scuttles up to me with a glass of water. I have the impression that everyone in the room is waiting, poised, as if another boot will drop.

Your illness, Mr. Hugo, William Howe says. I do not wish to be indelicate. A malady of the mind?

What could I tell him? That I was not ashamed, when I was indeed ashamed? That a few of my friends had similar episodes?

It's something that's going around, I say.

"Hysteria," the word to describe nervousness in women, had attained ready currency. Probably everyone knew someone so afflicted. The sanatoriums were full of sufferers, put away by harried husbands or fathers.

No such popular term had been devised for nervousness in men, though William James, my physiology professor, had a name for it. "Americanitis."

Causes: modern civilization, steam power, the periodical press, the telegraph, the sciences, the mental activity of women. Consequence: indulgence of appetites and passions. Symptoms: As far as I was concerned, violent fantasies. Fainting spells. Inanition. A terrible, stalking fear that I would lose my mind.

I have encountered an urge to false confession before, Howe says. Perhaps it soothes your affliction to take on responsibility for a heinous act of murder?

I am responsible, I say. My confession is not false. I killed my friend.

We shall reserve judgment, says Howe.

May I continue? I say, cross.

Howe and Hummel exchange a look. This is another feature of my infirmity, the certainty that others notice some aspect about me—that I have noxious body odor, for example, or that I am displaying a facial twitch—of which I myself remain unaware.

Shall we take an intermission? Howe asks, directing his question not at me but at Hummel.

No, we shall not, I say.

A train always harbors secrets.

I am no great believer in ghosts, or any aspect of the supernatural, no matter how popular such beliefs are today, being a rationalist to the death. Yet when one is working at one's drawing table in the dead of night, sketching sections of dissected human cadavers, and no other being is awake apart from the parlor brakeman, the assistant engineer and perhaps Colm Cullen, and one hears footsteps in the stillness, rogue thoughts do tend to cross the mind.

Next car up from me in the consist was *United States,* the Lincoln car. As I have said, we were taking it back for refitting at the New York yards as a favor to Collis Huntington of the Central Pacific. Our largesse was not entirely selfless, since as a collateral benefit of accepting the car we enjoyed a director's right-of-way on the line.

Several times, hearing or at least thinking I heard sounds from the empty and scrubbed-neat Lincoln car, I crossed over into it, only to find it deserted.

There the deceased president had lain in state. The outlines of the catafalque remained visible on the floor. When he was alive, he never saw or rode in *United States*. Yet could his great spirit haunt the living? I didn't think so. But the noises from the car next door seemed to contradict my most determined certainties.

It was Colm Cullen who put the mystery to rest. He was the solitary soul who patrolled Sandobar after we had all retired, taking regular late-hour strolls the entire length of the train. Checking trackside, observing our progress, seeing all was right. Our night watchman who never seemed to need sleep.

Colm's father had fled Galway during the first famine year, 1845, washing up on the Boston waterfront, inhabiting a wooden hovel in an alley off Batterymarch. He took a wife, doubling his misery, and together they spawned a family, Colm being the second of twelve. Cholera took off six of the children and then, finally, both parents.

In those brutal days, the North End acted as a proving ground for muscles, teeth, fists, heart. Colm joined the thousand or so child beggars in the streets of the neighborhood, hurling brickbats at the NO IRISH, NO DOGS signs that the good Yankees of Boston displayed.

"I couldna grown up faster any way but I did," Colm said. "Fightin' for every scrap. I used to slam my hands into buckets full of rocks to toughen 'em." Fleeing a criminal charge in Boston of precipitating riot ("A frame," he said simply), the twenty-five-year-old bruiser eventually wound up in Virginia City, handling security at the Brilliant Mine.

Colm told me he actually preferred his watchman duty on the train to being welcomed into its drawing rooms and parlors, having to make conversation with too many well-meaning people.

One night Colm performed his regular rounds, padding silently up and down the corridors of the sleeping compartments. He was midway through *The Brave*, he told me later, when he sensed a vibration above his head. A sound as soft as the footfall of a rabbit. Then a scratching, sliding noise. Some creature hiding in the insulation of the train? A rat?

Simply a rain of pebbles, Colm decided, falling off onto our cars from a cliff face in a cut of the track. A familiar sound, like rocks skittering down a mine shaft. He made to move on.

But no, it was footsteps. Colm halted. Whoever or whatever passed above imitated him, stepping, then stopping. He repeated his maneuver and the sounds again matched him.

"Well, I had a smile then," Colm told me. "I thought I knew what was what."

Sure enough, a hand appeared on the thick window glass immediately beside him, fingers spread, and a pale arm, white against the rushing black of the Utah desert. Then a face, upside down. And the face wore across it a broad, impish smile.

The wild little sprite!

Savage Girl rode the flat, smooth top of the train with total confidence, total ease. Feeling the dry night winds of summer gusting through her hair and turning her face up to the faint-burning stars.

For a quick second, she hung inverted, gripping the open clerestory vents all while hurtling forward atop Sandobar at forty-five miles per hour.

As quickly as she appeared, she pulled up and vanished. Colm heard the soft sound of her bare feet a few seconds more, then silence.

"That explains the noises in the night inside the Lincoln car," I said after hearing the story. "She must drop down into it. What do you think she does in there? Communes with Abe Lincoln's spirit?"

"I know she don't sleep much," Colm said. "Shall we tell Freddy?"

"Not just yet," I said.

✦ 8 ✦

Mostly, I stayed to myself and composed my anatomical sketches.

On the train, while I couldn't bring all the equipment I had at home, I had my trusty technical pen, India ink, compasses and metal-edged rulers, watercolors, sharp-lead pencils and enough high-rag, bright white stock to last me through half a dozen trips across the country. I loved the subject, its exactitude and precision. And I equally loved the materials utilized to evoke that precision upon the page.

My inks I could not use while the train was rocking, so I contented myself with charcoal. And watercolor washes.

My specimen jars contained human hearts (two), hands (six, a special study of mine), a flayed gluteus, a complete male reproductive system, assorted abdominal and thoracic viscera and, most rare, the cerebellum and brain stem of a ten-year-old child whose torso had been crushed in a streetcar accident.

My constant companion as I labored over my drawings, a gentleman I had requested join me on our travels, a fully articulated skeleton. I had named it Napoleon Bonaparte for its small stature. Boney had formerly hung from a metal hook stand in my study at home, and now he hung on a hook in my study aboard Sandobar.

Then I had my blades: lancets, scalpels and curettes, as well as carrying knives, everything from barlows to bowies.

Seeking to devise a new way of portraying anatomical subjects, I created a method by which the viewer might see the realistic portrait of the subject. An athlete stands in full fencing regalia in *en garde* posture—and then his skin is presented cut away to show the workings underneath, the muscles, arteries and bones that enable him to take his pose.

I planned to preview the in situ technique with Dr. James when I returned to class in the fall. He had praised my earlier sketches.

The hours rolled out dreamily. I'd bend to my drawing, look up at the passing landscape, bend to my drawing some more. Tennyson's "Lotos-Eaters" continually ran through my head.

> The Lotos blooms below the barren peak
> The Lotos blows by every winding creek
> All day the wind breathes low with mellower tone
> Thro' every hollow cave and alley lone
> Round and round the spicy downs the yellow Lotos-dust is blown.

Breaking our monotony, Freddy declared the stopover at the Great Salt Lake. We reached the depot at Kelton, there to be met with three excursion wagons, all arranged beforehand via telegraph.

The Kelton stop, west of Ogden, was one of those lonely, unpeopled outposts, at the same time the scene of some unlikely activity. A mountain man in full leathers waited for the eastern train. He was going back home, he told us, revealing his birthplace, surprising for one wearing a raccoon hat, as Flushing Park, Queens. His traveling companion banged tunelessly on a battered guitar.

> Toad in the road (he sang)
> Toad in the road
> Along come a wagon
> Whoopsie! (he yodeled)
> Road in the toad!

Anna Maria tossed him an unnecessary coin.

Kelton lay at the western piedmont of the Wasatch, a range of unsmiling, unpretty mountains, craggy and brown. Above us the sun already burned hot in an expanse of blue, and delicate bright-white clouds floated aimlessly on the horizon.

Our party had descended the three metal steps to the railbed and now stood stretching by the side of the train, taking deep breaths. The berdache, resplendent in a new dress, turned her face up to the sun. My father actually thumped his chest with pleasure. Anna Maria just stood there, eyes closed as if in prayer, her arms around Savage Girl.

The staff, too, tumbled out of the forward end of the train, laughing, talking, in high spirits.

Long days on a train, even so comfortable a one as ours, can get tiresome.

I myself felt my irritable mood lift and drift away with those small clouds.

To the south stretched the immense inner sea, its surface looking greasy and pellucid in the morning light. The Great Salt Lake.

"Stupendous!" said Freddy.

"Perfectly lovely," said Anna Maria.

And it was. The air was cool, almost cold when it hit the skin, refreshing even under the burning mountain sun. I removed my jacket, thinking ahead to stripping down altogether for a swim in the Great Salt Lake. I had heard many tales of it, and now there it was. How insane everyone would make me out to be as I plunged in splashing, naked as a newborn!

That was what I loved about the hunting trips I had been on with my friends in the Adirondacks. You could go about free and unclothed, embracing one's beasthood amid the streams and little lakes. It was expected. Everyone at home was so decorous, and I had no choice other than to fall in line. But in the wild, one could be free.

A strange incident at the depot: A dirty white cur rushed at us, barking, and Virginia suddenly erupted, snarling back at the thing, which ran yelping away, tail between its legs.

Freddy and Anna and I exchanged glances. What have we here? It took our breaths away, how quickly she had descended into viciousness. Savage Girl indeed. Was she at last beginning to reveal her true nature?

Anna Maria directed the loading of the excursion wagons and the dispensation of the staff. She had laid the plans for our picnic to be assembled a mile from the tracks, on a small hillock above the lake at the fringe of a stand of cedars. The railroad man Collis Huntington had recommended her the place.

We would take our luncheon there in the deliciously cool shade. This was not to be an ordinary picnic, though, but a grand endeavor, one that would re-create, out in the wastelands, the civilized features of our life.

Dowler and a few of his men went ahead in a dray, and by the time we arrived, the little hillside had become our gracious home away from home. The servants spread out a half dozen Oriental rugs, along with small tables, chairs and stools that had been stored in baggage for just such an occasion. Even the tiger rug from the parlor car took its place in our adventure.

My mother fell into a comfortable chair and opened her *Copperfield,* her face shaded by the mammoth brim of a straw hat, its cornflower-blue ribbons tied beneath her chin. Tu-Li and the berdache laid out on a carpet, beginning their inevitable game of ivory tiles. Freddy and I took a turn among the cedar trees, and not for the first time I wished I had my dog Hickory along.

We returned to our picnic, flopped into our comfort and drowsed in a pleasant stupor, spending the morning in "a land in which it seemed always afternoon" (as Tennyson had it). The lake, the sky, the murderous sunshine.

Savage Girl coiled up on her side on a thick, patterned rug, a little ways from the chair that had been set out for her, her eyes closed. I found myself staring and had to look away.

Freddy roused me for a swim. We headed down the slope to the Great Salt Lake, but as we did so, an immense stink rose up to greet us. Fetid, unbearable. Is this how it always was?

At the shore, disappointment. The lake was rimmed with an incredible mass of dead grasshoppers, their decaying bodies the source of the smell. From the actual shore, the mass extended forty feet into the lake.

"Well, I've swum in it before, you know," Freddy said. "Cold and bracing, extremely high salinity, as it is at the Dead Sea—you bob like a cork in it."

"Not today," I said. "I don't bob like a cork in that mess."

"Not today," Freddy said.

The stench was so bad it made us laugh, gag, dry-heave, then laugh some more.

"The Saints," Freddy said, laughing so hard that tears came to his eyes. "They've really made the desert bloom."

He meant the Mormons. Later we heard that a work party of Latter-day Saints harvested the dead bug carcasses with enormous skimmers, dried the husks and pressed the results into salt licks for their stock. Waste not, want not.

"Those people are clearly out of their minds," was Freddy's head-shaking comment.

Leaving the lake unswum and the dead grasshoppers commercially unexploited, we hiked back up the slope to our little campsite.

Finally, lunch. All of us gathered around a buffet table under the cedars, loading up our plates.

Back at the depot, Cookie had bargained with a hunter in a sand-colored cap and coveralls, gun still slung over his shoulder, hoisting his tray of quail. The tiny birds looked more like children's toys than edible meat.

Rose now laid down a platter of the cooked quail and paused. "Begging your pardon, ma'am," she said to Anna, curtsying. "Cookie asked me to apologize to you for the birds. We had a dozen, but two disappeared even before they was plucked."

She curtsied again and hurried off.

"Can you imagine?" said my mother. "Who would abscond with a quail?"

I felt an impulse to check Savage Girl's mouth for feathers.

We had more than enough food as it was, with the ten quail, grilled and scrumptious, as well as asparagus from the train's ice closet, drenched in sweet butter, plus orange fritters and chow-chow with green olives.

As we ate, we luxuriated in the panorama, inhaling the spicy scent of the conifers. Anna Maria and Freddy toasted our adventure with crystal goblets of icy Liebfraumilch. As a palate cleanser, licorice sorbet.

Gilbert Gates took over the fire, boiled water with a dash of vinegar, and blued the fish. These were fresh local rainbows (another depot purchase), and Gates explained that if you could parboil a catch like that quickly enough, when the natural coating on the fish's skin was still intact, the vinegar chemically reacted and rendered an effect that was startling and excellent.

Yes, it was. The trout showed bright, bright blue skin, bluer than berries, eye-hurting blue. Gasps and exclamations of pleasure as Gates presented the dish. They tasted good, too.

Savage Girl grabbed a fish in her fist and gnawed on the thing as though she were starving, mashing it into her mouth and devouring it bones, fins and head.

We all stopped eating and stared. We had witnessed the grossness of her manners before, of course—she had come to us never employing any utensil except her fingers—but this was something on a different level.

"Fork, dear," said Anna Maria gently. My mother had been previously trying to teach her. In vain. The girl merely picked up another of the blued rainbows and ate it with the same animal gusto.

After luncheon a few in our party scattered about the little lakeside meadows. Here was at least partial relief from the unending desert.

The berdache and Tu-Li wandered hand in hand. As it was the end of June, coneflowers and poppies and Queen Anne's lace mingled in a multicolored tapestry that came to nearly waist high on the young Chinese maid.

Breaking away from Tahktoo, Tu-Li began to select flowers, choosing carefully. As I watched her, I felt glad that she had brought some companionship to my mother. She was more than a maid. Tu-Li seemed ever calm, serious beyond her years. She was a listener, an anchor, and Anna Maria needed that.

Savage Girl joined Tu-Li down in the meadow. I watched her walk behind, the two of them wading through the luxuriant flowers, bending and picking as they went.

"Freddy," I said.

My father, his hat pulled over his eyes, pretended not to hear me.

"This business of nature versus nurture, don't you have to consider the part played by imitation?"

"Certainly," he said, his eyes still concealed. "Very good point. But that raises the issue of who is the imitator and who is the imitated."

Man, said Linnaeus, is a mimic animal. I looked down the slope to the two women.

"Perhaps she would make a suitable subject of study after all," I said.

"Mmn-hmm," Freddy mumbled from beneath his bowler.

I sketched a close-up view of one of the immense dead grasshoppers from the lake. The thing was the length of my hand. In its workings, the acute angle of its legs, the tripartite body segments covered in articulated armor, it appeared to me like a messenger from the future, a completely modern machine.

Tu-Li and the berdache came back up the hill. Virginia followed behind them, then walked directly up to me. Avoiding my eyes, she opened her hands and dropped the results of her flower-gathering efforts on the white lawn picnic cloth in front of my chair.

It was one of the rare times she paid me any mind. I felt myself blush with pleasure, then blush with embarrassment over my blushing. I reached out and touched the purple petals of a coneflower, about to thank her for the pretty thing she'd done, before I realized that something here was odd.

How right it was, and yet how wrong. A bouquet of wildflowers, yes, each one more beautiful than the last. And yet each bloom, you see, she had pinched off at the base of the blossom itself, not seeming to know what even a toddler recognizes: When you pick flowers, you gather them by the stem.

Savage Girl could imitate behavior without taking the sense of it.

The whistle sounded to let us know our idyll was at an end. We emerged from the Land of the Lotos sleepy and satiated and sunburned, and we began to make our way back to the depot.

Sandobar had taken on water and coal and was ready to depart. Father and Mother and I stood talking with Bob Cratchit, the engineer. His real name was Bob Crenshaw, but following the lead of my little brother, Nicky, we adopted the teasing nomenclature.

Tu-Li and the berdache had already boarded the train. The sun had gone aslant, and the servants were bringing the rugs and furniture and plateware back to the railcars under lengthening shadows.

"Where is Virginia?" said Anna Maria. Then, in a tone of rising concern, "Where is she? Has anyone seen Virginia?"

"Calm yourself," said Freddy.

"You calm yourself!"

"I am sure she is right here," said my father, beginning to look concerned as well.

"She has run off," Anna Maria worried. "She is a wild animal, and we've gone and lost her again. How will she survive?"

We first searched the length of Sandobar, looking under each of the cars. I climbed the shooting car's ladder and made sure the top of the train was clear. I crossed over and put my face to the depot windows, seeing only emptiness inside. Looked around the back of the building.

Nothing.

"Virginia!" shouted my mother. "Virginia, come along!"

Freddy wanted to pacify my mother but mentioned that even enjoying the director's right-of-way, we had to leave Kelton on time if we were to be through the mountains to Ogden that evening.

Bob Cratchit stepped up into the locomotive's cab and sounded another blast of the whistle, then came out to stand beside the tracks with me.

This time we had really lost her. And lost her in the middle of the chilly mountains, where night was falling, where there would be nobody to help her.

"Virginia," Anna Maria wailed.

And then I saw the girl, galloping across the field toward us, black mane flying like a flag, her brown feet bare, as always. She carried with her a long, thin branch, something she'd picked up in the cedar grove and trailed back with her.

"Virginia," said my mother as the girl pulled up beside us, holding her stick aloft like a torch, thrusting it out like a sword.

She didn't look at anybody, didn't meet our gazes at all. Small as she was, at that moment she appeared Amazonian, a warrior.

"Please don't run away again," my mother said, taking the girl's hand. "We so want you to be happy with us."

"All right," said my father. "Enough, Anna Maria."

Savage Girl wrenched herself from my mother's grasp, so roughly that Anna Maria gave a little cry. But the girl paid no mind, merely pointed her stick at a patch of sand near where we stood beside the railbed, an empty stretch scattered with clinkers and ash.

She had drawn two circles and a straight line.

Anna Maria tried to bring her away to the train, but again she pulled violently away. She took my mother's head in her hands as though she would crush it, physically making Anna Maria look at where she had been drawing.

"Wait," I said.

Everyone went quiet.

"Well, would you look at that," said Bob Cratchit. "Don't that beat everything."

What Savage Girl had drawn in the trackside dirt was, unmistakably, a *B*.

Or could it really be? Could this mute, wild creature know how to create an image that was more meaningful than two circles and a line?

She again wielded the stick, and an *R* appeared in the dirt.

We held our breaths.

She drew an *O*.

An *N*.

"Brown," Bob Cratchit guessed, and we shushed him.

W.

Y.

An *N.*

She looked up, finally, into the eyes of Anna Maria, poking her stick down at the pebbly, gritty, ordinary dust, pointing to the blow she had struck for the revolution, a word impaled in the sand.

Then around the circle, looking with great seriousness at all our faces in turn. Then again pointing. We had been yelling our heads off to her, but calling out the wrong name. She wanted us to know who she was.

Bronwyn.

Anna Maria was the first to break the spell. "Bronwyn? Your name is Bronwyn?" My mother broke down blubbering and took the girl into her arms.

"Would you look at that," repeated Tiny Tim's father. "Don't that beat all."

Bronwyn, I thought. Not Virginia.

Bronwyn.

I'm sorry, says my lawyer, he to whom all things must be confessed. But this really strains credulity.

Yes? I say.

This . . . this . . . this sylph, he says, struggling for the word and arriving at what I feel is an incorrect one. This wild thing can write her name? Who taught her? The lobo wolves?

You must free your mind, I say.

William Howe looks offended. Don't tell me to free my mind, young man, he says. My mind is free. I make my way professionally by the very freedom of my thinking.

Yet to judge the girl, I say, you accept the tale of some flimflam artist who titles himself "Professor Doctor."

So the Scott tale is entirely untrue? he asks, appearing, at that moment, like a petulant child. No Dollie Trent?

I propose to present my knowledge of Savage Girl, I say, the way I came to it myself—that is, gradually, piece by piece. You shall be like a man taken through a darkened house, me as your guide, with a lantern I uncover only occasionally, to illuminate a part here, a part there. But at the end of the story, you shall know all.

It strains credulity, Howe repeats, stubborn.

Let it be strained, I say. In sure faith that all will be revealed.

Howe snorts. All is never revealed. This would be the first time in the history of the world that all would be revealed.

He waves his cigar, which I take as a signal to continue my tale.

❦ 9 ❦

Freddy felt his mind was occupied with lofty questions. Are we fortune's playthings? Does a divinity shape our ends? Such concerns packed themselves tightly within the "nature versus nurture" debate, which was raging in the East Coast intellectual circles that my father frequented.

Not limited to the domain of natural science, the debate had religious, social and philosophical overtones. Were the poor stricken with poverty because they were born without moral fiber, or had their degraded environment corrupted them?

The answer mattered. If nature dictated our destiny, there was no use spending money on social programs, education or better housing for society's unfortunates, since what they were, they were, and there was no changing it. But if the destinies of the poor could somehow be reshaped by sufficient amounts of nurture, then charity became paramount.

For many of the more odious social philosophers of the day, an impoverished child removed from the dirt and filth of his home, scrubbed clean, clothed and taught his ABC's, would inevitably regress to the low condition of his birth. This was simply Calvinism tarted up in a political guise. Such a viewpoint considered social uplift useless or worse, since our characters, and thus our circumstances, were entirely preordained.

Many thought otherwise.

I saw Freddy's game. I understood how my father came to his excitement over Savage Girl or, as we were calling her now, Bronwyn. She remained a tabula rasa upon which Freddy could inscribe his theories.

If he could take this single-named creature, this rough-cut, un-mannered beast, tutor her, mentor her, shape her, present her to the world as fully accomplished and rendered human, why, it would be a triumph for one faction and a poke in the eye to the other.

Possibly Freddy would wind up writing a celebrated account of his work with this Bronwyn creature. Dr. Itard's 1801 book on Victor of Aveyron made the author hugely famous.

We continued to play, he and I, at listing what we knew about his new charge. In the parlor car, one morning after breakfast:

"Charmed by music," he offered.

"Dislikes dogs," I said.

"Oh, dear," said Freddy. "Can anyone be fully human and not like dogs?"

"I'm sure such people exist," I said.

"She is mostly pacific," Freddy said.

"Except occasionally," I said. I mentioned our excursion to the Great Salt Lake, when Bronwyn had once bounded suddenly ahead, seized a rock and hit a good-size jackrabbit, a mortal shot to the head. Cookie made it into a fricandeau, and we had it for dinner the next day.

"No, no, that's just impulse, not violence. Steadiness may be trained into her."

We both looked over to Bronwyn, stretched out on a chaise in a leonine pose.

"Could we discover, do you think, the details of her life?" I asked. "Say, for example, we search for a stolen girl in the American West, around '64, '65, mid-'60s—there can't be too many possibilities that fit the specific circumstances. Her family might have put out notices."

My father sighed. "Her parents might well be dead," he said.

"Someone will be looking for her." It felt wrong, or anyway there was a moral question lingering in our treatment of Savage Girl. She wasn't ours to keep. Or was she?

"I plan to put detectives on it," Freddy said. "There have been several instances, you know, of captives who insist, when they're found, on staying with the Indians that kidnapped them. They decline to come home."

"Ho-ho," I said, gleeful. "Given the choice, they choose wild savagery. Perhaps we should take that as an argument against the vaunted superiority of our culture, which we always so smugly assume."

"I sometimes think that Nicky, at least, might prefer a Comanche life," Freddy said. "When he was very young, he'd take off any clothing we tried to put on him. A real savage boy."

"It's our duty to find out all we can about her," I said.

Freddy wanted to switch the subject. "It will make it a great deal easier to train her up when she begins to speak English," he said.

God had to be invented, in order that men may play at being Him. Men such as Freddy.

With Kelton everything changed. Tu-Li and the berdache spent all their time with Bronwyn, modeling proper manners. Anna Maria and Freddy had her into their drawing room an hour a day for "instruction." In the art of being civilized.

How to behave (she wouldn't). The wearing of shoes (they killed her). Eating without making everyone else at the table ill (uneven results).

After the Wasatch came the Rockies, then the endless Plains. Comanche country. Bronwyn stayed glued to the window.

Once, far off, a swarm of black animal forms surged across the grasslands, but the big herds were gone. The bison didn't like the railroad, and the railroad returned the favor, killing them in hordes. Teams of men, blasting away off shooting cars like the one Sandobar dragged in its rear, only multiplied by a thousand. Death trains, hauling hunters, skinners, teamsters.

Everything but the skins they left to rot. The vulture, rat and coyote populations exploded. Not so the buffalo. Nor, for that matter, the Comanche. Soon teams of scavengers would pick over the endless bone fields, collecting wagonloads to be ground up for fertilizer.

We saw antelope, too, many within rifle range of the train, but the truth was none of us had much of a taste for shooting.

During our long trip across the American Plains, everyone else warmed to Bronwyn, and I found that even I could no longer remain aloof. I think she transformed me into a child again, something I resisted and denied but finally, in fits and starts, gave in to.

We had become chums, you see. Part of it was that we were bored, thrown together as the only two young people in the family quarters. We went on tiny adventures together. She was a spirited girl, always up for something. The most physical and acrobatic creature I have ever encountered.

I surprised her on one of those nights when she slipped into the Lincoln car. She saw me, bristled, and for a quick instant I thought she would attack me.

Instead she did something just as startling. Taking a long-legged head start, she ran up one wall of the car, getting quite high up before gravity pulled her back down.

She marked the spot she had reached with a swipe of her hand. Wordlessly challenging me. *I can race up a vertical surface in my bare feet this high. How high can you go?*

I felt we were somehow desecrating the holy realm of Lincoln's ghost. But then I thought this was precisely the kind of physical challenge Old Abe would have relished. So I doffed my shoes and tried the trick myself, matching her top spot.

She went again and set the mark higher. Then me. We went back and forth. Once she managed to touch the roof of the car with her foot.

Another day, one of terminal boredom on the endless Plains, she led me to the front of the train. She didn't need words; she pulled me onward with a glance, through the baggage car and past her bath closet, out along the rail of the tender, onto the locomotive deck to smile hello to Bob and Brownie, then onto the catwalk beside the boiler.

She moved easily and fearlessly, and I found myself admiring her grace. Slipping past the strutwork, she guided me to the little sleigh bench directly above the cowcatcher. It was a rare spot. The endless rails stretched ahead, rolled beneath us, vanished behind.

Bob went extra slow because we were up there, but Bronwyn kept pulling the bell cord connected to the cab, pulling and pulling on it: *Go faster, go faster.*

So Bob Cratchit balled the jack across the yellow Nebraska plains.

Fifteen, twenty, thirty, forty miles an hour. Too fast for me to esti-
mate how fast we were going. He said, later, fifty.

"Pound her out, Bob!" I screamed, laughing like a madman.
"Pound her out!"

If I squinted my eyes half shut, I could imagine that the train wasn't
even there, that my body was propelled over the Plains entirely on its
own. We held hands. We were flying together, she and I.

In the wake of such episodes of childishness, I always felt ashamed,
and I'd retreat to my anatomical studies.

Chicago. On the evening of the fifth day out from the Washoe. The
city had burned flat in 1871. Four years later we could still see patches
of blackened earth as Sandobar rocked into town.

Entering Chicago resembled nothing so much as coming into New
York, as after a long stretch of Great Plains isolation we were picking
up again on a big-city way of living. Urban world. Horsecars, fine
restaurants, people about the streets in fashionable clothes. My sensibility immediately readapted itself. Downtown Chicago had more in
common with Manhattan than it did with anywhere else in between,
or anywhere else in the world.

Palmer House, a fabulous, glorious, lyrical hotel. The hotel porters
floated us into the place on a cloud. Sprays of flowers in the lobby
stood as tall as a man.

"I do believe this might be the best hotel in the world," Freddy said
when we entered our suites.

Chicago impressed us. Union Stock Yard & Transit Company ran
at full capacity. Trainloads of cattle, sheep and pigs came in, some of
them over the same railroad lines we had just traveled. Freddy took
me down there, and we marveled at the efficiency of the butchering.
They did everything after the Cincinnati model, pigs hauled squeal-
ing by their back hooves onto a hoist, carotid artery opened, bled out,
gutted, quartered and carved, all within the space of minutes.

This went on without cessation night and day, Christmas and Easter included.

As an anatomist I approved; as a moralist I was confounded. A stench of death hung over the whole neighborhood. The South Fork of the Chicago River bubbled like a witch's cauldron from all the offal discarded into its depths. I was glad Anna Maria had not come along. Bronwyn, I was not so sure. Savage Girl might have enjoyed it.

We took Bronwyn instead to Marshall Field's to buy her a suitable wardrobe. In a major step forward (so to speak), she had through Tu-Li's ministrations learned to wear the soft black slippers of the Celestials, so at least she did not traipse through the store in bare feet.

While her dresses were being tailored, I squired her all over the sprawling establishment, each of the five stories, packed with dry goods, haberdashery, furniture, carpets, paintings, cabinet work, toys, tools, plus a regular Parisian café right there on the premises (we had tea, without incident).

When she and I came back to Freddy and Anna Maria, my father asked her, "What did you like best in the whole place?"

She looked down, stubborn. Freddy had been pushing her to say her first English words, to no avail.

He repeated the same question in Plains sign language: *What good here?*

Bronwyn grabbed Freddy and Anna Maria by the hand and led them to the drinking fountain.

We all laughed. Yes, of course. Pure, cool, fresh water, free and available at the push of a button, the most miraculous thing in the world for anyone who has lived in the Great American Desert. Much more wonderful than all the finery in the store.

Palmer House stood like the gilded queen of Chicago, enthroned at State and Monroe streets, all sparkling jewels, flounces and good bones, regal amid the innocuous streetside shops and restaurants. Freshly rebuilt, seven stories tall, with a grand lobby ceiling in Moroccan tile and a fireproof guarantee that was, given the town's recent conflagration, a comfort to its guests. The floor of the hotel's barbershop was embedded with silver dollars.

"Some of them minted from Brilliant blue," sniffed Freddy upon walking past it. He himself preferred that the barber come to him, and he was shaved, trimmed, clipped and powdered in the privacy of his rooms.

President Grant had stayed in our suite before us, and Sarah Bernhardt (though I rush to say not at the same time). Our penthouse chambers had a view of the lake, a freshwater-blue expanse a block to the east. It looked as bracing as an ice bath.

The black lacquer bar in my drawing room held bottles of whiskey and gin and a bucket of cracked ice, with a small ivory-colored card alongside that suggested if I needed anything I should pull the bell rope by the door and summon "our most dutiful assistance."

I had them take away the gin.

The lavish surroundings served to undercut my feeling of disappointment in leaving the microcosmic world of Sandobar behind. The spell had for the moment been broken. I think we all felt it, the sense that we could have rolled across the Plains forever, lost in time.

On the third night of our stay, when I emerged from my bedroom and entered the drawing room of our suite, Tu-Li and the berdache performed a mock-formal presentation of Savage Girl, her long black hair glossy and completely combed out at last, a cinch-waisted light yellow frock from Marshall Field's looking pretty on her slender silhouette.

Bronwyn performed an awkward, truncated curtsy.

Surprised and delighted, I smiled broadly and moved forward on impulse, opening my arms as if to embrace her.

But I was brutally rebuffed. She hissed at me like a snake—no, not like a snake, like a cat might spit at a threatening dog. Then she buried her face in Tu-Li's shoulder.

Both Tu-Li and the berdache laughed, but I was dumbfounded. I found the incident distinctly unfunny. I was further enraged to realize that, with her head still pressed against Tu-Li, Savage Girl was laughing, too.

I retreated to my parents' suite. They were in the midst of a discussion on whether Bronwyn could maintain her composure in a formal hotel dining room.

"I don't think so," Freddy said. "We'll have dinner in our rooms, as before."

"Nonsense, the child is perfectly presentable," Anna Maria said. "What do you think, Hugo?"

I thought it would at least be interesting. Maybe she'd hiss at the maître d'. "I vote yes," I said.

"Luckily, this family is not a democracy," Freddy said.

"The poor dear has been so patient with her instruction, she deserves a prize," said Anna.

We went down to the dining room. With Bronwyn. Not a democracy, no. Mother ruled.

Dinner proved lavish. Evening attire all around. I looked across the table and saw Anna Maria as others must see her, her handsome features complemented by a pearly satin décolletage and dangling emeralds. She beamed to be together with her family. Freddy, ruddy and exuding western health, in a stiff boiled shirtfront and jet-black clawhammer coat with grosgrain lapel facings, me the same.

"If Nicky were here, we'd be complete," Anna Maria said.

Tu-Li dressed herself in a pastel pink silk smock. The berdache, for once, took the masculine route and donned a tailcoat. Simpler that way, he felt, no jeers in the restaurant. Seeing him in male clothes had a feel of the tragic.

Bronwyn was at first glance just another ladylike young woman, in puffed sleeves of the lightest yellow and a rose velvet ribbon tied round her honey-colored throat. Tu-Li had lifted Bronwyn's black locks up at the back of her head and inserted a white gardenia behind one blush-pink ear.

The girl's restless fingers drummed upon the white linen tabletop. She gazed around the room. I could barely get her to glance at me. Her first faux pas: She lifted her water glass and downed it in a gulp, as though she had never tasted water before.

The headwaiter approached, his minions ranked behind him. "The boiled leg of mutton with caper sauce is excellent, sir," he began, addressing my father directly.

"Tonight we also have a beautiful joint of roast beef and a boned turkey with truffles and jelly. If you care for game, we offer woodcock and black duck. For fish the smelts are popular, of course there is lobster, and this evening we have something different: eels à la tartare."

I noticed Bronwyn noticing a junior waiter, a handsome, blocky young man who could have wrestled in a show on the Bowery. He parted his sandy hair severely down the center, but a strand of it wanted to stray to his forehead.

The wrestler-waiter, assigned to her side of the table, lavished attention on Bronwyn. The roast beef, as advertised, was delicious. Bronwyn, who had not yet become wholly accustomed to using a fork, forgot herself momentarily to seize a slice in her hands, pull it apart with her fingers, and gnaw on it so the juices ran down her chin.

The waiter rushed to the table with finger bowls in which slices of lemon floated. When Bronwyn moved to drink that down, too, I shook my head. Anna Maria took her hands and gently bathed them and with her linen napkin dipped some water and held it to her face to cleanse the blood. I had seen my brother's nurse wash his face in just this way a dozen times. Bronwyn stoically underwent the treatment.

That night my parents decided to turn in early, as we would depart on Sandobar the next morning just before dawn. I felt restless and took a turn down to Lake Michigan. Whiskey had begun to taste good to me again for the first time since my shooting-gallery tear, so I took a bottle along from the bar in my room.

As I strode the shoreline, sleek Chicago rats darted in and out of the bushes. My mind seized upon the wrestler-waiter who had paid Bronwyn such fawning attention at dinner. Slugging the drink, I brushed away the thought. Why did it even bother me?

Throughout my walk I had the persistent sensation of being watched. Thugs and footpads come out at night. I resolved to take Colm Cullen along on any future midnight strolls.

But it was just my imagination taking flight. No one was there; the thin sand beach remained empty. The moon had waxed for the whole time Sandobar traveled east and now hung over the rippling surface of the lake. Passing a shuttered fish shack on the beach, I saw the moon in the water mirrored in a dirty windowpane, the light of a weak, faraway sun, thrice reflected, from moon to lake to glass.

A thought occurred to me. Savage Girl might be mute, but perhaps words were unnecessary. That damned big-muscled server boy, she could seduce him with a smile, a look, by her mere presence.

As though they stood before me I summoned up the image of her and the waiter coupling like goats, smeared up against each other, face pressing upon face, bodies eager for the greasy sheets of lust.

A boozy jealousy tormented my mind. I left the beach and rushed back to the hotel, thinking I would check on the girl, knowing I was acting stupidly but unwilling to alter my course. The mighty hostelry stood silent, ghostly, its hallways inhabited by spectral shadows. The rising room, which took passengers up from the lobby to their floors, had shut down for the night.

Mounting the dark, empty staircase, my climb slowed to a trudge. I became short of breath, to the degree I felt I had to sit down. I uncapped the whiskey and took a long pull.

What floor was this? Only the third. On a dread whim, I opened the door onto the corridor.

She stood there at the dim end of the hall, twenty yards away, wearing the artful hand claws, clacking the blades together like a butcher at his knives.

Breathless, I slammed shut the door.

No, no, no. She hadn't been there. Not really. Weaving drunkenly, thinking that I must be hallucinating, I staggered up a flight and entered into the fourth-floor corridor.

There she stood once more, swallowed in the gloom but now with her long black hair streaming over her face. This time she started to run at me in loping strides.

Again I ran into the stairwell, panicked, climbing the flights, suppressing an urge to bellow out the alarm. The steps seemed to delight in tripping me up. I felt caged in the tight space, not knowing what I was doing or where I was going. A door slammed down below.

Giving up, I dropped to my knees, feeling that should she come for me, so be it. It was not her, not the she that I knew; it was some other creature. Which did not, it turned out, pursue me. The sixth-floor landing where I had halted remained silent and safe. With fumbling hands I located a barlow knife in my jacket pocket, opened it and waited.

No threat appeared.

My penthouse suite was one flight up, on the seventh. I rose to my feet, still dizzy, and opened the door into the sixth-floor corridor. Not wanting to know, not trusting my senses, not being able to help it.

A narrow corridor, lined with closed doors and golden, tomblike walls, receding into the darkness at the end of the hall. The lamps had been turned down low, the light was murky, the floor awash in red.

They were there, the two of them, just as I had prefigured them on the beach, a slight woman and a hulking man, clinging together. Her light yellow dress. Speeded-up time, both of them grinning wolfishly at me, white-pale teeth, blank-black eyes. Rage gripped me. I wanted to murder the man.

My mind must have walked away just then, for I have no consecutive memory of what happened. I regained my senses, which had been siezed with a killing fear. The lovers were gone. Whether my mind was disturbed by an actual incident or simply by the idea that I had just undergone a disruption of reality, I couldn't readily decide.

But no, no, this was all delusion. I had seen nothing, done nothing. I was alone in an empty hallway.

No terror exists so powerful as feeling that your grasp upon sanity might slip-slide away like a buggy on an icy road, not knowing what is real, not knowing what you've done.

Up in my suite, I examined my face in the room's massive, gilt-edged mirror. My nose appeared elongated, bulbous. I looked like a sad clown. My head felt full of sand.

Still shaken, still breathing hard, I poured myself another shot of whiskey, wishing I had my pen and ink, left behind in Sandobar. Anything to distract my reeling thoughts. Instead I sat down with the *Chicago Tribune*, wanting diversion, wanting normalcy above all.

I sat there, half reading, half musing, not wholly comprehending the printed words swimming before my eyes.

A commotion outside, rushing footsteps, and a muffled, horrified kind of shout. I opened my door and peered into the corridor, hoping desperately not to see the phantasms that had so recently afflicted me.

On the seventh floor, nothing. I took the stairway down a floor to the sixth. Four people stood in the middle of the corridor, speaking in hurried whispers, leaning into the open door of one of the guest chambers. Only too aware of my distracted thoughts, I proceeded toward them. But they ignored me, so intent were they on their activity.

Two males and two females in hotel livery, houseboys, maids. They gathered around a human form that lay twisted in the doorway, feet splayed out into the hall.

"I'm a doctor," I said. Not strictly true, but they stepped aside for me.

Crouching, the first thing I saw was blood, a lot of blood, staining the man's left leg. Cutting open the slice in his trousers with my knife, I found his adductors slashed at the artery.

Arteria femoralis. The femoral artery. One of the body's major vulnerabilities. Breach it and use your waning minutes to say your prayers.

The victim's torso also demonstrated signs of violence. Stripes across his chest, slicing through his shirt and vest as though it had been raked by a powerful and vicious knife attack.

The groin area had been totally destroyed.

I bent my ear to the man's mangled chest. No pulse, no hope. I judged him fifteen minutes gone, at least.

There was nothing I could do.

The wrestler-waiter lay dead, his sandy hair, formerly so carefully parted in the middle, now completely unkempt.

Something happened after Chicago, some sort of divide. In order to make a line connection, we left the Palmer House before daybreak, allowing me to avoid any immediate repercussions from the murder of the waiter. Though Chicago officialdom did not manage to question me, I was still rattled by the event.

What had happened? The terror of the sixth floor dissipated like wisps of a passing nightmare. I cleansed myself of the dead man's blood and wiped down my knife. Bundling up my room towels and stained clothes, I discarded them in a street-side trash bin as we took a carriage to the railhead.

And I told no one. Not Freddy, not Anna Maria, not Colm, keeping secret my involuntary excursion into a violent mental twilight.

Shut away also was a tiny, niggling, shivery suspicion. Did Savage Girl have a heavy-bladed hand in the death of the waiter? Was that the truth of it? No, no, the possibility was too absurd, too dark, too dangerous for me even to think on it.

What I saw were morbid fantasies, nothing more. My mind that night had been "disguised by drink," a phrase my grandfather used.

Sandobar traveled east, through the farms and small towns of the more settled part of the country.

But as I said, a divide. Bronwyn was no longer with us. She took to her sleeping compartment in the sixth car, did not come out, ate her meals there (I imagined Cookie tossing in a piece of raw meat, then running away).

Anna Maria, the berdache and Tu Li visited the girl briefly, but no one else—no men, not Freddy nor myself. My mother informed us it was a "female situation" and warned us to stay away.

Despite the violence in the Palmer House, I was careful to act normal and not display any inner turmoil around the family. None of them even knew of what had occurred in Chicago. I was unsure if I myself knew.

During this fallow period of her isolation, I was often in the parlor car, waiting for Savage Girl to appear. She never did.

As we drew closer to New York, like Bronwyn, I, too, became more and more withdrawn. The Palmer House nightmare, which I thought safely repressed, cropped up at unlikely intervals. Nothing had happened, I convinced myself. I had simply blundered into the aftermath of a crime.

What is your connection? Only that of the observer and observed. The witness is not, after all, a participant.

"You shouldn't moon about so much, dear boy," Freddy said to me, coming into the parlor car one morning. "You make it obvious how much you miss your playmate."

"It won't work," I said.

"What won't?"

"You and Anna Maria plan to groom and school her, in view of making her over into a polite young lady. Then you will introduce her into society as a test of your theories."

"We haven't exactly made a secret of it," Freddy said.

"They will never accept her," I said. "Because of her past." I spoke from firsthand knowledge of the snake-pit social world of Manhattan, where pedigree was all.

"No, you're right, they might not," said Freddy, shaking his head in what looked to me like pretend sadness. "The sentinels of propriety are known to be strict."

"That makes the whole exercise pointless, doesn't it? Your little game will be up as soon as the town learns what she was. A girl in a coochie show. In fact, they may run us out of town, too."

"Unless . . ."

"Unless?" Once again I had underestimated my father. "Unless they don't learn of her past," I said. "What will you do? Lie?"

"Oh, I don't think that will be necessary," he said. "Given the gullibility of our species, dishonesty is often superfluous."

"What then?"

"There is a difference between lying and not telling. I don't see what business it is of Caroline Hood and the Tremont aunts and all those crinoline pillars of the community."

"Oh ho, they will make it their business, you can count on that. And what about the girl herself? Have you asked whether she wishes to be displayed as a showpiece?"

"You know the incredible thing about Dr. Scott's production?" Freddy said. "She enjoyed it. Her performance was entirely deliberate."

"In order to go along with your plan, she must deny who she is," I said. "Who she has been."

"She might be in a hurry to forget it," Freddy said. "People enjoy transformation almost as much as a butterfly does."

"You're wrong about that," I said, probably a little too sharply for Freddy's taste. "Most people resist transformation as though it were the plague. What people enjoy most is being rooted in their own muck."

Freddy shrugged. "Professor Dr. Calef Scott's miserable theatrical on the one hand, the world of Manhattan's fashionables on the other. Which would you choose?"

"You don't detect any similarities between the two?" I asked.

Freddy put on his stentorian Dr. Scott voice. "See the Savage Girl! Raised from the Comstock gutter and transformed into . . . a Right Proper New York Lady!" He laughed at himself.

"She doesn't know the rules, nor the stakes," I said. "It's unfair."

"The choice will be hers to make, of course, at every step of the way, but I don't foresee any difficulty," he said. "I've noticed that the attractions of society often prove irresistible to human vanity."

He rose and halted next to my chair, looking down at me. "You'll play along, won't you?"

I should have stood up to him. I should have taken Bronwyn's hand and fled, released her somewhere into the wilderness, like some wounded beast we had nursed back to health.

I did none of that. I sighed. And, to my everlasting sorrow, nodded. As he knew I would.

"But, Freddy?" I said. "The sooner the better. She should debut this season."

"Really? I think not. I was going to hand her off to Cousin Karl for a year of finishing in Europe."

In New York City, wealthy, well-connected girls aged eighteen customarily had their social debuts in late winter. The elaborate process—lessons, calls, final culminating debutante cotillions—served to indicate to the wider world that the young lovelies were henceforth marriageable material. They could now "come out," literally, from the cloistered haven of their parents' homes.

"It has to be this coming season, January, February," I insisted, shivering as I thought of the scene on the sixth floor of the Palmer House. "Think of her as a bomb about to go off. The longer you try to keep it in hand, the more likely it will blow up in your face."

"Perhaps you're right," he said.

"You know I am," I said. If it were done, Macbeth says, better it were done quickly. The cardinal rule for all risky enterprises.

"Can we possibly have her ready in time?" Freddy asked.

"Anna Maria will help," I said. "Keep her off the raw meat and all that."

"And you?"

"Yes," I said, sighing once more. "I already indicated I would."

He smiled wanly and nodded. "I'm glad we had this frank exchange," he said, and left the car.

Freddy's sarcasm had a warm, blunt edge. He really was genuinely glad to talk to his son, but I feared he had no intention of listening to a word I said.

I wondered where Anna Maria stood on this decision. Watching her with Bronwyn would melt even the stoutest heart. It had always been my mother's dream to bring a girl out into New York society. I had seen her assist other debutantes in the process—cousins, daughters of friends—but thinking about it now, I realized that only her own daughter could truly satisfy her yearning. Of course she would side with Freddy on his quest.

Sandobar rumbled past the ominous stone prison on the Hudson River shore and ran alongside the Tappan Zee. I could see, miles to the south, the blocky outline of city buildings.

Manhattan.

A web of friendship and society waited there, ready to trap me once again.

Bev and Chippy and James and David Bliss. Jones Abercrombie. Cousin Willie. Delmonico's. The Maison Dorée. Harriet, Caroline and Camilla. All friends, and all in bitter competition. The Circle, we called ourselves, pompous even as green youths.

And Delia Showalter. Of course. Delia. Did I inwardly groan at the thought of her, or was that the feel of my heart leaping? The pale maiden, playing her role as the love of my life. What should I do about Delia?

I had been away only two months, but it felt like much longer. Had

I changed? Was I different now? What would my friends in the Circle think of me?

Another thought, which nearly unmanned me it was so disheartening. What would they think of her? Would they treat our recently plucked wildflower delicately, appreciating her fierce beauty?

No, I knew the sad truth. Asking such people to be kind only brought out the long knives that much sooner. They were the social equivalent of Chicago stockyard butchers, efficient at evisceration.

For the whole last leg of the trip to New York, I encountered Bronwyn only once, when she emerged briefly as we flew down the Hudson past the little river towns. I stood in the last car on the shooting deck, sunk in my thoughts. The Palisades, the grandest little chain of cliffs in the world, made me feel ill, I was so homesick for them.

Bronwyn came out onto the deck. I tried to read her face. A summery, end-of-June morning, just before midday, the river a lazy blue dragon asleep beside the tracks. The pink-faced escarpment, opposite, lit by white-yellow sunshine.

"Pretty," I said.

She took it all in for a long minute.

"Yes," she replied softly.

An actual word. Had she really said it, or did it float by on the wind?

She turned and went back inside. I didn't see her again until we were in the Grand Central Depot.

Southward, whistle howling, Sandobar rocketing and rolling, Bob Cratchit pouring it on, toward the island, toward the harbor, toward the sea. Whizzing directly alongside the wisteria-covered cottage where Washington Irving wrote, hating the new railroad when it went in back in the 1850s.

Thundering across the little stream at Spuyten Duyvil, onto the sacred ground of Manhattan, through the slot in the hills of Harlem, down the sooty trough of Park Avenue, down, down, down, into the quick-beating heart of New York City.

Home.

And there all our difficulties began.

Part Two

Madame Eugénie's Académie de Danse

🦉 10 🦉

After I talk myself hoarse, after I pursue memory to exhaustion, and after I witness Bill Howe take a voluminous lunch to match his voluminous breakfast, I finally sleep.

For three hours. It is late Saturday afternoon when I wake. I cross to the window. The pane is hot to the touch. The air in the street outside the Tombs has been struck still by the late-spring sun. Manic insects rub their legs together to produce their maddening frequencies of sound, which I can hear even inside the prison.

Blisteringly hot outside, in the prison director's office it is cool, almost cold.

At first I believe this is the effect of the marmoreal surroundings, but slowly, as my head clears, I realize that the source of the chill in the room is Abraham Hummel himself. Like Beelzebub, he brings his own winter with him wherever he goes.

His partner, Howe, is nowhere to be seen.

Waking to the realization that someone is watching you is always disconcerting, and having the onlooker be Abe Hummel makes it doubly so.

He stares me down. I can't pretend to go back to sleep, so I sit and face him.

You have left something out, Hummel says. Haven't you?

His first words to me during this, our latest encounter.

I suppose I must confess that Hummel and I have had dealings before. The reason Bill Howe took him on as a partner, the reason the pinched little man made himself indispensable to the already hugely successful barrister, was by means of a simple subterfuge Hummel invented and perfected.

He raised extortion to an art.

A wayward woman comes to the office of William Howe. Mr. Hummel, then a lowly stenographic clerk, takes down her story. She has been betrayed, says the woman, by a man of high standing. She mentions a name that could shake the halls of industry, the back rooms of business and the salons of society. The child aborning in her womb, she avows, is his.

Hummel is on the case. Not in the courts, no, he works in too fine a métier for that. He merely reaches out to the accused, whispers the name of his female client, promises discretion if . . .

The word "scandal" is never mentioned, only implied. Let the gentleman in question imagine the consequences for himself. Fathering a bastard with a light woman? How would his wife react, for example? His minister?

Blackmail by any other name would smell as foul.

The payoff is split, eighty-twenty, between the firm and the complainant, very much in favor of the former. Word gets around, and soon waywards are knocking down the doors of the offices of William Howe. And when the stream dries up, as it does occasionally (much to the disgrace of the city's goatish and licentious, who have fallen shockingly down on the job), why, Mr. Hummel is quite capable of hiring the seduction out. He puts a girl onto a likely target and reaps the results.

Bill Howe is sometimes frightened by his dried prune of a clerk, but never that frightened, and never for that long. He cannot deny the tides of money that are washing up on his shore. The firm of William Howe, Esquire, becomes the partnership of Howe & Hummel.

Alas, I played a small part in the matchmaking for that infernal marriage. Because yes, disapproving reader, I became ensnared in Abe Hummel's net along with the rest of *tout le monde*. While my mademoiselle was not in a family way, she did have evidence of our entanglement in the form of letters. So a few coins in Hummel's tide of gold came from my pockets. Or, actually, from Freddy's.

It is thus not without a measure of trepidation that I wake to find myself alone with Abe Hummel this hot-and-cold afternoon, and that

I find him speaking to me, since the last time we exchanged pleasant-ries the family coffers were poorer by a few thousand.

You have left something out, Hummel says. Haven't you?

I don't respond, but I do think, Well, yes. The lies one tells always pale in comparison to the truths one withholds.

I have left something out. To what miserable little detail could he be referring? I rack my brains. I already feel like a prisoner in the dock.

Do you have anything to say for yourself, wretch?

Yes! No! I don't know!

Hummel says, You crept into her room, didn't you?

At first I think he is accusing me of . . . But no.

One of those days, he says, when she was asleep curled up on the parlor-car divan, or perhaps one night when she was dashing about on top of the train. You went into her sleeping compartment while she was not there.

Hummel is the devil. He can peer through your soul like a pane of glass.

Yes, I say.

What did you find? he asks. Like a lawyer practiced in courtroom strategy, he poses only those questions to which he already knows the answer.

I found things that explained why she left us so soon after we freed her, I tell him. Why she had to vanish from the street in front of the International Hotel. Why she was gone for days before she came back to join us on Sandobar.

She needed to fetch something vital to her, didn't she?

She went out to collect her paltry belongings, yes, I say.

I confess the whole to story to Hummel, that I never planned to trespass, that one night as I headed down the passageway in *Night-hawk*, the personal servants' car, passing by her sleeping compart-ment's door, I experienced a sudden urge to turn the handle, to see if it was locked.

Inside, the smell of a lair, not unpleasant. A small, dark room, six by twelve, originally intended for a parlormaid. Bronwyn had taken all the linens from the cot and made herself a nest on the floor. No perfumes and potions bedside, but nevertheless a scent of oranges. No girlie things, no personal items at all.

Except . . . Kneeling down to investigate the swirl of sheets in which she slept, I spotted a dirty canvas bag shoved beneath her pallet.

Outside in the corridor, voices. Tu-Li, bringing Savage Girl back to her room. I am discovered!

But no, the voices continued forward.

Inside the bag, five items.

Her hand mirror. Two books, not whole but torn in half at the spine. The Holy Bible, minus the New Testament, Revelation and part of the Pentateuch. What looks like Thackeray's *Vanity Fair,* torn in half also, so that it is missing the first few and last hundred pages or so. Both half books are filthy and covered in grime.

And a rag doll. Dirty also, threadbare from heavy use. Pathetic, like the single toy of an impoverished child.

And? Hummel asks. One other thing was in that bag, wasn't it?

I nod. A set of the hand claws she used in Dr. Scott's show.

I thought as much, Hummel says.

William Howe sweeps into the room, trailed by his retinue of clerks and secretaries. He has bathed and changed his toilet from green trousers to scarlet, from a blue vest to green, and from a rose shirt to a yellow one.

For all I know, Hummel, too, might have changed while I slept, his black trousers and black waistcoat replaced by a black waistcoat and black trousers.

Howe glows with a robust pink freshness. He sits down and rubs his hands.

Never fear, he says, I have ordered up a tub brought in for you, young Hugo. Hot water and soap. We shall get you feeling like a new man again. Until that time, to business.

He confers in whispers with Hummel. Their firm's motto, *Fides apud fures.* Honor among thieves.

Howe motions to a clerk. By transatlantic cable, he announces, the wonder of the age, a telegram from your parents.

Freddy and Anna Maria are in London.

Waving the telegram, Howe says, They board Her Majesty's mail packet *Alhambra* by exclusive arrangement with the Court of St. James's and should be here within a week.

Patting my knee, he says, By which time we shall have you bailed, adjudicated, freed from the onus of these terrible crimes and able to meet Friedrich-August-Heinrich and Anna Maria (Howe rolls every *r*) with a clear conscience at the West Side docks.

He gives the telegram back to his clerk without actually letting me see it. To prevent distraction from the task at hand.

Now, he says, pray continue. What did I miss?

He was just telling me about his discovery of the murder weapon, Hummel says.

Howe blinks at him. A nasty business, he says. Shall I clear the room?

I'd much rather begin where I left off, I say.

Yes, yes, Howe says, arrival in New York, further machinations of this terrible starveling waif. Go on.

I feel as though I have gotten ahead of myself somewhat. All stories are about family, even those that pretend not to be. So I should tell you about mine.

The first rule with men: Put no faith in their words. Their words are only the wrapping of the gift, which must be torn away to reveal the truth. Look instead to their unspoken selves, secrets they believe they dissemble but which are in reality displayed for all to see.

The men in my family. Freddy's father you no doubt know, the fabulous August Delegate. And August's first son, also called August, or Sonny in the family, dead at the Christlike age of thirty-three, carried off by a sudden fever in the gold fields of West Africa, or who knows really how Sonny Delegate died? It is a mystery of the age.

Having accomplished more in his score-and-thirteen than most men do in their biblical allotment of three score and ten, Sonny existed as the world's marvel, a whirlwind, a genius. The Son King, they called him. For a shining moment, he walked the earth as the wealthiest creature on it. His true accomplishment was to make enormous amounts of money for all those around him, and this worked to make him famous and well loved.

Upon Sonny's death my grandfather was left with his other son, poor second-best Friedrich. An outcome so unsettling that Grandfather soon died of it himself. The African fever that took off Sonny, they said, reached out across the ocean for a collateral victim.

Yes, August Senior was left with Friedrich, and then Grandfather died and Friedrich was left with a fortune so high and tall that you could not scale its golden pile if you climbed for a whole sunlit Sunday.

Freddy was also left with me. As my father disappointed his father, so my father was disappointed in me. And none of us could help any of it. What a bottomless swamp a family is.

The Delegates' mining interests in Virginia City, first developed through Sonny's Midas touch, filled the coffers of the Boston and New York banks during the War of the Rebellion. This allowed the bankers to have money to lend to the Union cause. Thus it might be said the Delegate family helped win the war. They also serve who only stand and finance.

Because everyone knows we didn't have much else to do with the actual fighting. I was twelve when the war ended, and in that same week Lincoln was assassinated. My poor little sister, Virginia, had died of scarlet fever as Sumter's cannons boomed. My brother, Nicholas, came into the world in the war's second year.

The truth is that while the hostilities walloped the slaver states that were in revolt, across the North the industrial miracle was such that life churned on seamlessly. The mills ran twenty-four hours a day. Dry goods and groceries were never in short supply. Buildings were erected, rails laid, streets paved.

Only by the roll calls of the dead printed in the newspapers (which I followed religiously) could you tell we were involved in the hostilities at all.

And yet despite the war's remoteness, I passed a childhood awash in blood, my night dreams colored so precisely that they differentiated

between limbs blown off in battle (tattered, stringy) and those removed by a surgeon's saw (pinched, right-angled).

I had never before witnessed a man killed, not until Butler Fince
shot Hank Monk right in front of me in the club dining room of Virginia's International Hotel. But I had seen many deaths, gruesome and
bloody, in my nightmares.

The streets outside the windows of my father's library (we lived on
Thirty-first and Fifth then) might be thick with richly painted carriages, the walkways peopled by pink-faced men in gleaming top hats.
But as I followed the progress of the fighting, through Shiloh, the Pen-
insula Campaign, Second Manassas, Antietam, Stones River, I noticed
a shift in the view. Brass bands, oratory, nationalistic fervor, but also
the returning wounded.

More patriotic parades in the street always lead to more crutches
on the sidewalks. My anatomy instructor at Harvard told me there
were fifty thousand amputations during the war.

For once, practice outran theory. The nation's doctors, and especially its surgeons, were well practiced by the end of the conflict in the
use of bullet probes, bone forceps and conical trephines, their blades
rusted not by water but by blood. America had the finest anatomists in
the world. My teachers at medical school were former field doctors
who had tossed discarded limbs outside hospital tents onto piles that
rose to the height of a man.

Perhaps growing up in such a sanguinary time dictated my later
interests. All those shattered arms and legs in my dreams naturally
metamorphosed into a passion for anatomical studies.

When I draw, I defuse. Veins and sinews and flesh all get put down
safely upon the page. These days I no longer dream of severed limbs.

I've noticed a shared quality among my peers. We are a haunted
generation. We were too young to serve, or to be served up. A horror
happened, but it occurred behind the translucent screen that separates
the child from adulthood. We saw it only darkly.

The war took older brothers, uncles, fathers. There were riots,
speeches, broadsides. New York City was infested by Southern sympa-

thizers. Once in a while, during public unrest, smoke drifted up to us from burning buildings farther downtown. Once in a while, a ceremonial cannon boomed outside the Fighting Sixty-ninth's Armory on Twenty-fifth Street, but it was shotless, impotent, just a muzzle flash and a gout of white-black smoke.

We sat by the window and watched.

All this affected us in various ways, producing highly varied results. I grew up with a boy named Beverly Willets, around the same age as me, the oldest son in a family close to ours and a more or less constant presence throughout my early years.

The murder victim.

I hesitate, lately, to label Bev a friend, since we passed through several periods of estrangement, and his response to our common war-haunted childhood was so unlike my own.

I might have turned inward, or so others have told me. Bev I know turned outward. With a vengeance. He tore through the world like a princeling. He was too different from me to be a true friend and too close, with too many shared experiences, to be anything else.

It was to Bev Willets's country place in upstate New York that I went when I wished to cleanse myself of the prickly, shut-in emotions aroused by the western trip. I felt like Hamlet, too much in the sun. Too much Freddy, too much closeness. I wanted to breathe.

Returning from Virginia City, disembarking from Sandobar with my family at Manhattan's brand-new Grand Central Depot at the end of June, a restlessness immediately settled upon me. The city steamed, the cobblestones and stone façades forming the walls of an oven, radiating heat back and forth, multiplying it.

On our two-hundred-yard march within the depot, rubbing shoulders with all and sundry, to where our carriages waited on Forty-second, Colm ranged out front, clearing the way. Freddy had vanished, off arranging things. The berdache lay atop a mountain of freight piled upon a wicker baggage cart, borne along as though it were Cleopatra's barge.

I walked behind Bronwyn. I wanted to observe her. She was with Anna Maria and Tu-Li. I wished to see her cowed by the city. It would pummel and reshape and vanquish her as it did all of us, I felt sure.

Manhattan appeared more foreign than I usually saw it. The fashions looked strange. The surface of Forty-second Street had a thick, brown-yellow mat of horse dung laid over it. Crossing the crowded thoroughfare was like treading on a manure carpet. The ladies couldn't let down their skirts and walked hobbled.

Coming home meant coming back to myself and realizing I had changed. It took some getting used to. Part of it, I will not deny, had to do with Bronwyn. I could not connect her new presence with my old life.

We—all of us, my family and I—kept waiting for Bronwyn to be impressed. By the vastness of America. By our private train, its servants and luxury equipage. By the stone canyons and frenetic bustle of Manhattan. By something.

The first time I saw Bronwyn on the streets of New York City, the thought came to me, powerfully and with disturbing certainty: She's doomed for sure. She was too strange, too autonomous, too . . . something, I didn't know what, eerie.

I had visions of Frankenstein's monster and the chase across the ice floes. *A being which had the shape of a man* . . . The townspeople gather round with their torches. They hound Savage Girl until she goes to ground. Then they unleash the dogs.

Bronwyn proceeded down Forty-second Street not hesitantly, like a gawker tourist, but already walking with the velocity of a New Yorker, tromping along determinedly, shoulders hunched, maneuvering people out of the way. Paying no heed and being paid none.

It made me nervous to witness her loose on the unfeeling street. I had come to think more and more protectively of her. Who would protect her from harm? Was it my job? Colm's? My mother's? Freddy's?

Then, on the trip uptown, quite suddenly, the city grabbed me by the throat. As much as I was distracted by Savage Girl's reaction to it, my old home of Manhattan snuck up and claimed its prodigal. I was left breathless by my love for New York.

Rolling northward on Fifth Avenue in our carriages—my parents, Bronwyn, Tu-Li in one, Colm, the berdache and I following in a heavily laden coach—it all came rushing back, the traffic, the marble towers, the feeling of being at the center of it all, what my friends and I used to call "the zoom."

"I'm sorry," I said, opening the door of the moving carriage. "Tell my father and mother . . ."

Tell them what? I didn't say but leaped out onto the street like a gandy dancer, hailed a hansom cab and headed off into my own damned life. Laughter in a public room, a well-aged New York strip, champagne. Top priority! Be quick about it! And friends. Friends!

So I was absent for the Event, the kairos, Bronwyn's turning point, out with my Circle cohorts for porter and skittles at the Maison Dorée. I spent the whole afternoon at lunch.

Ça prends qu'un moment pour que le boulevard revienne. Who said that? It takes but a moment for the boulevard to come rushing back.

When I returned, exalted, to the family bosom early that evening, I was fully prepared to be immune to its charms.

The Delegate mansion on upper Fifth. The butler, Winston, the doorman, Paul. They ignored my rumpled state, welcoming me back. But I wasn't back, I wasn't there, I was already elsewhere.

"My good man, my good man," I mumbled to them.

Inside, I met with giddiness, tears, exultation. Everyone aflutter.

"What?" I asked Freddy, passing me in the stairhall, wearing a smile as big as a cigar. Something had happened.

"Wait, wait," he said, and disappeared up the center stairway. Another Freddy escapade.

The wine died in me then, the family uproar put me out of sorts. I realized they hadn't really noticed I was gone. Either Freddy had made some sort of killing in the market or it had something to do with Savage Girl.

It was left to Winston the butler to tell the firstborn son what had transpired.

"It appears Miss Bronwyn spoke," Winston said, the tone of quiet pride in his voice indicating that he, too, was swept up in the enthusiasm of the household.

Well, yes, I thought, she spoke. She spoke to me on Sandobar, said the word "yes," hadn't she? I wished that I had announced it then. She spoke to me first. And did I make a grand occasion of it? No, because it was our private moment. What was Freddy going to do, call in the newspaper reporters?

Later on, Tu-Li filled me in.

"She told your mother 'thank you,' " Tu-Li said.

"That's it?"

"Yes," Tu-Li said. "It was quite emotional for Anna Maria. The two of them were in the bedchamber in the South Wing, and Anna Maria told her that it would be hers and that they had commissioned a special bath for her use, and then Bronwyn said it."

Another special bath. I imagined the world dotted with them. You could trace her trail by the tubs installed for her soaking pleasure.

"Just those two words, 'thank you'?" I asked. "In English, not Comanche, not sign language."

"Yes, out loud," Tu-Li said. "Then, later on this afternoon, she said another two words in English to your father. Or three, I forget."

"The child is a prodigy," I said.

"I take your tone," Tu-Li said. "But you weren't there. It was— I can't describe it by any other word than 'sweet.' "

I wished at that moment that I had heard the girl. The bath, when I eventually saw it, was indeed a marvel, an enormous white-enameled claw-foot tub, seven feet in length, you could fit about four Bronwyns in it.

What she had said to Freddy that day: "I am Numunuh." Pounding her splayed-out hand against her chest.

Numunuh. I found out later that this was what the Comanche called themselves. She was telling Freddy that she was a Comanche girl.

"Her voice has a strange quality," Tu-Li said.

She spoke to me once.

Yes.

The miracle word, the word that is a miracle every time you hear it, the word that performs miracles.

"The thing is, her speech, it emerged out of nothing," Tu-Li said. "She has the whisper of an accent."

Of course, I thought. She would. She did.

For some reason I found myself becoming enraged. Perhaps because I had been left out. I was on the margin, and my first impulse was to leave my parents to their fantastically important pet project with my very best regards.

"Tell them I'm going out," I said to Winston.

"You don't wish to see Miss Bronwyn?" he asked.

I dressed in evening attire and left for Delmonico's, plunging back into Manhattan as into a steeplechase. I wanted them to witness me leave, but neither Anna Maria nor her new favorite was anywhere to be seen.

After a four-day stay in the city, just long enough to pass Independence Day and during which time I was only rarely at home, I left New York behind. Summer was not the season to remain in town anyway. The whole family made preparations to leave. I got out first.

"Delegate, old dog!" Bev Willets greeted me at his family's country place in East Chatham. Just returned from a late-afternoon hunt, his manservant trailing behind him with a brace of rabbits.

"Your keepers let you loose from the sanatorium, have they? Are we safe with you?"

"I come seeking refuge from my family," I said, ignoring the slight. A commercial train to Albany, an overnight stopover, a twenty-mile ride on a rented horse had put me at the Willetses' farm.

"Then you've come to the right place, since my revered progenitors are not at the moment present," Bev said. "We have the place to ourselves."

No parents, no family, no oversight. I had traveled to Bev's alone, having granted Colm Cullen two weeks' leave to smooth out his legal difficulties in his hometown of Boston.

Bev, pretending at the country squire, wore a comical Scottish-huntsman costume that afternoon, a hat tied beneath his chin with string ribbons. In his face I caught a first glimpse of his fleshy future self—rich, sensuous lips, a sloppy shock of blond hair falling over a lightly freckled forehead.

"Good Lord, Delegate," he said, "what is that creature you rode in here? Is it even a horse? It appears bovine."

My ancient chestnut, the only mount I could scare up in Albany on short notice.

"I shall put it out of its misery at once," Bev said. "Jookie, the Beaumont."

His much-put-upon manservant offered him the weapon, a beautiful blued carbine with a decorative stock. He made a show of aiming it at the head of the horse.

"Bev," I said, knowing he wasn't really going to do it and merely wanted to show off his new rifle to me.

"That nag is a disgrace to quadrupeds everywhere," he said, lowering the gun. "Come up to the house for champagne. Dad made me promise not to uncrate the new cuvée of Krug he pillaged from his British cousins, but this is an occasion."

"Dad" was Martin Willets, a reactionary financier so committed to his conservative brand of politics that he had erected, at East Chatham, one of his numerous country homes, an exact replica of Marie Antoinette's play farm at Versailles.

The main building had a rustic Norman inflection, an ocher tint, a thatched roof and fifty charming rooms tucked inside. Martin Willets considered this a modest endeavor compared with his mansions at Newport and Staten Island.

It was all too much, the dovecote and the dairy, the cozy little barn with its precious sheep and pigs, the tower in the shape of a lighthouse and an inscription in brass, QU'ILS MANGENT DE LA BRIOCHE, the martyred French queen's "Let them eat cake." All done up by Martin Willets in an effort to horrify his liberal friends (he had no liberal friends).

La Ferme, as the Willetses called it, The Farm, had long ceased to shock me. I had visited many times. Without Martin and his meek, willowy wife, Lillianne, at home, with Bev as its master, the place took on something of a carnival atmosphere.

We ate the fowl we shot, drank Dad's wine and smashed our glasses in Marie Antoinette's cold hearth. At a dinner party two evenings on, besides myself, were a crew of raucous and rough-hewn neighborhood friends, as well as Cindy Pokorski, Bev's nineteen-year-old mistress-in-residence, another local, introduced, with a sly wink, as his niece.

Also there, honored guests just in from Albany, two mulatto women and their retinue, a group of abolitionists rendered supernumerary by the Emancipation, left somewhat confused by the success of the Glorious Cause. Dedicate your life to a battle, win it, what's next?

The two regal and strikingly beautiful women had been made darlings during the war, notorious for having been purchased as twenty-year-old, light-skinned, mixed-race slaves by abolitionists, stripped naked and displayed at the auction block in Nashville, for all appearances entirely Caucasian females put forth as shaming spectacles to the slavers.

Sad figures, the little advocate party. Formerly the center of all the world's attention, now discarded amid the galloping rush toward the American future. The women and their handlers appeared dazed to be present at the Willets farm at all, unsure how they had wound up there. In Albany on a lecture tour, then suddenly transported to Versailles-in-the-Berkshires.

Soon enough, we were made so merry by the champagne that all uncertainty ceased. The host's suggestion that the women reprise their "performances" at the Nashville slave barn failed to give rise to violence, as I believe Bev, ever the provocateur, may have intended.

I envied him as a mind unmolested by doubt. He posed a danger to me, though. A profoundly bored individual, and thus one finely tuned to the possibilities of scandal as a form of entertainment, Bev Willets played no favorites in choosing targets for gossip.

The inclusion of Bronwyn within the family circle exposed us, rendering the Delegate name vulnerable. Adopting the berdache was one thing. But attempting to pass off a girl with a questionable past (and a combustible present) as fit to be introduced into society was quite another.

Fraught, the whole idea. I resolved to renew my efforts to talk Freddy out of it.

Bev avowed he wanted to be informed of "every trivial detail" of my transcontinental adventure. His attention then instantly wandered as I launched into the story. Just as well, since I had determined that I would withhold from him large portions of the family's recent experience.

Bronwyn I would keep as my secret.

❦ 11 ❦

The next morning, the quondam abolitionists and their two charming dolls had already departed when I awoke.

Bev was nowhere in evidence either but had somehow found a way to indulge in another bit of provocation. As I sat taking my tea in La Ferme's Temple of Love, an octagonal belvedere with a neighboring grotto, visitors arrived. Delia Showalter, her two cousins and her aunt rode up the driveway in a four-in-hand.

Their visit engineered by Bev, no doubt, as part of his endless campaign of mischief against me. He knew of my ambivalent feelings toward Delia, my intended, the erstwhile love of my life, and he wanted to see if he could sow trouble by throwing us together again after our long separation.

"I have chivvied you out, haven't I?" Delia said, looking prettily fashionable in a vermilion riding jacket.

I am not sure if I wanted to see anyone more than I did Delia at that moment, or anyone less. We had left a good deal hanging fire when I departed Manhattan two months before.

"You're looking well for someone who has just conquered the continent," she said lightly.

Her relatives, well trained, moved off to examine the Temple of Love, leaving us to stroll alone.

"Bev?" she asked.

"Off on a hunt, I think. Did he tell you I was here?"

"He telegrammed us to stop on our way to The Ditches."

The Ditches. Our family place near Lenox, just across the Massachusetts state line, five miles to the east. A fantastic mansion, the Delegate answer to La Ferme, to Newport, to Saratoga, and to every other rusticating venue where our set congregated.

Standing there in the fresh rural morning, Delia managed to exhibit the pale delicacy of a closed Manhattan drawing room, a translucency of skin tone that represented the height of fashion, and which in the past had thoroughly beguiled me.

She came to me forever breathless. I succumbed to her perfumed, feathery presence. Put a milkmaid's bonnet on her, pose her in the courtyard of La Ferme, and the ancien régime effect would be complete. Marie Antoinette come back to life.

"Are we friends?" she said as we walked along the shore of the little lake, its waters covered with lily pads and stocked with kissing carp.

"Seeing you again," I said, "I feel nothing if not affection."

She smiled a smile that lit the world. "Oh, I hoped so," she said. "I so hoped that what they say about absence and its effect upon the heart was true."

When I didn't respond, she added, "About its growing fonder."

"Yes," I said, attempting to keep the shade of exasperation out of my voice. Had she a need to spell everything out?

"Yes?"

To place into words such ephemeral feelings as our reunion had reawakened seemed to me a recipe for ruining their frail charms.

"You must have had all sorts of adventures with the wild women of the western territories," Delia teased.

I shifted instead to a description of my descent into the underworld via the Elephant, feeling myself closed within the steamy fist of the Brilliant Mine, the blue muck, a rataplan of black powder and nitro charges exploding in the caverns and galleries. The veins of silver ore embedded in the walls, hot to the touch.

"We brought someone back," I told her.

"Yes? One of your father's souvenirs?"

"One of my own," I said. "Colm Cullen, he's to be my hand when I return to school."

"Good," she said, trilling a laugh. "You need a minder."

Delia took my arm, and we walked on, and I felt myself drop

with a thud onto the track I had so recently jumped when I left for the West.

Delia Showalter had been marked for me (and I for her) when our families both had summerhouses amid the green enchanted woods of Staten Island. We played together, I was told, as toddlers on New Dorp Beach. At dancing schools, lemonade socials, skating parties throughout my youth, there was always Delia.

I developed a secret intoxication at the prospect of having her. Here was a prize being given up to me, obtained not through any effort on my part but as a birthright, a sacrifice offered simply because I was who I was. I could not adequately describe the level of flattery that such an arrangement entailed. It put me into a high state of arousal and smugness both.

"Won't you ride over with us?" Delia asked. "We have room in the landau."

Anna Maria had scheduled some sort of midsummer extravaganza at The Ditches for the remainder of the week, games, outings, a ball.

"I don't know," I said. I had a sudden urge not to attend at all.

Delia gave a short laugh. "Well, you are coming," she said, as though detecting my thought. "Being as it is your own family's affair."

"Bev and I will be over this afternoon," I said. "He has a new Kentucky racing mare he keeps going on about."

The man himself approached us across the lawn. "The brilliant young couple," Bev called out. "Wedded together like a button on a sleeve."

The Delegate country seat, a wood-and-stone Moroccan-flavored monstrosity, had been built near the end of his life by my grandfather and named The Ditches after a local Mahican village ruin.

Not a man given to half measures, Grandfather designed and constructed what was then (and for all we knew still was) the largest private home in America. A hundred rooms, an acre on each of its four floors, a two-thousand-square-foot ballroom. The place loomed over a crystal lake called Stockbridge Bowl.

After all that, it pleased August, in one of those ironic formulations that enliven the humors of the rich, to term the place "a cottage." Also after all that, he fell dead of a heart attack before he could take up residence.

The Ditches began as an experiment, part scientific, part emotional. Was it physically possible to build and maintain a structure of such vastness? To erect a private home large enough that a circus might come and set up within? And would such a home erase the stain caused by Sonny's death?

Where August Delegate went, fashion followed. Suddenly all of smart New York wanted a place in the mountains, and enormous cottages started to dot the Berkshire landscape: Fair Meadows, The Elms, Wyndhurst, Shadowlawn.

The Ditches dwarfed them all. "Why stint?" My grandfather's motto.

Viewed from the lake below, The Ditches resembled an unearthly, heavy-masted pirate ship approaching on the horizon. Among its hundred rooms, a billiards salon, a golf lodge, a walk-in humidor. Two chapels—we had some rogue Catholics in the family. In the private wing, a locked art gallery displayed scandalous French nudes.

When August needed properly weathered timbers, he secured them by salvaging a sunken French warship off the coast of Brittany, dismantling it and importing his choice of wooden beams to the work site. Dried out, the age-old timbers provided the antiquated look my grandfather thought delightful. The study where they were installed smelled faintly of the sea.

Alas, none of it brought back his much-loved son. Gloom hung over The Ditches like the fog on Stockbridge Bowl.

Bev and I rode the five miles from his family's place to mine at the height of the noonday sun. Anna Maria's midsummer festivities were to begin later that afternoon. The green fan of trees shaded us as we passed beneath, and the many cascades coming off the hills to the north cooled our progress also.

The racing mare, which Bev had named Tullia after the last queen of Rome, proved a magnificent animal, often executing excited little caracoles along the trail, flanks quivering as though she were only barely contained. In sprints Tullia went off faster than any other mount I had ever witnessed.

Bev had provided me with a black gelding, insisting on sending my pathetic rented chestnut back to exile in Albany.

"You're having a full thirty-piece orchestra," Bev said. "Vince Lopeman's boys, up from the Fifth Avenue Hotel."

He often did that, informed me of details about my family of which I had no awareness myself. How did he know which musicians were to play?

"And she has invited the Circle." She being my mother. I could soon expect to see the twenty or thirty cousins, friends and school-mates with whom we habitually associated.

There have been periods of my life when I never wanted to go anywhere with my family, never wanted anything to do with them; I just wanted to see my friends. Two months previous I had tried to wriggle out of the trip to Virginia City.

But now the prospect of meeting the Circle again left me feeling deeply ambivalent.

Bev and I broke out of the woodland and trotted alongside the shore of the Bowl, its blue surface showing off primrose glints of the sun. Sugary, unthreatening clouds massed in the sky.

Far off, in the fields that ran down to the lake from The Ditches, we saw a boy on one of Freddy's Cayuse ponies. At first I thought it might be my brother, Nicky. But the figure rode so well seated that I decided it had to be a groom.

Freddy had become enamored of the Comanches a few years back, during his first tour of the West, and he purchased a remuda of the tribe's distinctive, tough little mounts and had them brought back east, paddocking a dozen at the Berkshire house.

Everyone hated them. They were small, no more than fourteen hands, but they bit and kicked with a malevolence unmatched in horsedom. They smashed down fences like schoolboys and attempted to mount the ruck of our herd, once managing to foul a valuable broodmare.

The ponies would have been all right if they performed. But few of us could handle them. On top of it all, they looked scruffy, with shaggy three-inch coats, high withers and odd, sloping pasterns.

Left alone, they went wild.

But here was one, a pinto, ridden with blazing speed and astonishing grace, tearing along the open meadow parallel to the shore.

"What is that?" Bev asked, turning his mare to intercept the pony.

Seeing us, though, the rider altered his course, breaking toward the sparse, parklike forest above the lake.

Bev took up the challenge. We threw ourselves up the hill and into the woods. He let the mare have her head, and she crashed through the undergrowth like a banshee, thundering among the sunlit glades, getting after the pony. We galloped into a grove of beech, ducking under low boughs and dashing past tree trunks at great peril to life and limb.

The little pony was fast, and also much quicker on turns and maneuvers. It dodged effortlessly through the forest. We'd approach—or Bev would approach, since I lagged behind—and the pinto seemed to tease him, then veer suddenly away.

"If only . . . get him . . . on the stretch!" Bev shouted, huffing with effort.

He got his wish. The pony plunged abruptly downhill and emerged onto the shoreline of the lake, Bev and the mare galloping furiously in pursuit.

With a sickening jolt, I recognized the rider. The cross-dressing berdache had gotten to Bronwyn. She had taken to wearing boy's clothes, her hair tucked up under a cap.

I only hoped Bev didn't notice anything untoward.

We pounded on but couldn't seem to gain on the little pinto. A furlong, then another. Along the beach, sending up ricochets of stones and sand. The Ditches appeared above us on the hill.

The pinto pulled away.

As a last insult, Bronwyn lifted herself up and sat backward on the little horse, facing us, taunting and beckoning with no diminishment of speed, until she disappeared into the woods along the shore to the north.

Bev finally halted, his vaunted Kentucky mare flecked white, stomping at the pebbled shore and taking in great wheezing gulps of air.

"What . . . the dickens . . . ? Who was that kid?"

I didn't want to tell him. Here were all my fears and embarrassments come true.

"Whatever that was . . ." he said, still breathing as hard as his horse, "I want some."

We led our thoroughly blown mounts uphill through the meadows toward The Ditches, the pseudo-Moroccan hulk on the ridgeline. Human figures rendered small by distance wandered about the lawns and terraces. I dreaded encountering them.

Bev couldn't stop talking about what had just happened. He hated being beaten and kept badgering me about who had done so.

I nursed the fervent hope that Bronwyn would keep riding, into the Berkshire forests, over the mountains, out of my life. But I also experienced, so deep down it remained unconfessed, a glimmer of admiration.

I needn't have worried. As nervous as I was about the unsuitability of Bronwyn to society, my parents were more so. They carefully segregated the family from the Circle, leaving me and my friends to drawing rooms, garden terraces or beaches of our own.

That afternoon the inevitable archery competition among the young ladies. The sport held attraction by allowing for athleticism without exertion.

"Take a wager, you bounder," Bev said to my cousin Willie. Since the latter was enamored of Camilla Tracy, and Camilla did not know an arrow's blade from its shaft, Bev saw a mark.

"I've been burned before," Willie said, refusing the bet.

Chattering and laughing, the troupe of girls trailed lazily over the terraced lawn, quivers scattered on the ground. Each archer, all twelve or so of them, wore a shade of white—cream, frost or eggshell—each one dripped with lace, and each had styled her hair in some kind of complicated braided effect. They wore leather bracers on their arms and brandished regulation-size longbows, shoulder height.

Delia, the sun in her eyes, appeared in a high-necked white dress with an outlandishly pert bustle.

"The Amazons, you know, sliced off their breasts to make it easier to draw a bow," Bev said.

"You're irredeemable," Delia said.

"He's made the same remark at every archery match he's ever been to," said Chippy Wilson.

"And no one ever takes me up on it," Bev said. "You'd think in the spirit of competition, something could be done."

Harriet Smith-Croft sent a first arrow to the straw-filled target with a solid *thwock*.

"Who was it beat you two so roundly at the race along the shore?" asked Delia. "That pony didn't look healthy enough to stand, much less gallop."

The *thwocks* began to come in bunches, punctuating the conversation.

Archery represented only one element in the required armamentarium of every marriageable young woman. Piano. Watercolors. French. Perfect crewelwork. The quadrille, the waltz, the two-step. And *thwock*ing a straw-stuffed pasteboard target with a an arrow made of white cedar.

"Hugo refuses to divulge who the demon rider was," Chippy said.

"Twenty on my lady's next shot to hit the bull's-eye," I said to Bev.

"All right," he said.

Delia bent her head coquettishly, nocked her arrow and let it fly. Dead center at twenty yards.

"You dog," Bev said. "As if you need the filthy money."

Above us, on a walled terrace faced with Moorish stucco, the family played at its own little archery contest. With a shock I recognized Bronwyn among them.

She appeared swallowed up in her lace, her hem dragging and her sleeves too long. Wisps of her hair fell along the sides of her face. If she saw me there down below her, she didn't show it. She had a short bow in her hands and unleashed an arrow.

Huzzahs from the family terrace.

With a creeping sense of dread, I saw Bronwyn draw her bow again, shoot again, draw applause again. Her makeshift target, the U-shaped handle grip of a shovel dug into the earth at thirty yards. Her arrow passed cleanly through and embedded itself in the turf beyond. More huzzahs.

I realized that James and David Bliss had drifted out from the Circle's orbit, scaled the stone steps to the upper terrace and joined the family group. Davey made himself responsible for moving back the target, taking it up, pacing off ten yards, digging the shovel in again farther from where Bronwyn stood.

Well, yes, I thought. Horsemanship and archery. Comanche virtues. Of course. But have the damned Savage Girl face off with Delia Showalter at the cotillion and we'd see whose claws were longer.

From forty yards Bronwyn put another arrow through the palm-size space of the shovel handle. Louder applause now.

The Circle girls continued to *thwock* tirelessly away.

As I had in Chicago, I witnessed again the surprising attraction Bronwyn held for men. Chippy Wilson clambered up the terrace wall to join James Bliss beside her. James reached over to furnish her with an arrow as his brother moved back the target shovel ten yards.

"Who might that be?" Bev said, low-voiced, at my shoulder.

I had been prepared for this. Somewhat. Anna Maria and Freddy and I had talked it over.

"We decided we would introduce our dear young Bronwyn as a cousin," Anna Maria had said. "From the West."

"Not a lie, really," Freddy said. "In the sense that humankind is one big family and all men are cousins."

But the word "cousin" stuck in my throat. "Does the creature have a name?" Jones Abercrombie asked.

"More to the point," Bev asked, "is she out?" As in presented to society.

"For Chrissakes," I said. "She's just a child."

Up top, Bronwyn put her shot on target once again. Astonished laughter and cheers.

Delia approached the distracted members of her once attentive audience. "What's going on up there?" she asked.

Anna Maria had been organizing balls all my life, ginning up extravagant dances at the merest hint of opportunity. The Christmas Ball. The St. Valentine's Ball. The War Victory Ball. The Ball of Antiquity, a fancy-dress masquerade with a requirement of togas for the men and chitons for the ladies. The Any Old Occasion Will Do Ball.

She danced well herself, of course, and always hired the best orchestras. I can see her even now, train looped up to her wrist, smiling with genuine pleasure. As opposed to some other ladies, who maintained thin-lipped paralysis even as they waltzed. Dancing brought out the young girl in her.

As a youth I attended Madame Eugénie's dance academy, the only socially acceptable school in Manhattan for such purposes, running through the steps alongside Bev and Harriet and James and David and Camilla. But I actually learned to dance from Anna Maria. All except for the still-somewhat-scandalous waltz, of course. For that I was on my own.

At the Midsummer Night's Ball, Anna Maria lit the ballroom at The Ditches with low candles on the tables and placed sprays of wild roses and carnations and lilies of the valley in bowls on every side.

As a novelty the immense twenty-foot door panels at either end of the room were opened to the night, with a few of our boys posted at each with feather fans, Moroccan style, to bat away the insects. The breeze off the Bowl swept up the hill, cool and lake-scented.

The strains of the orchestra came up. Delia Showalter looked more beautiful than I had ever known her to be. My mind emptied of all other women but her.

I had made Freddy promise to exile anyone underage to the hinterlands of the second floor and to keep the adults well in the background. Unspoken but understood, the idea that Tu-Li and the berdache would occupy themselves elsewhere as well.

"Nicky will just have to stay away," I said. My annoying brother.

"Haven't you noticed?" Anna Maria asked. "Nicky is entirely be-sotted with Bronwyn. Follows her around like a puppy. I think he's almost as impressed with her as he is with Tahktoo."

I *had* noticed, actually. I had seen him toting the girl's hairbrush for her as though he were a royal page, trotting along behind Bronwyn, looking on while Tu-Li arranged her coiffure in the upstairs boudoir.

Savage Girl had once again descended into mutism, her verbal for-ays limited to occasional, unexpected phrases directed at a few select personages. She never spoke to me, for example. She barely looked at me. She ignored me.

At our midsummer ball, the gentlemen wore white tie. The ladies skimmed the floor atop their crinoline clouds, all milk-white skin and dimpled wrists, their gleaming hair pulled back to fall in fat tendrils down the napes of their necks.

Perhaps I had been reading medical journals too avidly, but the sight of the women's impossibly slim waists was slightly marred for me by a recent article on the "calculable harm" that overtight bone corsets wrought upon the internal organs. I felt as though I could cir-cle my hands around Delia's midsection and have my fingers meet.

Harriet Smith-Croft, on Bev's arm, wore rose taffeta with chantilly flouncing, while Caroline Howland, with Jones Abercrombie, was in black net over white gauze. Delia, with me, looked exquisite, a lily in her dark-blond hair, her apple-green dress exposing her shoulders, the powder-pale expanse of flesh accentuated by a choker of her mother's diamonds.

"Will you do me the honor?" I asked Delia as the first waltz began. We both smiled at the formality. We had danced with each other our whole lives.

I saw Anna Maria sitting at one of the small tables to the side of the orchestra, glowing beneath her tiara, making sure that everything was going well before taking to the floor herself. She waved her fin-gers at me and smiled.

Later on, far past midnight, I left the ball to pad down the endless carpeted hallways of the first floor, past the condemning portraits of Sonny and Grandfather (*What are you doing with your life?*), the sound of violins dying behind me. On either side of me stretched drawing rooms.

I had once commented to Freddy that The Ditches was one big drawing room. We had a series of interconnected ones on the ground floor, several more on the second level. They ran to themes: Alhambric style, Pompeian style, the Raj, a Roman one featuring bronze statuettes designated *Seedtime* and *Harvest*. Eight in all downstairs, too many for any reasonable utility.

"But more opportunity for assignations," said Freddy, arching his brow significantly.

That early morning, with the dancing still going on in the ballroom, I proceeded alone along the downstairs hall. Passing the seventh drawing room of the eight, I heard a crash. Then giggles, then shushing. I leaned through the open door and saw only dim shapes. Then, as my eyes adjusted, I could see my little brother, Nicky, brushing off his dark suit. He didn't notice me.

Next to him stood Bronwyn, appearing only as a small, narrow-framed girl, a little taller than Nick was, her thick black locks set off by the sky blue of her demure muslin gown. I could see the points of her white slippers peep out beneath her white silk slip.

The moon came in the window and cast a light on them. Nicky said, "Now, try again." She put her white-gloved hand on his shoulder, he put his hand on her waist, and they began their own cotillion there in the dark.

It was around this time the third murder was committed, although I did not discover it nor link it with the others until long afterward. One of our grooms, Graham Barton, disappeared from The Ditches without explanation. We thought, for various reasons indicated by his recent behavior, that he had simply left our employ. He had no family and had been talking a lot of late about the gold fields of the West.

Barton was a good man, a strong, strapping laborer of twenty with a great muscular build. He helped Bronwyn with Freddy's Comanche ponies. I had stumbled upon the two of them grooming the beasts one early morning, Bronwyn smiling gaily as she wielded the curry brush. Bronwyn, who never smiled at me.

I suddenly discovered myself upbraiding the fellow for his familiarity. Such strange impulses seized me at times. The girl, wordless as usual, flashed her eyes at me and stalked away.

Later, months later, that following winter, when Graham Barton's body was discovered by a local hunter in the muck of a little pond near the Bowl, animal predation had done its work. The mutilated corpus remained unidentified, unmourned and uninvestigated, buried in a potter's grave until Freddy and Anna Maria had it retrieved, a half year after the poor man's demise.

❧ 12 ❧

Even with the midsummer gala over and the celebrants gone, being at
The Ditches wore on my frayed nerves. During the remaining days of
summer, there would be more dances, more calls from neighbors,
more staying-over guests fleeing the New York heat. More opportunities, in other words, for Bronwyn to misbehave and for what I had
come to see as a reckless experiment on the part of my parents to end
in disaster.

The year before this, I had refused for health reasons the annual
invitation by the Bliss brothers and their friends for an Adirondack
wilderness sojourn. They took one every August, a time, Davey Bliss
said, "to go stark raving wild." We would depart the circus of civilization. Penetrate the northland wilderness by canoe. Live on the fish we
caught, the game we shot, the blueberries we harvested.

I wasn't quite sure I was up for it this year either, but I surely did
not want to sit around The Ditches. Since the ball, Bev Willets had
given every indication of becoming a pestering presence. He was like
an animal who scented blood. Who was this new ward of my parents?
What was her background? Could I do him the favor of tracing her
Delegate cousinage?

Delia also seemed rather too much interested in the mysterious
newcomer to the family circle.

So I went north with Jimmy and Davey Bliss.

Our entry into the Adirondacks, a first toe-dip into the wild before
the full-on plunge, occurred at Paul Smith's Camp, the celebrated
lodge on St. Regis Lake. An Erie Canal boatman, Smith had settled in
the region a decade before with a rough-and-tumble bunkhouse, leas-

ing canoes to athletic millionaires and their sons. Now he was a rich man, with thousands of acres to his name. You could drink whiskey and consume broiled foie gras in his lodge's main dining room while gazing out upon the soaring conifers and believe yourself a changed man.

Smith's was as far as many rugged outdoorsmen got. We planned to go farther. Outfitted with three canoes, five of us—the Bliss brothers, Bev's cousin Trip Willets, myself and an Algonquin guide named Johnnie Fishhawk—embarked on the first of August, a Sabbath Sunday, determined to leave all civilized constraints behind and worship at the true altar of nature.

I felt my gloom lift and my neurasthenia lessen as soon as we departed Smith's. Previous to this I had sometimes considered the wilderness to be too much of a physical challenge for me. But the paddle felt right in my hands, and digging it into the blue waters of the lake made my musculature come alive.

We camped that night on a deserted shoreline island. Johnnie Fishhawk made what he called a "white man's fire," a huge bonfire blaze. I felt shy at first but eventually joined the others in swimming au naturel. I ate with a relish I hadn't experienced since childhood.

Around the fire that night, Jimmy Bliss quoted Thoreau: "How near to good is what is wild!"

Davey said, "Does that mean 'near to good,' as in not quite good, and flawed?"

Trip Willets: "Or does it mean 'near to good,' as in sitting at the right hand of God in heaven?"

Thus our meandering and quite fatuous philosophical dialogues. Crude or not, everything, including conversation, felt truer in the outdoors. In camp we spent more time out of our clothes than in them, slathering our bodies with mud, as the beasts do, whenever the flies bothered us.

I had not a thought of The Ditches, I had not a thought of Manhattan, I had not a thought of Harvard, no thought of her nor anyone else.

Two weeks out I took a canoe, some flour, a little bacon grease and a packet of salt and pushed alone up Stony Creek and Raquette River to the falls. Fishing, paddling, camping, huddling in the lee of trees as magnificent storms blew through the mountains. I didn't hunt, not wanting the percussion of gunfire to desecrate the silence. I lived an animal existence.

I don't know why this kind of life appealed to me at precisely this time, when it only intermittently had before, but getting away from my family, at least, suited me well. Over the thundering cascade, at night, the aurora spangled the sky with ghostly green hallucinations and wolves called to each other far off in the cedar cathedrals of the forest.

No fear, my lupine brothers engendered in me no fear. Why should they, since with my bronzed body, my mud-slathered hide, the hawk feathers woven into my hair, I was at one with them? Besides, I had my rifle and my campfire.

I recalled Freddy's full-throated lupine yowl at Dr. Scott's and attempted to replicate it. I must have done a poor job, since the pack refused to answer me back.

Then, in September, Harvard.

It should have been a jolting reentry into civilization, but it proved not to be. I stopped off at The Ditches on my way to Boston, wandering the immense home's servantless halls like a revenant. Nothing renders a mansion more ridiculous than emptiness. The family had closed the Berkshire cottage for the season, decamping for the far northern climes of Canada, to our chalet at La Malbaie along the St. Lawrence. Bronwyn went with them.

With the legal cloud over him successfully dispersed, Colm Cullen met me in Boston, taking great delight in squiring me around his youthful stomping grounds. We set ourselves up in Cambridge, renting a floor of rooms at Mrs. Morgan's on Brattle Street. I took to punch and billiards at the Porcellian Club and generally slipped back into dear old homely Harvard as into a well-worn suit of clothes. A simple student once more.

Or so it seemed to me. My school chums kept remarking how

changed I was. "Why, Delegate, you've come quite near to health," the Roosevelt boy exclaimed to me, Teddy, a face full of grinning teeth.

"The Adirondacks," I said.

He brayed out a laugh. "Keep it up, old man! Up!"

A backlog of Anna Maria's chatty letters waited for me, some from Canada, some from the city. Hickory, our bull terrier, exiled to the country on account of trouble between the purebred beast and Bronwyn. Bronwyn herself, taken up by a trio of ministers from Grace Church on lower Broadway.

"They are very excited by the tattered Bible she possesses," Anna Maria wrote. "It lacks the New Testament, so Pastor Webb, in particular, pronounces her to be in a state of prelapsarian innocence, ripe for the redeeming power of the Word. There's good news, he tells her, and she repeats the Gospels after him."

While at school I more and more avoided my friends to spend time with Colm. We practiced the art of knife throwing together, using a stump in Mrs. Morgan's yard. He acted as my guide and protector on late-evening jaunts to the brothels and jilt joints of Ann Street, also known as "the Black Sea," Boston's harborside district and the one perhaps the farthest, in all senses, from Harvard Yard.

Not that we did not, often enough, encounter university students in the streets of the Black Sea who had traveled just as far as we had. But if I ever tried out academic discourse on my Irish friend, he would shake his head.

"I'll leave such matters to you, young master," Colm would say. "I ain't one for the impracticalities."

Acting nearer to that intellectual role, my mentor in the field of anatomy at Harvard, Dr. James. I would say that William James was the man I most admired outside of my father, though my admiration for Freddy waxed and waned with the moon, depending on his latest antics.

"I've noticed a marked distraction in your focus lately," Dr. James said to me one afternoon we spent at the dissection table.

He was perhaps more observant than my peers. They all thought I was the picture of health.

After returning from the wilderness, settling in for a term at school, I had slowly come to detect an increasing inner restlessness. I couldn't quite put my finger on the reason, but something felt amiss. An impatience with my studies. Not anatomy, no, but others, natural history, rhetoric. Then I noticed, sitting over my books, that my hands had begun to shake.

At the medical-school lab on Grove Street, Professor James and I worked on an unusual specimen delivered to him by Boston City Hospital, a teratoma taken from the uterus of a charity patient.

"Is anything off the beam with you?" he asked.

"No, no, I am perfectly happy," I said. "Well, no one is perfectly happy, but I am near to it."

He emitted a *hmmn* and went at the tumor with a set of dental picks. A teratoma is an odd little thing, one of the ghastliest growths known to man, a blood-infused ball the size of a child's fist, made up entirely of teeth and hair.

The two of us each wore a pair of ocular devices, inventions of mine that Dr. James commended very highly and adopted at once, high power magnifying lenses set into eyeglass frames and designed to be worn for dissection and surgery.

In fact, James tended to praise me often, perhaps too much for my equilibrium, since I admired the man so fervently. He liked my anatomical drawings.

"These are very good," he said when I presented some of the sketches I had done on the train ride across the continent. "Would you like me to speak to a publisher about them?"

Concentrating on the clot in front of us, we teased out its layers, peeling them back like the leaves of some rank, diminutive cabbage, flaying the epithelial tissues one after another. By an effort of will, I steadied my hands. It was fine work, but gross in the fastidious sense of the word, since the thing smelled foul enough to strip paint.

"Hair and teeth," James murmured. "The human irreducibles, sex and death."

I tried to understand what he meant. Hair, the alluring, and teeth, the slashing bloodletters.

"Except by fire, human hair is nearly indestructible," he said. Except by fire. Meaning: anger. The only force capable of destroying love.

"So love wins out," I said, speaking broadly. "Over violence, I mean."

"Oh, teeth, teeth last forever, too," he said. "Who has not felt the urge to tear and rip and maim? Do you know your Hindoo deities? Shiva, the Destroyer?"

I quoted a tidbit of Emerson: "If the red slayer think he slays, / Or if the slain think he is slain, / They know not well the subtle ways / I keep, and pass, and turn again."

He raised his head and beamed a smile at me, his eyes swimming behind the lenses.

I first encountered Professor James two years before, when he acted as my instructor in physiology. I took to him at once, and he, I thought, to me. I saw in him a like-minded figure, an intellectual, but one who felt emotions perhaps too deeply.

This year he had invited me to participate in a small, informal practical-anatomy curriculum, a course that often consisted of just the two of us, wearing our eyeglasses, cutting and prying, picking and exposing. Close work. The mere sounds made by a dissection—gelatinous, mucky, moist—have been known to send some people into a faint.

James kept a middle part to his hair and wore a pointed, well-clipped beard that made him look rather more Bohemian than less. His necktie, a striped creation that he let droop beyond his collar, would have elicited a laugh from Bev Willets, but though I didn't take up the style myself, it looked rather dashing on him. His face retained its youth (he was thirty-three that year) and normally wore a kind, soft expression.

"I wonder, Dr. James," I said after passing a silent moment working at the mass, "if the study of a wild child has any benefit for the furtherance of science."

"A wild child? You mean feral, one supposedly raised by animals?"

"Such as the Wild Girl of Songi or Victor of Aveyron," I said.

"Mostly hoaxes, I would have thought, though I haven't made any concerted study of them myself."

"But if we could posit the existence of such a creature, verifiable and genuine, would not the field of natural science be the better for a thorough investigation?"

"Certainly," he said. "However, these figures are almost always ruses, sideshow-carnival types of things, tricked up to inflame the popular imagination."

He stopped, propping his examination glasses on his forehead, making himself resemble some four-eyed beast. "I was assuming your query to be hypothetical, but perhaps not."

I was silent, bending to the work.

"Male or female?"

Again I refrained from answering, embarrassed that I had opened the subject with him.

"Is it planned to exhibit the creature?"

When I remained wordless, he rapped the table sharply. "Lord's sake, boy!"

I straightened, removed my eye device and met his gaze.

"I suppose," he said slowly, "that some compelling knowledge could accrue from a study of a feral child. Various propositions could be tested. One hypothesis that might be put to the proof, for example, is that some people have too much money, which they employ to toy and trifle with other people's lives."

We stared at each other until I dropped my eyes. "Shall we continue with the work at hand?" he said.

When we had stripped the whole tumor away, flattening it out on our examination table, James and I both remarked upon its peculiar shape at once.

"A homunculus," he said.

"Why, it's the shape of a man," I said.

We had fixed the product of our labors like an insect upon the table. The flayed tumor did indeed display a vague human outline, arms, legs, torso and head, a gingerbread man rendered in swirls of black blood, matted brown-blond hair and sharp, sparkling white teeth.

A little man.

I recited some popular doggerel of the day: "Run, run, as fast you can. / You can't catch me, I'm the gingerbread man."

"Except they always are caught, aren't they?" James said, closely inspecting the specimen, his eyeglasses only inches away from its mottled surface. "They are apprehended, then quite crunched down upon by pointed little teeth."

Later in the term, as Thanksgiving approached, James suggested I might be better off applying for a leave from the college.

"Is my work deficient in some way?"

"Not at all, not at all," he said, clapping me on the shoulder. "You only appear as if you want to be elsewhere."

"I am quite happy where I am," I said. I felt as though I were always having to tell him this. Though James was my anatomy professor, he very much tended toward the relatively new field of "mental science," or psychology, for which Harvard had no chair. He was a great reader of moods.

"You're not doing yourself or anyone else much good," he said, adding, a bit unkindly I thought, "Your head is in the clouds somewhere, you may want to change your academic focus, look into meteorology."

I didn't wish to be mulish, and after thinking it over I decided he was right. The ills that had afflicted me the previous term threatened to return. I couldn't deny that my mind felt somewhat unsettled.

Instead of waiting to go back to New York for Christmas, as I had planned, by mid-November, just days before Thanksgiving, I was on a train leaving Boston, Colm Cullen at my side, and me brooding the whole time.

On the way to the city, we changed trains in New Haven, recalling to my mind the sporting event I had attended earlier in the fall with Delia Showalter, a game of American football between Harvard and Yale.

Harvard won, 4–0, but the day should have been more successful than it was. The contest on the field was played with some sort of modified rugby rules that I did not wholly understand, involving a special oblate spheroid of a ball. I stumbled explaining the game to Delia, was caught out in my ignorance about field goals versus touchdowns and experienced an irritating sense of comeuppance.

Delia journeyed from Manhattan chaperoned by her aunt, and she elicited admiring glances all around by the eager male students on the stadium benches, but her quality of fatuous blandness (or bland fatuousness) grated on me for the whole visit.

We were allowed to sit together beneath an immense buffalo robe. Though the sense of physical closeness had its inevitable effect on me, I felt irritation even about that. As though I somehow resented her power.

Now, on my return trip to New York from Cambridge only a few weeks after Harvard-Yale, I decided not to telegraph the Showalters about my arrival. I wondered at my recalcitrance. Delia would surely be upset if she found out I was in New York without telling her, and she would indeed find out. I was being petty, and I couldn't understand why.

Well, I hadn't told my parents I was coming home either, but that was more in the way of a surprise. And also, I suppose, to avoid Freddy's displeasure at my leaving school.

Dear old New York, dear old Manhattan. Rumbling along the coast, past Greenwich, down through the Bronx and Harlem, I felt a rising sense of excitement all out of proportion to the event. Rather than arriving in the city with my tail tucked between my legs for having left Harvard, I had a sense of new beginnings.

Colm and I arrived at Grand Central Depot, then took a hansom cab up Fifth Avenue to Sixty-third Street.

A double château, our house and my grandmother's next door, both big enough for a regiment, together taking up the whole blockfront.

The Citadel, Nicky always called our half, not entirely in jest. It sat on that stretch of Fifth like a proud thumb stuck in the eye of social convention. With it, the family seemed to say, here be the Delegates, and let none dare to judge us.

Fashion had not yet caught up with our choice of neighborhood.

All around, especially to the north and east, were rock outcroppings, feral pigs, the poor. A favored specialized activity of the neighborhood, bone boiling.

The Citadel stood out. Built right to the sidewalk in mulberry-colored stone, two wings and four floors with a twenty-foot-high first story and a deep mansard roof, the residence reflected the iconoclasm of its builder, my grandfather.

Richard Morris Hunt, the architect responsible for all the important residential buildings in New York, had given The Citadel the likeness of a full-fledged sixteenth-century château, a fairy-book castle if there ever could be one in Manhattan, inhabiting a different world from the terrible cast-down hovels all around.

The trio of marble "white houses" on Fifty-seventh Street and Fifth, owned by a family of shipping magnates, were our closest neighbors or, as August Delegate had thought of it, our closest competitors.

Inside, the place was all Anna Maria. Tapestries, wainscoting, window dressings. Public rooms on the second floor, private on the third, servants on the top floor, stables at the back.

A space designed as a conservatory had been given over to an aviary for my mother's birds of plumage—parrots, cockatoos, chaffinches. It was immense, with little-visited, leafy corners where weather splattered the leaded skylights.

Freddy indulged in the training of a little kestrel in this sanctuary, taking the hawk over to the East River on occasion to fly. The back of our house sounded like a bird-thronged forest and was where we much preferred to live, away from the traffic noise of the avenue.

Stationed beneath the Fifth Avenue portal's copper canopy, Paul Rogers acted as The Citadel's gatekeeper and pig shooer. Freddy couldn't be satisfied with just a butler to receive callers, he had to have a doorman as well. A well-muscled slab of a man and a great favorite of Nicky's, Paul took an instant disliking to Colm, as someone who might be infringing on his territory.

"Back in residence, Mr. Hugo?" Paul said when I arrived.

"For the foreseeable future," I said.

Paul maneuvered aside the hansom hack trying to help with the luggage. "You there, boy," he said to Colm. "Servants' entrance at the back."

Colm just laughed, and we strolled in through the front door together.

"Mr. Hugo! This is a surprise," our butler, George Winston, said, nodding in a polite bow.

I put my finger to my lips and brushed past him, calling back over my shoulder, "Inform my parents they have a visitor in the front drawing room, but don't tell them who it is. And tea!"

I sent Colm away with my kit and took the stairs two at a time, feeling buoyant, exuberant. Unhushed by the gleaming mahogany all around, the burgundy Oriental carpets, the golden sunflower wallpaper.

I fairly burst into the upstairs drawing room, empty at this time of day, standing there, taking in the sights and smells of home, becoming infused with "Delegacy," as Nicky would have it.

Good old drawing room, full of good old furniture! The tall, curved cabinet of butterfly specimens, shrine to one of Freddy's serial obsessions. In one corner a full suit of armor, holding its lance as though it would charge across the room and impale the gilded statue of Diana in the opposite corner.

On the ceiling floated a large Chinese parasol—Anna Maria had filled the house with chinoiserie—and on the floor lay a fluffy satin pillow, one of many scattered throughout the house for our brindled mastiff, Rags, so that she never need bother herself to search for a bed when she wanted to lie down. The interior remained practically invisible in the murk of the evening, since none of the sconces were yet lit.

I startled at a figure in the room I hadn't immediately noticed. Bronwyn stood at a window on the Fifth Avenue side of the house, the washed-out light of the waning afternoon bathing her in fading gold. She was dressed in tightly fitted indigo plaid and wore a cameo that I recognized as belonging to my mother.

Our foundling had matured a great deal since I saw her last, over three months before. She looked at once more normal, less wild and at the same time more ethereal. She had grown out of her girlishness and into something else. She had a pretty figure. I could even believe she was taller by an inch.

Hearing me come in, she turned from the window. "Oh," she said quietly, "the other son." As if remarking on a cloud in the sky or a carriage in the street, something so very everyday.

Her words were like a punch to my gut, a gut that had already been sent flip-flopping by the new distinction of her appearance. To hear her speak at all was extraordinary. But on top of that, that she was so casual, so dismissive. The other son. As though I were totally uncentral to her life.

Shall I describe her voice? Husky, totally different from the breathy sibilance of Delia Showalter and her kind, velvet with some grit in it. An unplaceable, childish accent, enchanting.

I was about to greet her—we were old Sandobar pals, after all— but the words stuck in my throat.

Then Winston threw open the door to the central hall, and Freddy and Anna Maria came in, and Nicky spilled into the room also, and I was caught up in their surprised hellos. Rags filled the air with welcoming bellows. At least *she* recognized her master.

Towheaded Nicky plowed into me with a hug. My mother fussed, assuming that I had left school because of illness once again. I assured her I was fine.

"Then why?" Freddy said.

An embarrassed pause. "We'll talk about it later," Anna Maria said.

The berdache and Tu-Li entered, and the moment passed with their greetings.

"We have news for you," Freddy said. He gestured to Bronwyn and took her under his arm when she approached. "Hugo, we'd like to introduce you to your new sister. We've given Bronwyn the Delegate name."

Bronwyn performed the prettiest curtsy that could be demanded of anyone. Maybe she really had become domesticated, over the course of these months when I hadn't seen her.

"Kiss your brother, dear," Anna Maria said.

Bronwyn stepped forward and moved to place her lips to mine. Anna Maria said, "On the cheek, dear," and my new sister tacked to one side. A brief, whispery-soft warmth, the fragrance of oranges.

"We lost her governess!" Nicky said, an unaccountable note of triumph in his voice.

"And why would that be?" I had depended on the fact that a governess might provide a buffer, if one was needed, between my friends and the strange new addition to the family.

"Bronwyn stabbed her," Nicky said.

"Oh, shush," Anna Maria said quickly. "It was an accident."

"The cut was not deep," Tu-Li said.

Bronwyn turned her face to the window.

"Miss Peel called Bronnie a hellion," Nicky said. "She said she would never be a member of civilized society."

Bronnie? He calls her "Bronnie"? "What on earth happened?" I asked.

"It's too absurd even to recount," Anna Maria said. "No one's fault. It seemed Bronwyn carried a scissors of some sort, and Miss Peel turned around hastily, and they collided. . . ."

"There was blood," Nicky said. "I saw it. Miss Peel shrieked like a stuck pig."

"When have *you* ever heard a stuck pig?" I asked, mussing his hair.

"They never got along," Anna Maria said. "The woman could not appreciate the girl's qualities."

"Which qualities are those?" I asked.

"She's a ripping acrobat!" Nicky shouted, and attempted a cartwheel. He landed it, staggered and crashed against a lacquered Chinese stool, knocking it over.

Bronwyn laughed, something I had not often heard her do before.

By my lights Anna Maria's mothering impulse appeared to be entirely diverted to my new sister. I caught myself responding with a glimmer of jealousy that I could never express outright. But my mother sensed it, since she broke off favoring Bronwyn to place her hands on my shoulders and look searchingly into my face.

"But you're all right, Hugo, aren't you?" she said.

"Marvelous," I said, at least partially propitiated.

"I never know when you are being serious, dear," Anna Maria said.

"I love you, Mother," I said. She stood on her tiptoes to kiss me on the forehead, and I glanced beyond the crown of her head to the others in the room, my siblings, two of them now.

In his heart of hearts, Freddy did not care a whit whether I stayed in school or not, so wrapped up was he in his own inscrutable affairs. But he was my father nonetheless.

"Good you're home, son," he said, wrapping me in a bear hug. "We need you here."

ꙮ 13 ꙮ

Shakespeare tells us "it is a wise father that knows his own child," and wiser still, I'd say, is the child who knows his own father. In the days following my arrival home, Freddy showed himself to be fretful and worried over his new ward. I understood Bronwyn's rebellion in her studies to be the cause.

I sat in on one of her morning lessons. Deportment, or posture, or some such. Her teacher, an athletic woman named Genevieve Stebbins, had her cornered in the drawing room. Anna Maria attended for moral support.

They had set up a huge gilt-framed mirror and posed Bronwyn in front of it. My newfound sister stared blankly at her reflection. She wore a modest, lace-collared gray gown, her copious hair controlled in French braids.

"Now," said Mrs. Stebbins, directing her movements. "Drop forearm from elbow as if dead."

Bronwyn allowed her arm to fall limp, then stuck out her tongue and went cross-eyed. Her imitation of death, I supposed.

"Shake it," said the teacher. "Vital force arrested at elbow."

The world waited breathlessly as Mrs. Stebbins was in the process of writing a book. Her inspiration, a performer at the Paris Opéra-Comique named François Delsarte, whose method linked voice, breath and movement as expressive agents of human impulses.

The Delsarte Technique was all the rage.

"These are essential decomposing exercises," Mrs. Stebbins explained to my mother.

I thought the whole business complete bunkum. But Anna Maria loved to help with lessons; it was her favorite thing. She felt that it brought her closer to her daughter. Afterward they'd curl up together in front of an open hearth and my mother would read to Bronwyn for hours. All the fairy tales and children's stories Anna Maria had missed reading to her lost Virginia.

"Don't hunch, don't slouch," barked Mrs. Stebbins at her pupil. "It is rude and ill befits a lady. Also, slumping affects the voice." She reached out and physically pulled Bronwyn's shoulders back.

"Not so extreme," said Anna Maria. "She appears animalistic."

"He looks at me!" Bronwyn cried. Meaning that I was making her self-conscious.

Mrs. Stebbins told her to never mind.

Bronwyn sat down hard on a straight-backed chair and glared angrily across the room, once more reverting to a farouche child.

"She balks at her lessons and is headstrong in the extreme," Freddy told me over his after-dinner cigar that evening. "She will be proceeding along fine, making good progress, then suddenly regresses horribly. Anna Maria, really, is the only one who can do anything with her."

"I rather found her very much changed," I said. "I noticed it on my return home anyway. She speaks now, for pity's sake! What was I, fifteen weeks away? You are like a parent who sees his offspring every day and thus doesn't realize its incremental development, whereas a relative who comes only once or twice a year remarks upon how the child has grown."

"Well, yes, surely she has changed," Freddy said. "But when you start at zero, coming up to one or two is no large accomplishment. To be able to introduce her into society, we need her at a ten."

I suggested that the whole approach might be wrong. That before she could progress, Bronwyn had first to understand why she needed to learn. "You teach her table manners when perhaps she needs philosophy."

He snorted. "You haven't worked with her."

"I will if you want me to," I said.

He looked at me keenly. "Honestly, I have been contemplating aborting the whole venture."

"Shipping her back to Dr. Scott," I said.

"Well, no, that wouldn't do. Anna Maria would never have it. But, you see, that's part of the problem. What *would* do? How does one dispose of a half-finished human?"

"Your compassion leaks through your intent," I said, but I don't think he detected my sarcasm.

"She reads, you know."

I was shocked. "She does not."

"Yes, she does. Whether we have taught her or if she had some dimly remembered learning in her childhood, we don't know. But if sufficiently coaxed, she can understand a simple text well enough. More and more every day."

"That is great news, isn't it?"

"At times she demonstrates a voracious intelligence," Freddy said. "Quite remarkable. Except, notably, in the moral sphere, where she is an imbecile. And there's something else, too. I can't deny she has a quality of self that is very attractive to people. She has charmed the household staff. Winston is taken with her. They slip her delicacies when she is confined to her room."

"Do you confine her often?"

"When the occasion warrants, more often lately than before. I don't know what can be troubling her. We give her a place at our table, dress her sumptuously, she has every luxury. We spend a fortune on her toilette. Her willfulness smacks of ingratitude."

"You are asking a great deal of the girl, Freddy, attempting to cram years of education into just a few months. Professor James refers to the process as 'socialization.' It's very complex. She's not some trick pony."

"You said you would help, Hugo. Will you see what you can do with her? Perhaps a guiding hand, one nearer to her own age, a dear sibling, patient and understanding . . ."

"Don't lay it on too thick," I said.

"Anna Maria and I have been invited on a weekend away to Edward Livingston's country place. This is an example of a social affair to which we cannot possibly take Bronwyn in her present state. We have been terribly constrained in all our engagements, in fact, oftentimes having to leave her behind with Nicholas and Mrs. Herbert, the poor girl a virtual prisoner."

Mrs. Herbert acted as our head housekeeper and was a capable no-nonsense woman. Nicky had his nurse also, but somehow I did not feel them a match for Bronwyn.

"Take her into the park," Freddy said. "Take her on the ferry, read to her—that always soothes her—but take her in hand, will you? See what you can do, because I tell you right now, I am at my wit's end with her."

I had seen it before, one of my father's projects somehow not play-ing out precisely the way he expected it to, how he could jettison an obsession and move on as if it were only a passing whim. His collec-tion of exotic lepidopterans left unfinished, half the specimens un-pinned. He embarked upon a campaign against mediums who claimed they could communicate with the dead, dropping it abruptly. He be-gan and then abandoned an assemblage of Bibles that had stopped bul-lets during the War of the Rebellion.

Bronwyn would be discarded, too, relegated to the status of an urchin-in-residence or perhaps kept chained in the attic like Edward Rochester's mad wife.

Thus it was a few days after my talk with Freddy, equipping my-self with a bullwhip, a cattle goad, a pair of ready manacles and a flask of whiskey (only the last being the truth), I hied myself forth with Nicky and Bronwyn for an afternoon constitutional in the Cen-tral Park.

When we left the house, Bronwyn in a demure funnel bonnet with a satin bow, we all but bumped into a forlorn little group standing just outside the door, gaping upward at our windows. Two women, a man and two children, huddled together, looking at us as though we had stepped out of a dream.

"Coming through, coming through!" announced Nicky, holding out his arm as though to move them aside.

"A moment," I said. It was not a surprise to find them there. For as long as we had been at the Citadel, we had seen a steady stream of gawkers and curiosity seekers, some of whom trekked the eighty blocks from the East Side docks to see the house. Freddy employed Paul the doorman primarily to hustle such onlookers away.

As I fumbled past our admirers, Bronwyn paused and removed from the pocket of her cloak a little velvet purse. She untied its ribbon and with pretty, delicate movements, proceeding from one to the other, beginning with the children, deposited a coin into the hand of each. When she got to the father, finding her purse exhausted, she reached into her pocket again, this time pulling out a white handkerchief, which she solemnly conveyed to the man.

The gape-mouthed grouping parted for us then, and we moved across the avenue into the park.

Evidently my brother and my new sister had ventured into Olmsted and Vaux's American masterpiece many times before. The two of them walked confidently forward as we entered the commons at East Sixtieth, via Scholars' Gate, its name marked prominently on a stone plinth beside the portal.

"Do you know the role of the scholar in society, Bronwyn?" I asked, thinking to begin my lessons slantwise. In reply she scampered off with Nicky up Wien Walk, in a race toward the not-yet-frozen skating pond, leaving me trailing behind.

I soon realized that if I thought of taking them to the park, they in fact were taking me. The two of them treated the whole sprawling expanse as their backyard. Riding the bridle trails together almost every day. Bronwyn showing herself to be nowhere as much at home as on a horse.

We headed west, deeper into the park, skirting the Zoo and stopping at the Dairy for some fresh milk. I attempted to use the occasion for a discourse on the Dairy building itself, and Calvert Vaux's excellent grasp of Victorian Gothic architecture, but Bronwyn and Nicky were too busy comparing milk mustaches.

"Nicky wants the Carousel," Bronwyn said.

"I do not," Nicky said. "I'm too old for that business."

He turned out to be an eager child after all, however, since when we approached the amusement, he dutifully took his place in the line, leaving me alone with Bronwyn.

Gesturing to a black-streaked rock outcropping nearby, I was about to launch into a précis on the geology of Manhattan schist and gneiss, planning to crown my talk with a superb pun ("One is schist as gneiss as the other"). But Bronwyn abruptly took my hand and led me to the rear of the merry-go-round, where a dirt ramp descended toward an understory.

"I don't think the public is allowed here," I said. She dragged me down along the incline anyway.

The Carousel had a lower level. At the terminus of the ramp, a pair of weathered wooden doors hung half off their hinges. She dropped my hand, slipped one of hers into the gap between the panels and sprang the latch.

"You are going to get us into trouble."

She didn't listen but stepped forward into the darkened interior. Above, the calliope gave off its manic music and the painted wooden horsies went round and round. I felt the scene turning bizarre. Not knowing what else to do, I followed her through the barely cracked door.

Inside, one of the more curious displays in all of New York. In the musty basement, two ancient, swaybacked mules plodded around a circular dirt track, hitched to the center pole of the Carousel, their pathetic straining providing the power that turned the ride. I recollected the Toad, turning the tub at Dr. Scott's sideshow. The beasts performed their labors all out of sight of the merrymakers only a few feet above them.

No groom or boy watched over the mules. A bell rang, they halted. Two bells rang, they trudged forward again.

"Blind," Bronwyn said, approaching them during one of their respites.

The strangeness of the tableau trumped my thoughts of trespass, and I followed her onto the track. She fished into her frock and brought out a folded paper, which when opened proved to contain sugar. The first mule strained at its harness to get at the treat, lapping it eagerly with a hideous red-gray mop of a tongue.

The bell sounded twice, the mules lurched forward, forcing the Carousel upstairs to revolve. We walked alongside them.

"This one is Archie, and that one is Maud," Bronwyn told me.

The scene really did have a wonderful incongruity to it. I could hear the squeals of the children above us, my brother being one of them, though probably not among those so undignified to cry out.

The multicolored fantasia of the Carousel, its public face up top, contrasted sharply with the sad spectacle in the pit. The children, whirling about without care, while here underneath was the truth of things.

Archie and Maud had consumed their sugar and were chomping on the paper envelope. Nicky stuck his head through the door.

"Let's go," he said. "It's almost time."

Time for what? I wanted to ask, but felt myself borne along by their enthusiasm and by something else as well, their grasp of the secrets of a place that I had lived directly across Fifth Avenue from for years now but did not really know.

Shrieking with laughter, we raced goat carts on the Mall, scattering pedestrians left and right. I had a sense of triumph when I won one of the heats, although then I recalled that Bronwyn had counseled me as to which particular goat to choose, and I realized that she was the true author of my victory.

Its being a bright and warm autumn weekend, the park was thronged with visitors. On the graveled concourses that cut through the copses and green lawns, carriages passed by of every stripe: landaus, hansom cabs and open Victorias, the last predominating with the fashionables, the better to see and be seen.

"Bronnie, come on!" Nicky said, tugging the girl through the traffic on Center Drive. "It's time!"

I went along with them, not knowing or caring much what it was time for, willing to pass the day innocently with my two siblings, one blood, one adopted. We dodged across East Drive, avoiding the flying carriages, and approached the Zoo from the rear. Atop a small rise, we could look down into its enclosures and cages, seeing them ringed with spectators, some of whom aped and tormented the animals displayed.

As we passed down the slope, a thick blackthorn planting confronted us, backed by a dense hedgerow that skirted the Zoo along its rear boundary.

By this time I understood that Bronwyn and my brother disdained natural entrances to any of the park's attractions. They would rather improvise. We plunged directly forward into the thicket, following a faint track that had us bending and ducking all the way.

Emerging from the blackthorns, we hit the hedgerow, which I realized had a sturdy lath fence behind it. I considered ourselves stymied, but, taking up a secret path, Bronwyn and Nicky moved forward. I was about to suggest that this was altogether too much when the two of them stepped into an invisible break in the hedge and vanished.

Struggling to keep up, raked by blackthorn spines, after much difficulty I arrived at the lath fence to discover that it, too, had a gap. Nicky's hand reached back, grabbed the worsted of my suit and forced me to bend down toward him.

Slipping through, I arrived to where Bronwyn and my brother crouched, a narrow, trash-strewn alleyway behind the lineup of the Zoo's cages. The air had a heavy moschate stink, underlaid with a vinegary smell of piss. The alleyway angled and dead-ended there. A sign on a nearby brick building read RUBBISH, and groundskeeper implements leaned up against the wall.

"What are we doing?" I asked, but Nicky and Bronwyn both shushed me. I could hear the gabbing of zoo spectators just a few feet away, but we were invisible to them. We knelt beside a low concrete wall with bars embedded in it: the cage of some large creature.

A roar sounded from right near to us, a roar that would melt steel.

"We have to leave," I hissed. They merely waved their hands at me.

Another immense roar, a clang, and a lion came stepping through a small portal from its outside run. The cage beside which we crouched was the animal's interior den. The door banged shut behind the beast, the crowd booed, and we were alone with a jungle cat, within arm's reach, separated from us only by a low concrete wall and a few flimsy iron bars.

Near enough to feel the animal's body heat, I tried to back away but was constrained by the small space.

It was a lion, yes, with tensile flanks and giant paws and a flowing mane, but it was something else, too. A tiger. The huge haunches that rested a mere foot from my nose were streaked with dark tiger stripes, parallel bands running over the buff pelt of a lion.

"A tigon," Nicky whispered. "His name is Charlemagne, but everyone calls him Charlie. Tigons are much rarer than ligers."

"Tiger father, lioness mother," Bronwyn explained, "instead of lion father and—"

I clapped my hand over her mouth. *Shut up!* I wanted to shout at them. *Just shut up!* I had a terror of the creature's noticing us, although we were so near he no doubt already had. In such proximity the iron bars seemed to have diminished in size until they appeared as mere wires, easily broken through.

"Presented to the Zoo nine months ago by a maharaja in India," Nicky said, adding, for emphasis, "deepest, darkest India."

"They feed him every afternoon, then put him in here to sleep," Bronwyn said.

The tigon's amber eyes with their gulf-black pupils came up to rest upon us or rather, as I felt it, upon me. He stopped, gave a hollow sigh and sank to the floor. A low rumbling rose up out of his chest, sounding like faraway thunder.

"Bronwyn," I whispered.

"No," she said softly. "Wait."

The tigon flopped its enormous body toward us, rolling slowly over, taking its time. Still keeping its gaze fixed on me.

Bronwyn reached her hand into the cage. More specifically, she wrapped her fingers around one of the bars at about the height of the tigon's gigantic moon face. She let it remain there, and we all crouched, poised on the cusp of something great or awful, waiting.

The tigon gave a yawn that allowed us a good look at a pair of incisors the size of cavalry sabers. Well within reach of Bronwyn's arm.

Wait now, I thought. *Wait.* I seemed unable to unfreeze myself. How had I allowed things to go this far?

The creature raised his eyes to Bronwyn's. Gently but firmly, like to like, species to species, he rubbed his plush muzzle against the knuckles of her hand.

"Charlie," she murmured, over his purrlike rumble, which in the small space sounded enormous. She reached out to pet him then, a sensuous, rhythmic rubbing that the animal gratefully allowed.

"What are you kids doing here?" came a piercing voice, and I turned to see a stocky, bearded man in a blue uniform approaching us down the alleyway. "This area is forbidden!"

I stood up awkwardly, eliciting a worried growl from Charlie, and ducked my head submissively before the zookeeper's authority. But when I turned to collect Bronwyn and Nicky, they had somehow disappeared, leaving me to my stammering explanations as I was escorted from the Zoo grounds and instructed never to return.

"I'm afraid there is a detective in to see you, Mr. Hugo," Winston said, a mournful, disapproving look barely concealed on his face.

"Really?" I sat in Freddy's library the day after the Zoo visit. I had been occupied, all morning, compiling a list of books that I might read to Bronwyn. My parents were still in the country.

I told Winston to show the man in.

"In the stairhall below, young master," Winston said.

The stumpy little professional I met there wore a supercilious look and a bowler hat that appeared too small for his head. "If this is about what happened at the Zoo yesterday," I began hurriedly, "of course I can explain."

"None of that, sir," the little man said. "Don't know to what you are referring. This is on some other matter." He introduced himself to me as Otto Grizzard, "late of the Pinkerton Agency, late of Palmer House in Chicago, Illinois."

I felt myself being carefully observed so attempted nonchalance. Fumbling, I lit a cigarette from a box on the side table. "Smoke, Mr. Gizzard?"

"Grizzard," the man corrected, pronouncing the name in the French style. "And no, no tobacco. I'm temperance."

"You mentioned . . . late of here, late of there and now of where?"

"Now I am out for myself," he said.

"Sit, please, and tell me what I can do for you. I am afraid my father is not in town right at the moment." I motioned to the Gothic bench along the opposite wall.

He continued to stand. "It is to you whom I wished to speak, if you are Hugo Delegate. And you recently passed through Chicago, staying at the Palmer?"

"Well, I don't know how recently, but five months ago, I guess it was, I was with my family, and we spent a short stopover in the hotel on our way east."

"There was an incident during your stay," Grizzard said.

"I'm sorry, are you appearing in your capacity as an employee of the Palmer House? But you indicated you were no longer attached to the establishment, correct?"

"Correct."

"So I don't understand."

Freddy and Anna Maria had long ago taught me that the majority of humankind, when confronted with a possessor of wealth, immediately set themselves to securing a piece of it. The greater the wealth, the harder they came at you and the more incessant were the importunities.

We were, all of us in the family, attuned to the infinite guises that such approaches might take. At that moment I felt that, if I were not mistaken, Otto Grizzard, the former Pinkerton detective, late of Palmer House, was eager to reach his hand into my pocket.

"A member of the staff at the hotel, Matthew Donleavy, fell victim of a horrible attack during your stay."

"Yes, I knew that. I wasn't aware of the man's name, but in fact I came upon the crime in its immediate aftermath."

"Certain facts have come to light in the wake of your escape," Grizzard said.

"My escape!" I exclaimed. "My family and I were scheduled to leave from Union Station aboard our private train at five the next morning. I did not 'escape' from anything. I merely followed a plan predetermined far in advance of any unfortunate circumstance that befell Mr.—"

"Donleavy, sir," Grizzard said.

I remembered the shadowy hotel corridors, the blood. "I think I shall ask you to leave," I said. I rang, and Winston materialized at my side.

"Not until you hear me out, sir, I wouldn't."

"Good afternoon, Mr. Grizzard."

Winston stepped up to him. I waved him off. "Get Paul, will you, Winston? Or Colm, if he's around."

"Indications are pointing to you, Hugo Delegate," Grizzard said, stubbornly standing his ground.

He held up the splayed fingers of his hand. "One, the cuts what made the victim fall mortal was rendered with a surgeonlike instrument, such as a lancet or scalpel, a tool anyway of an expert, with which the body were horribly mutilated. Two, such instruments had been spied among your personal belongings in the time previous to the deed, bloody and well used."

"This is outrageous," I said.

"Three, you are a vivisectionist—I have checked on you, at Harvard College, in Boston, is it? You have a practiced hand at such matters. Four, another of your party, a young lady and your probable accomplice, had been seen up and around in the wee hours of the A.M. in question, when Matthew Donleavy met his end. Further—"

"Shut up and get out," I said.

"Further, such young lady was seen in the company of Matthew earlier in the evening."

"What?"

"Aye, you didn't know that, did you? Now, I ask you, seeing it objectively, what are we to think? Really, sir, what are we to think?"

I took another cigarette, my second, two more than I usually have on any ordinary day. "We were served by this man earlier at dinner, if that is what you mean."

The waiter's slicked-back blond hair recurred in my memory, his broad shoulders, the stupid expression he wore. She had a smile for him.

"The chippie was seen with him after that," Grizzard said. "Theory of the crime? We detectives are always big on the theory of the crime, sir. It helps us sort through the multiplicity of reality."

He again splayed out his fingers, checking off the chain of events one by one. "Young lady flirts at dinner, meets up later at an assignation, jealous suitor cuts down the object of affection. An old story, if I may say so, sir."

"You may not say so," I said, but my voice came out as a weak quaver. The whole instance brought the nightmare back to mind, disjointed and unreal. Could the woman I saw in the Palmer House maze (thought I saw? imagined I saw?) have been Bronwyn?

"Now, we don't know her name or her relation to you, but sooner or later the bottom of this matter will be got to, whether you like it or not. And wouldn't you prefer to be in control of the process rather than to be manipulated by the hands of others?"

Finally he was getting around to it. I said, "You must come out and say exactly what you mean, so I can thrash you within an inch of your life for saying it."

He was short, a half hand smaller than I even with the hat, but thick, and I doubted, if it came to that, whether I could take him. Where was Colm?

Grizzard only smiled at my threat, clearly not taking it seriously. He held out both hands as if they were the scales of justice.

"Well, sir, on the one hand scandal and notoriety, your name dragged around in the pages of the popular press, associated with if not accused in a macabre passion killing. The young lady were said to be very beautiful, so she would be catnip to the gentlemen kittens of the newspapers. Scandal and notoriety, sir, notoriety and scandal."

He allowed his left hand to fall as if weighed down by the immensity of this eventuality. Then he raised his right.

"On the other hand, there's only a few of us actually knowing the who and the why and the wherefore of this matter, only a few voices to be stilled, a few needy souls, working people all of us, housemaids and porters and such, needing to be taken care of, and all that scandal goes away as though the light of day never once shone upon it."

He bowed and turned toward the door. "I knew you would want to hear me out," he said. "I'm staying at the New York Hotel, not quite as nice as the Palmer House, I must say, and I'll only be there another week, should you need to contact me."

Grizzard turned at the door and gave me a broad wink. "Which I know you will."

Colm appeared in the doorway, a looming presence. Grizzard sized him up. "You needn't bother to escort me, my man. I can find the way."

At a gesture from me, Colm ushered him out.

🍃 14 🍃

Poor Grizzard, Bill Howe says, his voice dripping with feigned regret. So foolishly confident. He was fairly easily disposed of, wasn't he? It's a wonder that a man such as that would even try, when the outcome is so clearly preordained. When a verminous field vole comes up against the might of an eagle, what will be the result?

He rises to his feet and stretches. There could be no question of payment, he says, since money, once applied, tends to act as a stimulant, until it becomes an addiction and the poor victim becomes enslaved to it like a Chinese coolie to his hop.

Now, he says, a bath behind this partition here, a late repast, some coffee—or you prefer tea, don't you?—and we'll have at it once more. Are you tired?

The shadows of Saturday evening have fallen outside the Tombs. I tell him I am not. Are you tired, Mr. Hummel?

The question does not apply, since Hummel looks as though the very concept of sleep is foreign to him.

We are getting to the heart of it now, Howe says, to the very heart of it, which is where we want to be, eh, Mr. Hummel?

The sheriff of Nottingham, Hummel says inscrutably, astonishing both myself and Howe not by his words but by the very fact that he speaks at all.

Yes, yes, Howe says, the lawman from Virginia City. We will get to him. But first we must render young Delegate here wholly refurbished and refreshed. Replace that waistcoat with its nasty bloodstains.

Perhaps, he adds, ushering me behind a screen, where a scented bath has been prepared in an elegant copper tub, perhaps you might want to continue while you soak. I and Mr. Hummel will be right on the other side of this modesty panel.

I undress and slip into the scalding-hot water.

From behind the screen, I hear Howe's prompt: Grizzard's visit did unsettle you, did it not?

Grizzard's visit unsettled me a great deal, and I felt I had no choice but to lay out the whole affair to my father, as soon as he and Anna Maria returned from their country weekend upstate.

And yet, when it came to that, when my parents arrived and took up their busy city lives, asking me how my time with Bronwyn had gone, something prevented me from divulging anything more than bland and uneventful details. I told them we had gone to the Zoo, which was true. I left the freelance Chicago detective entirely out of the narrative.

I realized I had to do something to put Grizzard off, thinking briefly of paying him out of my allowance and then rejecting that as a last line of defense, to be employed only when others failed.

Instead I called upon two excellent, excellent attorneys of my acquaintance, genius lawyers, partners at the bar, to take care of the matter for me.

Which they did. Without, I may add, an unnecessary outlay of funds. The pair really are magicians.

You are too, too kind, Howe says, making a rare interruption in my narrative.

Not at all, I say.

Pray continue, Howe says.

I shall, I say.

And I do.

A stray thought nagged at me, and I turned out all the drawers in my wardrobe and searched through the contents of the desk I kept in the office off my bedroom. Finally I found it, tucked away in my copy of Suetonius, the newspaper article from the *Gold Hill News,* concerning the shooting I had witnessed in the club dining room of the International Hotel in Virginia City.

A word set off little dinging alarm bells in my memory. This was the phrase, in the second paragraph of the article: . . . *mutilated and headless corpse was found* . . .

Mutilated. I suppose it might be common enough for bodies to be mutilated in the course of murder, violence being a great disturber of persons. I did not know enough about homicide to be able to hazard a guess as to the incidence of mutilation attendant upon it. Still, it could possibly violate the rules of randomness, the fact that the word had cropped up twice in the past few months, first in the *Gold Hill News,* then from the gizzard of Mr. Grizzard.

I thought of calling Colm in, changed my mind and rang for Winston instead, asking him to summon a Western Union boy. I sent a telegram.

TO: SHERIFF DICK TOLLE, VIRGINIA CITY, NEVADA.

SIR, DURING OUR RECENT SOJOURN IN YOUR FAIR CITY LAST JUNE . . .

I couldn't think how to proceed. After several false starts, I settled on the following.

THE FATAL SHOOTING THAT OCCURRED IN THE INTERNATIONAL
HOTEL, WHICH I WITNESSED WITH MY OWN EYES, HAS CONTINUED
TO ENGAGE MY INTEREST [STOP] I WONDER IF YOU COULD FORWARD
TO ME SOONEST ANY DETAILS REGARDING BUTLER FINCE, PETER
FINCE, HANK MONK AND THE SURROUNDING CIRCUMSTANCES OF THE
INCIDENT, AS WELL AS THE SUBSEQUENT DISPOSITION OF THE CASE
[STOP]

Perfectly straightforward, and should Sheriff Tolle be so indiscreet as to share my communication with my father, a message that I could easily pass off as one of general interest.

From the back of my mind, stories of feral children surfaced, how both Victor of Aveyron and the Songi girl were subject to sudden fits of uncontrollable anger. I had witnessed Bronwyn's raging eyes many times, but so far she had indulged in no overt incidents of violence. At least not against human beings. I thought of her expertly braining that jackrabbit outside Kelton station. I wondered if the deprivations of her Savage Girl captivity might somehow lead her to shed human blood.

One evening after supper—this was two or three days following the fiasco at the Zoo—I ventured into the South Wing. Bronwyn had her rooms there, on the same third-floor corridor as Tu-Li and the berdache. Her windows thus looked out not only on Sixty-second Street but on the courtyard and stables at the back of the house.

I knocked upon her door, received no response, knocked again, waited, then entered.

Her private quarters. I felt like a spy.

Bronwyn's bedroom had been decorated by my mother and thus had little personal expression of its occupant. Against one wall stood a four-poster bed of dark walnut with a fringed yellow silk canopy and a set of curtains that could be pulled around the posts for privacy. A half dozen rose-colored embroidered pillows lay heaped up at the head of the bed, its satin quilt likewise rose pink.

Rooting through her room, I would have had a horror of her finding me, but the girl was quite obviously gone, probably next door in Tu-Li's bedroom or perhaps playing at Chinese tiles with the berdache.

A matching walnut armoire and chest of drawers ranged along the interior wall. A deep turquoise carpet made a circle in the center of the floor. Framed cameos and tranquil landscapes crowded the walls.

I passed through the empty, silent bedchamber, picking up and putting back down various objets. That was what was most arresting about the room, the collection of gewgaws and trinkets that stood arrayed on every surface.

Alabaster bud vases, tiny illustrated booklets of "ladies' rhymes," gilt clocks, spider plants in Chinese urns. Everything had come from Stewart's, or Macy's, or from somebody's trip to the Continent. A bottle of orange water.

Gifts from my mother.

Nothing in the room was of Bronwyn herself, except perhaps the indentation in the pillow where she had rested her head.

The room was cold. The big sash window on the eastern side had been thrown wide open to the night. I went to the window, stuck my head out and saw that it communicated to The Citadel's courtyard.

Behind me Bronwyn entered the bedroom from the adjoining dressing chamber. She did not see me at first, but I startled out a little cry, because I realized she was done up in a boy's clothes—shirt, trousers and boots—and was in the process of concealing her long black hair beneath a cap.

She stopped and stared at me as I stared at her.

"What do you want?" she asked coldly.

I was struck speechless.

"Don't be foolish about this," she said. Referring to her garb.

Gathering my wits, I said, "I saw you once before when you were dressed as a boy."

"On the back of a pony. You could not believe it. You asked yourself, Does she get smaller and smaller, like some shrinking person, or could she really be leaving us far, far behind?"

Gazing into the distance as at the horizon, waving her hand, she repeated, "Far, far behind."

She gave me a droll look and resumed bustling determinedly around the room, collecting a leather satchel, slinging it over her shoulder. Her appearance in those homely male clothes had an unsettling effect on me, especially when, completing the ensemble, she donned a leather coat.

"For Lord's sakes, are you going out?" I could not control the dismay and surprise in my voice.

Bronwyn didn't immediately answer. Reaching beneath her armoire, she extracted the dirty canvas bag I had first discovered in her sleeping quarters on Sandobar. From it she took out her set of steel razor claws, tucking the device away into the leather satchel.

"For protection," she explained. Then, again gesturing to her costume, "It's the only way I can venture out alone without people bothering me. I did it in the Comstock this way."

"No," I said firmly. "No, you can't leave the house. I forbid you."

She merely gave me a look, eyes blazing with purpose. The question rose unbidden in my thoughts, as if inserted there by some superior psychic force: *Who was I to forbid her to do anything?*

Nevertheless I babbled on. "This is just not done, Bronwyn, you could get hurt, something could happen, no, really, no, no, no!"

"Yes," she said. The first word I had ever heard her speak, back on the train.

"But it's nine o'clock! Where is there for a girl to go at night?"

She looked at me meaningfully. "Where do *you* go at night?"

Could she possibly know? Upon my recent return from Harvard, I had immediately taken up my old nocturnal habits, frequenting Delmonico's, meeting Bev or Chippy or Jones Abercrombie there, then going on to the shivarees at Mrs. Tolson's or the Dauphin, our favored brothels in the Tenderloin.

"That is entirely different," I said, not saying it, more like sputtering it.

"Is it?"

I realized later that she did not in fact know what I did with my evenings, that it was only my guilty mind reading into her words, but the effect was the same.

She crossed the room, heading for the window. I moved to block her, but she effortlessly dodged around to the side, making me stagger, in a move uncannily reminiscent of when the Toad servant had tried to prevent her from leaving Dr. Scott's barn.

"Bronwyn!" I called out.

She poised a moment on the sash, said "Hugo," over her shoulder, and disappeared.

I rushed to the window, in time to see her clamber downward on the ornamental crenellations of the exterior, cross the stable courtyard and slip out toward Sixty-third.

Thunderstruck, I rushed down the corridor to my own rooms in the opposite wing, dressed hurriedly in evening clothes and took the stairs down two at a time.

I found Freddy and Anna Maria in the aviary. Crossing the space quickly, spooking a fluttering cockatoo, I peered outside into the courtyard.

"Going out?" Freddy asked.

"Is there something wrong, dear?" Anna Maria asked.

"She's—" I began, then broke off.

"You look entirely out of sorts, Hugo," Anna Maria said. "Doesn't he, Freddy? Stop a bit, take a cigarette, you should never leave the house upset."

I'm sure I reminded her of the unhinged way I looked when I was carted off to the sanatorium.

"No, no, I'm all right," I said. "It's just— I must go!"

Freddy followed me out of the aviary as I crossed the stairhall. "Take the brougham," he called.

"I'll get a hack," I said back to him.

"Take Colm!" he called.

But this was not a night for Colm Cullen to know about. I needed his protection but more particularly wanted to keep Bronwyn's misconduct secret.

Once out on the street, I felt at a loss which way to turn. I proceeded the short half block up to Sixty-third, looked east, found the street empty. The whole district was quiet as a cemetery, as befitted a neighborhood of two homes only.

Winds shook the trees in the park and along Fifth. I pulled my topper close, tightened my scarf around my neck and crossed the avenue. I didn't know where I would find her. The only thing I could think of was that day at the Zoo, when she had known all the park's nooks and crannies, all the places a person could slip in and slide through unseen.

So I clambered over the gray stone retaining wall and entered the park, also empty at this time of night. I tried to make myself think like Bronwyn, act like Bronwyn. I hurried deeper into the wilder, sylvan precincts beyond the Zoo, hearing the caged animals snort and wheeze in the darkness, restless with the gusty wind.

Peering into the gloom, I saw nothing, no one, wandering for a full half hour.

On the verge of giving up, I reached Bethesda Fountain. Then the sound of music carried from somewhere nearby. I couldn't make sense of the direction whence it came. A Gypsy guitar, a bandoneón. In a nearby copse huddled a group of figures, gathered around a small, wavering campfire.

This, too, as with the rest of what Bronwyn had shown me of the park, was something new to me. Though I lived directly across from it, I had without thinking considered the whole park a dead zone at night, closed, depeopled, perhaps dangerous. Not a place of music and warmth.

Visible by firelight were dark men in the clothes of laborers, black-eyed women with black hair and colorful kerchiefs, wearing the same jackets as the men, brown and coarse. The guitarist played a fast, jig-like air, holding his instrument up near his face as he sang into the night. The women clapped rhythmically and took to dancing near the fire, one after another.

One of the men, a hugely muscled brute with a slouch hat and a sad, drooping mustache, swept into the dance with a girl in his arms.

Bronwyn.

They looked transported, the two of them whirling madly, the wild wind blowing her long hair about, the clapping tempo of the women keeping time, the assembled dancers and spectators crying out foreign, unintelligible words.

A dizzying scene. Before me I witnessed Bronwyn revert to Savage Girl, unloosed, abandoned, purely physical. I couldn't bear to look, and I couldn't look away. Weakness overcame my gut, my knees, my groin, and I sat directly on the ground. She had taken her hair down, but her male garb maddened me, as did seeing her smile at her partner. The music . . .

Bronwyn and the Gypsy dancer quit the group, breathless, practically staggering from exertion. They drifted off into the darkness around the Lake.

I could not help myself. I followed. I saw the Gypsy dip his whole head into the water, then rear back with a shout and fling his wet hair, glints of the far-off firelight playing upon the splashing droplets.

Savage Girl laughed. A rare event that spawned an agony in my chest.

Sagging against a tree, its rough bark digging into my cheek, I blanked out for a moment. Then I saw the Gypsy man walk away into the night. Where was he going? Where had Bronwyn gone? I pressed my fists against my eyes like a small boy doubting what he was seeing. Then I plunged deep into the woods beside the Lake.

I felt at the same time as if I were chasing someone and as though I were being chased. Complete and utter darkness. Visions, waking dreams. A black-haired woman appeared and then abruptly vanished.

A man lay sprawled out on a bed of autumn leaves, eviscerated. I swayed for a second over him. I smelled the ferrous stench of blood, thick as mucus, pooling beside the body.

Incarnadine stillness. Time suspended, adjourned. Far away, the group of Gypsies at the campfire. The silence of their open mouths.

A deeper darkness, into which I plummeted.

Waking at dawn in the Central Park after spending a chill November night laid out on the ground can never be easy. I had evidently been clubbed from behind, since a blood-pulped mass swelled from the back of my head. I was certain I had a concussion but was unclear as to how severe it was.

Of course I had been robbed, my shoes, coat and wallet stolen, my pockets turned out like the wings of flapping birds. My knife was missing. Poor me. A recollection tantalized the edge of my mind.

I had seen something terrible. I had done something terrible.

No sign of anyone. I tried to wash the black blood from my shirt-front, but the mucky water from the Lake seemed only to stain me further. In the Gypsy campfire, dead embers.

Summoning a cab on Terrace Drive cost me all the effort I had. Making it home at last, I woke Paul the doorman to pay the driver and staggered up to the third floor.

Not to my room, no, that would have been too simple. I must needs go to the South Wing and see what kind of damage had been done to Bronwyn—or if indeed she had managed to survive at all.

Not bothering to knock this time.

It must have been before six o'clock when I entered her room, since the light had not come all the way up and the streets of the city were not yet fully awake. Expecting blood and mayhem, instead I found a sweetly sleeping fairy nymph, dressed not in rough male clothes but in a frilly nightgown of candy floss.

Bronwyn lay nestled in spotlessly fresh linen bedclothes, warmed by her pink goose-down quilt. Her lips parted in a pretty dreamland pout.

My head throbbed like a steam engine. My first urge was to shake her awake and upbraid the girl for putting me through what I had just been put through. I wanted to demand what she knew of the man whom I saw gutted like a fish on the carpet of autumn leaves.

Instead I sank back into a satin-tufted chair at her bedside, the one Anna Maria used when she wanted to read Bronwyn to sleep. And soon fell asleep myself.

Between waking and dreaming, I suffered the awful conviction that I had somehow killed the Gypsy dancer. The images crowded my brain: me rushing furiously forward to assault him, slashing wildly with some sort of blade, dragging Bronwyn away. The blow to my skull had somehow scrambled thought and memory.

Groggy, I half woke and trailed my hands down my shirtfront, which did indeed have blood spatters on it. Was it my own blood or that of my victim? The whole idea was bizarre. But the scenes that beset my mind had a vivid reality about them.

Sleep took me again, and again I experienced that same strange, tension-filled hovering at the boundary of consciousness.

"Why, Master Hugo, sir, what are you doing in the miss's bedroom?" Shrieking female speech, crashing into my skull.

"Good glory, Jorny, lower your voice." The upstairs maid, midmorning. The sun slanted across the shutters of the window through which Bronwyn had escaped the night before.

"Why, it's not proper!" Jorny bellowed. Actually, she was whispering, as Miss Bronwyn was still fast asleep, no surprise after her spree. It was only the voice that I heard within my aching head that shouted so loudly.

"Stop, stop," I begged.

"You look a mess," she said. "Your ear is cauliflowered, in case you didn't know."

I attempted to keep the world from spinning off its axis. "She . . . she . . . had a low fever, didn't she? I was watching over her to see . . ." Trailing off, wretched.

"Had she really?" Jorny demanded. "I hadn't heard about that." She stepped over to Bronwyn's bedside and lightly laid a hand on her forehead.

"Well, she's all right now," Jorny said. "No fever, I don't think. You'd best remove yourself."

My head in my hands, I heard Jorny growl, "You are a low, filthy, dirty beast, aren't you, sir?"

I looked up. "What? What?"

"I didn't say nothing, sir," Jorny said. "Now, shoo, I have to wake Miss Bronwyn for her breakfast and lessons."

"Don't speak anymore, Jorny," I said. "Your voice is extremely grating on my nerves."

She looked crestfallen, and immediately I felt I had acted badly. "I'll tell you what," I said. "You go run me a piping-hot bath, and I'm sure I'll be human again sometime within the next week or so."

I could tell she didn't want to leave me alone with the sleeping girl. Me, the girl's own brother. "Keep the door open if you must," I said snappishly.

Checking under the armoire to see if the set of razor hand claws was inside the canvas bag (it was), I nearly passed out as I bent over.

Feeling my gorge rise—I had a concussion, for sure—I made it to the hallway of the North Wing before I vomited, discreetly, into a decorative Chinese vase Anna Maria kept near the door to her chambers.

The following day remained quiet chez Delegate. I slept until the afternoon, took a dry-toast repast, cadged a fingernail slice of opium tar from Tu-Li, which I admixed with brandy, and then slept again for a full round of the clock.

Colm checked in on me the next noontide. I was already awake, still in bed and brooding. The house was silent.

"The way things have been going lately," I said to Colm, "I almost prefer unconsciousness."

He told me he had Douglas the footman on the alert to bring me up a full breakfast tray. "Them's all upset on account Miss Bronwyn hasn't left her room, same as you, since the night before last," Colm told me.

"Them? Who might 'them' be?"

"Wouldn't come down for her lessons, wouldn't have Madam in to read to her. The maids swear they hear her weeping."

"What about me?" I said. "I haven't emerged from my room for two days straight, I haven't been able to see to my responsibilities, I could have shed a tear or two in the depths of dread night, and do the maids gossip and my parents show alarm over me?"

"What responsibilities might those be, Mr. Hugo?"

"Don't be insolent," I said calmly. "Tell Tu-Li to come visit me, will you?"

"She won't," Colm said. "She has cut you off, on account she says the American mind cannot handle the poppy but that it makes for a slide into horrible degeneracy."

I groaned, and he told me Mr. Bev had called looking for me, and Cousin Willie was offering his new chestnut gelding to me for a pop around the park, and Delia Showalter's aunt had left a card.

I groaned some more.

"Another thing," Colm said. "I don't know if you recall the heavy-bearded lunatic we nicknamed the Stone-Thrower, the one who chucked rocks at Sandobar while we was idled on the siding in Virginia. Sad kind of guy."

"Pining about his love for the girl," I said.

"He's in town," Colm said.

"You can't be serious."

"I chased him off from in front of the house," Colm said.

"Our house?" I said, incredulous. "Was he tossing rocks at the place?"

"What with railroads crossing the continent, it's becoming a little too easy for people to move around," Colm said, getting up to leave. He would come back to check on me, he said, that I should stay in bed, that I still looked a little peaked.

I ate a full breakfast, and though I didn't think I was up to facing my parents and the screeching birds of the aviary, I did venture to the drawing room in the South Wing that Tu-Li and Tahktoo shared as their own.

"She won't come out," Tu-Li said as soon as she saw me. "What did you do to her?"

She and the berdache appeared to be wearing matching green silk kimonos.

Song Tu-Li's great shame were her broad unbroken feet, flopping around at the ends of her legs, she believed, like a duck's. In the past this had led her to fraternize with Americans, who she felt were less judgmental about her hideous handicap.

Born in Kwangtung, smuggled as an infant across the sea to the "Gold Mountain" (the Chinese name for California), she worked for five years as a translator for the Central Pacific. Since being engaged as my mother's helpmate, Tu-Li had added a slight flavor of mockery to the family mix, something for which we all came to develop a taste.

She was always Anna Maria's girl; they were intimates, and a sense of deep understanding existed between them. Lately, though, that allegiance seemed to have shifted. How could loyalty to Bronwyn trump her loyalty to my mother?

I eased myself onto a chaise longue and called for tea.

"What did you do to her?" Tu-Li asked again, accusatory.

"Tell me something," I said, avoiding the question. "How often has she been going out at night?"

"What are you talking about?" Tu-Li said. "I don't see anything, I never saw her go anywhere, I don't know anything."

The berdache busied himself arranging the gambling tiles into the four-square pattern that began a new game. "You're not talking either?" I asked him.

The tea came, and I sat and savored it, soothed by the clacking of the tiles, the sound of hoofbeats passing on the avenue outside the window, the tick-tocking of the mantel clock. Underneath it all, an odd whispery sound—I've noticed it often before—of the city breathing.

My disturbing night thoughts gradually evaporated with the tea, the company, the light of day. I laughed at myself. Dreaming that I was a killer. Waking to think that she was.

Bronwyn was in the room immediately next to this one, with a communicating door between us. I could rise to my feet and open it, confront her. *See here, young lady, what is this business of shutting yourself in?*

"It's locked," Tu-Li said, reading my thoughts. "She locks it."

In a low voice, I said, "She won't attend her lessons, the whole project will fail, and Freddy will turn her out."

The tile clacking halted for a beat and then began again.

"No," Tu-Li said. "Madam loves her."

"If we all worked together, we could help her," I said. "We could be partners in the effort."

"Leave her to us," Tu-Li said. "You go about your business, we'll take care of her."

"But it isn't working, is it?" I said. "Whatever any of us is doing isn't working. She is just as wild as when we found her in Virginia."

They knew the truth of what I was saying but would not admit it. *Clack, clack, clack.* I had an impulse, not for the first time, to kick apart their game.

❦ 15 ❧

"I wish to make a Thanksgiving toast," said Freddy, who always made the holiday toasts for the family.

We had consumed the oyster soup and the cod with egg sauce, fallen hungrily upon the slivered carrots and celery in their crystal boats, and now an expectant silence had descended upon the table in preparation for the main course.

"To absent friends," I said, and Freddy stared me down.

"Hugo is correct, if impertinent. Not all of us are here this evening. That is a pity. We wish for her sake"—he made a vague gesture upward, toward the ceiling—"that our new daughter emerges out of her melancholy soon, to take her place *en famille.*"

"Hear, hear," I said, eager to get the champagne down my throat as quickly as possible. But Freddy still held his flute arrested in midair.

"We have much to be thankful for indeed," he said. "We have had a good year, we have survived the worst that Wall Street had to throw at us. We made a transcontinental voyage together, as a family, that proved stimulating, informative and inspirational."

Mary, in her white mobcap, appeared at the pass-through door holding the silver platter on which rested the golden, crisp-skinned turkey, so large that it was a wonder it didn't slip from her grip and skid across the floor. She hesitated, not wanting to interrupt what she supposed was the solemnity of the toast.

Winston took the turkey from her and laid the platter down atop the burgundy runner in the middle of the ivory-clothed side table.

"We do, however, have someone here to welcome anew." Freddy nodded at the wiry, satin-swathed, steely-coifed woman to his right, his mother, my grandmother. She sat examining the engraving on her silverware setting.

"Swoony. We are so glad to have you here again."

Cynthia Delegate, née Belmont, called Swoony ever since her childhood, carried on regally after Grandfather's death. Like him, she suffered mightily when my Uncle Sonny passed away prematurely. She hadn't been the same since she lost her son.

Having just arrived that afternoon from gilded Newport, leaving her bright marble mansion on the sea, Grandmother would take up residence for the winter in the house that adjoined ours, the mirror-image château occupying the other half of the block from The Citadel.

But as Freddy's mother, she had the run of the whole place, her home and ours. There was a door cut through from her second-floor central hall that accessed an upper corridor in our North Wing, a door that was never locked.

Swoony had lately become afflicted with the same sort of insomnia that often struck the elderly (she was seventy-seven), common when the footsteps coming for us all begin to sound louder and nearer. The previous winter we often found her trailing through the drawing room, the dining room, the library and the parlor, at all hours of the day and night.

Her thoughts were increasingly unmoored also. She soothed her afflictions with continual sips of Napoleon brandy, which she took out of a teacup that never left her side. Either the brandy was pickling her or age was.

"Swoony," we all said, lifting our glasses to her, while she lifted her teacup to us.

Winston supervised the serving. Rising above the opposite side of the table from where I sat, a whole wall of gilt picture frames displayed my father's collection of Meissoniers and the minor painters *français*. Nymphs cavorted in moonbeams that passed through puffs of pastel cloud.

"Winston," said Swoony, beckoning him. "Might we have the lobster salad?"

The butler appeared perplexed. A serving of the lobster salad already sat on my grandmother's plate, as did portions of the aspic and boiled broccoli, the stuffed apples and the superior biscuit. Everything was laid out on our gold-edged holiday china, which we used only a few times a year.

"Ma'am," Winston said, picking up the lobster dish nested in ice and holding it forward for Swoony.

"I didn't mean . . ." said Swoony, momentarily confused. "Oh, I meant the pressed beef."

Stewed peaches, ginger cake, pound cake, ribbon cake, figs, walnuts in the shell. The more that came on, the less I felt like eating.

"Where is the girl?" Swoony demanded loudly. "Virginia, the one in the pretty white dress and the hair ribbons. I like her. Where is she? Unkind of her not to attend."

"She's a shut-in," Nicky said. "Mrs. Kate says it's female trouble."

"Don't be ill-mannered, dear," Anna Maria said, a mild rebuke, I thought, for the insolence of the remark.

We retired to the drawing room. Anna Maria took to the upright.

"Tahktoo?" said my mother. " 'Here We Go A-Courting'?"

The berdache pulled himself up beside the piano and linked his hands in front of his chest. In a high, quavery voice, he began to sing the white man's song.

I gazed moodily out onto Fifth Avenue.

"Colm," I said, calling him over. I gestured out the window. "That's him, isn't it?"

The Stone-Thrower. Slouching along the Central Park wall, swaying drunkenly, staring up at The Citadel.

"I'll send him on his way," Colm said. "Or perhaps it's time to bring in the police."

I felt an inexplicable connection with the poor soul. "We should invite him in for our Thanksgiving," I said, but made no move to do so.

Later in the afternoon, Colm and I took a horse trolley down to the police headquarters on Mulberry Street, in a neighborhood of gun shops and cop saloons, normally haunted by newspaper reporters but quiet that day, with an air of sleepy holiday indolence.

"I've changed my mind," I said, hesitating at the police building's forbidding gray stone porte cochere. "You go ahead and make your Thanksgiving visits," I told Colm. "I think I'll go on to Delmonico's."

"Are you sure? Do you mark him?"

Colm gestured down the thoroughfare. Sure enough, our shadow the Stone-Thrower had somehow made his way downtown with us and cowered in an across-the-street doorway like a thief.

"One word from me and he'll wish he were back in Virginia slaving in the mines," Colm said. He had many friends on the police force, and I didn't doubt his word.

I told him no, I'd prefer the man not be bothered, bade Colm good-bye and headed off down Mulberry in the direction of Delmonico's. After half a block, though, and with Colm out of sight on his way uptown, I doubled back and entered the police building.

In the lobby the same sleepy air obtained as on the street outside. No one paid me any mind. An officer in a double-breasted blue uniform with copper buttons sat guarding the entrance into the bowels of the place.

"Officer," I said.

"Young gentleman," he said, not looking up from his perusal of the *Herald*.

"Hugo Delegate, sir." With sublime uninterest he looked up at me, then back down at his newspaper.

"I'd like to make an inquiry," I said. I felt oddly timid.

Sufficiently certain that I wasn't going away, he folded the *Herald* and looked up at me.

"Misdemeanor intake? Males, give me a name, the women are at Blackwell's. Is it a female you're after?"

"No, it's nothing like that."

"Felony?" he asked.

"I'm wondering about murders."

"I wonder about them, too," he said. "All the time."

"In the past few weeks, or months, have there been any odd murders?"

He stared at me. "What was your name again?" I repeated it for him.

"Yes, Mr. Hugo Delegate," he said slowly. "Yes, there has been a wealth of violence done upon the fair denizens of this metropolis, quite a few killings, in fact, as any student of human behavior might expect but which some of us more removed from the harsh realities of life would be surprised to hear."

A philosopher in blue serge. "Yes, well . . ." I said, faltering.

"Yes, well," he said. "Any murder in particular?"

"I'm thinking more in the line of gruesome crimes, with perhaps mutilation involved in the commission."

"Mutilation," he said.

"Mutilation." I nodded.

He fished out his newspaper and slapped it with the back of his hand. "What you want, young Delegate, is what the gentlemen of the press have. Garrotings, knifings, strangulations, assault by brass knuckles, random manslaughters, dear mothers placing their dear babies into the oven."

He shook his head and sighed sadly. "It's enough to make you question the good intentions of your fellow human beings, ain't it? I would give you my personal copy of this esteemed publication"—referring to the *Herald*—"but I haven't finished with its illuminating contents, and also, you might do better, for the lurid narratives you seek, by reading the *Police Gazette*."

Apart from sarcasm I understood that I could expect nothing more from that quarter. Leaving the police building, I crossed the street to where the Stone-Thrower sat, insensible with drink, on the brick steps of a shabby residence.

"You there," I said, and watched his consciousness struggle to return to him. "Would you like to accompany me?"

"Accompany?" A four-syllable word, too much for him. He blinked up at me. The odor of alcohol and sweat rose from his clothes.

"Will you come with me?" I asked again.

"She's . . . she's . . . she's . . ." he managed.

"Yes, yes, she is," I said. "But right now I am asking you whether you wish to come along with me on an errand I must run."

"You won't hurt me?" he asked.

"Certainly not," I said, helping him to his feet.

"Where are you taking me?" he asked. "I fear you'll do me harm."

"Nonsense," I said. "Whatever I do to you, I'll never approach the damage you habitually inflict upon yourself, now, will I?"

I guided him gently toward a hansom cab, and he came along willingly enough, but since he seemed uncertain of where he was, he might not have had that clear a grasp on where he was headed.

"Bellevue Hospital," I called to the driver. To the Stone-Thrower I added, loading him into the carriage, "I propose a visit to the city morgue."

Such facts as I extracted during our journey uptown to the Kips Bay neighborhood: The Stone-Thrower's given name was Karl Kleinschmidt, he was thirty-four, had made a small strike in the Washoe, sold out, and used the proceeds to finance his way across the country to haunt the Delegate doorstep. To what end I could surmise, but the subject felt like a sore one just at that juncture.

The magnet of Savage Girl. I imagined her drawing men to her, one after another from all over the country, admirers who had seen her just once, maybe, or those she had driven into folly. They couldn't forget her, so they performed their lunatic pilgrimages to her side. She had smiled at them. Or she hadn't. It didn't seem to matter. They came anyway.

There calls a small voice from deep inside every man, when facing the woman he loves, instructing him to fall flat on his face before his beloved and plead for mercy. As a romantic strategy, this approach seldom proves successful. But such was Kleinschmidt's choice.

Sadly enough, I felt some allegiance with him, which caused me to take him under my wing rather than beat him senseless, as men usually did whenever they encountered him.

"Did you just break wind?" I asked, the closeness of the carriage exacerbating the man's stench.

"No," he said.

"Do you always smell this way?"

"I'm sorry, I'm sorry, I'm sorry," he muttered, a thoroughly despondent individual. He kept repeating phrases. But one piece of babble among his many stood out.

"She beds them and then she kills them," muttered the drunken Kleinschmidt. "She beds them and then she kills them."

"She does, does she?" I said, trying to remain unrattled. "But I suppose that's better than the other way around, isn't it, my man? Kill them and *then* bed them? That wouldn't do at all."

Eventually his babbling passed to weeping.

When we made it to the morgue, I was glad to have an ally with me, even as hopeless a one as Kleinschmidt. We presented ourselves at the hospital's main pavilion and, with a small bribe, gained entry into the restricted area. To a tiled, well-windowed first-floor room, its dozen tables populated with cadavers of the unidentified dead.

The chemical reek of the place stung my sinuses, reminding me of dissections in days past. A stab of missing Harvard hit me. So simple, that life. Labs! Classes! Examinations!

Beneath the morgue's formaldehyde smell, a honeyed stink of death. Along the walls, immense blocks of river ice cooled the room to the point where I could see my breath.

"A moral visit?" asked the attendant, a gaunt man in a rubber apron.

"What?"

The attendant gestured to Kleinschmidt. "Him. Put the fear of the Lord into him, will you?"

I still didn't understand.

He shouted into the Stone-Thrower's face. "This is where you'll be if you keep on your degenerate ways!"

Kleinschmidt buried his face into the breast of my waistcoat, an extremely disagreeable development. I extricated myself as quickly as I could. The poor man gazed about at the surroundings as though he had entered a nightmare.

Perhaps, I thought, the visit could do him some good after all.

Small grave lights hung from the ceiling, illuminating the bodies. They lay carelessly shrouded, some half uncovered, men and women both, oaken blocks propping up their heads. Pale, pale, the faces of the dead.

"I wonder," I said in a low voice to the attendant, "if any of your charges might exhibit signs of peculiar violence. *Pudenda abscissa sunt.*"

This was an occasion for some delicacy. In the case of the Palmer House waiter, the genitals had been taken off and carried away. And with Peter Fince in Nevada, mutilation had also been mentioned.

The morgue doctor's Latin training might have been deficient, since I had to ask the question in the mother tongue. "The private parts cut off," I muttered.

The man gave me a frowning look. "Are you with the newspapers?" he said, low-voiced.

I shook my head.

"Then how do you know?"

"Just show me the corpus."

We were both whispering, a common practice with which I had become familiar in my anatomy studies, where loud voices and exuberance were considered anathema in the presence of the dead.

While Kleinschmidt stood gaping, I followed the attendant to the rear of the morgue. There a rickety wooden-framed structure supported yet more cadavers, a dozen or so stored in some sort of monstrous pigeonhole arrangement.

Pulling out a wooden body board from one of the cubbies, the attendant unsheeted the deceased.

"Police was here and gave up on him, seeing how he were just a Gypsy," he said. His voice took on a conspiratorial undertone. "The missing part was never found."

I had seen the man only a single time, in the dead dark of the Central Park wilderness, with just a campfire illuminating the scene. Yet I was certain that the well-mustachioed corpse, displaying deep incisions across its torso, the femoral artery expertly severed between the

adductor and the sartorius, the disfigured pelvic saddle a mass of clot-
ted blood, was Bronwyn's dancing partner of a few nights before.

"Would you like to tell me what's going on?" said a familiar voice
as I stood contemplating the dead man.

Colm Cullen. I felt guilty, as though I had been caught out at something, which of course I had.

"What might we be doing here, Hugo?" he asked. He had not gone
on his holiday visits after all but trailed me to see what I was up to.

"The Stone-Thrower . . ." I managed to say.

Colm poked his thumb toward the door behind him. "He just tore
out of here, white as a ghost. But that's not what this is about, is it?"

"No," I said.

"It's about her, ain't it?"

I nodded.

"Well, I won't tell you how you should run your life," he said. "But
if you let me in on it, maybe I could help. That's what you're paying me
for, ain't it? To keep you out of jams?"

So I laid it out to him, the two of us standing together in the chilly
morgue room. The killing I had stumbled into at Palmer House in
Chicago. The headless body in the Washoe. Finally the present one,
the Gypsy dancer.

Gesturing at the corpse on the slab, I said, "I saw her with this man
in the park just a few nights ago. Dancing like a bar girl."

Colm gazed down at the dead man. "You sure it was him?"

"Well, no," I said. "But don't you see? They're all being done to in
the same way!"

Colm shook his head, unconvinced. "You're telling me you think
the wee girl is capable of something like this? What does she weigh?
She'd blow away in a strong wind!"

"I know, I know," I said. "I think it's crazy, too." I omitted my other
crazy thought, that I myself might be capable of such crimes. But
Colm seemed to speak on it.

"Listen, I knew of a man back on Dudley Square, when I was
growing up in Boston," Colm said. "He was the jealous type, liked to
keep his girlfriends shut up in a room, and only he had the key. He was

attracted to a wild girl, really lively, out in the dance halls every night, everybody loving her."

Scratch an Irishman and he'll bleed a story.

"I used to . . . well, I mean, *he* used to dream up misdeeds this wild girl was doing, imagining all sorts of dark adventures just because she was fun-loving. A man's thoughts can run away with him. Do you see what I'm telling you?"

I did see. Colm Cullen, the workingman's version of a psychologist. I wondered what Professor James would make of him.

"Bronwyn ain't Delia Showalter," Colm said. "She ain't your fragile society girl. She might like her men. But that don't mean she's done deeds would make the devil blush."

It was all in my head, he was saying. My fantasies sprang from my own fears. Men normally like their women firmly under control. Savage Girl was simply too free-spirited for me, and that led me into dark suspicions.

"Now, for the sake of our peace of mind, let's go get a damned drink," Colm said. "This place is giving me the piss shivers."

All that Thanksgiving holiday, Bronwyn remained shut up in her bedchamber.

Mrs. Herbert kept the keys to every room in The Citadel on a chatelaine she wore at her waist, barrel keys for the silver cabinets, flat keys for the linen trunks, most of the room keys skinny iron skeletons. The head housekeeper was, as Freddy said, the rock upon which we built our home.

We had a small disagreement that evening, when I suggested that Mrs. Herbert accompany me to gain access to Bronwyn's quarters.

Freddy and Anna Maria had left the house on their Thanksgiving evening calls. Winston, too, seemed to be unavailable. Lacking appeal to superior powers, the formidable Mrs. Herbert had no recourse but to accede to my wishes.

"I'm worried about my dear sister," I told her. "We will only check to see if she is well."

"We're all worried, Mr. Hugo, but she insists on privacy," Mrs. Herbert said. "The Chinese maid goes in with dinner trays."

"I'm sure Miss Bronwyn is fine. But I'd like to speak to her directly."

Unlocking and opening the door, we came upon Bronwyn at a small writing desk on the far side of her bedroom. She was perfectly presentable, dressed in a pleated frock, the overskirt pulled up to a deep bow at her back. I noticed on the desk the torn-in-half Bible, propped open.

Mrs. Herbert waited at the open door as I ventured into the maiden's bedroom. "I'm sorry," I stammered, suddenly abashed. "Dear sister, you have been so secluded lately, I thought to make a visit to see if there was anything I could do."

"I want to be alone," she said.

"Yes, yes, surely," I said. "But too much aloneness can be mentally unhealthy, isn't that so?"

She appeared paler than when I left her last, when the upstairs maid turned me out of her room the morning after her escapade with the man now lying dead in the morgue.

"I wonder if it would be better to not only get out of this room but perhaps out of the house," I said. "I'd like to invite you to an evening on the town sometime, say, this Saturday, when we can sightsee the Young Patriarchs' Ball down at the Academy of Music."

She remained silent. In the doorway Mrs. Herbert coughed into her hand. "It might be amusing for you to see all the howling swells," I said. "Of course, we ourselves shall have to wear proper evening dress."

A backhanded reference to her going out in boy's garb.

"As you wish," she said. "But I'd like you to leave me to myself now."

"Saturday evening, then," I said, bowing backward out the door like a courtier.

Mrs. Herbert closed Bronwyn in her room once again. "Very good, young master," she said to me. "Very, very good. You've always been a kind boy. It will be a blessing for her to go out and about a bit."

Behind us we heard Bronwyn's door lock being turned.

That Saturday, the night of the Young Patriarchs' Ball, represented the traditional start of the Christmas social season. I was of course expected at the occasion myself but begged off, pleading illness. This was an untruth, though I was still feeling punky on account of the crushed-in noggin I'd received during the incident in the park.

Delia Showalter, with whom I was to attend, communicated her irritation by attending the ball instead with Bev Willets.

We finally had it out, she and I, Delia accusing me of shunning her and I protesting all sorts of maladies, among them one with which I thought she could not argue, tuberculosis of the bone.

The truth lay elsewhere. I was bored with her.

When Bronwyn descended the front staircase from the third floor to the second that evening, I had a thought that while she was not quite a woman, she was definitely no longer a girl. I recalled the body lying in the morgue. Perhaps killing a man matures a person.

Tu-Li stood behind her, watching her navigate the stairs. The Chinese maid had performed her part admirably. She'd ornamented Bronwyn's plain pleated dress with shawls and scarves and added accoutrements of gloves and jewels and other flourishes. Bronwyn wore no bonnet but had her black hair arranged in a chignon to which tiny blue flowers were affixed. The upsweep exaggerated the pale slenderness of her neck.

"Are you ready, sister?" I asked.

"Yes," she said.

A ride in a carriage was not a new experience for Bronwyn, but she seldom had gone out at night (except, of course, on her own). Now she wrapped herself in her mohair mantle and gazed out the window as we proceeded down Fifth. Our footman Randall drove. The smoky glow of the gas lamps, the cold black of late-hour Manhattan in autumn.

The Young Patriarchs' Ball at the Academy of Music started fashionably late. Guests arrived no earlier than ten o'clock, collected themselves, primped and chatted and took refreshments before the band struck up at midnight and they started in on the quadrille. They might well dance until dawn.

It was now eleven. We turned the corner of Fourteenth Street and proceeded crosstown past Union Square to the Rialto. I called for Randall to halt. Our brougham lined up among dozens of carriages on Irving Place and along Fourteenth. Chaises, landaus, whiskeys, even a fly or two—all of them disgorging the grandees of the city.

The zoom, in full force.

I reached across Bronwyn and slid open the window so that she might see.

Initially the splendid nature of the spectacle did not assert itself. Splatters of horse manure marked the thoroughfare, but the academy rolled out an elaborate purple carpet at the curb so that milady's train should not drag in the muck. Gaslight set the whole street ablaze. But the scene was too jumbled, too chaotic to be impressive.

Then something happened. Edwige D'Hauteville disembarked from a carriage ahead of her escort, DeLancey Kane. The lady looked a picture. A silver ball gown, a negligently bared shoulder as her stole slipped, and she stood poised, as if displaying herself to the crowd of gawkers held back from the entrance by big police.

"Oh!" Bronwyn exclaimed. I reached into my suit pocket and handed her some tiny mother-of-pearl opera glasses.

The D'Hauteville girl was damnedly handsome. But something more, she was caught there at the entrance to the ball as if frozen in a carte de visite or a tableau vivant, an emblem of something, the Evanescence of Beauty. A line from one of de Vere's sonnets applied: "Sad is our youth, for it is ever going . . ."

"Do you know that girl?" she said, holding the glasses to her eyes.

"I believe I know pretty much everyone going in," I said, not as a boast but merely to assert my fluency. "They are my friends."

It was the Age of Silver, silver was the color of the day, of accents and fabrics and jewelry settings.

"Over there is Elizabeth Rink, the older sister of a friend of mine," I said, indicating a young woman in a dress of white tulle (probably Worth) embroidered in silver, with pansies brocaded over the train.

Of another new arrival, I said, "I met Irene Davidovich, who is a marquesa, through my mother." The tall brunette made her way from her carriage to the doors of the academy in the finest satin, carrying a small bouquet of sweetheart roses circled round by, yes, a ribbon of silver.

"But her . . ." Bronwyn said as D'Hauteville entered the academy with DeLancey Kane.

I laid my hand on my sister's arm. "You could be that lady, Bronwyn. Come spring, if you apply yourself assiduously to your studies, if you learn to dance and speak and carry yourself, you could be her. You could be the one!"

She looked at me. "'Assiduously,'" she repeated. "You always use such big words, and I never know what you are talking about."

I laughed. "You will."

I wanted to tell her that to become fully human she needed more than vocabulary and dance steps and proper comportment, that one must look to the heart and the head, if not the soul. But on such basis her character appeared an unfathomable mystery to me.

She gazed out at the flamboyant parade around the entrance. "That blond woman has a bird in her hair."

"It's fake," I said. "Shall we go inside?"

"Us?" she said. I had never seen her react with timidity before.

"Let's go," I said, smiling. "I know a secret way into the lion's lair."

I handed her down from the brougham. She lifted her hem up from the dirt of the street and took my arm. We threaded our way through the crowd of spectators. We were dressed for the evening but not for the ball, and the gawkers dismissed us as unworthy of their attention.

Freddy told me it was a fairly new phenomenon, within his lifetime, this passion on the part of the mob to spectate on the affairs of the wealthy. The newspapers reported breathlessly about the "uppertens," as they referred to the wealthiest ten percent of the population. Caroline Hood, the reigning queen of society, told us she kept away from the windows of her mansion at Thirty-eighth and Fifth, in order to avoid the prying eyes of the public.

I guided Bronwyn around the block, up Third Avenue to Fifteenth, down the street to the rear of the hall.

"Now, don't ask where we are going," I said. "You are in perfectly good hands."

At the back of the enormous Academy of Music structure, a door stood partially open, yellow light spilling out to the street. A stage-hand loitered outside, a cigarette dangling from his mouth.

"We'll just be a minute," I said, slipping one of the new silver twenty-cent pieces into his palm.

Up one back staircase, then the next, then the next, all of them dirty and untended but with Bronwyn never uttering a complaint. We finally reached the door I was seeking.

It opened onto the manager's box, far up the side of the theater, one level above the parterres, so high the blaze of the orblike chande-lier struck us blind at first. We overlooked the nobby assembly down below, swirls of satin, men in stark and shining black, decorative ar-rangements of flowers so towering that you could smell their perfume even from our elevation.

Also in the air, a sensual electricity, from the touch of the men and women as they moved about the room together. But that might have been my imagining.

Bronwyn stared downward, cheeks flushed, eyes shining, clearly enthralled.

"They own the world," I murmured, putting my lips close to her ear. "The ones down there. It is not so much their wealth, though there is that. It is entrée. The ability to go wherever one wants."

I thought that would appeal to her, but it was not enough. "An-other thing: These people are bulletproof. If you join their ranks, whatever trouble you encounter, whatever threat you face, you can get out from under it merely by being one of their number."

She drew her gaze from the dance floor and looked at me, her ha-zel eyes searching mine. How pretty she was, I thought, how honest.

"Are you in trouble, Bronwyn?"

She shook her head. "Don't try to help," she said.

"But I want to. Whyever shouldn't I?"

"Because I'm poison," she said.

"What? What do you mean?" She looked away, and I let it drop. I decided I didn't after all really want to know what she meant by that.

"One last thought, very important," I said. "You cannot take society seriously. You must, must, must treat this all as a game. Otherwise you are lost. You can have it as long as you don't want it."

"A beautiful game," she murmured, looking down again at the elegant couples. Strains of music filtered up to us. The cotillion was about to begin.

"A bird in my hair?" Bronwyn asked.

"It doesn't have to be with a bird," I said.

Outside on the street, I realized I had made a blunder. Instead of directing Randall to bring the carriage around to the back of the hall, I had left him parked in front, at the entrance. Returning to the brougham, we encountered the two people I had no wish at all to see.

Beverly Willets and Delia Showalter.

They spied us just as we slipped into the carriage.

"Delegate!" Willets roared out, alerting the whole crowd to my presence. Delia looked stricken. I waved uncertainly.

"Go, go, go!" I called to Randall, wanting him to get us out of there before I was forced to engage in what would have been an awkward conversation.

❧ 16 ❧

I wanted Bronwyn to come into my world, the real world, the precisely cut diamond of Manhattan society, and I now believed she wanted it, too. We recognized a shared goal. The alchemy of that evening spent spying upon the Patriarchs' Ball rendered our relationship much clearer.

Later that night, into the early morning, as if in reward for our newfound intimacy, we sat before a dying fire in Freddy's library and Bronwyn told me her story.

Her words, while she traced her background from childhood to the present day, served to bind us as close together as any brother and sister ever could be. To say that the facts of her life newly altered my feelings for her would be misleading, since those feelings had been in constant transformation since the day I first set eyes on her in Dr. Scott's barn.

We did not finish talking until the dawn came up, imbuing the leafless winter dogwoods in the park with a ghostly materialism. The recounting had a good effect. In the weeks that followed her confession, Bronwyn applied herself to her studies with such focus and enthusiasm that everyone remarked upon it, from Freddy to the tutors to the household staff.

Bronwyn was, in a word, tireless.

"You've worked a miracle, dear boy," my father said, giving me all the credit.

Freddy and Anna Maria set the last day of February as the date for her debut, and all our efforts were geared toward that. Bronwyn had progressed to the degree that by New Year's week we felt she was ready to take her first tentative step into society.

Dancing school.

Specifically, Madame Eugénie's Académie de Danse, attendance at which was de rigueur in our circle—

Wait, wait, Bill Howe interrupts me again. You're jumping ahead.

Yes?

Well, you can't do that, he says.

Do what?

Tell it that way. Mention that the girl has told you her story and then slide over it as an inconsequential detail.

Bronwyn's story is well known by now, isn't it?

Howe splutters. But . . . but . . . but—there are so many different versions, from the newspapers, the authorities, even the clergy, it is imperative we hear the account she relayed to you. With utter completeness, if you will, Mr. Hugo, with utter completeness.

Might that not derail the momentum of the narrative, I say, by entering us into a previous chronological period? Doesn't Aristotle preach a strict unity of time?

Bugger Aristotle, Howe says.

From what I've heard of the great man, I say, he might enjoy that.

Howe says, Go back, if you please. Leave nothing out. That evening after your visit to the Patriarchs' Ball. What she told you.

Bronwyn's Story

My life comes out of a cloud of not knowing. The truth is, I don't have a birthday, I don't know how old I am. Sixteen or seventeen or eighteen. Which means I was born sometime before 1860.

I don't remember my papa. I remember Mama better. My father had a beard, a black beard. He used to come into where we were, in whatever camp it was, all dirty from work. He did mining.

I think we came from Wales. That's what occurred to me during my geography lessons with Freddy. Mama talking about Wales. Or maybe Cornwall, since either Cornwall or Wales is where the mine workers in America always come from. But I think I remember her telling me about our village in Wales. Her mother and father. They were coal miners.

This is hard for me, since all I have is pieces. A baby cradle in front of the fire. Mama could never nurse, she had no milk. The baby cried. My mother's hands smelled clean from the washtub. My father's smooth, dark hair and his eyes that were serious so much of the time. Once I was able to look into mirrors, I came to believe that I had his eyes.

I'm not sure about any of it. We lived first back east, and I don't remember how we got west. There was a lot of walking, but it could have been anywhere. Both my parents pushed wheelbarrows full of our things, and at night we'd turn the barrows on their sides and put our canvas over them and that was where we slept. Glynn, the baby, died.

We were in Colorado. After all the flat country, seeing the mountains for the first time was one of my clearest early memories. Standing there staring at them. I can close my eyes right now and see them still. The peaks with snow on them made me feel tiny.

We were very poor, but everyone was poor, so it didn't matter. We'd go to a camp, stay for a while, then move on. I don't remember the names of the camps. Leadville, I think. They were sad places.

I learned to read from the family Bible, sounding out sentences to Mama as she did her work. I could write my name. I was always smart, always ahead. My mother gave me instruction, as much as she had time for. She handed me a stick to write with in the dust. The letters came easily for me.

In Colorado they hung my father and three other men for stealing gold they dug but that wasn't theirs. They made the whole camp watch the hanging. Mama covered my eyes, but I looked.

We went south along the mountains. Somebody called them the Blood of Christ Mountains. And there we found paradise. Like in Genesis: "And a river went out of Eden to water the garden." Everything was beautiful and sunny and fresh.

Mr. Hugh Brace, my next papa, took care of us. He was a hunter, and there was always lots of game and fish in the streams. We even had a cabin. I sang a hymn to the camp. I can see the close, dark walls we lived within. I remember the window and how the sun came in and made a patch on the dirt floor, and how glad we were for the sunlight. For a miner, light is precious.

Then Mr. Brace said we all had to go. I couldn't understand why we had to leave, but we went south again. Along the mountains. Every sunset was like fire. And that was when I was taken by the Numunuh. I must have been about four or five. They rode down on the train of wagons we were with, and first they drove off the stock. I didn't know what was happening, but everyone was crying, so I cried, too. Darkness and a storm of horse hooves.

Rough hands yanked the back of my pinafore, throwing me across the pony behind the rider. This was Tabekwine, Sun-Eagle, my next father. I cried, and he cracked me across the cheek, so I didn't cry anymore, not out loud anyway.

We rode for days and nights, changing off ponies. I slept tied to the mane. I was thirsty, hungry. He gave me some chopped-up corn from a little pouch and a piece of greasy dried meat.

After a while I ached so and was exhausted and sunstruck. I wanted nothing apart from getting down off the pony.

Until that day I had never been on a horse before. After that I was rarely off one. I cried every day for the next month. A woman took care of me sometimes, Nautda. I called her "Old Mother." Her children, Cos and Ogin.

My white skin made me strange, but I soon burned brown. No one harmed me, no one beat me, I was free. They let me keep a doll, the only thing I had from my old life. I made deerskin clothes for it, learning to sew with sinew.

It is difficult to believe, I am sure, the way you live here in New York City, that my life among the Numunuh was anything but a hardship. It wasn't. After a time I began to be happy. The children were let go. We could do anything. We raced ponies in the arroyos. We all had our own bows. I could put an arrow into a knothole better than any of my brothers. They called me Naivi, which just means "girl." They loved me.

Let's say you are like the wizard Merlin in the books Nicky reads to me and had magic and could say to me, "I will fly you back to life among the Numunuh." You would think that I wouldn't go, that of course this life now in New York City is better. The one in the lodges, where everything smelled like smoke, where I was wild, that is a poor life, you would say.

But for me, in my heart, it's different. I might go or I might not, but it would be a hard choice. I am a Numunuh girl. Those years made me who I am. They made me free.

We never called ourselves Comanche. That was the name others gave us, the Mexicans, I think. It means "Those Who Want to Fight Us All the Time." Given all the horses we stole and the wars we fought, I can't blame anyone for naming us that. We were Lords of the World.

After I had spent two summers with them, Sun-Eagle and Naudta took me as their own daughter. I might have been seven. They led me into a lodge, and an elder lifted me up in the smoke of the fire four times, saying, "Her name is Hutsu." It meant "bird," and after that I was really a part of the clan.

We began to move. Something had changed. I heard the word *tai-boo,* meaning "white men." I think this was at the end of your big war, when the cavalry came west again and pushed hard against my people. We ran, but there seemed nowhere to run.

Then Sun-Eagle began to follow a wise elder named Victory Dance, who had a vision that we must cross the mountains and the great desert to find peace from the *taiboo.* Some of us went and some others did not. I left behind many of my friends then.

The march across the desert killed us all. Nautda died, then Sun-Eagle. And there was no peace, no paradise. At the end of the desert, only more mountains and more *taiboo.* The soldiers captured Victory Dance and scattered the clan. It was a disaster. I was lost among these new mountains in a land I had never known.

Then, for a long time, I was alone. This will be the part you will choose not to believe. I knew what berries and green shoots to eat, I could fashion a bow and arrows, and I could hunt, but I still felt a lone-liness in my heart. I went deeper into the hills. I found a valley, huge and empty of people. I thought if I ever saw another *taiboo,* I would be murdered. So I made this big valley my hidden home.

I discovered a group of caves. In one of them, a hot springs formed a pool all the way at its back, warm and clean year round. The pool I named Kaatu, and it was holy to me. It was my religion. I bathed every day as if I were worshipping.

This is the part I hesitate to let anybody hear.

It is not that I am ashamed.

But it is so difficult, I think, for people to understand. You have not been in my shoes, is that how you say it? Funny, since I never wore shoes until I came to you.

One day I hunted in the forested hills near the caves, searching out a kind of mushroom I knew grew under the trees there. I heard something then that I didn't think possible: the crying of my infant brother, Glynn, a soft sobbing when he was beginning to get hungry but when my mother couldn't nurse him.

Maybe solitude had made me crazy. I walked in the direction of the sound. I looked to the ground, to see if there was really a baby anywhere nearby.

And, in fact, there was.

The cat crouched near the body of its dead mother. When I say cat, I should say kitten. This fuzzy creature had giant ears as big as yours, Hugo, and stood about as tall as my knee. She just kept up her crying, the most forlorn sound I ever heard.

The Numunuh taught me caution as the first rule of the wild. I wasn't sure it was a wise idea, coming up on an untamed animal, even a young one.

But with its mother gone, I reached out to the kitten. The animal lifted her head but continued her crying. I went down on my knees. Very slowly I reached out and touched the cat's fur. Soft, softer than anything, a newborn softness.

The kitten's pelt might be tawny-colored, like a cougar, but the dead body of her adult mama bore a quilt of dark spots, some looking like paw prints, others a single black rose, and every shape in between.

Jaguar. That is the name I have since found in one of Freddy's books here in the library. The Numunuh would have said *wah-ew*.

Terror, delight, mother feelings, these all rushed through me as I began to stroke the little cat. Her whiskers were the length of my fingers. Her paws were almost the size of my fists. She showed me needle teeth already as long as my thumb.

The kitten now quieted, rolling over to have her belly scratched. Downy, cream-colored tufts.

I wasn't going to go back to my cave alone.

I buried the mother (dead from I couldn't find out what, no marks on the body) and picked up the kitten (she squalled in my arms, complaining loudly).

I fed her bits of smoked fish. She refused the berry mash I presented her. Greasy strips of dried rabbit meat, yes.

Jaguars, it turned out, love nothing so much as water. She didn't like the hot springs as much as the cold streams nearby. But she swam like an otter and sometimes joined me in my ritual baths.

For a long time, I had to keep her on a length of deer sinew to stop her from going back to the pile of rocks over her mother's grave. I called the kitten Mallt, my Welsh mother's name, but also sometimes Nanatunaboo, "She Who Proudly Shows Her Spots."

Together we would travel along the streams in my valley. Mallt became an expert fisherman and shared her bounty. She grew fat and long, until she was about the same size as me. Her spots came up, dark, pretty circles. She could roar as loud as thunder.

We were often troubled by crows and ravens, whole flocks of them. They had picked clean the bones of all the dead buffaloes, and now they were hungry. Mallt thought it was magic when I brought one down with my bow.

Two summers passed. In winter we took to the cave. The Numunuh always stayed in their lodges whenever snows or storms came, telling stories and making each other laugh.

The Washoe was six valleys away from mine, but I ventured to its edges occasionally, perhaps once or twice a summer, in order to obtain the three things I needed yet could not secure in my wild routines: clothing, metal tools (knives, mostly) and salt.

A few times Mallt traveled with me. We would sneak up on a brush house or a cabin that stood alone, take what was necessary and then flee.

I possessed a couple of treasures I had taken from an empty cabin when I hunted outside the valley. Two books, both of them dirtied and broken in half. The Bible. And another, a storybook. I didn't know its title or the ending, since those parts were torn away, but it was about a girl named Becky Sharp.

My third spring Mallt disappeared. Now I cried for real. I searched the whole valley, the hills and mountainsides beyond it, but she was gone.

After a week of searching went by, I returned to the valley, taking my broken heart back to the cave. But still I loved the sunlight flooding the hillsides, I loved tracking game and spearing fish, wandering the meadows and, especially, the baths that were how I marked my day.

Mallt reappeared one evening as I sat in front of the cave. She rubbed herself against my shoulder. By the next morning, we were fishing together once again. Soon she became heavy with young. After three months I watched in horror and wonder as she gave bloody birth. Two of her furballs came into the world dead, but the third lived, with a pelt that was solid black.

Tukaani, I named the little one. "Night." Or sometimes Puna-Petu. "Only Daughter." The Numunuh always called things by a lot of different names.

Now we had a family, Mallt and Tukaani and me. I was no longer so lonely. I usually had a full stomach. I couldn't puzzle out everything in my books, but I tried. I read to the cats, and what was more strange, they listened.

When I fell ill with fever that autumn, Mallt brought me food and allowed me to nurse alongside Tukaani. She saved my life.

Spring, another spring, another spring. It was summer when my disaster happened.

I had just come out of one of the other caves, a cool place where I stored food, not the one with the hot spring. I had retrieved some dried wild onions. Then Mallt leaped on me from a crouch. I don't know why she did it or what I had done wrong. But she closed her jaws around the back of my neck and my skull, taking my whole head into her fangs.

I knew what came next. I had seen her do it many times to javelina, the wild pigs we loved to hunt. She took their skulls into her mouth and crushed them as easily as you or I would crack a chicken egg.

So I would be killed. I felt her teeth break the skin at my neck and my scalp, closing downward. She rested her enormous paws on my shoulders.

"Ke!" I shouted. No! I still had the dried onions in my hand, and I swatted Mallt on her muzzle with those.

She released her bite, tearing her fangs away from me, and with two enormous leaps bounded off into the brush. My wounds were not deep, but cuts to the head always bleed more than those on other parts of the body.

My mothers. My Welsh one, Mallt. My Numunuh one, Nautda. And then Mallt again, for my jaguar mother. And now Anna Maria. Of all four, only one of them ever nursed me, and that was the one that tried to kill me.

The slashes Mallt gave me grew infected. I raged with fever, dying as I lay beside the hot spring in my cave. Mallt and Tukaani came back as if nothing had happened, nuzzling and worrying over me. But I could never feel the same about them.

If I hadn't been sick, I would never have been captured. But the fool mountain man Jake Woodworth blundered into my cave, chasing silver. He took me, packing me on the back of his mule as if I were a dead antelope, bringing me down to the Comstock, where I fell under the care of the Sage Hen and was sold to Dr. Scott.

I never have breathed a word of this to anybody.

Breathed a word. Is that how you say it?

❧ 17 ❧

That Christmas, the holiday after Bronwyn's disturbing revelations, December 25, 1875, I shall always think of as the Christmas When Nothing Happened. It was a calm, small, family celebration. After the multiplicity of events that had afflicted my life of late, and especially since I learned the details of my sister's past (which I was still struggling to digest a month later), the holiday proved a welcome respite.

Diamonds were very much the fashion that season, having recently come in cheap. They were everywhere—shopgirls had them, babies wore buttons inset with chips, and many of the gifts we exchanged featured the darling sparklers. I presented Colm with a diamond breastpin. Anna Maria gave Bronwyn a diamond choker. Tu-Li bestowed a diamond-embroidered silk gown upon the berdache.

Nicky gave Bronwyn an odd gift. An Indian-style short bow, evidently an artifact of some kind, which he had taken and had the stave set with diamond festoons.

"It's the genuine article, made of Colorado ash," he told her. "The very bow Chief Niwot carried at Valmont Butte, when with Bear Head and Many Whips he met with Captain Aikins."

I feared that his gift did not in fact represent that very same authentic bow; rather my brother had gotten swindled by some unscrupulous peddler of native relics, but I refrained from spoiling the holiday atmosphere with my doubts. After all, what other debutante in archery-crazed Manhattan possessed a diamond-adorned Indian bow?

For my gift to Bronwyn, I did not have to venture farther than Freddy's library, the room where she had told me her story. I simply chose a particular volume, wrapped the book in gay paper and presented it to her. She did not seem overly impressed, merely placing the volume aside and uttering a perfunctory "Thank you," not immediately realizing what it was. Among all the diamonds, my present failed to shine.

For our holiday dinner, Cookie outdid herself. Roast duck succulent in its onion sauce, baked potatoes with their jackets crisped in duck fat, chicken pie, stewed carrots and a dozen other dishes. Bronwyn threw herself at the dessert candy along with Nicky and the berdache, gobbling up hickory-nut macaroons and chocolate drops. I instructed Colm to take a plate of chicken pie out to the Stone-Thrower, and he told me that the Stone-Thrower had disappeared. The morgue visit must have spooked him.

Later that evening, when the servants were let off for the half day and everyone fell dazed and sleepy from our feast, we gathered in the aviary. I retrieved my present from Bronwyn's gift pile and went over to sit next to her.

Opening the volume to the chapter entitled "Family Portraits," I began to read:

> Sir Pitt Crawley was a philosopher with a taste for what is called low life. His first marriage with the daughter of the noble Binkie had been made under the auspices of his parents; and as he often told Lady Crawley in her lifetime she was such a confounded quarrelsome high-bred jade that when she died he was hanged if he would ever take another of her sort . . .

Out of the corner of my eye, I watched Bronwyn. Paying little mind at first, she suddenly became very animated.

"It's Miss Becky?" she asked, incredulous.

It was indeed. The book I gave her was Thackeray's *Vanity Fair*, whose partial pages she had treasured and nursed and puzzled over during her years in the wilderness.

"I can't imagine a more cruel state of affairs," I said, "than to be allowed to know part of a story and not be able to get at its end."

She rose from her seat, grabbing the book out of my hands and planting a kiss on my cheek. "Oh, thank you, thank you!" she said, her eyes shining.

My parents failed to understand the exchange. It was odd that for all their involvement in Bronwyn's life they were ignorant of many essential elements of her existence. They had no idea she crept out at night. No awareness of her real story. No grasp on her emotional life. They made her their darling, monitored her studies, but had little appreciation of her, as I did, as a human being.

I kept her tale to myself. What could I think after hearing it? That she was a fabulist or, more bluntly, a liar? This biography of hers was clearly too fantastic to credit. Suckling a jaguar?

Yet to look at her, to ruminate upon her behavior, I wondered. That quality of self she demonstrated, so different from other young ladies of my acquaintance, was it animal grace? That she herself seemed not to care whether I believed her worked strangely in favor of my accepting her remarks.

I thought of her easy communion with the big cat in the Central Park Zoo. How she could make him roll over, do her bidding.

That Christmas season found me of two minds. I felt little confidence in the prospects for success of Freddy's "project"—introducing Bronwyn into society. This odd, winsome creature, with her fantastic history and untoward habits, would be no one's choice for a triumphant debut. The fearsome gatekeepers of our world, Mrs. Caroline Hood, the Tremont aunts, not to speak of minor deities such as Delia Showalter, would smoke her out immediately.

Freddy's impetuous nature once again tipped the scales, proposing to bring the debate over Bronwyn's pedigree into the public sphere in a particularly disturbing manner.

Darwin arrived in America as a gift to social conservatives, who construed his "survival of the fittest" principle as a sort of civic boosterism, a tribute to American progress.

In our rough-and-tumble nation, and especially in the business atmosphere of Wall Street, only the fittest could survive. It was the way of the natural world, and who were we to fool with the rules that guided the universe? Survival of the fittest, to these philosophers of commerce, meant the triumph of the wealthiest.

Freddy, among the richest of the rich but way out on the progressive wing politically, itched to take on these self-congratulatory gasbags, if not in open battle then at least in public debate. Coined in 1869 by Darwin's cousin, British polymath and fingerprinting pioneer Francis Galton, "nature versus nurture" asserted itself as the dominant question of the day.

The issue was personal with my father. His opinions were formed in rebellion against the rock-hard conservatism of his own father. Freddy despised the reigning financial moguls: the crude cattleman-turned-speculator Daniel Drew; the rapacious "Commodore" Cornelius Vanderbilt; and this new man, the cadaverous Baptist, John D. Rockefeller, a con man's son gobbling up the kerosene reserves in the wilds of Ohio.

All of these men piously cited religion as encouraging their actions. "God gave me money," quoth Rockefeller.

"Men's truths rather too neatly fit their convenience, have you ever noticed that?" quoth my father.

So it was inevitable, after attending holiday services at Grace Church, during a stroll with the family north toward Union Square, that Freddy should break off from us to confront a conservative apologist named Arvald Stockton. Bronwyn, Nicky and Anna Maria walked behind us, surrounded by a protective quartet of Grace Church pastors and deacons.

"Stockton!" Freddy called out, crossing Broadway to where the man walked alone, cane in hand. Their intercourse offering more in the way of entertainment than any passel of Episcopalian ministers, and cognizant of the fact that Arvald Stockton had often used his walking stick against his enemies, I went along with my father.

"Ho, Stockton," Freddy greeted the man.

"Delegate," Stockton said simply, squaring himself off as if he knew what might be coming.

"Read your piece in the *Tribune,* didn't I?" Freddy said.

"I don't know, did you?"

Preliminaries. The boxers circled each other in the ring.

Stockton, the same age as Freddy but with a shock of white hair, square-faced, somehow babylike in his affect, acted as a prime spokesman in the press for unfettered capitalism. As president of the high-domed Merchants' Exchange on Wall Street, he knocked down all government regulation and blasted any publicly espoused sentiment that he could label antibusiness. This included, within his far-reaching intellectual range, the idea that the positive effects of nurture could offer a balancing ideal to the vicious rigors of nature.

"You outdid yourself with that article, my man," Freddy said. "I didn't know such flights of reasoning could possibly exist."

Stockton, cautious, mistook my father's irony but remained uncertain of praise emanating from that particular quarter. "I've had a very good response."

"No doubt, no doubt," Freddy said. "The kind of hogs you surround yourself with usually enjoy the kind of hogswallop you dispense."

I saw the cane quiver in Stockton's hand. In another age, and one not too distant either, such a thrown-down gauntlet would have resulted in an invitation to duel.

"Good day, sir," Stockton said.

"I wonder if you would care to air your views in an open forum," Freddy said. "Test our positions in the crucible of debate. Name the venue and I will be there to demolish the cant you call argument."

Stockton went rigid. He glanced over to me. Depite the frail presence that I was, he felt himself outnumbered.

"You, sir, are a traitor to your class," he said to Freddy.

"Better than a traitor to all humanity," Freddy said.

"Come now, gents," I said. "I am a poor audience for your quarrel. Mr. Stockton, my father challenges you to a debate on the subject of your article, nature versus nurture. Better to hash out the question before a genteel gathering of philosophers than here on the street."

Stockton twirled his cane in a quick, insolent arc, making me flinch. Freddy stood his ground.

"I suppose I must accept, Delegate, if only to silence your silly nat-terings," Stockton said. "You shall hear from me."

He bowed stiffly and strolled away.

"Good Lord, Freddy," I said. "The man will take you apart."

"Not if I bring Bronwyn to the podium with me," he said. "Exhibit A."

My stomach turned. "You're not serious, I hope."

I looked across Broadway to where my sister and mother walked with the flock of black-garbed ministers. At the urging of the clerics, Anna Maria appeared to be admiring the new Gothic steeple of Grace Church, the pride of all Manhattan. Bronwyn, I noticed, had her eyes fixed on the pigeons that infested the grounds. Luckily for the birds, my mother had her arm linked firmly in her daughter's.

Dust kicked up from the thoroughfare, thick with omnibus traffic and coaches. I didn't want Savage Girl hauled into public, at least not in the way my father had planned. She remained still so unformed. I thought to keep her out of the communal fray for at least a little bit longer.

"Perhaps Cooper Union," Freddy said, musing on a suitable venue for what he envisioned as a Clash of Titans. Lincoln had secured his presidential candidacy with a speech there in 1860, before a packed house. Freddy pictured his debate triumph along the same lines.

"I was thinking more of our drawing room at home," I said.

Whether I sought to shield her from public exposure or not, I found it increasingly entertaining to squire my young sister around Manhat-tan. Not to social events—not yet—but to the kind of unusual, nook-and-cranny attractions that make wandering New York City so agreeable. On occasion we would take Nicky, or Tu-Li and the ber-dache, though rarely all three.

Bronwyn very much enjoyed the Block of Cowboys, that stretch of East Forty-second Street near Lexington where stables, blacksmiths and corrals concentrated and where a proliferation of Stetson-hatted, spur-wearing western characters walked the streets. Shipments of horses for the city's businesses and residents arrived there, and a mar-ket in equine flesh went on six days a week.

The dray horses took our fancy especially, immense Belgians, Percherons and Clydesdales. Bronwyn had only to glance at one of the cowboys to find herself swept up and seated on one of the heavy-maned beasts.

We also went to view the ice-yacht racing on the Hudson, rode the rising-room passenger elevators to the dizzying top of the seven-story Equitable Life Assurance building on Cedar Street, played at hide-and-seek (Nicky was with us) amid the vast, snow-powdered Christmas-tree markets of the flower district, near the Thirty-fourth Street ferry landing.

Like a pair of truants, we snuck into the construction site for the Catholic cathedral they were calling St. Patrick's, on Fifth Avenue at Fiftieth Street. The white marble structure as yet had no spires and no stained glass, and it rose from a lot that was wooded and remote from the bustle of downtown. I trailed the nave aisle behind Bronwyn like a forlorn groom.

For New Year's Eve, Freddy brought us out to the West Brighton Hotel on Coney Island. An odd choice for a winter holiday, but he was supposedly investing in a streetcar line and had come to inspect the road. The hotel itself was closed for the season, but they opened part of it for us, with great roaring fires in every hearth.

Bronwyn said she thought she had seen the ocean once, in dim childhood. As we walked along the shore, she told me it called to her in her dreams.

A pack of wild dogs troubled us, coming out of the wind-swirled snow.

"Watch, now," Bronwyn said. "You see there are a dozen of them? I can tell you which ones will snarl at me."

The mongrels approached.

"The two on the left, the white one and the dirty gray," she predicted.

Sure enough, the ones she had marked out rushed her with bared teeth. She reacted as I had seen her do before, way back at Kelton station, shouting at them and backing them off.

"How did you know?"

"Beware of pink-skinned dogs," she said. "I've always had trouble with them, I don't know why."

She explained that with some dogs you can see the pink flesh under their short fur. I recalled that our white bull terrier Hickory was pink-skinned, and because of Bronwyn he had been exiled.

We left the dogs behind and kept walking along the beach.

"Too bad it's too cold to swim," I said then. Pellets of sleet and sand blistered our skin. She did prove to be a regular fish later, in the hotel's saltwater pool. When the two of us swam races, we came up even. Deal of a good swimmer.

A few times during that holiday season, we stayed quietly at home, sitting in Freddy's library, reading, the hush of snow outside the windows. Bronwyn came in to find Nicky and me there one afternoon during New Year's week.

"Do you think it matters that we have an insane drunk for a doorman?" Bronwyn asked, flopping down on the tiger rug in front of the fire.

"No, I would think it rather makes sense," Nicky said. "Keeps the riffraff away."

"He *is* riffraff," I said. Often one floated into The Citadel on a cloud of Paul's brandy breath.

"You two lay off Master Paul," Nicky said. "He's the only man who stands between us and the mob."

Nicky loved to fill Bronwyn's head with his trenchant analysis of Manhattan's social strata. He did so now.

"The whole purpose of society," he lectured her, "is to keep everybody else out of the cream so the cats can have it all to themselves."

"Meow," said Bronwyn.

"There's a lot of people out who want in. They are called climbers and strivers, and we turn up our noses at them."

He demonstrated, holding his nose in the air with two fingers and prancing around the room with exaggerated superciliousness. Bronwyn imitated him.

"Very good," he said. "You think it's enough to have fancy clothes and filet mignon? It's not. Money isn't everything. These days even the worst kind of people have money. If you have money but no standing in society, it's a terrible sort of limbo. We call these folk arrivistes, and parvenus, and we turn up our noses at them."

Once again he paraded and Bronwyn followed.

"Much more of this, I'll lose my mind," I said.

"So," Bronwyn said to Nicky.

"So," Nicky said to Bronwyn. "If you're outside, like you are, Miss Bronwyn, how do you get in? You need first of all a patron. Grandmother holds the key, because she knows all the old families. And the old families are the gatekeepers."

He pantomimed knocking at a door. "May I come in?" he said to the empty air, shouting out "No!" in reply and slamming an imaginary door in his own face.

"Poor Nicholas," Bronwyn said.

"But, but, but!" Nicky said. "If you have an old family angel looking over you, inviting you, approving you . . ."

Bronwyn approached the imaginary door, and Nicky opened it for her in a sweeping motion. She performed a full curtsy.

"You two ought to take that act down to the Bowery," I said.

"Envy is a most disagreeable human emotion, is it not?" Nicky said to Bronwyn, looking at me with exaggerated pity.

"'Tis," said Bronwyn. "But I'm wondering, dear Nicholas, who these fearsome old gatekeepers might be."

"Ah, yes," Nicky said. "Right now in Manhattan, they number three. The two Tremont aunts, Fabrice and Gladys, and Caroline Hood, Mrs. Donald Hood, a woman so toplofty and refined she even powders her butt."

"Nicky!" I warned.

"She does, I saw her do it myself," Nicky said.

"You did not," I said, scoffing.

"No, really, I've seen her, her grandson Eric and I used to be friends. We hid in her boudoir."

"You did not," I repeated. "Don't listen to him, Bronwyn."

"Behind the arras," Nicky said in his Shakespearean voice. "Her heiress behind, spied from behind the arras."

"For pity's sake," I said, laughing in spite of myself.

"Lucky for you," Nicky continued to Bronwyn, "Swoony and Caroline Hood debuted together. And if Caroline Hood receives your call and returns it, you're in. If not, you are loaded onto the oblivion express. Back to the Comstock wid ya!"

"Oh, no!" Bronwyn said, dragging her hand across her forehead. "Anything but that!"

"We love well in the higher echelons of society, Miss Delegate, but we hate even better. You think the Washoe is savage? Wait until you come out in Manhattan."

"You've never been to the Washoe," I said. "You know nothing about it."

"I know that the quality of meanness here in Manhattan is superb," Nicky said. "Really first rank, tiptop. You haven't been well hated until you've been hated in New York City. Are you ready for that, Bronwyn?"

I was about to tell Nicky to leave her alone, but Bronwyn shook her head and took his hand in hers, a serious expression crossing her face.

"Ah, Nicholas," she said. "Don't you know?"

"I know everything. What don't I know?"

"The opposite of love is not hate, dear Nicky."

"No?" Nicky said.

"The opposite of love is loneliness," Bronwyn said. And she flopped back down in front of the hearth. She who knew a little about loneliness.

I took her to my New York, and at times Bronwyn surprised me by taking me to hers.

"Tahktoo has a job," she said to me one morning when I sat with her in the South Wing drawing room.

"I can't quite believe that is so," I said. I had noticed the berdache absent from The Citadel rather more of late.

"It's true, and I'd like to go there," she said. "Will you take me tonight?"

Secretive about the where and what of this startling new development, Bronwyn herself arranged for us to take the fly out that evening. The lightweight pleasure carriage obviated the necessity of a driver, so no report of our activities could redound on us back at home. She wore black, the better to fade into the night.

I understood the need for mystery when she directed me on our way. "Downtown on Fifth," she said, very much the little New Yorker by now, "then west on Twenty-eighth Street."

The Tenderloin.

The neighborhood of faro casinos, saloons, sporting houses and dance halls had long been a haunt of mine, a favorite as well for many of the more unbuttoned young males in the Circle (Bev Willets was a regular). But the idea of visiting it with a female, and a family member at that, struck me as so outlandish as to throw me into mental disarray.

I should have immediately turned back the fly. That I felt myself, lately, increasingly under the sway of Bronwyn did not excuse the fact that I drove on, though I grew moody and silent.

She, for her part, began an athletic process in the seat next to me, changing out of the gown in which she had left the house. She garbed herself not in the rough laborer's outfit of her adventure in the Central Park but in a quite respectable suit jacket and trousers of black worsted.

"What are you doing?" I asked, though I well knew.

"My disguise," she said.

Performing her transformation beneath her cape, she managed to slip her male clothes over her female ones, resulting in a lumpy, disordered costume, but one that could pass muster in the dim gaslight for which the Tenderloin was justly famous. Bronwyn tucked her hair beneath a tight-fitting black bowler.

With her thus reconfigured, we were simply two young swells out for the evening, one perhaps a little sweller than the other but both well within the normal range of the demimonde.

The streets of the Tenderloin roared every night of the week, including the Sabbath. Vice stopped for no man, but quite a few stopped for it. Men of the cloth liked to rail against the neighborhood as "Satan's Circus." Twenty-fifth between Fifth and Seventh was for faro, Twenty-sixth for dice, Twenty-seventh for low brothels and Twenty-eighth for high. Unescorted light women of all price ranges roamed the sidewalks, some in bosom-baring dresses, some in chaste gowns.

"Ho, hi there, you handsome devil!" hailed one of them I recognized, sending me into choking embarrassment. Bronwyn pretended not to notice, taking the reins as I coughed myself red in the face. I felt paradoxically both mortified and aroused to be with my sister amid such company. The effect would only grow more pronounced as the evening wore on.

"Here," Bronwyn said. She pulled up in front of a three-story brownstone on the far western reaches of the Tenderloin, a louche precinct to which even I had never ventured before. The stoop risers of the entrance were painted a lurid shade of purple.

Inside, it was all scarlet and flame. Even the glass of the lampshades shone red. The heavy velvet window dressings, pulled tight, were darkest crimson. I recognized the atmosphere instantly—a luxury sporting house, for sure—and knew there would be curtained cubicles lining the hallways upstairs. But the clientele proved wholly alien.

Women were as rare here as in Virginia City.

A massive bar ran along the wall of the first floor, with a cracked, spiderwork mirror that had pictures of current vocal stars pasted up to the glass. Men of all stripes congregated at the rail, mostly of the middle class but also gents in elegant evening dress. Among the milling crowd, a half dozen individuals stood out, strange rouged men wearing the full makeup of women, like Elizabethan actors on the stage.

And Tahktoo. The most outlandish of them all (I caught myself, briefly, actually being proud of his flamboyance), standing posed beside a grand piano in the conservatory past the bar, one hand placed gracefully upon the instrument, the other reserved for gesture.

Costumed in the sexually ambiguous dress of his station, the Zuni flourishes on his flowing gown acting as bizarre accents, he stood erect and sang.

Or warbled. Or yodeled. Whatever it was, it could not be found in any other throat this side of an insane asylum. His register wandered from baritone to soprano in the course of a song or, really, in the space of a refrain. When we came in, he had just launched into "Dixie" and drew the song out, singing every verse two or three times, favoring his audience members.

Which were, surprisingly, many and, astoundingly, enthusiastic. At the berdache's feet crouched a young man with curly blond hair whom I might have recognized as the brother of an acquaintance had not the rules of the Tenderloin strictly precluded recognizing anybody at any time. Staring up at Tahktoo, the catamite wore an enthralled expression on his face.

"Baths upstairs on the third," Bronwyn murmured into my ear. "Tahktoo told me he likes the cold vodka rub, the rock salt massage and the *platza* beatings, being whipped with a branch of dried oak leaves."

"Don't tell me any more," I pleaded.

"This house is called The Point," she said. "The *New York Sun* labels it a debauch, but you know what Tahktoo says? 'I don't read the *Sun*,' he says."

She laughed.

The berdache went into a novelty song, a strange histrionic number with verses that always ended the same way: "Come up, you fool." He'd give a come-hither gesture, the crowd said it in unison along with him, and I understood it was his favorite identifying phrase.

Come up, you fool. I tried to carry off our visit with something like Bronwyn's brand of savoir faire, but at first I wasn't quite up to it. A pair of triple brandies aided the process.

I thought Tahktoo might be abashed in the setting, but I was wrong. It seemed that he knew everybody and that his own strangeness simply accented the strangeness of everything else. A plump man-woman in a goatee and Chinese pigtails. Boys that looked to be as young as my brother, bewitching sirens of the soused. Shirtless men transiting through the place. A gaggle of Yalies.

The berdache finally noticed us in the crowd, and his face split open in a huge smile. Instantly he crossed the room, maneuvering among his admirers, and took Bronwyn by the hand. He brought her to the piano, introduced her as "my muse" and launched into a popular number, "O Were My Love a Sugar Bowl."

Upon the second refrain, she joined him! Making a mess of the German accent required of the song, but still.

> *O vere my lofe a sugarpowl,*
> *De ferry shmallest loomp,*
> *Vouldt shveet the seas from bole to bole*
> *Und make the children shoomp.*

The whole raucous crowd joined on the chorus.

> *O it vouldn't be no dime at all*
> *Before I'd shoomped the fence!*

At the end of the second verse ("*She is de holiest animile dat rooms oopon de earth*"), Bronwyn wowed the crowd by doffing her bowler and shaking out her hair, revealing herself to be, among all the outlandish creatures in that house, a true girl.

Wild, shocked applause. She was a hit, a palpable hit.

On our way home, the chill night air clearing off my brandy haze, I said, "Those are the very types of places that a proper young lady can never attend."

"No," she said. She drove while I sagged backward in the seat. No? Did she mean, *No, I will never go to such places when I am a lady?* Or, *No, I will not have you telling me where I can and cannot go?*

"This whole neighborhood," I said, swinging wide my arm drunkenly.

She looked back at me. "Then it will be our secret, just between the two of us." Touching me lightly on the arm.

I thrilled. I was inebriated. I hauled myself upright, peering at her in the gaslight gleam of Fifth Avenue.

"I wonder, Bronwyn, how many other secrets do you harbor?"

The frigid air on my face, our exhalations pluming in the night.

"How many secrets?" I said, the question floating off in a cloud like my breath. I didn't expect her to answer, but she did.

"Everything," she said.

Delia and I had several brief, pouty encounters in passing, at Delmonico's and once on the promenade around the top of the Murray Hill Reservoir at Forty-second Street. I had to admit that one reason I still held on to Delia, beyond all logic and kindness, was that I knew Bev Willets had been waiting in the wings for her. If there was ever a hint of trouble between me and Delia, he would pounce.

But finally I dropped a card at her home, suggesting I wanted to speak with her, giving a time I'd call. Later that afternoon, at the appointed hour, I arrived at the Showalter place on Twenty-eighth, off Madison.

"My, you're formal," Delia said when the butler opened the door. "A calling card and all. And your forehead looks positively scrunched."

She came up and gave me a light buss on the cheek.

"Can we go someplace?" I said.

"Hmmm, that's an interesting suggestion," she said, teasing me a little.

"The drawing's in use?" I asked, refusing to play along.

"Well, Mother and my sister are in the drawing room, entertaining the mayor," Delia said. "Anything but that."

"Will it be too chilly for you outside?" I felt an automatic gentlemanly posture take hold whenever I saw Delia.

"I have my wool wrap," she said. "And the most cunning new fur bonnet. You'll see."

Her words were gay, and she tried for her usual light breathiness, but her voice had a wavering quality. Did she know what was coming?

Delia turned quickly to get her things and made her red dress and petticoats fly up behind her in a whirl. I caught a glimpse of an ankle, trim in its white stocking and high-heeled black slipper.

I tried to flatten out the flutter in my heart.

The winter sun shone weak and remote. We made our way to

Gramercy Park from her house. I couldn't hold back until we got to a place more private, more appropriate. I told her the truth.

"Delia," I said, "this isn't meant to be."

"I know," she said lightly, but with a slight look of concern rising in her eyes. "It's just too cold out here. Not the day for a walk."

"No, it's just— You know what I mean." I looked at her and saw that she did in fact know. She realized, I think, that this break had been coming for a long time. Even so long ago as the midsummer ball at The Ditches, when we waltzed and behaved to all the world as though we were engaged.

"I don't think—" I said, and then, strangely, my eyes filled with tears even before hers did.

We held hands and spoke for a good half hour. The neighborhood sidewalks were deserted on this frigid afternoon, aside from lone pedestrians who hurried along, looking past our faces. Freezing tears on cold cheeks. Across the gated park enclosure stood the mansion belonging to the Willets family, a place Delia and I knew well, having visited, danced, had dinner parties there many times over the years.

"Are you sure?" One of the things she repeated several times.

"Sure? What is sure?" I said sadly. "But—"

"You'll always be my friend, I know," she said, interrupting.

I was silent.

"May I tell you something? Will you promise not to get angry?"

"How can I promise if I don't know what you are going to say?"

"Before this you'd promise just at my asking," she said.

I shrugged. "What is it?" Trying not to sound impatient.

"Watch out for that sister of yours," Delia said. "You think you know everything about her? But you don't."

I did indeed feel a pulse of anger.

"She has nothing to do with this, or with you," I said. "You'll always be my pet, even if we can't be together."

What a wretch I was, pronouncing that insipid phrase.

And how my spirits rose! as I detached myself from Delia Showalter at her front door and wordlessly we went our separate ways.

❧ 18 ❧

In that first week of the New Year, Bronwyn took her initial step into the public sphere.

Prior to this she had remained safe within the family. After her archery triumph at The Ditches, the Bliss brothers tried to call on the new prodigy, but we put them off. They had come pestering by our house, dropping their cards. With Bronwyn safely cocooned in the South Wing, they never made any headway.

Bev Willets was more subtle, and therefore more dangerous. He had buttonholed me at school a few times (he was also at Harvard, when he bothered to attend), probing my family circumstance. He, too, wanted to know about the archery girl. Realizing that to discourage him would only put the scent of blood in the water, I had affected a casual offhandedness.

"You know Freddy—he collects people like Greek sculpture," I said. I had described Bronwyn as a distant cousin from San Francisco, a summer visitor.

But rumors and gossip persisted about a new ward of the Delegates. Freddy managed to keep her actual name out of the newspapers. That didn't entirely eliminate interest in her existence. Money was the draw, of course, since anyone associated with us, especially a female, might conceivably act as a doorway into our countinghouse.

More than that, high society just then felt itself under siege. Nicky had been right. Climbers of every sort sought a way in. All interlopers were treated as a species of burglar. Any new figure within the stockade invited intense scrutiny and, until proven otherwise, was assumed by the hens to be a fox.

From when I first came to understand my father's audacious plan for the Savage Girl, back in the wilds of Nevada, I declined to believe that it would work. Initially I stood cynically apart, then became swept up in the effort myself. At every turn, as I watched it move forward, I thought the project would crash.

Yet here I was, in the first week of January, sipping a cup of weak Ceylon in the gallery of Madame Eugénie's Académie de Danse. This cultural institution lodged itself off Washington Square and was perhaps fading with the neighborhood but still retained an almost mystical significance for our set. I had attended there. Nick would also, though I could hardly credit the idea.

In Madame Eugénie's ancient ballroom with its smoothly varnished oak-wood floorboards, the rosebud petals of the prominent New York families first came into bloom, gently bred young women of seventeen or eighteen, sent forth for a final round of finishing before their social debuts.

This was the season, the short two months after the holidays and before Lent. This was the first and last best chance. To come out successfully meant love, security, standing. Really, it meant life itself, since failure was a sort of death.

Entering Madame Eugénie's was, for these girls, a miniature debut. It resembled the claiming races of the season's Thoroughbred three-year-olds at Saratoga: a chance to survey the field. Who will my horse be running against when the derbies begin in earnest? Which entry will be the strongest? Where may I locate the competition?

I sipped my tea and waited for Anna Maria to show up with Bronwyn. When I left The Citadel around noon, they were involved in a fitting, and now, at the two-o'clock bell, they had still not arrived.

Below me, drifting across the floor in clouds of white, the first few nervous daughters had entered the arena. They were, to a girl, irresistible, denizens of that fairyland that is the female coming-of-age period. Desire washed over me like a blush.

"Delegate, the man of the hour," Bev Willets said, sliding onto the divan next to me. "You have a bitch in this hunt, don't you?"

"Employing your usual delicacy of phrase, Beverly."

"Your ward who was only a summer visitor, a Miss Brennan, correct?" he said.

I smiled inwardly, thinking that our strategy of secrecy had not been fully a failure if Bev Willets hadn't been able to ferret out Bronwyn's correct name.

He gazed down at the dance floor below where we sat in the gallery. "You are a cur for keeping her from us. Why all the secrecy? Which one is she?"

I told him that my sister had not yet arrived.

"'Sister' now," Bev said. "I thought she was your cousin. You Delegates have to get your stories straight."

He was just tweaking me. That my parents had adopted a ward was by this point commonly known. I could just as well have questioned Bev as to why he was there, since entry into the dance academy was ostensibly carefully controlled. He would probably have pleaded cousinage of some sort to one of the belles below, but his real purpose was titillation.

The balcony gallery at Madame Eugénie's was the proper territory of mothers, brothers and chaperones of the girls à l'école. A variety of ottomans, chaises and divans, all Second Empire castoffs, all antimacassared to the inch, were scattered throughout, alternating with frowsy palms that had seen better centuries.

Madame Eugénie Brochet never took to the dance floor herself, having long since vanished into a twilight of chintz and phlebitis. She sat to the side, ensconced in a thronelike armchair, one gouty leg propped up before her, muttering about the glory days of the world when she was young. Her companion and opposite number in a Boston-style marriage that had drifted south to Manhattan, a Miss Renée, trotted forth from her side with instructions, imprecations and random irrelevancies.

The two ladies occupied a downstairs garden apartment to which they strictly forbade admittance.

The true powers at the school were the dancing masters, Messieurs Henri and Sébastien, cousins and rivals. Conjoined almost to the same degree as Chang and Eng Bunker, they differed from those celebrated Siamese twins in the fact that they actively hated each other.

Dressed formally and identically in ditto suits, pleated ascot ties and wing-collared shirts, they strolled among the growing crowd of mothers and daughters on the floor below, being introduced, bowing flamboyantly, keeping an eye out lest one gain some imperceptible advantage over his adversary. The only way to tell them apart: monocle (Henri) or pince-nez (Sébastien).

Anna Maria glided in with Bronwyn, and at the same moment Delia Showalter appeared at my side.

"Hugo, Beverly," she said, her inevitable aunt hovering in the background. "At last we see the new crop of fashionables."

"Some of them less fashionable than others," Bev said, always a precise judge of couture.

"And yours," Delia said to me. "She comes to us quite without experience, I'm told."

"Don't believe everything you hear," I said. It was the first time we had spoken since we broke it off.

"Why, she's really very pretty," Delia exclaimed as Bronwyn passed beneath us. "She must be a nurse, since she accompanies you out and about when you are sick." This was Delia's pointed reference to the evening she saw Bronwyn and me in a carriage outside the Young Patriarchs' Ball, an event I had begged off of, pleading illness.

"Yes, what was *that* all about?" Bev asked, twisting the knife.

"So fresh and unworldly," Delia said, still on Bronwyn. "I shall have to put her together with my sister."

Young Marcella Showalter had taken her place among the debuting mademoiselles on the dance floor.

"A tragic figure, Marcella, in that her beauty can never approach that of her older sibling," Bev said.

"Thank you," Delia said. "Marcie can very well hold her own."

I turned from them and approached the rail, eavesdropping on the chatter below. Anna Maria had left Bronwyn and, accompanied by an elderly battle-ax named Mrs. Blight (of the Philadelphia Blights, grand-mother of debutante Penelope Blight), headed toward the stairway to the gallery.

I have to admit my heart caught in my throat, seeing my little sister cast off to sink or swim on her own.

She sank. Anna Maria had left her with a cousin of ours, Beldonna Griswold, who immediately jettisoned her wallflower relative and set off to seek smarter company. Bronwyn remained alone, directly below me. Clots of debutantes formed themselves into hierarchies, throwing off furious hooded glances at their competition. The musk of female rivalry rose from the floor like a rain squall on the ocean.

I had the impulse to leap like Booth from the balcony, take Bronwyn's hand, stand beside her, act her champion. The same refrain occurred, the one that had sounded ever since I'd first encountered the girl.

Who will protect her from harm?

Oh, no! Danger! Danger! I wanted to shout. A certain Miss Croker, singularly ill-favored, perhaps the one girl in the whole coterie without prospects or grace, approached Bronwyn. She was the kind of young lady who wore spectacles to dancing school. Edna Croker was social death, her family tainted by financial reverses in the latest panic, enduring the additional onus of an overly public suffragist uncle.

"Will we do the Lancers, do you think?" Edna asked Bronwyn. "I quake at the Lancers."

Bronwyn smiled at the girl and said that the Lancers dance steps gave her difficulty, too.

"I'm so very shy and nervous," Edna said. "Will you be my friend?"

It was hideous, gruesome, but Bronwyn merely said that she would. Marcie Showalter and one of the Buchanan twins detached themselves from a chattering clutch of pretty girls and approached the two outliers.

"I must say hello to you," Marcie announced, addressing Bronwyn and ignoring Edna. "Your brother Hugo was fated for my sister, Delia, in which case you and I would be relatives of sorts."

"But Hugo Delegate isn't your real brother, is he?" Pauline Buchanan said. "Just a cousin?"

"It must be romantic, to be the poor ward of a wealthy man," Marcie said. "Like in Sir Walter Scott."

"Who is Sir Walter Scott?" Bronwyn asked, and I groaned inwardly.

"What an ignorant boobie you are! What a foolish question!" Pauline exclaimed.

"Baronet Scott, the great author?" Edna said helpfully. *"Peveril of the Peak?* I love *Redgauntlet!"*

"Oh, do be quiet, you homely mouse," Pauline said.

Marcie assessed Bronwyn coolly. "Miss Delegate might have a wee bit of catching up to do, in order to come level with the rest of us," she said. "Whatever do they teach you way out in San Francisco?"

"They teach us not to bully our lessers and that there is no such thing as a foolish question," said Bronwyn.

"She's quaint," Pauline said, and made to turn away.

Bronwyn reached out and laid a hand on Marcie's arm, and the girl froze at the impertinence. My sister leaned in close and murmured something I couldn't catch. Marcie gave a look of horror and flinched backward. But Bronwyn had her toe on Marcie's slipper, so the girl lost her balance and stumble-stepped.

And with that they were finished with each other.

Later on I asked Bronwyn what she had said to cause such a reaction in Marcie. "I asked if she wanted her pretty little nose bloodied," she said. After this initial encounter, the younger Showalter girl gave Bronwyn a wide berth.

Madame Eugénie struck a small gong at her elbow. She then fell back, exhausted by the effort. The dancing masters took to the floor, clapping their hands. The well-practiced girls and boys assembled themselves in cotillion lines, facing one another across the floor, separated by gender.

Once again Bronwyn blundered, being out of place and finding herself lined up alongside the boys. Titterings. Monsieur Henri had to guide her physically to her mark.

But something happened then that worked to retrieve the whole afternoon.

Monsieur Henri cleared his throat. "Gentlemen, advance."

The boys lumbered across the room to pick their preferred partners. Much jostling and elbowing, and suddenly—the waiting girls watched, dismayed—a dozen of the young men clustered in front of Bronwyn. There would have been more, but there wasn't space.

Observing from the railing above, I saw the dynamics in the room shift. The girls could carp all they wanted and disdain the newcomer as "the poor ward of a wealthy man." The boys had other ideas.

Bronwyn took the first suitor in front of her by his shoulders.

"Edna is a very accomplished dancer," she said, guiding him to the diffident (and wholly partnerless) Miss Croker, extending a kindness to her new friend. She enlisted the second boy in line for herself.

"Now, mesdemoiselles, messieurs," said Monsieur Henri. The piano struck up softly behind him, and he held one finger aloft, as though testing the air. "The origin of the accomplishment of dancing has never been traced. Probably it is coeval with legs and feet—"

Cousin Sébastien interrupted him. "We don't need all that!" he cried. "Anyone can manage to knock up a hop of some kind or other. We will begin."

He leaped to the piano, shoved the recitalist aside and launched into a sevillana.

Monsieur Henri went from couple to couple, ostentatiously adjusting their positions, placing a hand on a shoulder here or turning a face there.

"Lancers Quadrille!" shouted Sébastien.

"Oh!" gasped Edna, looking at Bronwyn.

"In the first figure, the Rose, the ladies and gentlemen advance four steps to the right. . . ."

"Dance is the poetry of motion!" called out Monsieur Henri.

Watching the action, I sensed not poetry but latent cruelty, the flavor of Darwin present in the incessant, insistent pairing-off. Thus do fledgling humans make their first tentative claims to positions in the social hierarchy. Or, perhaps a better metaphor, they string the needle with a particular thread, and ever afterward their lives will be stitched with the color they choose. Destiny awaited. At a dance academy!

Later, as the flush-cheeked dancers came off the floor, I reacted with something akin to panic when I saw that Bev Willets had cornered Bronwyn. I registered a slow-moving disaster as my malevolent friend was able to have a good few minutes conversing with my sister before Anna Maria came and fetched her.

Miserable, I let my mother and Bronwyn leave without wishing them good-bye.

At least I got to Bev before he could reach Delia and pass on his newfound gossip. "Where are you going after this?" I asked him.

"She has never in her life been to San Francisco," Bev said, a congenital mean streak showing in his tone. "From what I gathered, she is no blood cousin to you and is definitely not related to your mother's side of the family. So the question naturally arises—what or who is she?"

"I have my carriage," I said. "Why don't you take a brandy at the Lotos with me?"

He cast a glance at Delia, still waiting in the balcony, a golden opportunity for him to pour poison. Wouldn't Delia love to hear that the Delegate family ward was a sham! In the wake of our breakup, Delia Showalter furiously scented out rivals to blame and, ridiculous as it was, had formed a clear antipathy toward the girl. Equally clear was Bev's ardent interest in Delia since the canceled engagement.

"Let's go," I said. "My sister's real story is rather more interesting than the one that has been put about."

Between present evil and future mischief, Bev chose the latter, and we were off, both of us giving a wave to Delia as we went.

✿ 19 ✿

In mid-January, two weeks after that first dancing class, Bev and I proceeded down Fifth in the Thirties, heading for the atelier of a London-based couturier, the House of Richardson. We were to meet Bronwyn and Anna Maria there. An essential step of the debut season required that the prospective debutante be provided with the full wardrobe of a lady.

Bev manfully volunteered to advise in the process. He and Cousin Willie and I and others among our male friends had dressed many women, many times—light women, kept women, mistresses, whatever you'd prefer to call them. We usually steered clear of the House of Richardson as too public for these purposes, but we all had open accounts at Kate Reilly's, just down the avenue, and a licensed importer from Worth in Paris named Victor Goldthorpe.

It was one of Bev's many pretensions to know more about couture than any dressmaker, to be abreast of fashion in such a way as to be able to anticipate it, play at it, make others stand in admiration of his taste and discernment. He pored over *Godey's Lady's Book* with the passion of a schoolgirl and took notes when he visited Paris on whatever look was then dominating the scene.

He fussed over his own wardrobe, of course, but was known as a lethal judge of female style. In any other man, this facility might have been revolting, but with Bev Willets it was merely another aspect of his fixation on power and thus recognized and accepted by the paragons of society.

Our conversation at the Lotos Club after dance class that first day began with him hurling scorn at my choice of venue. The Lotos was one of my affectations, a mutt of a club, near the Union, the Knick and the Academy of Music at Irving and Fourteenth, but miles away from the other venues in terms of prestige.

"I'm ashamed even to walk by here," Bev muttered. The place had been founded by literati, a class of people made for the sneers of cynics such as Bev Willets.

Ignoring the sally, I proceeded to lay out the truth of Bronwyn Delegate's life. Not the whole truth. I cut and tailored the fabric to suit my needs. Nothing about jaguars, for pity's sake, and certainly nothing about the Comanche. That she was a waif, a foundling, an orphan plucked from the wilds of Virginia City. Brought here and shaped up by Friedrich Delegate in order to advance into society.

"Something in the nature of a challenge," I said. "See if we can sneak her past the old goats who guard the ramparts."

"You won't be able to do it, my man," Bev said. "Never." Then he added, as I'd bet everything that he would, "Not without my help."

Foreseeing certain disaster in having Bev as a spoiler in Bronwyn's transformation, I was forced to take him on as an ally.

With enough champagne, Bev turned enthusiastic about the project, gloating at the idea of "putting one over" on society, then becoming ruminative.

"You know, there's a quality about your girl," he said. "She's different. Do you know 'duende'? A Spanish term, they use it about music. Something like authenticity. When I stood talking to her at Miss Eugénie's, I felt it."

He shook his head, as if to clear from it a memory. "I had an uncanny feeling that she wasn't taking me quite seriously," he said. "At any rate, she's not one of our fading violets, is she?"

With that he promised to help, "throw my whole being into it," as he said, vowing that in his "role as *arbiter elegantiarum*," he would make Miss Bronwyn Delegate the success of the season. He had even agreed to meet with my mother, at The Citadel, to look at fabric swatches and advise her on what might be à la mode.

We arrived at Richardson's, a street-level emporium with a bow window that held a display of samples. The bell at the door tinkled as we entered to see my mother and sister, already arrived.

"Here you are, here you are," called Anna Maria. "Mr. Richardson, this is my son Hugo, and here is his partner in crime, Beverly Willets."

"I know Mr. Beverly well," said Richardson, a gentleman who displayed every bit of the primness required of his trade. That and a trim Vandyke beard, which left him with more hair on his face than on his pate.

"Mr. Hugo," he said, bowing. "Your sister, the lovely young Miss Delegate, she is the prize." He made a display of seizing Bronwyn's kid-gloved hand to kiss the air above it.

Bronwyn blushed prettily and yet managed to look calmly down at the top of Richardson's egg-bald head, as though such men kissed her hand every day.

Three bowlegged chairs had been arranged around a small table, which supported a pitcher of ice water and a plate of untouched butter cookies. In the center of the room lay a circular mauve carpet with a triptych of mirrors beside it.

"This is how we will proceed, my ladies and my gentlemen," Richardson said. "With masterly strokes of genius, laboring night and day, I have created couture based on the materials Mr. Bev and Mrs. Delegate chose earlier in your gorgeous palace so far uptown on the Central Park. The mademoiselle will try them in sequence."

A woman in a narrow black dress stepped forward to lead Bronwyn to the back dressing rooms of the shop.

"Very nice, very courteous," said Anna Maria. She took some ice water. My mother always appeared a little subdued around Bev. He had dressed for the day as a man-about-town, in a pearlescent morning coat, checked trousers and a bowler not of black, as everyone in the world wore, but in the most delicate dove gray.

I had been only tangentially involved in the arrangements. I wanted to allow Bev a free hand, knowing that the more time he spent at it, the less likely he would be to spoil the whole project. I had never seen my sister in anything fancy or womanly, at best a plain day dress with simple lines and a high-rising neck, topped with a modest little bow-tied bonnet.

So I was thunderstruck when I saw Bronwyn emerge from the

recesses of the store and glide toward the mauve carpet, a long train trailing behind her. Bev had demanded, Anna Maria had accepted and Morgan Richardson had executed a cerise walking dress with tiers of ruffles. The elaborately draped overskirt produced a swag at the front, and the form-fitting sleeves flared fashionably at the wrist.

I had never seen anything like it. The gown's squared-off neckline showed a few more inches of Bronwyn's skin than the New York world had ever seen. A magenta ribbon encircled her neck and drifted down her back almost to the bustle, which consisted of a hump that I doubted would allow the girl to sit down.

The woman in black knelt beside Bronwyn with a mouthful of pins, fluffing out the skirt's flounces with the utmost concentration.

Anna Maria clapped her hands in delight.

"Well, I wondered," Bev said. "But the girl can carry off cerise."

"This, this," said Richardson, hurrying to Bronwyn's side. "It is perfect." He proffered a chapeau of dark straw that tilted from the crown of her head down her forehead, to be fastened, before it slid away, by a length of wide magenta silk.

Bronwyn looked at me, puffing out her cheeks and raising her eyebrows.

"Sister," I said, "you are a vision."

She examined herself in the mirror, turning slowly around.

"This will do," Bronwyn said, and we all broke out laughing at how regal she sounded.

"But there are so many more!" Richardson said. "Go! Reveal yourself to us."

"She'll be dressing for a good half hour," said Bev to me, retrieving a silver brandy flask from his morning coat as Anna Maria went off with Richardson to investigate accessorizing the gowns.

"I well know the mysteries of the corset, if that's what you mean," I said. I'd had plenty of fumblings with it at Miss Cora's sporting house down on Twenty-seventh Street. Among other places.

"It's more than that, much more," Bev said. "A chemise first, then drawers. Without . . . um . . . ahem, with no center to them. The corset and the busk that opens it. A corset cover. A decency skirt. Then the petticoats. Crinolines. Then the gown and its garniture. Finally hat, gloves, parasol."

"Don't tell me any more," I said. Every insane person I ever met always talked too much.

"And don't forget the bustle," he said. "Metal and canvas stuffed with horsehair."

"A necessity," I said.

Bronwyn arrived from the back of the store and stood in front of us. She had taken much less time than we imagined, prompting the thought that perhaps she had skipped a few of the underlayers.

"What's a necessity?" she asked.

"Your adorableness," said Bev.

She walked to the mauve carpet, faced us and glanced over her shoulder into the mirror.

She wore what would become among the most celebrated garments of the age.

"Magic," said Bev.

"Bravo," said my mother, returning with Richardson.

A long, floor-sweeping gown of creamy silk, off the shoulder, with short puffed sleeves that exposed her whole ivory-pale arm, and a décolleté that plunged, so that her breast was disguised only by a scrap of lace. Suddenly Bronwyn had a voluptuous figure, thanks to a steam-formed corset.

A tight cuirass formed the upper part of the outfit, which snugly circled the hips and trailed off to a riot of satin ribbon and fabric frills. But the masterpiece was the jeweled embroidery of the bodice, encrusted with a shimmering panoply of diamonds and pearls.

Bronwyn had been made into a priceless bauble. It would be a wonder if a thief did not steal her.

"For the debut," said Richardson, watching our reaction. "Yes?"

"Oh, yes," Anna Maria said.

"They only do this kind of work in Germantown," Bev told me.

Bronwyn turned to the mirror then, and we saw the back of the gown. Bev and I exchanged looks. The posterior displayed an enormous bustle—gigantic, really—a cream-colored, audacious powder puff, all the more exaggerated because it emerged from a back that was so slender.

"Allow me," said Bev, jumping over to the mauve carpet.

"Now, now, Mr. Bev, please wait," said Richardson.

"No, really," Bev said. "See and learn." He put his hand on Bronwyn's bustle and, in a slightly obscene gesture, massaged it flat, collapsing it to a more natural appearance. "And so. Much more modern."

The woman in black looked stricken. Anna Maria appeared appalled. Richardson considered. "Perhaps."

"No 'perhaps,'" Bev said. "This is in Paris today, and tomorrow it will be on the Ladies' Mile. After all, Miss Bronwyn is not an animal, is she? She doesn't need to accentuate her hindquarters to attract a mate."

Bronwyn looked over at me. "Tahktoo would love this shop," she said. "I want to bring her here."

She tried on half a dozen more outfits that morning. A princess sheath dress, a purple-striped day gown with a lilac polonaise, a tea gown in the artistic style, with uncorseted lines and appliquéd daisies. She took some of them with her in the carriage, wrapped in white tissue paper, to await her coming-out.

The pearl-and-diamond-festooned debut gown remained at the shop to have its bustle trimmed.

I returned home to find Freddy and Colm assembled in the library with a visitor.

"You remember Sheriff Dick Tolle, Hugo, don't you?" Freddy said, throwing me a frown and gesturing to the fellow. Large drooping nose, larger drooping mustache, painfully erect posture.

"I ain't a sheriff no more," Tolle said, crossing to shake my hand. "Turned out of office by a thieving Democrat."

"You repeat yourself there, 'thieving Democrat,'" I said. Colm, at least, laughed.

"I believe you've made Tolle your correspondent," Freddy said. I felt instantly on guard, more so than when I first walked in and discovered that the Virginia City lawman had journeyed across the country to show up at our door.

"Alerted by your telegram, which you saw fit not to share with me," Freddy said in a thin, forced voice that I recognized from childhood. When I had done something wrong.

"Oh, I didn't want to bother you," I said. "A minor matter, a query about a memorable incident of our western sojourn last summer."

"Yes," Freddy said, drawing out the word to indicate he remained unconvinced by my blithe manner. "At any rate, in connection with that 'memorable incident,' Tolle has an extraordinary tale to tell. I wonder if you'd mind repeating it, sir, for my son's sake and for my own, since I could hardly feature it upon first telling."

"What I came for," Tolle said, and he launched in. "I thought it a remarkable coincidence, Mr. Hugo, when I received your telegram about the Butler Fince affair, part of which you witnessed."

"The shooting in the club dining room," I said.

"Yes."

"At the time I considered it a confirmation that tales of the Wild West were actually true," I said.

"Thing was, I had been caught up in that very affair when your telegram arrived," Tolle said. "Fince had remained at large in Virginia since he shot Hank Monk, and he didn't stop there. He raged about, demanding justice for his dead brother."

"I wonder that he wasn't brought to court for murder," I said.

"There were political reasons for that," Freddy put in. "But go on, Tolle, tell us how the ravings of a lunatic ex-lawman might possibly concern our family."

"Fince was mad for revenge. His brother Peter—part of him anyway—had been found dead in his cabin out by American Flats, past Gold Hill."

"'Part of him'?" I asked.

"He'll get to that," Freddy said.

"Butler Fince spent his days drunk and accusatory, knocking heads with everybody in town, including myself, alleging a wide complicity in Peter's murder. I put him in jail a couple times to sober him up, but he'd go right back on the bottle and on the warpath as soon as I left him free."

Tolle paused to light up a western-style cheroot, puffing it awake until the stink of cheap tobacco filled the room.

"Finally, though, Fince run out of steam. He was leaving town, going back to Reno whence he come. I was thinking good riddance. There was enough trouble in Virginny without Butler Fince adding to it."

"But something happened," I said.

"Something happened to start him off again. He visited a certain barn in a certain peddler's alleyway off 'A' Street. His brother Peter had gone there often when the Savage Girl show was up."

"The domain of one Dr. Calef Scott," Freddy said.

Let him tell it, I thought.

"Oh, well, the man Scott had cleared off after he lost his prized exhibit," Tolle said. "His barn got took over by a stable, which is what it had been before the showman established his spectacle in it. Fince visits this barn, and he comes across a piece of 'evidence,' as he calls it, that lights him up and sets him off on his revenge tear all over again."

"What evidence was that?" I asked, thinking I might know the answer.

"Odd parallel slash marks, deep triple gashes left in the walls of the barn there, as if by some wild beast."

"Sound familiar, Hugo?" Freddy asked.

"Thing was," Tolle said, "Fince had seen identical markings in his brother's cabin, blood-soaked as it was, up in American Flats, which he visited over and over to try to glean the truth about the circumstances of the death."

"So he's set off again," I said.

"That's right," Tolle said. "Fince wants to know the reason for those odd-looking marks. We all told him that a cougar had kilt his brother to begin with, since there was animal signs around the cabin, and since those slash marks looked cougarlike, but he never could accept that explanation, and insisted upon human agency in the killing."

Tolle took a few fresh pulls on the cheroot. "Now that line of thinking got refreshed and reinvigorated in Fince's mind. He was shouting and carrying on. 'Who was it left those marks on the barn wall? How did they happen to be there, the same ones as in my brother's cabin?' "

"A certain set of hand claws," I said.

"He didn't have to go far to find out the truth of that matter," Tolle said. "So suddenly he's raging on the trail of Savage Girl."

I started to feel a little sick to my stomach then, as Tolle's story veered closer and closer to home.

"Butler Fince tracks down the mountain man Jake Woodworth," Tolle said. "Takes him at gunpoint on a little ride into the wilderness. Wants to find the exact cave where Woodworth found the Savage Girl."

"For pity's sake," I murmured.

"One thing about the brother Peter Fince, when we found him dead, the cabin looking like the inside of a slaughterhouse—"

"He was slashed at the leg, and his private parts were missing," I blurted out.

The action in the room stopped. They all looked at me a little strangely.

"That body was pretty much too destroyed to tell what was cut up and what weren't," Tolle said. "And I don't know about his private parts. But one thing for sure that was missing was Peter Fince's head."

I put my own head in my hands.

"Which Butler Fince found . . ." Freddy prompted.

"Which Butler Fince found in the cave where Woodworth had earlier discovered the Savage Girl," Tolle said. "The missing head was battered and rotted and chewed up, but Fince recognized the thing by his brother's blond hair, which he wore long and stringy."

I recalled what my professor had said during our dissection of the teratoma: *Human hair is nearly indestructible.*

"You all right, son?" Freddy asked. "You look a little green."

Tolle continued, clearly feeling the momentum of his tale. "Fince now thinks he knows for certain who killed his brother, this Savage

Girl of Dr. Scott's. He pursues his detective crusade, finding out that his brother was a regular at the Savage Girl show. Peter and Hank Monk had fistfights over her, which is what led to Butler Fince's killing of Monk even before he had the whole truth of the matter."

"You said animal depredations were present in the cabin?" I asked.

"I saw the signs myself," Tolle said. "Hairs, paw prints in blood, and them slash marks."

"So it's clear what happened," I said. "Peter Fince was murdered by persons unknown, or perhaps died at his own hand. His body, left to rot, was fed upon by scavenger beasts. The head was carried off to the cave by an animal—a coyote, perhaps, or a big cat."

"Hugo . . ." Freddy cautioned, shaking his head.

I couldn't stand it. The suspicions I had been harboring boiled over. "Because otherwise we are left with the idea that she had some involvement!"

"If you're talking about 'she' meaning the Savage Girl, that is certainly the conclusion reached by Butler Fince," Tolle said. "He spent many days making a pest of himself around the Comstock, asking the whereabouts of the creature displayed by Dr. Scott, she who murdered his dear brother, Peter Fince."

"It's too insane!" I cried.

"Insane or not, it's what the man Fince believes," Tolle said. "He had no shortage of informers to tell him just what became of Dr. Scott's prized exhibit, that she had been taken off by wealthy easterners by the name of Delegate."

"Couldn't you stop him?" I asked.

"Right in the middle of all this happening, along comes your telegram. And then fraud at the polls stripped me of my office. So I come out here to warn you."

"And I suppose you wish payment for this service?" Freddy said.

Tolle shook his head and rose to his feet, an offended look on his face. "I'm at the Cambridge Hotel, if you want me."

"You're selling a load of rubbish," Freddy said. "A human head batted around like a football! This Fince fellow is a madman. I wonder you credit anything he says."

"Freddy . . ." I said, but he would not be stopped, a barrage of words.

"There is no Savage Girl here, Mr. Tolle. I don't know why you approached us. If I judge your purpose to be financial gain, I tell you, sir, I'll have my fellow Colm here toss you out on the street."

"You probably don't want to be speaking to me like that, Delegate," Tolle said, glancing over at Colm. "The bad man Butler Fince is headed this way with blood in his eye. I thought you'd want to know. Now that I've done my duty, I'll bid you good-bye."

The three of us remained sitting in the library after Dick Tolle departed, leaving behind the bitter smell of his tobacco. That and numerous questions.

Colm thankfully remained mum. It fell to my father to disturb the silence.

"I don't believe it of her," Freddy said. "I'll never believe it of her." He smoked a cigar of his own, rather more complex in its aroma than the former sheriff's bargain cheroot.

"We took delivery of her wardrobe today," I said. "For her debut. She tried them on. She looked . . . angelic."

"The debut is going forward," Freddy said, rising from his chair. "Bronwyn will come out as planned—I don't care what this business portends. And I'm not going to trouble Anna Maria with any of it, nor the girl herself."

Clapping both Colm and me on the shoulders, he said, "Do you hear me, you two? Not a word to Bronwyn. She has enough to worry about."

Tossing his unfinished cigar into the fireplace, he turned to leave. "I think I'll take dinner in my rooms tonight."

"Colm and I have an engagement," I said.

Freddy halted at the door to the library. "This blackguard Butler Fince," he said. "I saw him kill one man in cold blood. Perhaps, Colm, you could recruit a few of your police friends, ask them if they'd like to make extra income working for us in the off hours, providing security."

He walked out. Colm and I remained in armchairs by the hearth, staring into the fire.

We were not alone but rather were haunted by ghostly presences, joined there in the library by the victims of a string of murders. The waiter at the Palmer House. The Gypsy dancer in the Central Park. Now a wildcat miner in Virginia City. Where, oddly enough, I had also been present, as I had been for the other two.

In pursuing evidence of Bronwyn's involvement, I thought at the same time to conceal from Colm my own self-suspicion. I who was at hand for each incident, I who was unstable of mind, I who was . . . what, a raving maniac?

A series of three mutilation murders in the space of eight months. How many would the country average in an ordinary year? I would have to put the question to Professor James. Boston Corbett, the soldier who shot the assassin John Wilkes Booth in the burning tobacco barn back in '65, I knew to be an odd-duck preacher who had castrated himself and thrown the offending organ into a fireplace. So perhaps it wasn't that unusual.

And Colm, I realized, Colm, too, had been at the scene of every murder. At least in the same general vicinity. I looked over at the stolid soul sitting next to me. "One may smile, and smile, and be a villain," said Hamlet. Although, truth be told, Colm didn't smile that much. He was more all-business.

After a long stretch of silence, I said, "I propose we continue our previous supposition. That the girl is innocent of any wrongdoing."

"And meanwhile carry on with our investigations," Colm said. "How long do we have before this debut shindig of hers happens?"

I counted up the days in my head. "Six weeks," I said.

"It probably wouldn't hurt to hire a few more hands," Colm said. "I know this man Fince by reputation. I don't care if he ever was a sheriff. There's a thin line between the law and the outlaw in the West, and I know for a fact he crossed it several times. Once he hung all the Negroes in Rockertoe, Utah, for the fault of a single one."

I wasn't thinking about Butler Fince. I was brooding about Bronwyn.

"I could hit the bricks, track the man Fince down, break his neck for him," Colm said. "He's a loudmouth, and if he's here in New York, he shouldn't be too hard to find."

"I want you to stick close to her," I said. "Whenever she goes out, wherever she is, I want you nearby. I'll tell Anna Maria that Bronwyn has a new chaperone."

"What about you?" Colm asked.

"I'll be all right," I said.

Colm favored his LeMat, so I was a little surprised when he took an entirely different handgun from his pocket, a nickel-plated Colt revolver with a stubby two-inch barrel. He handed it to me. The compact piece fit easily in my grip.

"It's a .38," he said. "It'll stop anything coming at you. Called the Sheriff's Model, but bloody desperadoes have been known to carry one. Folks nicknamed that gun 'The Last Word.'"

"I'll try to measure up to its reputation," I said, pocketing the pistol.

✣ 20 ✣

In railroading there was such a thing as twinned tracks, rails that went parallel before they diverged, trains running along on both as if unaware of their ultimate fate, upon which track they would eventually be switched.

That winter I experienced the double life of the Delegate household, one caught up in a frenzy of organizing for Bronwyn's debut, while Colm and I pursued an altogether different purpose, one with darker overtones.

Freddy prepared the way for his triumph with Bronwyn, participating in the debate against Arvald Stockton regarding nature versus nurture. The venue had been set, at the Union, the city's most exclusive men's club. I was surprised at the flurry the occasion set off in the popular press, fanned, no doubt, by Stockton's newspaper connections.

"'Resolved,'" Freddy said, quoting the proposition, "'that nature and heredity dominate nurture and environment in determining human character.' Mr. Stockton speaks in favor, I in opposition. Thirty minutes each for argument, fifteen for rebuttal, five for summation. Audience declares the winner by acclamation. I plan to carry the day."

We sat with Anna Maria and Nicky, just the four blood Delegates for once, not in the aviary but in a second-floor drawing room.

"I would make hay with the words 'dominate' and 'determining,' as inexact and fraught with misinterpretation," I said.

"Niggling pettifoggery," Freddy said. "I'll do nothing of sort. I will simply inform them that I can take any human creature, no matter how feral, from the wild, and with enough care and education I will give them a fully formed, fully moral, fully proper human being."

"You know, I wonder at that 'fully moral' business," I said. "Don't you think Bronwyn might have a little problem with—I don't know how to say it—the biblical virtue of chastity?"

"You beastly boy," Anna Maria said, rapping her knuckles on a side table for emphasis. "Don't speak like that about your sister. Of course we had her examined by Dr. Bulton. She is intact. She is in fact as virginal as Blake's 'pale virgin shrouded in snow.' Which is a whole lot more virginal than you, I might suggest."

"You can't modify 'virginal,'" Nicky put in. "No one can be 'more virginal' than someone else. Either you are or you are not."

"I can't believe I am discussing this at all, much less with a thirteen-year-old present," Anna Maria said.

"I am more 'the youth pined away with desire,'" I said.

"Once fallen, forever lost," said Nicky.

"Oh, do be quiet, Nicholas," Anna Maria said, fussing. "I won't have a word said against her virtue."

I had to leave the whole thing there.

Later in the week, the blue-blooded Union Club members being firmly in the "nature" camp, Freddy lost the debate.

It turned out that Richardson's was only the beginning. As the month progressed, a steady parade of delivery boys came through The Citadel's servant entrance, their arms piled high with hatboxes, brown-paper-wrapped parcels, oblong white cardboard cartons with articles of clothing nested in tissue paper.

"We can hardly blame her for not knowing a thing about money," Anna Maria said graciously as the stream of packages turned into a flood. "She goes out to the shops, they show her their wares, she says yes. She's always saying yes. And that Willets boy. He's even worse."

Its provenance was a mystery, but an article appeared in the World that allowed Bronwyn her first brief taste of celebrity. It was, in the way of newspaper stories, something of a fabrication, which did not prevent it from becoming accepted as gospel truth by numberless readers. The real problem, the phrase that set off a scramble of enthusiasm and notoriety, was the headline THE MILLION-DOLLAR WARDROBE.

"I don't think so," Freddy said dubiously upon being confronted by the piece. "The bills are still coming in. I suppose it's possible. More like half that, I would think."

But the damage had been done. The newspaper reported that Bronwyn's jewel-encrusted debut gown, not yet seen but eagerly anticipated by the public, represented a fifty-thousand-dollar creation. It quoted Hampton Lowell, the self-crowned king of the fashion commentators, as saying that while money wasn't the key to taste, it could hire a damned good locksmith.

And then the picture accompanying the article. An engraving, actually, of a photograph commissioned by Monsieur Richardson. Bronwyn in a slim-profiled dress, looking back over her left shoulder, a parasol propped on her right. She had a heartbreaking, shrouded-in-snow look, very much caught in the moment. Nicky bade Richardson to furnish him with the original photograph upon which the *World*'s portrait was based. He kept it bedside.

My sister's favorite color for her frocks, according to the *World*, was the deepest green, straying past forest to verge upon black, a dark emerald named Delegate green in her honor that season, for the simple reason that she spent so much in the stores.

"Pray bring me the feather of a peacock," the ludicrous article portrayed a very un-Bronwyn-ish Bronwyn as saying to a couturier. Pointing to the shimmering green of the plumage, she was said to have proclaimed, "This is the color I must have!"

A week after the *World* report appeared, Fifth Avenue saw itself flocked by green-hued outfits, ladies abroad resembling so many just-settled iridescent night moths.

The Million-Dollar Wardrobe. The man in the street pronounced himself appalled. In a city where three-quarters of the population lived on less than a dollar a day! Man in the Street dearly wished the press would tell him more about this absurd extravagance, a lot more, in order that he might base his outrage upon a firm grounding of facts.

I have often noticed that journalists are like sheep. Where one goes, others must baa-baa after. The *Sun,* the *Herald,* even the *New-York Tribune* followed with stories of their own. Miss Bronwyn Delegate, the new sensation. Step right up.

When I returned, later that month, to the balcony gallery at Madame Eugénie's academy, I noticed a subtle shift in the dynamics of the dance floor. Bronwyn had established herself as a power with which to be reckoned. Given her popularity among the boys, the girls grudgingly submitted to her dominance. You could see it in how the groupings formed, moons around a sun, and in the sidelong glances everyone gave to her, as though checking upon the mood of a duchess.

From my post amid the potted palms of the balcony, I pretended omniscience, a god lazily monitoring the follies of mere mortals down below, the splitting-ups and coming-togethers, the pairings, the alliances of convenience and those of passion. Only a few years previous, I had gone through the same labored, youthful upheavals. They had seemed to me important then. Now, happening to someone else, they appeared trivial.

Bev Willets was thankfully absent that afternoon. I thought of him immediately, though, when I saw Delia Showalter enter the hall and move along the border of the dance floor. Bev and Delia had, predictably, taken up with each other. My jealousy was such that I could still feel enraged by this, even though I had officially ended my engagement to the lady in question.

Delia looked ill, a fact that embedded a shaft of guilt into my conscience. I had seen girls used and discarded by Bev Willets before. Like a clean white linen napkin crumpled and wine-stained after a dinner party. I wondered if it had already happened.

My former love moved like a ghost amid the dancing students. I watched Edna Croker break off from her practiced steps and cross to her. The two fell into an intense tête-à-tête. Edna returned to the floor and retrieved Bronwyn, then in the midst of a mazurka with a spotty-faced youth.

Monsieur Henri, dismayed at the disruption to the class, clapped his hands imperiously. The girls ignored him. Taking Bronwyn's hand, Edna guided her over to Delia. The three of them took up the furious, whispering conversation that the first two had begun.

I watched it play out in dumb show. Uncomfortable as I was with these particular girls becoming familiar with each other, speculating on what rumors might pass between them—my former intimate, Delia, pouring dark thoughts of me into Bronwyn's ear—I somehow felt that gossip might be the least of the perils involved. The little trio looked to be seriously plotting, contemplating the overthrow of the government, maybe, or arranging for the demise of Monsieur Henri.

When Bronwyn's debut mania became too much for me, I simply switched to the other Delegate track. Toward the end of January, Colm and I consumed some Zuni cactus buttons with the berdache and went out to Coney Island after a murder.

It was time for me to return to Harvard. But a family consensus developed that I should not go back to school. I continued to display a mental rockiness (something that Tahktoo said would be soothed by the ingestion of peyote). Plus, my parents relied on me to help with Bronwyn.

Colm told me that the body we were after had washed up at Coney Island in early January. Why he had picked this one, out of all the deaths in New York, he didn't reveal.

"A hunch," he said, but I knew that could be code for inside information from the Manhattan district attorney's office. Colm had used his connections to search for mutilation murders in the city, all while we both still maintained that it was absurd to think Bronwyn had anything to do with them.

Coney Island, so well peopled in good weather, hibernated in the winter. I thought back over our recent New Year's holiday there, Bronwyn on the seashore. It was even more barren now. The winds blew in slantwise from the Atlantic, pitching up sand, giving the whole scene the feel of a freezing wasteland.

Colm, Tahktoo and I took to the beach through Norton's Point, which was probably a mistake, given that it was the most degraded few blocks in the whole of Brooklyn.

Bedraggled denizens roamed the streets, looking hungry and cold. Under the effects of the cactus buttons I had ingested, I perceived them in weird guises, alternately piggish, bearish and, finally, dolphinish. I had the uncomfortable idea that every person I encountered knew all about me. The dwarflike children on the corners played not with toys but with rocks and bits of bark.

"My teeth feel funny," Colm said. He grinned painfully. The peyote gradually loosened its grip. The berdache (who walked within a pulsing halo of silver light) had said the cactus buttons might make me feel better, but in fact I felt worse.

We finally staggered out of the decrepit neighborhood and headed onto the empty sands, where the sunlight was hammered into a flat sheet of gray. The berdache strayed to the surf, leaving Colm and me to ourselves.

"You were here when?" Colm asked.

A month back. Christmas week.

"And at night . . ." Colm said. "Was she ever alone?"

"She had her own room. We were in separate wings, actually, Nicky and I in one and she and my mother in another."

I paused to remember an incident that I had failed to confess to Colm.

Restless after dinner, I had ventured out to the storm-lashed beach. My mental state oscillated between nervous exhilaration and nervous exhaustion. After struggling against the wind, I huddled in the lee of a stone breakwater, a small refuge invisible to the nearby stretch of sand.

A woman had gone by me where I hid. Her hair showed black against the black sky, and her dress lifted in the wind. She seemed magically unaffected by the howling gale and walked past as if floating. I had been thinking intently of Bronwyn and wondered if here appeared the incarnation of my thoughts.

"Bronwyn," I had called out, but the gale swallowed my words as if they never were spoken.

The wind blew, the woman vanished, the wind blew some more, she reappeared once again. I can't explain the desolation I felt, the horror of this solitary figure on the darkling beach.

But she was gone, only a vision, taken away by the storm, blown wildly above the white-capped waves and wheeling into the black clouds over the ocean.

The next morning I had crept into Bronwyn's quarters while the family sat downstairs at breakfast. Next to her bed, a heap of wet, sandy garments.

Should I now tell Colm Cullen about all this? What would I say? A ghost flown off like a succubus in a tempest, plus some beach clothes discarded at our girl's bedside? What was that? That was nothing.

I remained silent. We trekked to nearby Gravesend, Colm, Tahktoo and I, where we located a police station among the storm-brutalized buildings of the beach town.

We queried. Yes, there had been a recent death.

A corpse had been dragged up out of the ocean in tatters, gnawed at all different angles by all different beasts—crabs and sharks and fishes. He was the Human Polar Bear, a big brute who made a living diving into icy waters and hoping passersby would toss him two bits. The police we spoke to all thought it was odd and, in the way of gallows humor, funny.

The Gravesend sergeant said, "Middle of the holidays, cold as a witch's tit, only a few people on the beach, this brazen hero who swims so good drowns."

Bronwyn and I had in fact met the victim when we'd walked the same beach back in December. Bronwyn told him he didn't have to swim, it was too cold; she gave him a dollar anyway. He immediately dove in, coming out streaming, the water icing on his skin.

Dick Pollard, the Human Polar Bear. His corpse long gone now, collected from the coroner by a tubercular wife, mother of his brood. "Him the family's only earner, and them with six under the age of ten," the sergeant said.

"Can you tell us where Pollard lived?" I asked.

"Norton's Point," said the sergeant. "You don't want to go there."

"We have just come from there," Tahktoo said. The sergeant looked at him oddly. People were always looking at Tahktoo oddly. For the berdache the customary human expression must be one of puzzlement.

"Look here, I'm from the Harvard Medical School," I said to the sergeant. "I'm studying wounds in a criminal context, and I wonder if you have a postmortem on the body."

"You're wasting your time," he said. "Officially, the Human Polar Bear drowned."

"Unofficially?" Colm said, slipping a folded sawbuck across to him. The Gravesend sergeant pawed his desktop, came up with a document and handed it to me.

The Brooklyn coroner's office had miraculously produced a full autopsy report, labeled "Death Narrative." Among other details, "deep incision to the femoral artery," with the hand-scrawled notation, *"mort."* Meaning fatal. But the coroner had ruled for drowning, since the lungs were full of seawater.

"I've seen corpses bumped on the breakers here, battered around pretty good, seawater gets beaten into them before they're finally fished out," the Gravesend sergeant said. "Doesn't matter they're dead before they went into the drink. Coroner's finding is always drowned."

While I had murder on my mind, Anna Maria and Bronwyn conducted the arduous social preparations of the debutante.

Calling and returning calls represented a chief occupation. Acting as Anna Maria's social secretary, Tu-Li had spent much time this season in Anna Maria's North Wing drawing room, plotting the social strategy of my mother and Bronwyn. She calculated that there were one hundred twenty homes at which they had to pay calls.

To accomplish them all before Bronwyn's debut in late February required an exercise of military precision, a quick march of three visits a day (excepting Saturday, the day for shopping the Ladies' Mile, and Sunday, for the late service at Grace Church).

Coming back with Colm from Gravesend, I was present at one such call, a triumph of Anna Maria's life at that time, since it virtually secured the success of Bronwyn's coming-out.

My mother skillfully employed Swoony's status as a society power, knowing all and being known to all, in order to receive a call from the Tremont aunts, Fabby and Gladys, perhaps the ultimate social arbiters of our day (Caroline Hood notwithstanding). For Bronwyn to be introduced to the Tremonts, and for them to accept her introduction, was an imprimatur of the highest order.

A wicker basket sat on a credenza in the front stairhall, holding the cards deposited by the society ladies and their daughters awaiting their debuts. These cards displayed a remarkable uniformity, as did the ladies' dress and their decorum. Each card was no more than two and seven-eighths of an inch long, each bore the lady's name and, written in script in the upper left-hand corner, the name of the debutante daughter, granddaughter or niece.

The Tremonts came to The Citadel, they saw, and Bronwyn conquered. The aunts brought their own debutante to show off, a great-niece, Gertrude, a girl with uneven skin and bouncing brown curls. Bronwyn knew her from Madame Eugénie's.

"Darling," said Swoony, kissing Fabby Tremont on the cheek. Darlings all around from Swoony to Gladys, Gladys to Swoony, Fabby and Gladys to Anna Maria. I stayed out of the line of fire, introduced but ignored.

"My nephew's daughter, Gertrude Debry," said Fabby Tremont, pushing forward her prize. The Tremonts both wore royal blue gowns and matching beribboned hats in a style that had gone out with the war. Their grandniece seemed a smaller imitation of them, in a lighter shade of blue and similar matching hat.

"Please do come in for a cup," said my mother.

"Gertrude, remove your mantle," said Aunt Gladys. "No one will do it for you."

Gertrude looked about for a servant. Ours had vanished in the direction of the tea service, and Colm was the only man left standing. When he stepped forward into the center of the drawing room, all six foot three of him, dressed not in livery but in a dark suit with a pistol bulge at the hip, she looked to faint.

Gladys Tremont stared him up and down before handing off her own wrap.

"I believe you know my godchild, Edna Croker," Fabby said to Bronwyn. "She calls you courteous and warm."

"Thank you," Bronwyn said, performing an artful curtsy. "Her I love, and you are very kind."

Fabby Tremont's massive sculptural head nodded slowly up and down, and Bronwyn was made.

"We are parched," Gladys Tremont said in the direction of my mother, as Randall and Douglas came in to serve. "We come from calls at half a dozen houses, and no one was at home."

"All out on calls themselves," Swoony said.

Anna Maria gestured to the tea service. "The silver came from our mines in the Comstock," she said airily. "We had it fabricated in London."

Aunt Fabby looked dubiously into the bone china cup with which she had been presented. "If this is tea, bring me coffee," she said. "If this is coffee, bring me tea." A shopworn Lincoln witticism, dated now like everything else about the Tremonts. But we Delegates were known for our weak tea.

Bronwyn wore the "artist's gown" she had purchased at Richardson's and slippers without heels. She looked positively Pre-Raphaelite. The niece Gertrude, as a rival debutante, stared at the dress as though she would tear it to shreds.

"I admire your hat," said Bronwyn, a creation that young Gertrude had poised like a pillow atop her skull.

"Stewart's," said Gertrude, touching its brim. "The milliner called it champignon style."

"Yes!" Bronwyn bubbled with laughter. "A mushroom!"

From across the room, the drone male brother (myself) had to laugh with her. Proud of her also for the French. Finally Gertrude laughed, too.

And that was that, that was enough. Peace between the young ladies at least.

Nicky thrust his head in the doorway closest to me. "You know how old I'll be in 1930?" he demanded loudly. "I'll be sixty-eight years old. Sixty-eight!"

He was shooed away. Swoony held up her cup for replenishment and beckoned to Colm, whom she had entrusted with the brandy.

Tomorrow, in the *Herald* perhaps, or the *Sun,* or (knowing Anna Maria's energy at such matters) both, notice of the afternoon tea would appear, Madam and Mademoiselle Delegate hosting Mesdames Tremont. Orders for artist's gowns worn without corsets would emanate from numerous households.

And Bronwyn Delegate's debut, in the eyes of Those Who Matter, would be granted legitimacy, her coming-out ball marked upon the calendar as Not to Be Missed.

✿ 21 ✿

Lorenzo Delmonico had recently opened another restaurant to save us all from having to traipse down to the old place on unfashionable William Street.

The new venue took up the length of Twenty-sixth Street between Fifth Avenue and Broadway, looking out over the wintry flower beds and callow, shivering trees of Madison Square Park. This season it also overlooked the copper arm and torch of Liberty, the gargantuan allegoric statue (*La Liberté éclairant le monde,* or *Liberty Enlightening the World*) that organizers were trying to install on an island in New York Harbor.

They had not yet the money subscribed for the full sculpture so put this small part of it on tour to raise funds. There it stood in all its unlikely glory in one corner of the park. A metal flame poured out the top of the torch, and sightseers were welcome to climb a cat ladder up fifty feet to take in the view from the top of the marvel.

Inside our private dining room at the new Delmonico's, all was lively and lovely. Mirrors lined each wall, and silver chandeliers hung from the frescoed ceiling, beside golden sconces, swags of shot silk and fringed shades pulled down halfway. An urn of lilies and roses stood atop a column to one side of the room. And there, out the window, Liberty's torch burned under a splash of moonlight.

I could see Colm outside, pacing the walk, scanning the landscape, ever on the alert for our bogeyman from Virginia City, Butler Fince.

We made a strange crew that evening, assembled in honor of my Harvard anatomy professor. William James was in town to squire his sister, Alice, a dark-eyed chronic invalid in her mid-twenties, to a series of medical treatments, including something called a "blistering bath."

James invited a pair of notorious women, Victoria Woodhull, the spiritualist and sometime presidential candidate (on the Equal Rights Party ticket), and Woodhull's sister, Tennessee Claflin. The two of them were up to all sorts of shenanigans—a radical newspaper, scandalous "free love" advocacy, a Wall Street brokerage firm underwritten by Cornelius Vanderbilt.

The sisters arrived in black waistcoats and jackets and long black crepe skirts, but they behaved as charmingly as any high-society ladies. Alone, without men, as was their wont. Victoria's husband, Colonel James Blood, was busy dying in the gold fields of West Africa, the same miasmic precincts that took the life of my ill-starred uncle, Sonny Delegate.

I brought Bronwyn.

I wanted to expose her to the kind of intellectual soiree that she might encounter as she made her entry into New York society. Coming out was really a series of small, aggregate debuts—at an afternoon tea, at the dance academy, at a call to a great lady's home, at the final culminating ball. And at intimate gatherings such as this.

When I heard that Professor James would be in town, I told Bronwyn I wanted to take her out to a real Manhattan dinner party.

"I read about one of those in the *Herald*," she said. "Mrs. Hunter Beaumont from Dallas and P. T. Barnum, the showman."

"It's different when there's real people," I said.

"At Delmonico's," she said. "The new one on Madison Square." She already knew everything.

"You remember we went to the traveling circus in the Hippodrome at Coney Island? The lady tightrope walker?"

"The one who carried an umbrella and did somersaults on the wire," Bronwyn recalled.

"Right," I said. "Your performance at the dinner party will be similar to hers."

"I can do that," she said, laughing.

Even now there were times when she was like the old Bronwyn, my friend of the transcontinental trip. We could still be easy with each other. Tahktoo's trademark phrase, "Come up, you fool," had become a well-used joke between us, invoked in casual, quite silly ways, when we climbed stairs together, say, or when I stepped on her toe as we practiced dance steps.

All the different roles she played in my life . . . Her laughter might make me happy that night in Delmonico's, but I thought back to how miserable I was, how beset and confused, lost beside the bloody Lake in the park or crouched that night on the beach in Brooklyn. She was tearing me apart, yet I could sit next to her at a restaurant table and appear perfectly normal.

To make Bronwyn more comfortable, I brought along Tu-Li and the berdache. Tahktoo caused a stir when he sat down at the table (dressed impeccably in white tie) and Tennessee Claflin recognized him from his appearances at The Point.

"Gentlemen and ladies, we are in the presence of Zuni royalty," Tennessee announced sententiously, actually rising from her seat and bowing to Tahktoo, who took the attention in stride. I had presented him (her?) with a diamond brooch for Christmas, and it gleamed at his throat, providing a feminine counterpoint to his otherwise male garb.

Bronwyn's friend Edna Croker met us at the restaurant. She had removed her eyeglasses, by which simple act rendering herself much prettier. For a chaperone she brought along her cousin, the strapping footballer Percy Roehm. Aware of Bronwyn's taste for hulking men, I seated them as far away from each other as was possible.

The radical sisters, Percy and I all drank the Moët Imperial Brut. James abstained, as he never took alcohol. His sister, Alice, looked as though a glass of champagne might cause her to expire. The others in the party sipped chocolate out of demitasse cups, excepting the berdache, who nursed a succession of absinthes throughout the evening.

We began the feast with East River oysters, eight dozen for the table. Edna did not partake, but the rest of us, Bronwyn included, tossed back our heads and slid the oysters down our throats, one after the other. We went on to the menu I had ordered in advance, the terrapène à la Maryland, the canards à tête rouge, the artichokes for which the restaurant was famous, the turbot and the grouse, with petits pois, fleurette. And the steak Delmonico, of course.

James held his sister's hand under the table. "Sweetlington," he called Alice, cooing like a schoolboy. She addressed him as "Willy."

"I like the drapes," the berdache said to Alice James, who winced out a smile.

Tu-Li attacked her artichoke. "You place them between your teeth?" she asked Tennessee Claflin.

"Like so," said the woman universally known to the press by the punning tag of "Tennie C."

The conversation, and the inebriation, became general.

"That nefarious project you mentioned," James said to me. "The domestication of a wild child."

"Oh, that," I said. "That never came off."

"I'm very glad of it," James said. "You have better things ahead of you."

I looked across at Bronwyn, certainly the most striking young woman in the room, displaying what I considered a faultless grace and civility, even while quaffing oysters.

"Your sister," James said, following my gaze. "Very fine, very self-possessed, with some ineffable quality . . ."

Words failed him. "Duende," I said.

"That's it exactly!" James cried. "How astonishing that you mention this concept, as I have just been thinking of it."

He looked over at Bronwyn again. "Duende."

James told me he had recently taken on an Irish setter pup, Dido. "I don't know why a dog should bring out the human in one, but it's true," he said. "I find myself wanting to return to Cambridge for no greater reason than to see the creature."

I said, "How goes the phrase? 'Plus je vois les hommes, plus j'admire mon chien.'"

I saw Bronwyn across the table trying to puzzle out the French. The more I see of men, the more I like my dog. When she had it, she smiled and mentioned to Edna that she preferred cats.

"'What's time?'" James asked, quoting a poem by Robert Browning. "'Leave Now for dogs and apes! / Man has forever!'" To read these lines always strengthened his backbone, he said.

"Miss Delegate," said Percy, actually moving his chair around the table to pull up next to Bronwyn. "May I ask whence your Christian name derives? I've never encountered it before."

"I suppose my parents gave it to me because they hadn't any other," said Bronwyn.

"Rather," Percy said, apropos of nothing. "The name sounds magical. Out of a fairy tale."

"Oh, my," Edna said.

That evening Bronwyn wore a nutmeg-colored ensemble with long sleeves and a modest skirt, lending her more of a schoolgirl appearance than I would have wished, given the elegance of the evening.

"Bronwyn," said Percy, pronouncing it with savor. I wanted to strangle the wretch. Making love to her like a ham.

"But you do possess magic?" asked Percy. "You must."

"Only the most ordinary kind," Bronwyn said.

"She has every kind of magic," said Edna.

After the main courses, brandy. James addressed Woodhull, who lit a cigarette in a tortoiseshell holder. "Alice has asthma, Mrs. Woodhull. If you extinguish that tobacco, I promise to vote for you in the next general election."

Woodhull complied. This evening was the first I had gotten an up-close look at the infamous suffragist rabble-rouser. She had talked a straight streak since we sat down and now, with the alcohol empowering her, trained her considerable analytic powers upon the young women at the table.

"Look at these two, ready to debut this month, and they stuff their heads with dance steps and embroidery patterns and popular musical airs. Nothing useful, nothing vital." She called across the table. "You, Miss Croker, tell us your philosophy of life."

"Oh, my," said Edna. That being pretty much the sum of her conversation all evening.

"Female education must be revolutionized," Woodhull said.

"Oh, my," Edna said.

"Do not keep saying that," Woodhull commanded sharply.

"May I take a thought from Plato?" Edna suddenly said. "'Be kind, for everyone you meet carries a heavy burden.' That's my philosophy of life."

The sentiment, pronounced with such pretty diffidence, managed to silence the sophisticates at the table for a quick beat.

"Plato said nothing of the sort, Miss Croker," James said gently.

Woodhull: "And you, Miss Delegate?"

"I'm afraid I am still arriving at my philosophy," Bronwyn said.

"Regale us with the process," Woodhull said.

"Something about balance, I would think."

"Balance," Woodhull said.

"When I look deeply into nature, I see balance as an ideal," Bronwyn said.

"Emerson?" James asked.

"Bronwyn Delegate," Bronwyn said, and we all laughed.

James said, "And you might apply this insight how?"

"Politically."

"Politically?" Woodhull hooted. "Very good, Miss Delegate!"

"From my reading of history—" Bronwyn said, and I couldn't help myself but burst out with a laugh.

She froze me with a glare and began again. "From my reading of history, human beings will always cozy up to the rich and powerful. They justify their actions with oratory and great flights of words, but the truth of it is transparent. Groveling before the top dogs is a natural, understandable impulse. I can't blame anyone who indulges in it."

"I can," Woodhull said. "I can blame them."

"But to balance this natural inclination of fearful bowing to wealth and power, I propose we must favor the poor and weak whenever we can. Not because one course of action is wrong and one is right but simply for the sake of equilibrium, that the toady population not outnumber us all. For the weak, against the strong. That is my philosophy in a nutshell."

Woodhull, quite under the influence, leaped to her feet, knocking over her chair, and applauded.

"Very apt, Miss Delegate," Tennessee said. "We believe that the suffering of women is the suffering of all humanity. You must allow us to send you *The Communist Manifesto,* by Marx and Engels, which we publish in this country exclusively."

"Because all other damned publishers are afraid of it!" Woodhull exclaimed, sitting down and nearly missing her chair.

"Why don't you go ahead and have some more wine," James said to her in a nicely acerbic tone.

As dinner's sequel, glaces fantaisies and chilled d'Yquem. Our happy company slowly broke up, Professor James and Alice remaining behind at table, the rest of us drifting into the frosty February night. Percy, I noticed, still mooned around Bronwyn. The berdache had convinced Lorenzo Delmonico to let him take along one of the dining-room valances and wore it as a cloak.

South of us loomed the elegant Fifth Avenue Hotel, in the ball-room of which, in a week's time, Bronwyn would accomplish her formal coming-out.

She would debut with girls from five other families. Other debutante balls at other venues, scattered over the weeks of late winter, brought out other groups of debutantes, but our Fifth Avenue soiree would easily be the grandest and gaudiest, the most heralded, the one that crowned the season.

We took a turn around the square, Edna Croker on my arm, Bronwyn with Percy, Tu-Li and the berdache coming along behind. I seethed at the big lout's flirtation with my sister.

As we arrived back at our carriages, Percy bade his "magical Bronwyn" good night, having the effrontery to kiss her hand.

I crossed Fifth to where Colm stood at the edge of the Madison Square Park. He peered into the darkness toward the immense copper rendering of Liberty's upturned hand.

"Up on the catwalk," Colm said. "Do you see him?"

A far-off figure, raffish, square-hatted, in black outline only, leaned on the railing around the gigantic sculpted flame and seemed to be gazing at us as we gazed at him.

"Butler Fince?" I asked, and Colm shrugged.

The figure had disappeared by the time we threaded our way through the bare trees of the park to stand beside Liberty's torch.

☙ 22 ❧

"Hugo," Bronwyn said, silently mouthing the words. "I need you."

Come up, you fool.

She stood atop the balcony of the Fifth Avenue Hotel ballroom. Two curving staircases of white marble swept downward to the dance floor. I ran up one, and Bronwyn tried to bring me along into the ladies' parlor, where no escort was meant to venture on this night of nights.

It didn't matter, since I found I could not wedge myself through the door, there were so many bell-shaped belles inside, their skirts of gauze and tulle fanned out, occupying the whole of the small powder room that the hotel had set aside for the evening's debutantes.

"I need my mirror," Bronwyn whispered, my way to her blocked by several egregious bustles. She had asked me to carry her hand mirror, as it would not fit in her evening bag. I gave it over and returned back downstairs into the ballroom.

"How is she?" Anna Maria asked.

"Fine," I said. "Cool as a cucumber."

"You really should not have gone up there," Anna Maria said.

Midnight on the leap-year evening of February 29, 1876. Bronwyn's debut. Everything we had been working for found its culmination in this ballroom on this night, all of us—my parents and myself, Swoony our secret old-guard weapon, Tu-Li and the berdache, Bev Willets acting as Beau Brummel for the endeavor, Colm lending muscle—and Bronwyn, Bronwyn the Savage Girl, Bronwyn most of all.

I had been to these affairs before. The glitter took one over until the whole business entered into an exalted reality. It may have been frivolous in the grand scheme of things, but you could never tell that by us while we were swept up in it. Life, cruel, degraded, ordinary human existence, sets itself apart for a brief moment and becomes suddenly and unexpectedly ravishing.

On the adjoining sidewalks, the hordes. All of New York, those not on the inside, were outside with their noses pressed up against the windows of the Fifth Avenue Hotel, their curiosity inflamed by the newspapers. What gown? Which jewels? Who was the heiress, the ingenue, the debutante of the moment? Who waltzed with whom?

The process of coming out in Manhattan was as tightly scripted as any religious ritual. By Lent the whole crop of that year's young women would be presented to society—for harvest, to complete the rather awkward metaphor. The dozen or so debutante balls each gathered together hundreds of swells to review the maidens and grant their tacit approval. The occasion was also for dancing, drinking and making merry.

But it served a serious purpose. The women—the mothers, the grandmothers, the aunts—sponsored and introduced their prospects. The whole coming-out process, offering up younger members of the tribe as potential mates and breeders, thus exercised and displayed matriarchal power in society.

It all made me glad that there was no concomitant ceremony for young men.

The male role at a female debut was in fact limited. Observer, meet the observed. Dance with her (but only once), admire her (from afar), allow her to excite your enthusiasm for possessing her. Within the year, or at the very outside within two or three, all of the sixty or so mesdemoiselles of the season should become mesdames. If not, they would be taken out into a field and killed.

Well, not really. But you get the idea.

At our Fifth Avenue Hotel ball that evening, a half dozen debutantes readied themselves to descend into the bon ton assembly. I stood below with Bev. All around the room were ranged stiff white gentlemen in stiff white shirtfronts and mature women in jewel-toned gowns. Almost every member of the Circle was there—though Delia, I noticed, was conspicuously absent.

Swoony, Fabby Tremont and other society grandes dames, including the well-powdered Caroline Hood, took their places on the pol-
ished floor and turned their faces up to the balcony.

Draped in maroon taffeta, bustle and train elongating her small
figure to drastic proportions, Swoony already fastened onto her teacup as though we had prematurely arrived at the dessert course. She
appeared positively thrilled to be present for the coming-out.

By means of pale silver reflectors, the lighting of gas lamps and
candles had been fixed to evoke moonlight. On the round supper tables that ringed the floor, crystal and bone china gleamed on crisp,
snowy linen, a bevy of gilt-wrapped favors beside each place setting.

Also on display, a profusion of monstrously expensive hothouse
flowers. Garlands mounded in great tumbling masses, hundreds upon
hundreds—lilies of the valley, gardenias, carnations, glads.

Freddy stepped up beside me, tears shining in his eyes, the old
softy. We had pulled it off. Finally my father was proud of me and I of
him. We embraced manfully.

A cornet sounded. The evening's debutantes began to make their
way down the crimson-carpeted steps, each one holding her train
over her arm, each one dazzling in white. Edna Croker, Bronwyn's
great friend from dance class. Gertrude Debry, the Tremont niece.
Sally Gildings and Emma Vanstyle and Georgina Worrell.

They descended carefully, slowly, one brittle doll after another
finding her place beside her mother, aunt or grandmother, whichever
woman had been charged to usher her from one stratum of society to
the next.

Bronwyn halted at the landing for a moment. A small shiver ran
through the assembly. It was the dress, its jeweled bodice catching the
light of the gas jets and throwing it back into our eyes. She shimmered,
all creamy silk and creamy skin, her satin-gloved hand resting lightly
on the white marble of the balcony. Her eyes blazed dark, and her lips
must have been painted, because they were red, much deeper than
their natural color, which effect only rendered her skin paler and more
ethereal.

A delicate, sparkling tiara encircled her forehead. Perhaps the gasp from the assembly came in reaction not to the dress but to Bronwyn's coiffure. Unlike the other debutantes, with their tightly fixed tresses and artificial curls, Bronwyn had allowed her locks to flow freely.

No one had ever seen anything like it, not at a coming-out ball—daring, shocking, a little unreal. Her black mane fell in soft waves halfway down her back, like some kind of mystical mermaid. Tu-Li had put it up earlier, but the deb herself wanted it down.

"Bronwyn Delegate," I heard someone behind me murmur. "Bronwyn." "Who is she?" "Good God! Can they do that now?" "The Delegate ward."

She began her procession down the steps, slowly, as though she were gliding within a silken bubble, looking out over the cavernous room all the while.

"Perfection," said Bev, at my elbow.

"Thank you," I said.

"Well, that wasn't a compliment for you," he said.

"No, I mean, thank you for all you've done," I said, tearing my eyes from my sister to turn to him. "Really. Thank you."

He gazed around at the crowd. "We've put one over on them, haven't we?"

"I'm not quite sure we haven't put one over on ourselves," I said.

I moved toward the bottom of the stairs to give Bronwyn my arm. I felt as though I were floating, too. My sister looked eager, like a child at Christmas, although I then recalled that after age four she actually had been wholly deprived of Christmas mornings.

"Nervous?" I asked her.

"I only hope they put blood in the punch," she said. "All mine's gone to my head."

Many grand bouquets had been sent to The Citadel for her, as was the custom—from Bev, from the Bliss brothers, from Percy Roehm, from every damned Tom, Dick and Harry who had ever encountered her. I had ventured into the fray myself with an arrangement of wildflowers, imported from the West.

The bouquet she chose was a simple one, presented to her by Freddy, a clutch of white rosebuds and white violets bound in japan paper and trailing a pair of long silver ribbons. The scent of the flowers enveloped us as we walked.

We crossed to Anna Maria, and Bronwyn embraced her with a kiss. I fear this might have been the apogee of my mother's life. I expected her to ascend heavenward in a beam of white light. Her hopes for her adopted daughter had been fulfilled and surpassed.

We let Bronwyn go at the side of Swoony, who exercised her grandmotherly duty by spending the next hour formally introducing the girl to the Manhattan uppertens, a flock of impeccably feathered turkeys, presented to her one at a time.

"Virginia, my granddaughter," Swoony would say.

"Bronwyn Delegate," the Savage Girl corrected mildly, performing a deep curtsy. Over and over again, never failing with her "Very pleased to meet you" and "So happy to have you here."

The fashionables pressed forward to get a better look at the bejeweled beadwork on her gown. They made her turn around. Over and over.

The dance followed supper. My sister and I waltzed. Bev took her for the mazurka. In violation of etiquette, he took her again for a quadrille.

But as her escort I had rights, and I reclaimed her for the German. Monsieur Henri of Madame Eugénie's had been assigned to call the figures. The dance was an eccentric sort of performance. At the climax the ladies held a stout rope, which the men tried to get over, under or around.

As the dance then demanded, Bev and I show-wrestled while Bronwyn watched, her hands clasped. A handkerchief was tied around my eyes while the other dancers marched in a tight circle.

In a gesture of her high regard (for Swoony at least, if not for Bronwyn), Caroline Hood had given over to the Delegate family the use for the evening of her four-in-hand coach, an old-fashioned affair imported from Germany, gilded and black-enameled over every inch, with the Hood family crest emblazoned on its doors.

It was the dead hour, four o'clock in the morning, when we finally emerged out of the ballroom into the frozen night. Snow dusted the park across the avenue. The front stairs of the hotel filled with euphoric ballgoers, Freddy a veritable peacock in his thrill of accomplishment.

I looked for Colm. Across the street, in the park, still illuminated by gas jets, Liberty raised her torch.

Bronwyn stepped outside, took one look at the outlandish carriage waiting for her and emitted an appalled laugh. "That is for me?"

"Your fairy godmother has come through," Bev said.

Even in the wake of her triumph, I was happy to see she still treated the whole thing as I had suggested, as a game, as a lark. Some girls might grow vain with all the fuss. Not she.

The crowd of gawkers had thinned but not entirely dispersed, a few journalists sprinkled in among them, identifiable by their predatory look. "Bronwyn!" they called. "Miss Delegate!"

They wanted her to display her gown. She shrugged the wrap from her shoulders, and it dropped away as a cloud might move from in front of the sun. It would have fallen to the pavement if I hadn't caught it. She turned, posing, showing her profiles and backside to the multitudes.

A gasping sort of cheer rose from the sidewalk assembly, similar to the one I had heard inside the ballroom. I saw the newspapermen scribble furiously, sketching the flatter, diminished bustle, the new style Bronwyn (and Bev) had wrought.

I thought it all a bit much and moved to cloak her again.

Several things happened at once. I saw a man in a Stetson Boss hat push his way through the crowd. He had on a long leather greatcoat and didn't wear a tie. Milling spectators blocked his way, but he plowed ahead.

Butler Fince.

The shooter I had last seen in the Comstock, murdering a man. As then, in his hand he held a pistol.

Behind the intruder, Colm Cullen raced forward, a desperate look on his features. He wasn't going to make it, I realized.

A curious effect: Time slowed to a crawl. Bev Willets moved up next to Bronwyn. My parents turned away to bid good night to the hotel stewards, perhaps to tip them with a bit of coin.

The man Fince extended his pistol at my sister and fired.

Bev flinched back. I stepped forward, trying to shield Bronwyn.

The bullet smashed into her bodice. I felt the embroidered pearls explode into a hundred pieces, some fragments of which stung my face. But the diamonds held.

Screams, chaos.

Bronwyn staggered backward, caught in Anna Maria's arms. I reached for my .38, but it got fouled in my belt and shirt back. I realized there was something wrong with my right foot. Colm grappled with Fince, stripping the man of his weapon but receiving a blow to the head that put him down.

He struggled to his feet, but by that time Fince had run off, shouting, "I'm mad! I'm mad!" Colm trained his LeMat at him. But the crowd was too general, and he pulled the gun up. Knocking over gawkers and ballgoers like tenpins, Fince tore through the panicked throng.

Tu-Li met him at the edge of the sidewalk. As he dashed past her, she extracted a long, thin dagger from the sleeve of her simple silk gown and drove it directly into Butler Fince's heart.

The man's momentum pitched him forward, and he staggered out onto dung-carpeted Fifth Avenue. He lay dead by the time Colm reached him. The thinness of the blade, the strike directly to the heart, meant little blood was spilled.

I stayed with Anna Maria at Bronwyn's side. She remained remarkably unhurt, having only had the wind knocked out of her. Saved by a cuirass of embroidered diamonds.

"You're bleeding," she said to me. Feeling weak, I sank down on one knee in front of her as if asking for her hand. Then I looked at my foot and toppled over into a faint. The last sound I heard was my handgun clattering to the paving stones.

A squeamish anatomist, William Howe says lightly. I fear for your future in medicine, young Hugo, if you faint at the sight of blood.

Hypovolemia, blood loss, I stutter, laughing sheepishly at the memory. My shoe entirely filled with blood!

But she did not die, Howe says. The newspapers call it a miracle. The bullet is meant for her, but it ricochets off her bejeweled gown and strikes you in the foot.

We can thank the Comstock for that, I say. My parents' wealth is what I mean, being able to afford pearls and diamonds sewn into silk for a bulletproof frock.

The fifty-thousand-dollar coming-out dress, Howe says.

Yes.

I pause in my narrative, contemplating the vagaries of fate. Outside the Tombs the self-satisfied silence of a Sunday evening grips the streets of Manhattan. Most of the residents have been fed, fortified with spirits and, earlier in the day, forgiven their sins.

So Bronwyn Delegate tucks herself into bed that morning . . . Howe says.

. . . And wakes up that afternoon famous, I say, completing the thought.

Only to become more and more so as the week progresses, Howe says. Her story splashed across the pages of the popular press.

She had but a single moment, I say.

Before scandal descended with its ugly truths, Howe says. Not a San Francisco cousin after all. Merely an urchin from the West, without standing or family, a nobody.

She was allowed to feel triumph only briefly, I say. The few golden hours from when she was introduced to when she left the ballroom.

Scandal! Howe cries, entering his histrionic courtroom mode. Society withdraws its regard! It casts the pretender out! The newspapers still love her, but what is that? Notoriety! Not fame but infamy! Scandal! The fall from grace!

Yes, I say. All that and more.

In these degraded days, Howe says, this decadent time of ours, infamy is celebrated, notoriety cozened.

What followed next, I say, was worse. Much worse.

Part Three

The Hunter's Camp in Lansdowne Ravine

❧ 23 ❧

Stories spilled liberally across the pages of the *Herald*, the *Sun*, the *World*, flooding New York in the days following the debut. DEBUTANTE DISASTER! was a favorite of the headline writers, but the focus shifted, as the week progressed, from the ball to Bronwyn herself.

The reporters soon ferreted out the facts of her life in Virginia City. This was delicious beyond all deliciousness. She was not a blue blood after all. "My Bronnie Lies," was one of the milder taunts in the press, punning off the momentarily popular ditty of the day, "My Bonnie Lies Over the Ocean."

My sister came to be known in the popular imagination by a singular epithet, "The Wild Child of the Washoe." The telegraph wires between New York and Virginia City melted with all the traffic. What the newspapers knew of her stopped with Dr. Scott's freak show. Nothing of jaguars or Comanches. But that was enough.

When they couldn't glean new truths about her, they made up lies. Tu-Li, sleuthed out by the press and labeled the "Dragon Lady," came in for her share of attention. The fact that she habitually concealed a stiletto about her person was made much of.

But the newsmen really couldn't get enough of Bronwyn, especially the luscious gulf between the debutante and the wild girl.

Engravings of Bronwyn in the gem-encrusted gown (on one side of the card) and on all fours with streaming hair (on the other) appeared, to be traded among shopgirls and delivery boys. A photograph reproduced from a stolen carte de visite was popular, too. Representations in burned wood, stereopticons, sheet music ("The Wild Child of the Washoe: A Ballad"), silhouettes.

Alone among all New York, Victoria Woodhull and her sister, Tennessee, took up Bronwyn's cause. With friends like those two . . . I regretted the evening I ever put them together. They gave copious space to the affair in their newspaper, *Woodhull & Claflin's Weekly*.

"Miss Delegate is a free, untrammeled New Woman," Woodhull wrote, "and therefore she strikes dread in the heart of every male."

Bronwyn received an enigmatic if ostensibly sympathetic note from Professor James's sister, Alice. "The cuckoos imitate the clocks to perfection," it read.

Amid all this Bronwyn, Bronwyn, Bronwyn, I found myself sullen and ignored, hobbling around on my bad foot with a borrowed cane of Freddy's. A couple of my metatarsals had been fractured by the spent bullet, according to the bone doctor whom Anna Maria brought in (and who asked if he might meet Bronwyn).

Serious, the doctor said of my wound. Might limp for life if I didn't stay off it.

I woke every morning, foot throbbing, sunk deeper and deeper into humiliation. Some days I could not move myself to get out of bed. Fifth Avenue in front of The Citadel crawled with gawkers and news hacks. The latter repeatedly attempted, with some small success, to suborn the servants for the "inside story." Colm told me he was bid a hundred dollars in an attempt to secure his cooperation.

I felt upset in general and irritated with Colm in particular.

"Why weren't you there?" I asked him. "The one time when Fince knew exactly where'd she be."

"I know, I know," he said.

Colm told me his strange story. The morning of the debut, on his way out to accompany Bronwyn on her day of days, he received a piece of bad news. Sheriff Dick Tolle had been shot and killed in a low tavern on Pearl Street. Rushing there, he found the man very much alive.

"Why, Dick, they told me you were kilt," Colm said.

Tolle had gotten a similar note at his hotel, that Colm Cullen had been murdered at the Red Lion tavern on Pearl Street downtown.

The two men had the same thought at once. "Fince is here somewhere," Colm said.

They glanced around the Red Lion, an ancient, low-ceilinged place with inch-deep tobacco stains on the walls and pockmarked rafters that looked as though they had been attacked with hatchets. A few waterfront drunks, but none who looked like Fince. Colm and Tolle spilled out into the street.

"There," Tolle said. Up the curving cobblestoned block, a tall, leather-coated man in a Stetson Boss hurried away.

"Well, he gave us a merry chase," Colm told me. "The streets down there have no sense to 'em." They pursued Fince across Exchange Place, losing him in the daunting neighborhoods of the financial district.

"But we seen a Boss Stetson on a ferry just pulling out of the slip, crossing to Brooklyn, so we took the next one over. That hat of his . . . well, it just made it easy for us to track him in a crowd."

"Brooklyn," I said.

"Yup," Colm said.

"That's where you were when you should have been with Bronwyn."

"I thought I was doing the right thing," Colm said. "Tolle had a lot of information that Fince was living over there. We picked up his trail."

"And when I saw you coming up out of the crowd at the Fifth Avenue Hotel . . . ?"

"We soon enough realized it was a hoodwink," Colm said. "Fince had costumed up some drunk to look like himself in order to lead us astray. I raced back to Manhattan as fast as I could, but I was just a step too late."

Almost lost amid the flurry of Bronwyn reports was the death of Edna's escort, poor Percy Roehm, his body discovered in the Fifth Avenue Hotel the night of the ball. Edna, beside herself, retired for a sojourn at an upstate rest resort.

The details were enough to send anyone running.

Percy Roehm's body had not been intact, had been separated from its manhood like the others. A hotel maid found his corpse discarded among cast-off dirty linens, a flood of blood pouring out when she tipped a laundry cart trying to deposit a soiled tablecloth.

To the newsmen it all seemed to blend into one rolling, tawdry mess—a beauty with a scandalous past, a street shooting and, at the same venue, a mutilated dead heir stuffed into a closet.

Confused as usual, the press blamed Fince for Percy's death. But even without a hint of suspicion of guilt falling on the girl, it was one more element to taint Bronwyn—and the whole Delegate clan—even further.

"I can't get my police sources to tell me what's what," Colm said.

"We know the Percy Roehm killing was grisly, and we know where they found him—off the second-floor balcony, above the ball-room."

"Bronwyn was up there, wasn't she?" Colm asked. "In the little powder room at the top of the stairs?"

"Every deb was in that room," I said. "The atmosphere was intense. More like a gunpowder room."

"Did Bronwyn leave the receiving line when you were there?"

"No," I said. "Yes. Maybe once or twice. I don't know!"

"Did you accompany her when she left?"

"No," I said, despondent. "No one did. She's so damned free, she just walked off upstairs."

"So she could have . . ."

"Murdered the boy and then calmly gone back to the quadrille?"

"Well, I don't see Fince for it," Colm said.

"Neither do I," I said. "But lucky for us, everyone in the world does."

I might not have trusted Bronwyn, but I wanted to make sure no one else suspected her.

Quelle horreur, the words on the lips of the society matrons. The highest echelon of their ranks, Caroline Hood and the Tremont aunts, had been tarred by the scandal—the former had even lent the offending lass her coach!—which rendered the affair all the more titillating.

"How did this Delegate girl possibly believe she'd ever be accepted?" the society ladies said, one to another. "I saw through her from the first."

A few days passed, and Colm was able to duck his way out of The

Citadel through the milling crowds of the curious. None of the rest of us could venture out. We couldn't even go near the windows. We were all marooned in the house, but each alone, not taking our dinners together.

Anna Maria and Freddy kept to themselves in the aviary. I lost myself in an intricate anatomy drawing of the chambers of the human heart.

Nicky clung to Bronwyn as though she were his life preserver. I recall a paroxysm of jealousy I fell into around this time, when I happened to be in the South Wing one morning and I bumped into Nicky emerging from Bronwyn's room, bed-haired and sleepy-eyed.

"Brought her some tea, did you?" I asked.

"Couldn't sleep, so I crawled in with her," he said.

No, old man, no. Not done.

"Don't worry." Nicky laughed. "Nothing happened."

I told myself my brother was just a child, they were both just children. I couldn't believe I had lowered myself to the point where I was jealous of my little brother.

It wasn't the first time. Everyone said Nicholas Delegate was the spitting image of his Uncle Sonny. Sonny had made much of the boy, and the two of them (Sonny died in 1869, when Nick was seven) had an easy, conspiratorial friendship. Sonny had taken him down to the Merchants' Exchange on Wall Street, settled a trust fund on him, taught him the rudiments of investing, declared the boy "a natural Midas."

I was envious then. The dynamic between my father and his brilliant brother was beginning to be played out between myself and Nicky. Nicky was always the funny one, the bright one, the lucky one. I was the one who fainted and spent time in a sanatorium. I was the one rickety on my pins.

Perhaps family relationships are handed down like heirlooms, to turn up in generation after generation, enacted again and again, ad infinitum or, more to the point here, ad nauseam.

"It would help if you weren't so damned chummy with her," I told my brother one day soon after I caught him coming from our sister's bedroom.

"Help whom? Poor Hugo. You should have stuck with Delia."

"Shut up," I said, suddenly thirteen again. We were in the aviary, but for once our parents were elsewhere.

"You can't marry her," Nicky said. "You know why?"

"Don't be filthy-minded," I said, becoming flushed. "She's a child. She's our sister."

"You can't marry her because I am going to."

"Shut your mouth!" The problem was, I half believed him.

"You're pathetic," Nicky said. "Everything you know is wrong."

I hadn't been moved to hit my brother since we were children together.

He effortlessly parried my near-powerless blow, knocking my fist from the air, then rose to his feet and struck a pose. Uncle Sonny had taught him boxing as well as the stock market, the principles of which were, after all, similar.

Feeling shamed, I left the aviary. A blue parrot squawked, commending my retreat.

"Everything you know is wrong," Nicky called after me.

In March, just as the gawkers outside The Citadel were beginning to thin out, the showman P. T. Barnum put in an appearance on our block one afternoon. Playing to the spectators and shouting his offer up at our curtained windows through a red-white-and-blue megaphone, he proposed that Bronwyn appear for an exclusive engagement in his "Grand Traveling Museum, Menagerie, Caravan & Hippodrome," a combination circus and sideshow of "freaks" and *lusus naturae.*

Nicky said he considered it a "smashing" idea. "Bronnie should go with Barnum, and I could go with her!" he cried. "As her manager!"

The ignominy deepened, and the press did not let up. Weeks after the debacle, I found Anna Maria weeping, collapsed on a divan in the aviary, Freddy pacing in front of her. As I entered, Freddy stormed out.

I comforted my mother. "It will be all right, dear," I said. "This will all blow over."

Sobbing, she rose to her feet. "You don't know anything," she said, and rushed out after her husband.

That should have been my first inkling that something else had gone seriously wrong. But in the rolling crisis surrounding Bronwyn, I missed it.

I hobbled up to the South Wing drawing room. No one around, Tu-Li and the berdache off in their own chambers. I knocked at the door communicating to Bronwyn's bedroom.

"It's me," I called out.

She startled me by opening her door and surprised me more by her unperturbed demeanor. No tears, no rending of garments. Through her doorway I could see discarded newspapers littering her floor. But she herself seemed the still eye of the hurricane.

"Dear Hugo," she said, emerging from her bedchamber into the drawing room and plopping down on an overstuffed chair, tucking her legs beneath her. She wore one of her artist's gowns and an embroidered pair of silk slippers.

"How are you holding up?" I asked.

"I'm reading your Suetonius," she said. "I like it: 'The die is cast.' Ancient Rome makes Manhattan appear positively civilized."

"You don't feel . . . I don't know, besieged?"

"Oh, I can get out when I want to," she said. "My bowler and waist-coat are my passports."

"For pity's sake, Bronwyn!"

"What?"

"They'll eat you alive if they discover you!"

"Or I'll eat them," she said. "The *Sun* had me as a cannibal today."

"Please, please, take this seriously."

"I thought you told me to play it as a game."

Maddening as she was, I admired her ability to remain unfazed. "I came here to offer you a way out," I said. "To offer us all a way out."

She remained silent, resting her chin on her hand, her long hair winding over one shoulder, a pert expression on her face. I had the uncanny idea that she knew what I was going to say.

"It came to me last night, when I couldn't sleep."

"You do look fatigued," she said.

"Please, just let me speak my piece," I said. I took a breath. "I thought about what's going on, and I decided it will solve our problems if I marry you."

"Ah," she said. "How noble."

"Don't you see?" I cried. "Your getting married will settle the scandal immediately."

"I'll be rehabilitated," she said.

"Yes! I can't stand it," I moaned like a schoolboy. "I can't abide what's happening. Your marriage prospects have otherwise evaporated. Society has taken a stand against us. The other debs complain that they have been tainted with scandal simply by coming out at the same time as you."

She stood up and walked across the room to the south-facing windows, silent a long time, considering, I believed, the ramifications of what I proposed. Looking slantwise, west on Sixty-second Street, she could see just a sliver of Fifth Avenue and the park.

"There's a man wearing a sandwich board down there," she said. "Selling my picture for twenty cents."

"Exactly what I'm talking about!"

She turned back to me, a soft look on her face, and took up my hand. We had touched only rarely of late, and the heat of her skin contacting with mine momentarily overwhelmed me.

"What you all have done for me, giving me a family, Tu-Li, Tahk-too, I can never repay," she said.

She leaned close and kissed me lightly on the cheek. My thoughts tumbled over one another in utter confusion. I had her! She was mine!

"But, dear Hugo, I could never accept an offer made out of obligation," she said. "You laughed when I said, 'From my reading of history.' All right, it was a foolish thing to say, when I haven't really read even a single percent of what I should. But from my reading of the poets, the authors, the chroniclers of the deepest human emotions, I know one thing, that love must be freely given and received."

Her words made no sense to me, as though she were speaking a foreign language.

"It's Bev Willets, isn't it? Don't you know he will never marry you now?"

"He might take me as a lover," she said.

I made a move to slap her, but my hand could not complete its stroke. I collapsed into a chair.

"All right, I don't want to upset you, but I will put it in plain words," she said. "That sandwich-board man down there? He can't harm me. And your believing that he can makes me think less of you. Your offer is insulting, the desperate ploy of a small child who just wants everything to be put right."

A carriage went by on Fifth, the hoofbeats deadened by the dirt and muck of the street.

"Come to me as a man, Hugo," Bronwyn said.

She patted my head and left me alone, heading off down the hall toward the North Wing, cool, calm and undestroyed.

A week later, just past midnight, I stood holding two horses, a roan gelding and a gray charger, trying to fade back into the shadows of our stable courtyard.

Colm had informed me that Bronwyn had once again taken to going out at night. We had nailed shut her bedroom window, but still she somehow managed to roam.

Standing there in the dark, I witnessed her do it yet could not readily tell how it was accomplished. A human outline moved across the crenellated façade of the South Wing, disappearing, reappearing, vanishing again, then suddenly a boyish figure in a bowler hat was slipping through the courtyard archway onto Sixty-third Street.

Colm stepped up beside me. "You see her?"

I nodded, and we quickly mounted. We needed to give her enough of a head start not to spook her but not too much that we would lose her. We went around the block the other way, on Sixty-second, and lay in wait in the shadows off Fifth, assuming she would head downtown.

We were not wrong. Bronwyn climbed into a cab a block away. The uptown streets were so empty at that time of night that I thought it unlikely a hansom would have been in the area trolling for customers. She must have arranged for the driver to be waiting.

Allowing the cab to pass by on its way down Fifth, we fell in behind it, keeping a good twenty-yard gap between us. Plunging through a ghost Manhattan in the moonless dark, I saw a world of half-built cathedrals, barren undeveloped stretches of avenue, the brick-clad Murray Hill Reservoir looming to our right at Forty-second Street, all sites of our more innocent past.

Downslope at a canter as the hansom ahead of us picked up speed.

Past Delmonico's, Liberty's lonely torch in Madison Square and then the venue of our recent disaster, the Fifth Avenue Hotel, brightly lit and bustling even at the late hour. I wondered how the denizens of the area would react had they known that the notorious Wild Child of the Washoe had even then returned to the scene of the crime. I had an awful moment thinking this might be Bronwyn's destination, but the cab didn't linger, heading farther south.

Fourteenth Street marked the Rialto, a neighborhood of more activity, more people on the streets, yellow gaslight illuminating the thoroughfare. We pulled up as the hansom bearing Bronwyn stopped.

She descended from the cab without a look our way and, to our surprise, immediately entered another carriage waiting curbside on Fourteenth, an expensive private coach drawn by a matched set of docked and plumed grays.

"Do you know it?" I asked Colm.

He nodded. "Mrs. Woodhull's," he said, and we followed along behind. Only a brief journey, across Fourteenth and up Irving Place, finally to arrive at the Willets mansion on the north side of Gramercy Park.

"That Bev fellow has been cultivating them," Colm said. "He calls on the Woodhulls almost every afternoon."

"And when did you think to inform me of this?" I cried.

"I've been keeping my eye on it," Colm said.

Bronwyn at Bev's. I had been dreading the eventuality as soon I discerned that the Woodhull coach was headed for the rich-if-faded Gramercy neighborhood, knowing the domicile of the Willets family intimately, having whiled away many hours there throughout my younger years.

Bev's parents spent little time in Manhattan, handing the Gramercy Park place almost wholly over to their reckless son. Located on the lip of the Tenderloin as it was, the luxurious home served as a convenient jumping-off place for nighttime forays and had itself hosted its share of riotous parties.

Colm and I held back, peering between the spikes of the iron fence that surrounded the private park. The coach disgorged its occupants, Woodhull and her sister, Tennessee, then my own sister. Somewhere along the way, Bronwyn had ditched her boy's outfit and reverted to female dress.

Laughing and chattering with the others, Bronwyn entered the lion's den—a metaphor that, given her history, seemed especially apt. I had a brief, jealous glimpse of an effusive Bev Willets, welcoming the three women to his humble, million-dollar abode.

We waited outside considerably longer than was dignified. The horses nickered, impatient. Colm kept silent watch, and I said little, inwardly seething.

It pained me to stare up at the shaded windows, painted with moving silhouettes. I did not want to look, did not want to hear the faint, dying laughter, but could not help myself.

"With those three women, what naturally comes to mind is the witches in *Macbeth*," I finally said. "But I don't believe she's up to murder most foul tonight, do you?"

"You're mixing up your tragedies, ain't ye?" Colm said.

Then suddenly he gestured down East Twenty-first. "I see her!" he yelled. "What color is her dress?"

"Black!" I shouted, but he was already galloping away.

The roan balked and would not go. Colm came back after only a few minutes.

"What?" I asked, breathless, still trying to get my horse in line.

"Someone was there," he said. "A woman."

"Was it Bronwyn?"

"I couldn't tell," he said.

I slipped off the skittish roan and tossed the reins to Colm.

"Don't," he said.

But I was already on my way across the street, up the steps of the Willets town house, blowing past Margolis, Bev's beleaguered butler.

"Mr. Hugo," he managed. I didn't stop, racing up the steps and into the drawing room.

"Where is she?" I shouted.

Woodhull, Tennie C., Bev.

With a shock I recognized one of the mulatto women we had hosted at East Chatham. Several assorted others, epicene men and daguerreotype women. A Mameluke servingman in harem pants. A male-female couple in complete dishabille, her richly nippled breasts spilling out of her stays.

No Bronwyn.

"Misplaced someone near and dear, have you, Delegate?" Bev said.

"You know damned well," I said. Wild-eyed, out of control.

"How men lose their heads around her," Victoria Woodhull murmured.

"You shouldn't go looking for something you may not want to find," Bev said.

"Poor little man," said Tennessee. "All the proud penis owners."

I felt, suddenly, deflated. It came upon me in a rush. They were all laughing at me! Wild-eyed, out of control . . . and pitiable.

I turned heel and left.

Bev caught up with me on the stairway. "Bloody hell, Delegate," he said. "Show some self-respect."

"What would you know about that?" I yelled. I waved my arm in the direction of the salon, crowded with Woodhull and her group of layabouts. "You don't believe their claptrap, do you?"

"Please don't underestimate me," he said. "If I know one thing, it's that those two words don't go together—'free love.' It's rarely love, and it's never free."

"Then what?" I said.

Bev shrugged his shoulders. "You're behaving as if you don't know your own mind."

"Just stay away from her. Stay away!"

Bev shook his head in mock sadness, infuriating me further. "Margolis!" he called. "Show young Mr. Delegate out!"

Where had Bronwyn gone? There was another way out of the town house, I knew, a back entrance that led via a lane to Twenty-second Street. Was she at dinner with some rounder at Delmonico's? Wandering the streets, sad and lost?

Or out employing her hand razors. I couldn't always think of her as a murderess. If I did, I would go crazy. More than I already was.

Colm and I turned our mounts uptown, the party within the Willets place still going strong, lights blazing, Bev's laughter ringing in my ears.

A small, cheerless fire crackled in the grate when I arrived in the dining room early the next morning, and Freddy sat at the end of the long table with the *Sun* opened before him.

Anna Maria filled cups of tea from the sideboard—we followed the English way in having no servants at breakfast—laying one down in front of Freddy and one at her own place beside him.

Outside the windows the gawker circus hadn't yet begun its performance and the sky threatened an early spring rain.

"Late night, dear?" my mother asked me. "Or are you feeling unwell? You appear highly disturbed."

"We just need tea," Freddy said to her. "Not talk."

Freddy looked as though he'd had a few late nights himself. The pouches beneath his eyes had grown darker, more swollen. With a shock I realized that the scandal of the past weeks had aged him.

I sat down beside Nicky. "No news for you today, chum?" I said. Nicky usually scanned the paper front to back alongside my father.

"Banal," he said, no doubt imitating a grandee he had encountered somewhere on his rounds. "So terribly banal."

"Is that right?" I said. "Well, eat your grapefruit."

The last grapefruit of the season, shipped direct from Safety Harbor in Florida.

"Too bitter," Nicky said. "Don't you think, Freddy?"

Freddy, distracted, *hmmn*'d my brother.

"Needs a spoonful, eh, old chap?" said Nicky, offering his father the sugar bowl.

Still immersed in the paper, Freddy piled the top of his grapefruit with sugar and passed the bowl to my mother.

Nicky started to slide on his chair until only his head remained visible and he was holding on to the edge of the table white-knuckled.

Freddy took a segment of citrus into his mouth, twisted up his face and choked. "Bbbwhatt??" Sputtering.

"April Fools'!" cried Nicky, laughing.

The old salt-for-sugar trick, hoary from childhoods past. Normally every one of us would have been on the lookout for it, this day of all days. A distracted Freddy was easy prey.

He swiped at his tongue with his linen napkin and shook his head violently from side to side. "What? What?"

Nicky ducked under the table.

"April Fools', Your Eminence," we heard from beneath us.

Freddy usually had a sense of humor, even at his own expense. This morning he became enraged, jumping up with his hands gripping the table, then swatting the grapefruit off his plate onto the floor.

"Up, sir!" he said. "I want you here. Now."

Nicky struggled out from under the table and went to Freddy's side, ducking his head in contrition. "Cookie helped," he offered.

"Darling," said my mother. "It is April Fools' Day, after all."

"Good morning, everyone." Bronwyn stood at the dining-room door. She was elegantly dressed, not in morning clothes but in the striped lilac outfit from Richardson's. She wore a cloak, short gray gloves and a peaked hat of the kind a woman adopted when she went out about town.

Embarrassed now, Freddy sat down.

"I got him!" Nicky crowed, dashing back to his seat. "I nailed Freddy, Bronnie!"

"Tea?" said Anna Maria.

"I won't," said Bronwyn. "Or rather I can't. I'm leaving."

Anna Maria gave a sideways glance toward Freddy. "I thought we said going out wasn't such a good idea just now," she said. "Freddy?"

"What?"

"I won't be back," Bronwyn said.

"It's just, everything is at sixes and sevens, with the newspapers," Anna Maria said. "You know that."

"Wait," I said to Bronwyn. "What do you mean? What are you talking about? 'Won't be back'?"

"April Fools'!" said Nicky.

No. It was something else. A sick, panicked feeling crept over me.

"I guess, if you are careful and just go for the afternoon, perhaps wear a veil, it may be all right," Anna Maria said. "What do you think, Father?"

"No," said Bronwyn. "It's not that."

"April Fools'?" asked my father.

I noticed that Bronwyn's dress was looped up to knee height and she wore what looked like Turkish slippers, as well as some sort of outlandish lacy trousers above her white stockings. Exactly like underwear, I thought, except that she was on her way out into decidedly public New York City.

Bloomers. Or, rather, to render it as it occurred in my mind, *Bloomers!*

"I can't bring this trouble down on you anymore," Bronwyn said. "It isn't fair."

"Oh, dear, none of us feels that way," Anna Maria said. "It's not your fault. It's those wretched journalists."

"This is just something I've decided I have to do," Bronwyn said.

"It's all too banal, Bronnie," Nicky said, employing his new favorite word. "Too, too banal."

"But I don't understand," Anna Maria said. "You're going?"

"She's going, Mother," I said. "Didn't you hear her? She's moving out."

"But where will she . . . Where will you live?" a bewildered Anna Maria said. "This is your home."

Nicky went back under the table.

It had begun to rain, a sparkling, sunlit downpour, the kind that required boots and a voluminous umbrella.

"You'll get wet . . . Your slippers . . ." Anna Maria had tears forming in her eyes, we could all see them. Bronwyn stepped up to her and laid her hand against my mother's cheek.

"Well, it may be for the best," said Freddy gloomily, rising to his feet again.

"Oh, Friedrich!" Anna Maria said, blubbering now, clutching Bronwyn's hand and pressing it to her lips.

Freddy said, "This episode, this thing that has taken us all over, it must come to an end."

"But where will you go?" Anna Maria repeated.

"I'll be perfectly all right," Bronwyn soothed.

"Answer her!" I cried.

"I know two ladies who want to take me in. Very elegant, very civilized ladies."

"Who?" I demanded. "Who is bringing you away from us?"

"You know very well, Hugo," said Bronwyn. "Since you and Colm saw me with them last night."

Anna Maria: "What? What? What is going on?"

"Victoria Woodhull," I said.

"Oh, my Lord," said Anna Maria, seeing fresh disaster looming.

"Running for president when she can't even vote," Freddy sneered. "That makes a lot of sense."

"Don't forget her charming radical sister," I said. "The one who advocates legalized prostitution."

"Hugo!" wailed Anna Maria.

"April Fools', April Fools'," Nicky said weakly. Bronwyn dragged him out from under the table and hugged him.

"*Tami,*" she whispered to him. Comanche for "younger brother."

"*Patsi,*" he said back to her. Older sister. Then he dove back under the table so the rest of us couldn't read his distress. He began kicking methodically at the table leg.

"It's better for you all if I go," Bronwyn said. Approaching Freddy, who tried to turn away, she seized his arm and kissed his cheek.

"I'll always remember what you did for me," she whispered to him. His eyes brimmed with emotion.

Bronwyn walked out of the dining room and down the stairs that led to the front door, her train flowing over each step like a waterfall. Anna Maria and I pursued her, my mother holding the girl's hand and promising her that things would change if only she were to reconsider.

In the stairhall, Bronwyn kissed my mother. I pitied Anna Maria. She had opened her heart to the girl and had gotten so little in return. Now this. A second daughter was deserting her just as the first one had.

Nicky came plunging down the stairs after Bronwyn. She ruffled his hair.

"Tell Tahktoo and Tu-Li that I will see them soon," she said.

She reached out her hand to me. But I kept my mine at my side, saying only, "You have no bags."

"I have everything I need," she said.

❧ 24 ❧

And then, disaster.

It rolled up on us slowly. Or at least it did on me. Freddy and Anna Maria knew all along what was happening, like a giant wave they saw far out in the ocean, coming closer, rising, rising, until it towered over them and they realized it was going to crash.

There could have been signs that I didn't notice, mired as I was in a brown study, my thoughts poisonous and morose. I embarked upon a project to draw a complete human musculature, after Vesalius.

At one time in the not-too-remote past, Andreas Vesalius had been my god. He was the founding genius of anatomical art. A sixteenth-century Flemish physician based in Brussels, he published in 1543 *De humani corporis fabrica* (*On the Fabric of the Human Body*). The book exploded like a thunderclap in the storm of ideas that was the Northern Renaissance.

Vesalius did the dissections, but no one was precisely sure who drew the brilliant, shattering, diabolical illustrations. Most definitely a student in the studio of Titian, probably a Dutch painter and draftsman named Jan Stephan van Calcar. Here in these superb anatomical drawings was the human being demystified, man as meat, man as animal.

Vesalius gave us human muscles, bones, organs. He did not manage to picture the human soul. He peered into the heart of man and found . . . muck. Blood, sinew, tissue.

It is possible the heresy of humanism was born with the publication of *De humani corporis*. Certainly the drawings furthered the radical idea that man was the proper study of man—not God, not theology, not the divine. *Sanguino ergo sum*. I bleed, therefore I am.

Freddy had given me an eighteenth-century copy of the Vesalius when I was fourteen, and I don't think I ever recovered. In those early days of April, with Bronwyn abandoning us, I returned to Vesalius as to an old friend.

At first, sitting at my drafting table, I thought the rising ruckus outside The Citadel was more Wild Child of the Washoe nonsense. The crowds seemed larger, more vocal, angrier. But I was locked in my study trying to get a rectus abdominis right, and locked also in the misery of my own mind. I tried to ignore what I considered petty distractions.

Until the crowd started to toss bricks at our windows. By the fourth of April, things came to a head. I ventured out of my study to find the house in an uproar.

"What on earth is going on?" I asked Randall, who merely ran past me down the hall without bothering to answer.

I proceeded downstairs and encountered a struggling crew of servants trying to board up a smashed window in the front parlor. Venturing to the entrance hall, I surveyed the crowd in the street outside.

A moblike clot of laborers, with a scattering of gentlemen among them, completely blocked Fifth Avenue. Mounted police officers forced the mob to the sidewalks, but the rabble reasserted its blockade as soon as the horses passed. A man in a slouch hat roused the crowd, screaming that my father was a crook. Another man ran, pursued by a cop with a cudgel.

What new nastiness could this be? Whereas the Wild Child crowds ran on vicarious urges, the current mob seemed downright threatening. A bolt of fear ran through me, and I withdrew from the front hall and went looking for Freddy for an explanation.

I found him, Anna Maria, Tu-Li and the berdache assembled in the aviary, along with a small clutch of servants. It was as far as we could get from the madness at the front of the house.

"Hugo, old man," Freddy said. "I'm glad we could pry you out from your anatomical studies."

"That riot in the street isn't about Bronwyn," I said.

"I'm afraid not," Freddy said.

"Sit down, dear," Anna Maria said.

"What's going on?"

"Well, you've been rather holed up the last few days," Freddy said. "There've been developments."

"Developments about what?" I asked. "Is Bronwyn all right?"

"We know you've been upset," Anna Maria said. "We've all been heartbroken."

"This isn't about your sister," Freddy said. "At least not directly."

"For pity's sake!" I said.

One of the servants, a houseboy named Georgie, addressed Freddy—an unlikely occurrence that indicated incipient chaos in the household. "You sent young Master Nicholas away, sir," he said.

Then Annie, the kitchen girl, said to Anna Maria: "We're afraid for ourselves, madam." The mood in the room veered toward open rebellion.

"Please, let Master Friedrich speak," Winston said.

"No one needs panic," Freddy said, raising his voice in a bid to gain control. "We are perfectly safe. We did send Nicholas away to his cousin's, merely as a precaution. I have contracted with a force of Pinkertons, who should be here shortly to clear the loiterers from in front of our door."

"But why are they out there?" I was practically shouting. "I have to know—has something happened to Bronwyn?"

"She is all right, for all we know," Anna Maria said. "Tu-Li has seen her."

"She prospers," Tu-Li said, a comment, in the present heightened circumstances, that seemed oddly out of place. She prospers?

"I am sorry to say I have not been completely forthcoming with you," Freddy said. "I thought I could remedy the situation and all would be well. But lately it has deteriorated past remedying."

He laid out the whole sick story then, a tangled tale of financial sleight of hand and attempted monopoly that I had to believe few in the room could fully understand.

Events had gone on right under my nose that had ruined us.

During our trip to the Comstock the previous summer, when I

thought Freddy was consolidating the family's mining interests, he was in reality engaged in a highly risky conspiracy to game the world silver market.

Working in alliance with Michael Hart-Bentley, Oliver Stringfist, Stanley Beales and Dixon Kelly, the same moguls with whom I had shared breakfast in Virginia City, Freddy had concocted a scheme that worked like this: His combine sought to buy up as much silver and as many silver contracts as it could. Some of these were newfangled financial instruments called "forward contracts," meaning they bought the right to buy silver in the future at a prescribed price.

It was all done at a very high level, with the collusion of the Chicago Board of Trade. Normally such forward contracts dealt in grains—wheat, corn, barley, rye and oats—seeking to smooth out volatility in the markets. Freddy's group sought to do the same with silver and come out ahead in so doing.

They made an audacious attempt, in other words, to corner the market and develop a monopoly on the supply of the precious metal throughout the world. By withholding their stockpile, they would drive up the price, enriching themselves to an impossible degree.

Incredible as it might seem, the insane maneuver very nearly worked. By the winter of 1875–76, the Stringfist-Delegate cabal had managed to gain control of an astonishing sixty percent of the world's liquid reserves of silver, some 500 million dollars' worth. All the fat moguls had to do then was sit on their pile and gloat, watching prices spiral up, the market firmly squeezed between the jaws of supply and demand.

Freddy didn't bother to lay this all out during that talk in the aviary. He merely sketched the broad outlines. Later on, digging into the details myself, I learned the outlandish scope of the plan. And I realized that I had never really understood my father.

As much as Freddy gloried in his status as a dilettante, a dabbler in a green satin vest, inwardly he seethed. He was seen as the man without a job, who didn't have to work, who collected butterflies and birds of prey and odd, comical people. His brother, Sonny, was the serious Delegate, the successful one, the famous one.

How my father must have grown sick of that endless refrain. In death, Sonny's reputation grew ever more resplendent.

The silver fandango, I realized, was Freddy's attempt to assert his own primacy. In a single stroke, he would double the family fortune and be hailed as a financial genius who ranked alongside his famous brother.

Instead he lost it all.

Halfway around the globe, an unforeseen event occurred, a historical happenstance that even Oliver Stringfist could not control.

It was actually more a chain of events. The French had been beaten badly in the Franco-Prussian War. The victors forced the vanquished to pay an indemnity. France transferred to Germany a huge portion of its national gold reserves, which had been piling up in French coffers since the time of Louis XIV. Otto von Bismarck, the German minister, in receipt of all this incredible wealth, decided his country would much rather use French gold to mint its ubiquitous thaler coins, rather than American silver.

Suddenly, in early spring 1876, Friedrich Delegate and company saw silver prices heading downward, rather than upward as they had planned. The end came surprisingly quick. Their bet went sour. Forced to make good on their forward contracts at set prices that now lost them millions, each of the five men involved went bankrupt. They witnessed their personal fortunes sucked away by the voracious demands of the market.

Freddy turned aside that day in the aviary, away from the crowd of servants, putting his forehead against mine, hugging me with forlorn desperation.

"I wish I could tell you that I gave all your money to the poor," he said.

"How much?" I asked, a strangled whisper. "How much did you lose?"

I never actually heard him say it, but it didn't matter, because the word would be out on the street soon enough.

A number: 60 million.

Sixty million dollars, the whole Delegate family fortune, vanished, like one of those streams out west that don't end in the ocean but wind up just draining into the sand of the desert. Swoony's fortune remained relatively intact, but it was just a matter of time until that, too, would be fed into the maw of the banks.

The swindle's failure led to a widespread financial collapse, which led to a panic, which led to an even more widespread financial collapse. The men in the street outside The Citadel had been put out of work by the greedy folly of Freddy and his friends.

My father turned back to the household servants. "I'm afraid we shall have to let some of you go," he said. "And for the others, it might be newly difficult for us to appear in public for the next few days."

The threat of retributive violence loomed. If the promised Pinkertons did not arrive, the situation might become dire. He was sorry, he said, to put us all into an unpleasant fix. Better days would come.

The deflated servants shuffled out, more stunned than angry. We heard them burst into dismayed chatter as soon as they were out of sight.

"So we're poor," I said when they had left.

"No, no, not poor," Anna Maria said.

"We are no longer rich," my father said simply.

A sequential catastrophe descended upon us during the month of April, a stunning succession of blows that sent us all reeling. I would think, Well, now, that's the worst of it, only to wake the next day and find new torment in store.

The Ditches, mortgaged, foreclosed, sold to a Vanderbilt scion. Our Fifth Avenue residence, mortgaged, foreclosed, to be sold or rented out by the bank. We would be able to find refuge right next door at Swoony's, but still, the displacement rankled.

The poison at the tip of the barb was Bronwyn. I could not help but think of her as the evil angel of our misfortune, at that very moment rejoicing somewhere in the completeness of our disaster. She had spurned us and now stood with her loathsome new friends, glorying in the Delegate decline and fall.

Yes, she prospered, as Tu-Li had said. Despite my self-imposed hermitage, I read the popular press, obsessively tracking down every tidbit of information on my dear departed sister.

Her scandal and Freddy's own rolled themselves up into a single ball of dung, smeared across the pages of every newspaper in town. The Wild Mogul of the Washoe joined the Wild Child as a figure of universal derision.

I witnessed Bronwyn leveraging her infamy to higher and higher levels of celebrity. Competing stories cropped up in competing papers. She would appear on the stage, it was announced. No, she would not. Queen Victoria wished to meet her. The queen did not wish it, being unamused. She walked the streets of the Tenderloin, offering her favors. She walked the streets, but with Tennessee Claflin and her people, extending charity to fallen women.

Later the night of Freddy's confession, I found a small group of our not-yet-let-go male servants gathered in the back courtyard, near the stables. Several of them, Cheevil and the Laughton brothers, gave me black looks and stalked aggressively away as I approached. But Paul the doorman remained, a half-empty whiskey bottle in his hand, a surly, deal-with-me-if-you-dare expression on his face.

I said not a word at first, just stood there in the horse-smelling dark, and eventually Paul said, "I guess you's just as worse off as us," and passed me the bottle. We proceeded to descend together into a blotted-out sea of alcoholic oblivion. When we tossed his empty bottle on the manure heap, I ventured back into the house and got another.

There can be a grim joy in drinking alongside a serious drunk. It is a mutual test of wills, a comparison of two men's concept of the color black. At first we nursed our parallel angers, imbibing in seething, silent rage. Later our twin furies appeared to merge.

People often misinterpreted my silence as an invitation to speak. Paul began to mutter, a stream of words so filthy that I marveled as each one came out of his mouth. I only gradually became aware of whom he talked about.

"Like attracts like. The fallen moves among the fallen. Why do you think she works with hoors? Because she's one of them! I don't have to know it. The whole town is talking about it. She mixes with light women—she's one of the lightest."

He was speaking of Bronwyn, speaking as no servant should ever speak of one of the family, nor one human being of another. I should have stopped him right there but found a stinging comfort in hearing my darkest thoughts pronounced out loud.

"Every night a different man. She don't *welcome* advances, she *makes* advances. You seen her walk. Right there, that's an invitation. She's got a come-on smile, don't she?"

"Yes," I said, only it came out "Yush." Self-pitying, I considered that Bronwyn never smiled at me.

"You need to bring her to heel, young master. It ain't proper, the way she lords it over us. You look in the Bible, a woman is a tool of man. Oh, she's a girl that can gull you. She's gulled all the family, I know that. Pretty Bronwyn, dear Bronwyn—what a laugh. You ain't to blame. The whole world got taken in. But here's the thing: She's poison."

That rang a bell. "What did you say?"

"I said, she's poison. P-o-s-e-n—I don't know how you spell it, but you know what I mean."

Paranoia flooded in. I grasped Paul's lapels drunkenly. "She used to say that. She herself said she was poison. Did she put you up to this? She wants you to warn me off her?"

"What? I'm just trying to tell you. Don't you see? She hoodwinked all of us. Everything she wanted has come to pass. She didn't like the dog Hickory, Hickory is gone. All girls'd love a rich wardrobe, she's sitting on silk. She wanted to come out grand, she's come out grand. She controls your parents and young Master Nicholas. She's evil, I tell you."

He muttered and cursed all the way through the second bottle.

The next morning at breakfast—or, really, the next hungover noon at tea—I encountered a harried-looking Anna Maria.

"We have to fire Paul," I said.

"Oh, you poor dear," Anna Maria said. "We have to fire them all."

Now everything went dark. With Bronwyn gone amid the roiling uncertainty about our family future, I withdrew into my room, alternately lying paralyzed in bed or obsessively cataloging and recataloging my anatomical specimens. I was like a moth with no flame, my life an emotional wilderness, a desert, really, the type of psychic landscape one crosses slowly and painfully.

It didn't help that I was abandoned, just at that moment, by two friends and allies, Tu-Li and the berdache. Our estrangement might have been partially my doing, but still it stung. I went to them in the midst of our family uproar and carefully enumerated my suspicions that Bronwyn might in some way be connected to nefarious crimes.

"Too many circumstances have come together for me to think the girl is entirely innocent," I said, trying to be mild and less sensationalistic at least than the newspapers.

We were in their drawing room in the South Wing. In preparation for our move out of The Citadel, the space had been almost stripped clean of furnishings. But I got the impression that as long as the two of them had their gambling tiles, it wouldn't matter what else was taken from them.

"You now believe Bronwyn is a criminal?" Tahktoo asked. Not incredulous, really, more stony-faced. "I've seen you oftentimes stupid, Hugo, but never mean."

"You hate her, like the rest of them do?" Tu-Li asked, gesturing outside the window, to Fifth Avenue, New York, the world. "She who is only faultless?"

I could tell this wasn't going to be easy. I was saying Bronwyn might be crazy, and clearly they were thinking that *I* was. Was I being so unreasonable? Bodies were piling up as if on a battleground. Someone had to do something. I tried to convince them.

"Young master," Tu-Li finally said, "you are wrong, and wrong in such a way that until you leave this folly behind, it is going to be difficult for me to look at you again."

"Or remain in the same room with you," the berdache said.

And with that they both rose solemnly from their game, leaving the ivory tiles scattered on the floor, and walked out.

"Wait," I said, trailing them into the hall.

But they wouldn't wait, and when I caught up to them, they looked at me without seeing, two faces each closed like a door.

They left The Citadel that day, never to return. Anna Maria was inconsolable. First Bronwyn, now Tu-Li and the berdache. All her pets. The South Wing stood in rebellion against the North Wing, and the divided house could not stand.

The betrayal was so complete, so bitter, that I cast about for additional explanations. It could not be wholly my fault. Bronwyn, Tu-Li and the berdache had left because the scandal burned too hot. Or because the family had lost its wealth. Maybe they knew something they didn't want to tell. They were the petty ones, not me.

By the third week in April, our move from the residence began in earnest. Whenever I emerged from my room, I would encounter strange groups of men in shirtsleeves and arm garters, watched over by the still-faithful Winston. They carted away pieces of furniture, examined the premises, measured the rooms with tape measures.

Creditors. Our collapse was complete.

We opened the communicating hallway between our house and Swoony's to the north, transferring our much-diminished possessions in a sad parade.

Swoony's place was the twin of ours, with the exception that the furnishings in our house had been sparkling new and in use while hers were covered with canvas sheets. She lived in just two rooms on the first floor. Perversely, I could relate to the surroundings, everything masked and thwarted and old.

One of my last acts before we shut the hallway and departed The Citadel forever was to venture into Bronwyn's old quarters in the South Wing. Here, alone among all the rooms of the house, nothing much had been disturbed. Anna Maria couldn't bear to pack away Bronwyn's things. She still hoped for her pet to come back.

I lay down on her bed. One or another of the now-dismissed servants had kept the furnishings dusted and neatened, and it resembled a place whose occupant had just stepped out, shortly to return. The room still smelled of her. Like beach sand, oranges, mown hay.

She had left everything behind. The million-dollar wardrobe hung in the dressing room we had created for her. The special bathtub Anna Maria had commissioned remained, empty and dry. A book—a translation of *The Letters of Abelard and Heloise*—lay cracked open on the bedside table.

Bronwyn's casual rejection of the things we had given her shocked me, demonstrating a lack of normal human sentiment that brought to mind a snake sloughing off its skin. I thought of a favorite phrase of Professor James: "the unbribed soul."

We had tried to buy her, but she would not be bought.

I reached beneath the armoire, hoping somehow that she might have left her totem items: her pathetic books, childhood doll, lethal razor claws. The battered little canvas bag was gone. She took only what she came with and left behind destruction in her wake.

Fury rose in me, a white-hot anger that felt almost pleasurable, because it had been weeks since my inner life had become dulled and pinched off. And as I could not bring myself to hate Bronwyn herself, I focused upon Bev Willets. He was the one. He had poisoned her mind against us, encouraged her rebellion, seduced her emotions.

He had taken up with Delia Showalter. Now he would do the same with Bronwyn.

Why? Why did Bev Willets do anything? Because he could. Out of some Iago-like motiveless malignity. Because, even as a young child, he liked to break things.

My new quarters in Grandmother's house I left undusted and closed, the canvas covering still on the bed. I slept in a chair. I didn't bother to unpack my belongings. I simply brooded, allowing my anger, distress and petulance to mature until they wholly took me over.

I pawed through a lifetime of Bev's perceived slights, picking at each scab until it bled afresh. Beverly the scoundrel, Beverly the mean, Beverly who had presided over one of my signal childhood humiliations, a depantsing in the bathroom of Collegiate School.

The age-old riddle: You walk in upon your love in the embrace of another. You react with mindless rage and happen to have a pistol in your hand. But which one do you shoot?

Your mate? The interloper? Both? What satisfies your sense of hurt, your wounded honor? Your choice reveals an essential aspect of your character. Who are you, Leontes or Othello?

Women, I am told, tend toward killing the rival, while men usually shoot their betraying spouse. It is not a hard-and-fast rule. Some years ago, you will recall, Congressman Dan Sickles killed his wife's lover, Key.

I've always found it a trick question. My forlorn response to the riddle, which I would never publicly admit to, my answer, my secret, hidden, unconfessed answer: I would shoot myself.

There exists a very deep level of the human mind where homicide and suicide are one and the same thing.

I finally bearded Bev Willets at his club, the Union. Not wishing to relive the indignity of the recent evening when I burst in on him at his town house, I planned an ambush. I contrived to enter the hushed, thickly carpeted and tobacco-flavored precincts of Manhattan's most exclusive gentlemen's establishment, sneaking in like an impostor. A big leather armchair in the parlor off the billiards room provided a useful blind in which to conceal myself.

I knew he would come. I simply waited. And, stupidly, I must have dozed, since I woke to Bev shaking me roughly.

"Delegate, old dog!" he said jauntily. "If you're looking for her, you won't find her here. We don't allow women in the Union, though I see they've made an exception for you."

"Be quiet and listen to what I have to say," I told him.

I noticed that even though he affected a casual indifference, Bev's eyes roamed to my hands and belt, checking for weapons.

"Come to give me what for?"

"I've come to tell you what an odious swine you are," I said.

"In that case let me call for brandy," he said. He motioned over a waiter.

"Shut up!" I shouted. In my frustration I failed to notice that we had drawn an audience. In the billiards room next door, the balls had stopped clacking. A half dozen young Union Club swells gathered in the doorway, amused expressions on their dull faces.

I tried and failed to lower my voice. "You forget that I know you," I said to Bev. "I know your vile ways with women, how you use them and then throw them away as if they were garbage."

The random "I say!" and "That's rich!" emanated from our audience. I put my face close to Bev's. He affected an unruffled air. "This time you've gone too far," I hissed. "I won't have it."

"Have you spoken to Bronwyn about this? Because even though *you* won't have it, I'm afraid *she* will."

Rude whistles from the billiard boys.

I almost struck Bev then but held my hand. "You've disturbed my sister's mind to the point she is not thinking clearly."

"Your sister! You really are mad, do you know that? You've lived with her, given her the immense benefit of your acquaintance, yet you don't know a thing about her. Do you know she prefers coffee to your stupid weak Delegate tea? That she has trouble with the kind of pink-skinned dogs your family persists in keeping? That the color you see on her lips is not rouge but strawberry juice?"

"Shut up!" I shouted again.

"If you're so in love with her, you should really shave off that ridiculous beard of yours. She doesn't like fuzzy bears. How could you not know that? How could you not know anything about her? Are you so lost in yourself not to realize what you have right in front of you?"

"Sir?" The waiter, upset that our disagreement had disturbed the tomblike stillness of the late-afternoon sitting room, had summoned help, two burly club doormen.

"All right, Delegate," Bev said. "This evening, nine o'clock upstairs under the eaves at my place, come ready to fight."

He turned to the doormen. "Could you escort Mr. Delegate to the door and see to it he's not allowed to return?" Applause from the billiards room as I left.

Escorted roughly out into the streets of Manhattan, I charged around, down to Washington Square, back up Fifth, finally settling in at the Madison Square Delmonico's. A despised member of the notorious Delegate clan now, I was cut repeatedly by acquaintances and waiters alike, but I didn't care. I ordered a steak and, when it finally came, examined it for kitchen spittle before tearing into the beef like an animal.

Replaying every thrust and parry of my verbal clash with Bev.

"Under the eaves." The Willets mansion came equipped with all the fashionable touches, including a top-floor racquets court illuminated by skylights. A pretty space, the site of many previous competitions as well as incidental parties and random debaucheries.

At ten after nine, I arrived at the town house and was charitably welcomed by Margolis the butler. Marching up the stairs to the garret at the top of the house, I experienced the hollow-stomached, weak-groined sensation I always got before a boxing match. Margolis waited below as I climbed the rickety fourth-floor stairway to the court.

"Best of luck, sir," he said.

"We who are about to die salute you," I called back.

Stepping into the gymnasium, I experienced fresh humiliation. Spectators. A few of the billiard-room boys, the Bliss brothers, Jones Abercrombie.

And Bronwyn. She stood to one side with Victoria Woodhull, Tennessee Claflin and a small clutch of other women. Just to distract me, wearing bloomers again.

I would not be spared, it seemed, any possible opportunity for shame.

"Delegate! Finally!" Bev called out with false heartiness. "We thought you might back out."

"Let's get to it," I said, ignoring the audience, which had gathered at the far end of the space. There for amusement and entertainment. I thought back to when Bev and I performed our mock-combat dance during the German at the debut.

"Oh, I like the fights," I heard Bronwyn chatter. "My old mother told me women always enjoy watching the fights because they like to see some man get what's coming to him."

Laughter from the assembly. They loved her.

The overheated racquets court made my head swim. Bev always kept the whole town house blazing, as if to declare himself separate from those faceless poor who could not afford coal. Even before the contest, sweat had broken out on my skin. I'm afraid I appeared nervous.

When Bev stripped off his shirt, I realized I had underestimated him woefully. Lately he had taken up the gymnasium training craze, employing a medicine ball and Indian clubs. His gym master had him running around a wooden track like a dog.

Next to him my physical shortcomings were thrown into high relief. In the court's mirror, I appeared hollow-chested, spindly. I had violet shadows beneath my eyes. My beard was in disarray, as though a porcupine had assaulted my face and then stuck itself there.

Bev and I had fought many times throughout our childhood. He always eventually gained the advantage. The rule is that a boxer will beat a brawler every time, but with us such distinctions went out the window, our antipathy for each other quickly taking over, making us flail.

We had done so before in this very same space. Some of the dark stains on the hardwood floor were no doubt the old unscrubbed outlines from blood spilled in childhood, which as everyone knows is ineradicable.

We both oiled. No signal, no bell, simply a "Yup" from Bev and we went at it, larruping each other mightily. For a good five minutes after we started, the only sound was the solid whack and slap of our blows.

Some fights are determined not by skill but by which combatant is angrier. I believed I was gaining the upper hand. Bev was punishing me, though. I could feel my brain caroming around inside my skull like a cue ball. My bum foot was a handicap.

Then we both swung wild punches and, with simultaneous lucky shots, knocked each other out.

The last sensation for me, before a woozy spiral into unconsciousness, was Bronwyn's chiming laughter and her saying, "Excellent, gents, very well done."

❧ 25 ❧

At seven o'clock on May Day morning, slipping past the few hardy souls who still hung in ambush about our block, not waiting for Swoony's dry-toast-and-weak-tea breakfast, I shook off the gawkers and took a hansom cab down to the East River docks, to board *Saxon,* of the Sprague Line, the last steam coastal headed for Boston that would arrive in daylight.

When I reached the dock and was waiting to board, my skin suddenly bristled, as the skin of a mouse must crawl when it's around a cat. I felt somehow observed, stalked. I darted a glance over both shoulders, quickly, in order not to attract attention to myself. Nothing.

All the murders, all the bloody gashes, all the obliterated organs. The thought had preoccupied me for the past few weeks, that I had been present at every crime scene. Matthew Donleavy, the waiter at Palmer House in Chicago. Our groom from The Ditches, Graham Barton, his body only recently identified. The nameless Gypsy dancer. Percy Roehm, the young heir at the Fifth Avenue Hotel. Pollard, the Human Polar Bear at Coney Island. Even Fince's brother, Peter—well, I had been in the general vicinity of Virginia City when it happened.

By some lights, by some narrowly suspicious lights—by a policeman's lights, in other words—I could have done them all.

That the police had not caught up with me yet was tribute only to the gross incompetence of the law. But that didn't make me feel much better. I often thought the day would arrive when some eager detective would come knocking at my door.

Or the Savage Girl would. Because the only other person I could think of who was at each and every crime scene was Bronwyn. She might suspect that I knew too much, that I understood there was some kind of a link between her and these horrible murders. Plus, she had a sharp instrument in her possession that she could employ against anyone, including me.

Whenever I saw a young, shapely woman from behind, approaching her so that I could not glimpse her face, seeing only thick black hair pinned up under her hat, I would always think of Bronwyn, the savagery in her waiting only to come out, seeking the opportunity to claim her next victim.

On the dock one such woman triggered in me staccato thoughts of fear and flight. I looked again. Not her. *I am mad. I am mad.* What Fince shouted before Tu-Li finished him, the words now ringing in my brain.

I occupied my time on the way up by reading Professor James's lecture notes on paranoia. I planned to throw myself on his mercy as a patient, though the only sure cure for what I had would be for me somehow to turn back the clock.

The coastal went along at a fast clip, breasting the shallow gray waves, past Long Island, Connecticut, Nantucket, Cape Cod. The speed of the boat helped me forget my fears, at least for now. By the time I arrived in Cambridge, it was four o'clock in the afternoon. I had gotten over the feeling of being tracked, but I still felt poorly, agitated to the degree that I noticed my hands trembled more than usual.

The James house on Quincy Street had generous proportions, a gracious yard behind a glossy black gate, with banks of late-blooming forsythia all around the verge. I climbed the steps and rang the bell, wondering if escaping my troubles by falling upon the hospitality of my professor was the best idea.

Alice James, attired in spider-gray velvet, came up promptly behind the houseboy.

"Hugo, we were so glad of your telegram. Come in."

"Ho!" sounded a deep voice behind her. Not Professor James but an older man who resembled him, his father, Henry James Sr. "I have heard about you, young man." He shook my hand with vigor.

"Have you?" I offered.

"I know that you provided William with an excellent pupil in Cambridge and with excellent fare in Manhattan."

I had heard something of the senior James, too, that he had gypsied his family around Europe and America while the children were growing up, settling in no place for more than a year or two, parking them in experimental schools and with private tutors and somehow giving them a marvelous education in the middle of all the upheaval.

William told me that he had already toured Europe five times and that he was fluent in five languages. His brother, Henry James, relocated permanently to London, was well on the way toward becoming a serious writer. Within the family, though, the two geniuses were merely "Willy" and "Harry."

The interior of the house was light and warm, the atrium entry hall toasting under the early-May sun streaming in through a greenhouse-style roof. I remembered something James once said to me when we worked in the science laboratory, our papers spread out in front of us, a beautiful snowfall pressing up against the bank of windows. "The light is shrieking away outside."

It has been my observation that when you are feeling bad, no environment, no matter how pleasant, can lift the pall. I suspected that these two people, Alice and her father, could not help but notice the corners of my mouth sagging, that they feared I might break into tears at any moment.

"Let our man take your overcoat," said Mr. James Sr.

"Hugo." Professor James had joined us. "Glad to see you. A delightful break from reading examination papers." All around the entrance hall towered a series of palms in square containers on a glossy parquet floor. Three collegial armchairs stood clustered in a corner, with a shawl thrown over the back of one. It was easy to imagine Alice sitting there alone, awaiting company. Me.

"Mary!" shouted William's father in the direction of the stairs. "We have a guest!"

"She needn't come down," said Alice of her mother. "We've planned a walk anyway."

"No, please," I said. "I've just come to consult with Dr. James."

With that I physically pulled my professor into the little receiving room to the right of the front door.

"Delegate?" he said, baffled at my abrupt treatment of his family. "I thought we might take a stroll around the Yard."

I shut the door. "You have to help me," I said. "I believe I am going mad."

For fifteen minutes I spewed forth a steady stream of anguish. James was fast becoming America's premier authority on psychology and the human mind. I grabbed at him like a drowning man.

"Can there be such a thing as a dissociative state, a trance a person goes into and afterward he has no awareness of what he has done?"

Certainly, Professor James said. He had seen it occur.

"Can there be two selves in one body?" I asked. "And one goes out and does things, horrible things, and then wakes up to become the other, without memory?"

I ran through it then, the fact that wherever I went, murder seemed to follow. I could not be certain what I had done, but with the memory gaps, the uncanny coincidences, the serial procession of dead bodies, I was beset by doubts.

"It all seems bizarre," I said. "I know that I've been gripped with horrible rages lately. I feel like my head has been in a vise. Could it be paresis?"

"But isn't it a common characteristic of paresis not to recognize the symptoms of paresis?" James responded.

He questioned me. About the concussion I suffered after the Gypsy killing in the park, whether the memory gaps had been more serious since that time. Did I link the incidents mentally with any other person? My mother or father?

I had left Bronwyn out of the whole story.

He listened. Bless him, he listened. When I finished, he offered no palliatives, but I somehow felt relieved. We fell into a long silence.

"Well, Hugo," James finally said. "I am truly sorry. Of course, we couldn't help but hear about your tribulations at home."

"It's not good," I said, choking up slightly.

"I would suggest you remove yourself from the fray a bit. You've been up at St. Alban's before, I recall?"

St. Alban's Recuperative Home, in Wellesley, an asylum for those beset by nerves and exhaustion. I had retreated there almost exactly a year ago. My doctor-torturers induced seizures, fed me copious amounts of butter, put me in cold baths for hours, afterward covering my body with wet canvas. Strict silence enforced at all times.

None of it helped. My instability of mind had persisted.

Professor James suggested that he should take charge of my pistol, the one that Colm Cullen had given me. "Someday when you tell me you don't see the need of it anymore, I will give it back to you."

"That doesn't make any sense," I said.

"Your keeping a pistol is what does not make sense. Guns are like thermometers, only instead of measuring body temperature they measure our fear."

I gave him the weapon. He slipped it into a desk drawer. It was easier to give up the pistol, knowing I had a trusty sliding knife in my breast pocket.

"Shall we walk out?" said Professor James. "Alice will be anxious for us, and I thought you might want to reacquaint yourself with your school, which has dearly missed your presence."

We exited the little room into the residence's entry hall. The professor's mother, Mary James, peered from behind her full-bearded husband. "Very pleased," she said. "No tea, then?"

"No, Mother," said Alice. "We must go if we want to catch the last of the light."

"Very nice to meet you," I said, and once again the elder Mr. James gripped my hand.

We crossed the street to the campus, and I was immediately flooded with memories of my Harvard days, of plunging myself into studies so completely that everything else in the world—most of all my small fears and worries—melted away. I rarely socialized when I was at school. Unlike in New York, where there was always temptation, a group of raging young fashionables ready to invade a restaurant or a club or take a rollicking dive into the Tenderloin.

We turned in among all the old familiar red bricks, the Yard greening up with the season. The warm weather pricked at my mood.

Alice said, "The ancient superstition as to spring and youth being the most joyous periods is pretty well exploded, don't you think?" She took William's hand. "The one is the most depressing moment of the year, so is the other the most difficult of life."

"I suppose," I said, "but my own difficulties are . . ."

"Overwhelming?" asked James. "You know, you can speak before my sister with perfect confidence. Crises and debilitating anxieties have long been my bosom companions. Alice, too—do you mind my saying, Alice?—has struggled often with the idea of self-death. Haven't you, dearest dear?"

"What to do about it is the question," said Alice. "My best answer: clothe oneself in neutral tints, walk by still waters and possess one's soul in silence."

Well. Another prescription.

"That is precisely what I have thought," said James.

"Nonetheless I have found that of all the arts," said Alice, "living is the most exquisite and rewarding."

"Again, what I was thinking," said James.

"And your sister, Bronwyn?" Alice asked me. "I was very much impressed to meet her in New York. Such an interesting, intelligent, fierce presence."

We rounded the corner past Massachusetts Hall. And Harvard Hall, where I had so often labored late into the night, immersed in my studies, never imagining the troubles in my future.

"Let me tell you a beautiful, touching tale," said Alice.

"Here we go," said James. "Now, listen."

"An old couple near Boston who had lived together for half a century became destitute and had to sell all their things, and had nothing before them but the dreaded poorhouse, where they would have meat and drink, to be sure, but where they would be separated. They could handle all but that, so one day they went out together and never came back, and their old bodies were found tied together in the river. How perfect a death!"

"Alice is having a good day," James said mildly. We silently parsed her tale.

A loose-limbed fellow with big teeth and shaggy brown hair ambled toward us across the Yard.

"Oh, not that fool Roosevelt," I muttered. I took James's elbow, he took Alice's, and we guided ourselves in the opposite direction.

"The newspapers came to attack your sister like wolves," James said.

"It makes me glad to be of such small moment in the world," said Alice.

Professor James said, "Tennessee wrote us that Bronwyn had moved in at their town house."

I searched his words for irony or disapproval. How could I explain?

"She was so beautiful at her debut, so perfect." I said. "Everyone loved her. And then it all fell apart."

We stood in the middle of the Yard, in front of Mass Hall, and the shadows tumbled stone blue all around us. A ripple of coolness passed through the air. Alice pulled her shawl close.

I said, "A shooting, a stabbing, a boy's body and all the flood of stories—it's no wonder she went away." I wiped my eyes. "She went to the Woodhulls, yes."

"Is she unhappy?" asked Alice.

"The odd thing is, I don't think so. I don't know. When she left us, it looked as though she were embarking on a grand adventure."

"She'll have an adventure, certainly, with those women," said Alice as we resumed walking back toward Quincy Street.

"And my heart is so sick," said I. "I wanted to protect her. To care for her. But those things are impossible."

"What will you do?" asked Alice.

"What *is* there to do?" I said. I suddenly remembered Bev's absurd words of advice: All you've got to do is shave your beard. But where would that get me?

"There is only one thing for it," said Alice.

"Tell me," I begged. For some reason my heart felt totally open to the tiny woman with the sad eyes, my professor's invalid sister.

"You have got to fall in love," she said.

"Funny," said William James, "I was just thinking that."

I did not resort to St. Alban's sanatorium. I took the night train home from Boston and walked out of the Grand Central Depot into a brand-new springtime morning.

Manhattan in May. I wondered, for an uncharacteristically eu-phoric moment, whether there could be any more exciting place on earth. I had to remind myself I was miserable. The mildness of the air tempered the usual street cacophony. Calm self-satisfaction showed on all the handsome passing faces. The lions in the jungle were happy.

Half a block toward Fifth, I entered a storefront barbershop and had the man render me clean-shaven. The strop of the straight razor, the hot towel, the blade at my throat. And I was a newborn babe.

As I walked north, a hot, soft pretzel materialized in my hand. Eventually the green of the park rose up into view like the opening of a picture book. We Delegates could pull through this financial night-mare, I thought bravely. Plus, Bronwyn was in the world, she was somewhere in this city, drinking coffee and wearing Turkish slippers (though not bloomers, I hoped) and smiling her Bronwyn smile.

I had been told to fall in love. It wasn't hard. I discovered myself already there.

Swoony's manservant, Mike, shut the door behind me, and I dropped my bag onto the floor and sighed. A deep and dark stairhall, taste that hadn't changed in years.

"Hugo, dear," I heard Swoony call. "In here, darling!"

Swoony's downstairs parlor was the usual place to find her now. I walked in the door talking. "That coastal to Boston *is* really fast, Grandmo—"

Bronwyn sat on the divan beside my grandmother. Clad in a dress of tangerine silk that fell in a pool around her feet. Her lustrous, wavy hair she wore loose around her shoulders. She had changed her ap-pearance, though. I realized that she had cut her hair in a fringe across her brow, the new style called "bangs" that all the girls would now describe as "charming."

She rested her hazel eyes on me, a luminous gaze that worked to stop me in my tracks every time.

"Oh," I said. For some reason I began to back out, as if I had blundered into a private place.

"Hugo, stay, stay, of course," said Swoony. "We have a guest." She toasted me with her teacup.

I hadn't noticed, being overwhelmed by the mere fact of Bronwyn, but there was another woman present.

Seated across from the divan, in the soft velvet chair that we called "the comfortable one," the elderly lady wore black from head to toe, shabby black, offset by a bright white handkerchief in her lap. At first I thought that Swoony in her unpredictable way had invited a potential housekeeper in for an interview and was now feeding her tea. The woman's hair, too, was black, a deep, wavy black, pulled up and pinned in back.

Bronwyn's black hair.

"Hugo," said Bronwyn. It was the first I had heard her voice in a month. "This is my mother, Mallt Bowen."

I stood there. Her mother now. So. She didn't spring from a god's forehead after all.

"I'm grateful to make your acquaintance," said Mallt. Her voice faint, with a Gaelic lilt.

As in a dream, I stepped over and bowed to Bronwyn's mother. Her real mother. Even if I hadn't been introduced, it would quickly have become obvious. I looked into her face and saw Bronwyn's brow, Bronwyn's nose, Bronwyn's mouth.

"Excuse me," she said, and spit bloody sputum into the handkerchief.

"How did . . . ?" I said—to the mother or the daughter or Swoony, whoever knew—asking how this impossible reunion had come to pass.

"Freddy found her," Bronwyn said.

"We missed our daughter," said Bronwyn's mother. "We missed

her ever so much. We knew she was taken by those terrible savages. We thought she'd been kilt for sure."

Swoony petted Bronwyn's hair. "That's our Virginia," she said.

Looking momentarily puzzled, Mallt said, "We heard all the mining jobs was down in Argentina, so we went there."

"But how did you hear about Bronwyn?"

"A man come looking for us," she said. "A man your father sent. And Bronwyn kept her name, you see. Didn't you, darling?"

"Virginia," purred Swoony.

"I lost Hugh Brace along the way, Bronwyn's stepfather. He had the consumption. But I made it here, I did."

"Yes, you did, Mother," said Bronwyn.

"And there's only one Delegate family in town," said Mallt. "You was easy to find."

"Virginia Delegate," said Swoony, sipping.

"I don't like those folks that crowd the streets here," Mallt said. "Ugly people, ugly."

"It's all right," said Bronwyn.

A coughing spasm racked her mother, the daughter moved to position the old lady more comfortably in the chair, and Mallt Bowen lapsed into a closed-eye meditation.

My emotions piled up like storm clouds. I cannot let anything unsteady me, I told myself. I crossed to the window.

"And Bronwyn," I said, finally facing her. "You've returned."

"I missed Nicky," she said. She joined me at the window.

"Really," I said.

"Those women are false," she said. "Woodhull and Claflin. I couldn't trust them after all. Then Freddy sent for me, and I heard I might have a living mother. So here I am."

Her eyes held me. "You've shaved."

I trembled inwardly, standing so close. The scent of oranges. "You know, you have a small macula," I said.

Bronwyn stiffened. "A what?"

"A speck," I said. What was I saying? Babbling on. "Just a little black bar on the rim of the iris. In your left eye. I've noticed it before."

She appeared alarmed. My face felt hot.

"It's nothing," I said quickly. "I'm sorry I mentioned it."

Bronwyn turned away, flustered, and went to Mallt, then knelt and laid her head in the woman's lap. "I'll never leave you," she murmured. But she still looked strangely back at me.

I didn't know whether to put my arms around the two of them or warn the mother that she had a killer for a daughter.

"What should we do now?" I asked.

"Drink tea," said Swoony.

❦ 26 ❧

I wish I could tell you that it was all sunshine and roses from there on in. Nicky returned from exile at Cousin Willie's. We were a family again, he and Bronwyn and Freddy and Anna Maria and I. But we were like a vase cracked and put back together without glue. One touch could make us fall apart again.

How I read it: Bronwyn had left us in order to be free, and she returned because she was willing to sacrifice that freedom to be with her mother. She knew we would take Mallt in.

Toward me she appeared skittish. When I entered a room, she often as not left it. During the day she stayed by her mother's side, making sure she was comfortable, helping the nurse whom Swoony had hired. We came slowly to grasp how completely illness had taken over the woman.

We could thank Freddy for Mallt Bowen, and for the few details that she summoned forth regarding Bronwyn's early life. It took a while, but Freddy's hired detectives finally tracked down the story of a child taken by wild Indians, a couple bereft, their subsequent travel to South America. Found, too late, the stepfather dead, the mother dying.

Bronwyn had been born in the Port of Philadelphia on July 19, 1857, on the first day of Dan and Mallt Bowen's arrival in the United States from Wales. The family relocated to the coalfields of northeastern Pennsylvania, then, with the Civil War raging, to the mining towns of Colorado. In an unheralded Comanche raid, she was taken, aged four, in late spring 1862.

So her real name was Bronwyn Bowen. Her real age, eighteen.

Bronwyn might have acted the dutiful daughter during the day, but in the evening she continued to leave the house. Not covertly, dressed as a boy, as she used to, but openly, brazenly.

The ostensible reason, she said, was her charity work with women of the night. She had recruited Edna Croker into the task. Recovering after the Fifth Avenue Hotel tragedy, Edna felt well enough to engage in the pursuit, especially since it meant spending time with her beloved Bronwyn. Several times Colm went with them as a bodyguard, if their target neighborhood was particularly low.

"They pass out bundles," Colm said when I asked after Bronwyn's nighttime activities. "She's keen to get them fallen ladies engaged as seamstresses. They have a doctor with them, and some nurses."

"And afterward?" I asked. "She goes out?"

"Afterward she comes home," Colm said. "At least she did when I was along."

I didn't entirely trust his account. He appeared to have become a complete Bronwyn partisan. I was surrounded by them. I was also stung she hadn't invited me to accompany her on her missions of mercy.

Love is a coin played often for its obverse, jealousy. My lovesick neediness appeared not to impress Bronwyn. She continued to avoid me and, when we spent time together, to act distracted and remote.

I swear that I did not actively spy on her. Knowing at least that much, that a sure way to kill love is to worry it.

Why did I follow her that particular night? All that day and the day before, there had been a flurry of activity on her part for which I could not fully account—hurried meetings in the stairhall with Edna Croker, notes sent by messenger, notes received. Something was clearly up.

"The last two missives were to the Showalter place," Mike the butler told me when I buttonholed him.

"Showalter? That can't be," I said.

"Before that, two from Croker, then two more to Croker," Mike said.

Colm told me he had no idea what was happening, if indeed something was. "Young ladies," he said, as if that explained it all.

Which it very well could have. But my feelings for Bronwyn were not to be denied. I could not simply settle into an evening of anatomical drawing and forget about her.

A thunderstorm hammered in from the west, bringing hail that afternoon and a drenching rain afterward.

"I hope you have the good sense of staying in tonight," Anna Maria said to Bronwyn at dinner.

"I'm going to Edna Croker's," Bronwyn said. "Her family is having an evening at home."

"I suppose that's all right," Nicky said, assuming the pompous air of a social secretary. "Although I might wish for a more exalted company. The Crokers remain not quite comme il faut."

"Don't be precocious, dear," Anna Maria said.

"They are the only family that will accept me as a guest," Bronwyn said.

"A recital?" I asked.

"You shan't come," she said to me, a tad abruptly, I thought. Softening, she said, "You'd be extremely bored. Bel canto, not to your taste."

You are lying, the green-eyed monster within me said.

"Take the barouche," Freddy said, forgetting we had already sold it.

"She's picking me up in her coach," Bronwyn said.

Stormy as it was that night, I made it my business to be waiting in the darkness of Sixty-third Street as the Croker coach pulled up in front of Swoony's. Mike helped in a heavily veiled Bronwyn. Edna herself, whom I glimpsed as the coachman passed down Fifth, appeared veiled also. I followed them downtown.

The pelting rain transformed the graveled avenue into slop. My suspicions rose to new heights when the coach stopped at Forty-second and Fifth for a new passenger, a woman who left a second carriage parked alongside the reservoir and quickly climbed inside the coach with Edna and Bronwyn. In the rain, that it was indeed a female was all I could see, since furthermore her face remained totally obscured by veils, scarves and wraps.

The coach abruptly swung back north, turning in the middle of the thoroughfare. I had to pull my mount smartly around to prevent myself from being seen. I needn't have bothered, for in the next moment the Croker coach pulled to the curb. The trio of occupants got out and, shielding their heads from the downpour, transferred to a hansom cab.

More and more strange. I couldn't imagine what it was all about, but I didn't like the feel of it. Back up Fifth Avenue, a block past the rising scaffolds of the Catholic cathedral a-building, to arrive at an elegant, four-story chocolate-stucco mansion at the northeast corner of Fifty-second Street.

The place's somewhat forbidding aspect stemmed from the dearth of gaslight around it. Oddly, that specific stretch of Fifth lacked streetlamps. Most houses at least illuminated their own doorways and grounds, out of a sense of display or for simple safety. Not so this one, which stood well shrouded by the night, to be only occasionally lit by fissures of lightning.

The three women left the cab, did not approach the front door of the house but instead proceeded along a dark walkway to the side until they were swallowed by the gloom.

The caper began to feel dangerous to me. Whatever they were up to, it did not involve a stay-at-home vocal recital under the watchful gazes of Mr. and Mrs. Croker.

Thoroughly drenched, acting entirely on impulse, I hitched my mount across Fifth Avenue and plunged down the little walkway myself, wishing at least to establish into what door my quarry had disappeared. But when I rounded the back corner of the mansion, I blundered directly into them in the dark.

I make a poor footpad, but in my defense the three of them were dressed head to toe in black, the entrance they stood before was unlit, plus the rain obscured all.

Edna Croker emitted a little gasping shriek as I collided with her.

"Hugo," I heard Bronwyn hiss. Two things happened. The anonymous woman with them collapsed into a faint, and the door in front of which we stood cracked open, allowing a thin gleam of yellow light to emerge.

By that illumination I saw that the third veiled woman, slumped lifelessly now in Edna Croker's arms, was Delia Showalter.

I felt weak in the knees myself.

"Don't you go down, too, damn you," Bronwyn said, seizing my arm.

"What's happening here?" I asked. I meant it as a demand, but it came out more resembling a yelp.

"Bronwyn Bowen," Bronwyn announced to the maidservant who had opened the door. The servant nodded but then reclosed the door sharply.

"Bronwyn," I said.

"Oh, my God," Delia moaned, coming back to life. "Oh, my precious God." She turned her face to the corner of the doorway.

"Why'd you have to come?" Bronwyn asked, her voice fierce.

"Now that he's here, we need him," Edna whispered to her. "We need a man."

Bronwyn shook her head, dismissive. "He won't be able to take it."

The maidservant opened the door again, beckoning us in.

"I have to know what's going on," I said.

Bronwyn hesitated, then put her face into mine. "We're in trouble. You make a scene, you do anything except keep your mouth shut and look pretty, I'll slice open your guts and feed them to Rags."

The imperative in her words impressed me—authoritarian yes, but with a desperate pleading mixed in, too. Such was her sway over me that I could not, at that moment, do anything except exactly as Bronwyn commanded. I meekly followed them into the dark-lit mansion for I knew not what purpose.

A parlor or waiting room of sorts, replicating the gloom outside by utilizing only a single candelabrum for its uncertain glow. The hearth unlit. Flowered carpets, velvet curtains, engravings of Dutch masterworks hung on the wall beside the ormolu mantel clock. An air of restrained opulence. It did not feel to me like a brothel, but there was something mercantile about it, not a private home. A smell of carbolic in the air.

The maidservant had disappeared, and when she returned I caught a quick glimpse of the interior: two women walking side by side in loose kimono-style white robes. From somewhere deep within the house, the squall of an infant.

"Madam Restell will soon be with you," said the maidservant.

With those words the scales fell from my eyes and I felt the world crashing down upon me.

Everyone knew Madam Restell. She had become wealthy even before the war, but after that time her fortune, one of the first big mail-order fortunes ever, rivaled those of some of the wealthiest men in Manhattan. She didn't earn respect for it, though, but hatred.

Madam Restell helped women to adopt out babies, and she helped women avoid having babies, too. People commonly jeered and spit at her elegant carriage as it conveyed her openly about the town.

I felt it impossible to recover my equilibrium. Madam Restell! "The Most Evil Woman in New York!" A living, breathing, walking scandal, a tempting target for every preacher and Puritan, subject of tirade after tirade in the press.

Naturally, I did not track the exact movements of such an odious personality, but the last I heard, she operated out of an unassuming yellow clapboard house in Greenwich Village. Now here she was on Fifth Avenue, having come up in the world.

Madam Restell, who advertised as a female physician in the *Herald*, promoting herself as a dispenser of pills and nostrums:

> Madam Restell's experience and knowledge in the treatment of cases of female irregularity, is such as to require but a few days to effect a perfect cure.

Madam Restell, abortionist.

I flung myself into one of the upholstered chairs in the waiting room. A boiling wrath erupted inside me and I leaped back to my feet. Somehow I directed my anger not against Bronwyn, the guilty party, but against Delia.

"How could you bring her here?" I snarled, seizing Delia by the arm, wrenching her hand from her weeping eyes.

Delia shrank away as if in horror. "Please, please, please, we must leave!" she cried.

Bronwyn moved in between us.

"No, no, this is not right," I said. I grabbed Bronwyn and looked her square in the face. "You must have the child!"

She took a single step back.

I spoke quickly to her, a flurry of pleading. "I don't care who knows, we will accept it into our family, your lying-in, everything will be taken care of, but not this! Not this! Please, Bronwyn. Keep the child!"

Competing angers battled for my attention. Anger toward the man who had spoiled my love. Bev? One of the Bliss brothers? The Gypsy dancer? The candidates were many. Anger toward Delia and Edna, conspirators who had brought Bronwyn to this awful house of shame.

And then the woman herself entered to us, Madam Restell, in a rich black silk gown, lace mantilla trimmed in fur, white satin bonnet. The very luxury of her costume enraged me. It seemed the height of indignity that this woman, who I featured at that moment should be flung into the pits of hell, instead walked the earth in finery.

"Miss Bowen," she said in a calm voice, moving forward to take Bronwyn's hand. "This must be too, too sad for you and your"— looking at us, choosing her words—"friends."

Wanting to pound her to the floor, I remained paralyzed in her presence.

"All will be well," Restell said. "I have stood in this room with countless weeping females and seen those same young ladies but a short month later, all gay and laughing in carriages on the concourses of the Central Park."

"We should go!" Delia cried out.

"Now is not the time to lose your nerve," Restell said, still addressing Bronwyn. She turned to me. "And this? Is this the man responsible?"

The strangeness of the surroundings, the appalling circumstance I found myself fallen into, most of all Bronwyn's degraded status served to rob me entirely of words. I could not answer Madam Restell. I would have known my lines, if I could have but said them, drawing myself up like the hero in a melodrama. "Me, madam? I am not her betrayer! But I shall be her avenger!"

"Yes, yes," Restell said, as if responding to my unspoken sentiment. "It is always the same. The men are always right, but it is the women who are wronged."

Edna wept, too, now, the whole waiting room awash in emotion. Clucking, Madam Restell said, "Who comes with her to the examination?"

She glanced at me. "Not you. You look as if you like to faint. You had better sit down."

"No!" I shouted, and took Bronwyn protectively in my arms.

Restell shrugged. "Then her," she said, indicating Edna. With that the abortionist gathered up Delia Showalter and, Edna Croker following, conducted her into the examination room.

I had been well pummeled by blows the whole evening, serial realizations that led me into ever darker regions of my mind, but now I formed a new understanding that staggered me all over again.

It was not in fact Bronwyn who was here for Madam Restell. It was Delia Showalter.

"Tell me something, Hugo," Bronwyn said as we were left alone. "Have you been a fool your whole life?"

I sank back into a chair, all clear thought thwarted by emotion.

"We're lucky the poor girl didn't die of shame simply from your presence," Bronwyn said.

Bile rose in my throat, and I felt sick to my stomach. Bronwyn kicked a spittoon over from a corner and positioned it in front of me.

"You could actually help, you know," she said. "Instead of being a drag on the whole enterprise."

"The enterprise!" I wailed.

"She needs a strong arm to lean on," Bronwyn said. "Let's leave judgments and upsets and anger behind for now, all right? Let's just get through this night."

I looked up at her. I am sure my face was a mask of distress. I could not understand her expression. It appeared cold to me. Savage. Yes, yes, all very well to say, leave judgments behind. But here she was, judging me!

"I am sorry we ever brought you here from Virginia City," I whispered.

"You didn't bring me," she said. "I came."

Bronwyn told me to do nothing but sit upon the small chair in the waiting room, exactly where I was, not to move until I was called upon. Then she went into the examination room.

"Don't stir from this place," she said as she left. "But be ready."

How could I not? The weeping in the next room, the doom-laden striking of the ormolu clock, the certain crime in which I had become involved worked on my mind incessantly.

Time passed, the weeping died, then was replaced by wretched, impossible, horrible shrieks of pain, choked and pitiable.

"Mama, oh, Mama, Mama!" Delia cried. I could not just sit there helplessly! But I did.

Four A.M. The deserted hour.

Bronwyn burst through the door. "Hugo, come quickly," she said.

What I encountered in Madam Restell's examination room will stay with me for the rest of my life.

Restell, in a gore-streaked surgeon's apron. Delia only semiconscious, her legs splayed under a stained sheet and flopping pathetically whenever they were repositioned. Edna Croker standing alongside the abortionist, her eyeglasses splattered with flecks of blood.

From some dim recess, I summoned up the memory that Edna volunteered as a nurse, and she seemed to be steady and stoic, holding up better than even the grim, worried Restell. I feared for Edna, though, thinking that another trip to the rest home might be in store for her.

Bronwyn stood at the head of the table, holding tight to one of Delia's bloodless hands, whispering desperate soothings into the girl's unhearing ear.

"She's bleeding out," Restell said to me. "You're a medical student, they tell me. Can you do anything?"

Four A.M. The desperate hour.

Yes, I tried. Edna and I tried. I attempted to locate and stanch the bleeding at its source, but it kept coming, not pulsing, not arterial at least, but venous, a slow draining-away of life. Finally, after I packed her wounded uterus with a tamponade of gauze, she stabilized.

At dawn, as the light rose . . . well, you really couldn't call it a rally, but Delia came around sufficiently to be able to talk.

"I want to go home," she whispered. "I want my mama."

"You can't be moved, darling," Bronwyn said.

Madam Restell was frantic not to have the dying girl there. "A litter, a closed coach," she said. "We have done it often before."

"No, no," said Delia. "I can walk."

We did get the poor patient to her family's Twenty-eighth Street brownstone, Edna acting as friend and nurse, smoothing the way for Delia, holding her up for the few steps from hired coach to home.

Halting briefly at the Showalter back door—the servants' entrance, I noticed, less public that way—the sick, ruined girl turned and gave a wave and an ashen, uncertain smile, then disappeared inside.

Dawn after a big rain. The city washed fresh and clean. Ice and coal wagons on the street. The sidewalks just starting to become peopled. Bronwyn and I proceeded by hansom cab from Twenty-eighth north up Fifth toward Swoony's. I tied my mount on behind. Inside the cab we were largely silent.

Hugely silent. The kind of silent filled with empty words. I had a lot to say to her, but none of it mattered.

Instead, after a few blocks, when we reached Thirty-fourth Street or so, she began to talk. "Nothing in her life prepared her for any of this," Bronwyn said.

Delia.

"Her mother counseled her, but only delicately. The needs of her future husband. Her mother said to open her heart to her spouse, don't smother him, physicality is not wrong, nor is it paramount. Delia hoped fervently that she would make a good wife. But she was a girl sent out into the world without defenses."

"Please," I said. "I'm not sure I can bear it."

A blow, another blow, then one more.

"Beverly Willets wrestled her down in a closed carriage on a cold night last February. He parked on an empty street at the far western edge of town, by the docks. He held her hard by the neck, squashing her windpipe while unbuttoning his trousers. She had no way of responding, it was so far out of her ken. She was strong, you just saw in there how strong she is, but she wasn't raised to fight. And the man she thought was her friend simply outmuscled her."

Stupid fool. All I could think. Not about Bev—there were harsher judgments reserved for him—but about myself. I had been foolish in regard to Delia. Not realizing that by jettisoning her I had made her vulnerable to any predator who happened by.

"Afterward she straightened herself and he walked her into her family's home, the perfect gentleman."

"I want to kill the man," I said.

"I have, too, ever since I finally heard the whole confessed truth from Delia," Bronwyn said. "But of course the coward has fled town."

"How did you get involved?" I asked. "Surely there were others who could have helped her."

"Who? Do you really think this is rare, Hugo? A girl spoiled? Come along with me and the Crushed Daisy Alliance some night, see how common it is. What's rare is people willing to help instead of condemn."

"Crushed Daisy? Could you possibly have come up with a more ridiculous name?" I said.

"You're avoiding the issue," she said.

"It was you who knew Madam Restell," I said. "You who arranged it. Victoria Woodhull taught you all this."

"Don't worry," she said. "I kept your holy Delegate name out of it."

She saw that the shot hit home and laid her hand on my arm. "I'm sorry," she said. "You were fine in there at the end. Really fine. I felt as though it was a privilege to know you. You saved her life."

I sobbed silently. "She doesn't have a life," I said. "Not anymore."

"Sure she does," Bronwyn said. "Look, Hugo darling, the strong savage the weak. Men brutalize women. What did Restell say? The men are always right, but the women are always wronged. What can you or I do against any of it? This was nothing. This was only doing what had to be done. She will survive."

"I feel like an outlaw," I said.

"Me, too," Bronwyn said. "I think it might be safer for us right now if we did what outlaws tend to do."

"What's that?"

"Leave town."

Not right away, she said. That might arouse suspicion. The Showalters would be as anxious as we were to conceal the truth of what had happened. But given the awareness that Bronwyn had of being stalked continually by the press, it might be better simply to leave the field of battle for a while.

"An expedition," she said. "We'll take Nicky to the fair."

I stared at her. After the abattoir of emotion we had just been through, to be able to pronounce that word, "fair." To be able even to think of it. Bronwyn's heart was truly ice. There was indeed a massive world's fair in Philadelphia just then. But how could she suggest a visit?

Against gallows humor nothing measures up so much as a physician's dark brand of sardonic observation. I have witnessed words spoken in an operating theater, the patient lying etherized on the table, that would have carried the poor soul off just to hear. A method of coping, no doubt, but an extreme one.

Around Harvard Medical School the previous term, a doctor's satirical witticism got repeated over and over, passing from student to student as a sort of common reference that demonstrated the cool-hearted knowingness of the teller.

"The operation was entirely successful, but the patient succumbed."

Ah, yes, boys, very funny, that. With Delia Showalter the sentiment came brutally true. We were, in fact, successful in ending her pregnancy. We got her home. Pale to ghostly, complaining of terrible pain, she spoke, walked on her own, even appeared at dinner once, all the time bleeding, seeping into her menstrual rag.

Two nights later, at the hour of sleep, the blank hour, four A.M., the patient succumbed, her heart struck by a clot and stopped like a broken clock.

❧ 27 ❧

Sandobar, poor Sandobar. It would be the last journey we would make in our magical machine.

I thought of Vesalius's drawings in which the skin and skeleton and arterial systems are all stripped away, leaving only the nervous system. That was what was left of Sandobar, that was what was left of me.

The train at least had her still-twitching torso: the parlor car, sleeping compartments for my parents and for Bronwyn, a separate car containing a shared compartment for Colm, Nicky and me. The stoves were cold, though, and the boiler heating system disconnected.

The Lincoln car long gone, reclaimed by Huntington.

We were down to six cars. My father had managed to sell the others at auction in New York, and he had a buyer in Philadelphia for the rest of the consist. We would live on board as we had during our trip from Virginia City. Since the galley was unstaffed, we would order in our meals.

"Why spend money on a hotel?" said Freddy, who had not, in fact, the money to spend on a hotel.

It was hard to say whether we were visiting Philadelphia or escaping New York. The plan was to spend a weekend at the fair, after which my parents and Nicky would sail from there for Europe.

"Our time to the City of Brotherly Lu-uh-uvv: three hours, three minutes, three seconds!" Nicky announced, acting as our bombastic conductor.

If you crave anonymity, the best tactic is to locate the nearest large crowd of people. Philadelphia was putting on the biggest, most lavish fair ever mounted in the United States, the Centennial Exposition of 1876, a party for our country's one-hundredth birthday.

It was the age of exhibitions. Similarly ambitious world's fairs had been held in London, Paris and other international venues. Vienna's, the latest, attracted well over ten million visitors in 1873. Ever eager to tub-thump America's vast superiority, local civic chauvinists wanted our homegrown exposition to outstrip them all.

Bronwyn's erstwhile friends Victoria Woodhull and Tennessee Claflin would be present at the fair, both as scheduled speakers and in a booth, shilling their newspaper. There were over three hundred such exhibit booths, featuring everything from phrenology to new-fangled potato peelers. All in the space of Philadelphia's Fairmount Park.

"Colossal" was the word bandied about in the press.

We shall go to the fair. As spectators or as exhibits? See! The Amazing Delegate Family, oddities, ironies, a collection of freaks and wonders.

As soon as we left Pennsylvania Station and headed south, the deluge began. Another furious downpour, lightning stitched across low thunderclouds, sheets of rain drenching the windows that made it feel as though we were not in a train but in a ship on a gale-beset ocean.

Naturally, Bronwyn and I relived the storm of the tragic night we had just endured. We were chary with each other, I believe that is the word, two bruised people delicately attempting to avoid contact lest we exacerbate our unhealed hurts.

Hard to confess, but I felt sorry for myself. I missed Delia, my childhood sweetheart. I rediscovered her in death as a friend, our early days on Staten Island, a picture in my mind of her and her black-bearded father in his sailboat, just offshore, cutting through the bright green waves of the Lower Bay.

There had been no public funeral. That was how the Showalter family attempted to diminish its disgrace.

I had struggled with my love for Bronwyn, then finally stopped denying it. In reply she had tossed a gauntlet at my feet. You think you love me? See if you can handle this, boyo. And this. And this. A shoot-out at a grand debut? How about a little trip to Madam Restell's? How does your precious love hold up under something like that?

Challenge after challenge, crucible after crucible. Starting anew almost every day. I despaired of ever getting truly close to her.

Ten miles out of Newark, Sandobar was confronted by a flood of storm runoff overflowing the tracks. We halted in the middle of a vast expanse of empty New Jersey marshland, bluebirds flying in the rain, terns passing over in sullen flocks.

"Here we are again," said Anna Maria as brightly as she could. She had the lamps lit in the parlor car even though it was still early morning. They glowed against the outside gray. Nicky lay on the floor, reading his new book, *The Adventures of Tom Sawyer*, exclaiming "Cracking!" every once in a while.

No jolly Sandobar tableau this time. As fat-bellied black clouds rumbled along the horizon, we gathered around the piano in the parlor car and sang sad songs. Anna Maria did a passable version of the Easter aria from Handel, "He Was Despised." Colm sang "Londonderry Air." Nicky, of all people, flattened them both with a thirteen-year-old's reedy-voiced turn on Stephen Foster's "Hard Times Come Again No More."

Bronwyn got up and sang the old tavern ballad "The Weary Whore."

> *The light is dim*
> *As the gold he pays.*
> *She welcomes him*
> *With a weary gaze.*
> *The night has come*
> *Like the one before.*
> *A glass of rum*
> *For the weary whore.*

Standing there, one hand resting on the baby grand, she sang in her pleasantly husky voice. Then, on the chorus, Colm joined her with a harmony tenor.

The weary whore cannot lie down,
Not one time more, not one time more.
The weary whore can't find the peace
That she longs for, that she longs for.

Afterward a cold-meat lunch. The storm-dark afternoon closed around us, the tracks were still blocked, and every other second the interiors of the cars were lit as if by bonfire. An ennui set in, and I dozed.

Dreaming suddenly, seized by her, I woke. She was gone.

"I need to get my drawing materials," I announced, feeling foolish upon realizing that no one cared. I escaped from the parlor car to the front of the train. I passed through our living quarters, knocking lightly on all the doors.

No response. Where could she be?

I made my way up to the locomotive deck. Getting shouted at by Cratchit and thoroughly soaked in the process, I clambered forward onto the sleigh bench above the cowcatcher, where Bronwyn and I had once flown together toward New York.

Nothing.

The yellow swamplands ran on forever, stark and friendless. Impenetrable even in good weather and terrifying when lit by stroboscope lightning.

Coming back, I stopped in Sandobar's baggage compartment to extract my drawing paper and pencils from my kit bag. I was cold and wet and couldn't wait to towel off, but I desired something with which to occupy my mind. There was nothing to do but think, and I didn't want to think.

"I see you," I heard from the corner, a playful, spooky voice. Bronwyn. Her words seemed to emanate from the air. Was I really hearing her, or was it my own sick mind?

"In here," she whispered.

I found her inside the oversize tub that my parents had installed for her back in Virginia City, when they first understood her love for bathing.

I peered over the side. The tub was dry. She sat on the floor of the receptacle, her feet stretched out in front of her. Wearing her artist's gown, the only dress she would put on of late. She had had it with corsets.

"Here," said Bronwyn, patting the floor of the tub beside her.

I climbed over the side but stayed opposite her. I leaned against the copper wall, shivering.

"The parlor car feels so close," she said.

Silence.

"No one knows what to do," I said.

Silence.

Was this what love did to you? Made you stupid and dull?

"I thought I'd draw," I said. "Maybe I could draw you sometime?"

"Now? In the dark?" Gloom had settled in the windowless bath closet.

"I could draw you by lightning flash." Perhaps the dumbest thing I'd ever said to her.

It had been a stormy spring on the East Coast, one of the worst in recent memory. I could hardly make out Bronwyn's face. She was over there in the shadows, probably grinning like the Cheshire Cat.

"I'm so in love with you," I said.

A long, heart-stopping beat. Lightning flashed, and I saw that she was looking right at me. Not smiling.

"Big secret," she said when the blackness fell again. "You've been in love with me . . . well, at least since that evening stroll I took back in Virginia City, when I saw you emptying your stomach behind Costello's Shooting Gallery. A lovely image, I haven't been able to get it out of my head."

My half-strangled feelings. "Are you in love with me?" I asked.

"You can't be in love with me," she said, sounding impatient. "Do you know why?"

"Because I'm my sister?" I said, fumbling up the words.

She laughed. I so much wanted to kiss her, there in the dark.

"I'm not your sister, Hugo," she said solemnly. "You better stop thinking that way, or your Professor James is going to have at you in his psychological laboratory."

I insisted. "Why can't I love you?"

"Oh, because I'm poison," she said. "Didn't I already tell you that? Everybody who loves me dies."

No answer for that. Or an unacceptable one: that I would willingly sacrifice myself for her.

Silence. Paralysis. Three hours, three minutes, three seconds. It was impossible to judge how long we waited.

A sudden insane clatter as Nicky tore through the baggage car, shouting at the top of his lungs like a newsboy. "Extra! Extra! Fierce *Hadrosaurus* dinosaur sighted in the Jersey meadowlands! Read all about it!"

"But I'll tell you what," Bronwyn said, leaning over.

She gave me a long, deep kiss, caressed my face for a moment, then abruptly bounded up in one athletic leap over the lip of the tub and out of the little bath closet, howling along after Nicky.

"*Hadrosaurus* coming!" she shouted.

Leaving me alone in the lightning-streaked dark.

Vesalius has an anatomical drawing where he has stripped away the muscles around the skull, peeling them back and letting them hang. It looks as though the subject's head has exploded.

I floated through the fair. How could it be otherwise? I went to the greatest exposition ever mounted in America, a sprawling, multifold event with untold thousands in attendance, marvels at every turn, and for me the sole attraction stood only a few feet away.

I saw nothing else. I had kissed many women in my life, mock-kissed light women and actresses and ladies of the night, bussed my lady friends in the Circle, but that one on the train with Bronwyn I swore was my first real kiss. I still felt the heat of it.

"You need to fall in love," said Alice James. Or, earlier, when I bemoaned my nervous mental state to my brother, Nicky had said, "You think you're going pots? You're just in love, that's all, you idiot!"

So we attended the fair. I am fairly certain of that, ha-ha. We parked Sandobar on a siding west of the grounds and entered into the Centennial Exposition of 1876.

Freddy and Anna Maria acted as if the whole weight of New York had lifted off them. Nicky, of course, Nicky was over the moon. I was cognizant of the others being there but was really actually wholly oblivious to everyone—the crowds, the performers, my family.

We all got to see something we wanted. Nicky, being the loudest, steered the course first, to the Machinery Hall, where the monstrous Great Corliss Engine, raging with the power of twenty-five hundred horses, hummed like hellfire.

"Sixty-five cars required to transport it from Providence!" Nicky informed us, reading from the official program. He stared slack-jawed at the Krupp Gun. But what he really loved there—although not so much as Colm—was the cone of hot sugar-popped corn sold from a cart near the entrance.

At the Nevada Quartz Mill, Freddy determinedly steered us elsewhere, the memory of his Comstock collapse too raw. The crusher at the mill furnished silver for exposition souvenir coins, an exhibit tout announced, at two dollars apiece.

Anna Maria sighed over the statue of the Freed Slave in Memorial Hall and insisted we spend an hour (it felt like a week) in the Women's Pavilion. Freddy lingered by the manufacturing exhibits. The science of silk was under heavy promotion, it seemed, and he had many questions concerning making a go of silkworms. Perhaps he'd get into the trade himself.

Reinvention. The true American pastime.

He appeared at times like the old Freddy, mercurial and optimistic about all the "marvelous opportunities" that awaited him in the world. But then he would turn away, quiet, with a hollow look about his eyes.

We followed my father to the Turkish Pavilion, where the coffee was "clear as amber, black as ebony." Freddy fell into a seat and somberly fingered a tobacco hookah.

Outside, in the midway, stood the hand holding Liberty's torch, transplanted from Madison Square.

Walking the grounds, Bronwyn enjoyed the sunken gardens with their vivid blooms. I had been thinking of her as the strongest of all girls, but amid the flowers I had a brief appreciation of her fragility. In the Pavilion of the States, she stood before the "oldest doll in America," molded in pure wax, imported to Rhode Island in 1792, with eyelids that still batted. I thought of Bronwyn's own pathetic rag doll, hidden away like a secret in her canvas bag.

Dolls and murder. It seemed both conceivable and inconceivable at the same time.

Freddy and Anna Maria sampled a few glasses of champagne at the French exhibition area. At Nicky's insistence we left them nodding off to an orchestral performance in the Main Building. The four of us—Colm, Nicky, Bronwyn and I—felt less constrained without the parents.

I was aware of my brother only as a vague, buzzing presence, repeating his wish to journey into town on the trolley to see the fossilized *Hadrosaurus* skeleton at the Philadelphia Academy of Natural Sciences. Bronwyn made much of him, and I tried to be affable.

On our way to the Sawyer Observatory tower, reachable by elevator and perched four hundred feet above the Schuylkill River, Bronwyn pulled up short.

"Hugo," she said. Nicky scampered ahead.

She took my arm. "Over there. Isn't that . . . ?"

"Who?" I asked, looking where she gestured.

"The Sage Hen."

Was it her former keeper? Hard to say. The stubby little form made its way along the riverside toward the stockyard at the edge of the grounds, where we had been earlier in the day to see some of Bronwyn's favorite exhibits, the quarter horses and the bulls and buffalo.

"Colm," I said, calling him over from where he walked with Nicky. "See her?"

"That's a familiar figure," he said.

"She's heading on that little path into the woods," I said.

"Let's not catch up," said Bronwyn.

"We'll just see where she goes," I said.

☙ 28 ☙

The path wound down a small incline, at the end of which lay one of the fair's more idiosyncratic attractions, a compound grandly called "The Hunter's Camp in Lansdowne Ravine." Bronwyn and I had wanted to visit earlier but were distracted by Nicky's engine and Freddy's silkworms and Anna Maria's statuary.

We now passed a small sign made of rough-hewn wood, guiding us in the direction of the site. A stream flowed below the bank, and a log cabin, one of its walls left open for display, sat square in front us.

The Sage Hen had vanished.

"Howdy, miss!" called out a handsome mountain man in a skunk-fur cap and an outfit of buckskin and denim.

He stirred a pot over a smoky fire. Behind him, in the half cabin, were arrayed the horns of Rocky Mountain rams, buffalo hides, stuffed mallard ducks. Outside, a knocked-together plank table and a rope hammock that was strung between two trees.

"I've got my little friend over there to help protect the camp," said Mountain Man. Tethered to a stake, a small black bear, about the height of my chest, preoccupied with gorging on a bucket of slops. "Don't you worry, I've got him pretty well trussed."

"What goes on here?" said Colm.

"Well, sometimes we take a ride," he said, motioning with his thumb to a canoe tied up at the bank of the stream. "Other times we sit and whittle."

Bronwyn looked as if she would have liked to move right in, and I suddenly became irritated by the fake young Mountain Man. His buckskin-wrapped muscles.

"What would you like to do?" he asked, coming up beside Bronwyn.

"That," she said, pointing to an animal hide pegged out on the ground and in the process of being tanned.

"The wolf pelt?" he said.

Bronwyn nodded.

"Sure."

Three additional men emerged from behind the cabin. One, shorter and slighter than the others, held a banjo with a collection of small game birds hanging off the neck of it. The other two carried shotguns on their shoulders.

"Hey," said Mountain Man. "My buddies."

Upon seeing us, they tossed aside their irons. Banjo Boy hit it, and Mountain Man produced a jaw harp and began a stomping rhythm. A bandy-legged cowboy creature in chaps and a red-checkered shirt immediately swept Bronwyn up in a dance. One of the others grabbed me, and I found myself jerked forward and back by a smelly slob of a mule skinner.

Nicky choked himself laughing, then ran off to investigate the canoe. Colm raised his hands and stepped back when a third camp character tried to get him into the square dance.

Bronwyn smiled as she spun around with the bandy-legged cowboy. Breathless, they fell aside and stood together over the staked-out wolf pelt.

"We use brains to cure the hide," Mountain Man said, going back into guide mode.

"I know," Bronwyn said.

"Missy," Mountain Man said, eyeing her, "you ain't never cured a wolf pelt in your sweet little life."

"You'd be surprised," Bronwyn said.

Putting his arms around her from the back, the bandy-legged cowboy dancer guided Bronwyn's scraping of the hide.

Colm and I looked at each other, having the same idea at once.

"Maybe I'll stick around here some," Colm said. "Keep an eye on that checker-shirted cowboy, see if he runs into trouble later on tonight."

"It's been known to happen before," I said, watching the two of them.

Nicky ran up, having escaped drowning himself with the canoe. He had gone totally fair-wild, overexcited, red-faced.

"There's a cat head mounted in the cabin," he announced breathlessly. "Its teeth are like razors, and I think it's a Mexican jaguar."

Her hands wet with cow brains, Bronwyn stopped scraping the wolf pelt and shrugged off the bandy-legged cowboy.

"Time to go?" I said.

As we took the little path out of the ravine, a ragged urchin dashed up, thrust a handbill at me and ran off again.

I was about to toss it away unread when Bronwyn stopped me. She took the paper, and we looked at it together.

"The Wild Child of the Washoe!" read the handbill. "In person, revealing all, the scandalous wolf-girl who shocked the world." And, down below, in smaller script, "Professor Dr. Calef Scott's Traveling Spectacle, direct from appearing before the Crowned Heads of Europe!"

The handbill steered us to something called the Street of Wonders, outside the exposition grounds proper, one of the numberless commercial attractions seeking to siphon coins off the free-spending fair-goers.

"Do you think it really can be?" I said.

"Well, that was the Sage Hen we saw earlier," she said. "I was sure of it."

"Let's all go," Nicky said. "It's you onstage!"

"I'm here with you, Nick, I'm not onstage," Bronwyn said. "Get us some lemonade, will you? You look like to drop dead of heatstroke."

He dashed off.

"Let me ask," I said, brandishing the handbill. "Does this make you feel like running the other way or running toward it?"

She shrugged. "The Street of Wonders," she said. "Doesn't that sound worth a look?"

It did, and it was, though the "Street" wasn't actually a street and the "Wonders" weren't all that wonderful. Along a decrepit alleyway inches deep in mud, near the stockyards outside one of the exposition's back entrances, the attractions presented were mostly extremely sad affairs, pigment disorders, misshapen people, accidents of stature.

The Half Lady. The Lion-Faced Boy and His Snake. The Human Owl. I was curious, as an anatomist, about Juan Baptista dos Santos, the Man with Two Penises.

Nicky wanted to see them all.

Most engaging to us, of course, as we approached a sagging canvas banner advertising THE WILD CHILD OF THE WASHOE, was Bronwyn's return to her former milieu. For my part the tension spiraled almost out of control.

But the Savage-Girl-Who-Once-Was remained a cipher. Bronwyn resembled a traveler in time who could see it all from a level distance. Here were the same eager men, the same lurid come-ons, the same handlers who had once dished her up to the world. She responded with no tears, no balking, no spilling out of emotion.

"Have you a veil?" I asked. Given her notoriety from New York, Bronwyn had already been recognized, once or twice, but we had so far managed to avoid a mob scene.

She unraveled a band of black netting around her hat, bringing it down over her face. Nicky helped her position it.

At the entrance to the show, where I expected a Toad, we met a gangly boy in his late teens. "You're too young," he said to Nicky, and to Bronwyn, "We don't admit no women to the afternoon or evening shows, ma'am, but you can come back tomorrow morning."

"Let's leave," I said, thinking I was doing Bronwyn a favor by getting us out of there.

"Run tell Dr. Scott something for me, will you?" Bronwyn said, sweet as butter, smiling at the gangly youth. "Tell him Savage Girl is outside wanting to come in and say hello."

As if under a spell, the youth left his post and trotted through the canvas doorway, but he almost collided with Dr. Scott, bursting out to greet Bronwyn with an immense, beaming smile on his face.

"My dearest, darling girl, you've come back to us!" he exclaimed, seizing her hands in his and kissing her on both cheeks, European style. She stepped back to avoid a full-on embrace.

He lowered his voice. "We've followed your exploits in the East," he said. "Very nicely done, missy."

Then he turned to me. "Young Delegate! The lady's paladin, whisking her away from her livelihood to ever greater fortune in the vast metropolis of Manhattan!"

Again, sotto, his wet lips near to my ear. "Though of late I hear of some reversals. If you wish to borrow a sum, I let out loans at twenty percent."

He gave a formal bow to Nicky. "I have not a doubt this is young Nicholas Delegate. He exhibits the family intelligence, handsome look and, most importantly"—extracting a silver Seated Liberty dime from behind my brother's ear—"their wealth."

A corny trick, but one with a hidden sting, as if a thin dime were all we had left of the family fortune.

I had been unsure of our welcome, and the one that occurred seemed innocuous enough, though beneath the dappled surface of the encounter between Scott and Bronwyn I detected darker eddies and undercurrents. These deepened when the Sage Hen emerged and gave a silent curtsy to Bronwyn.

"The Sage Hen," Bronwyn said in a strained voice. "We saw you this forenoon at the Hunter's Camp, but you were too far away and we lost you in the crowds."

"I weren't never at the Hunter's Camp today, your ladyship," the Sage Hen said.

"Come now, it's me," Bronwyn said. "No need to be so formal."

"Oh, you have rose to 'nother different level than us folks, haven't you?" the Sage Hen said.

Neither Dr. Scott nor I liked the trend of the conversation. "Why don't you see the show? Free of charge, my compliments," Scott said, all false heartiness. "We have a secret box next to the stage, specially rigged for our incognito visitors."

"A stage, you say?" Bronwyn said, taking Dr. Scott's arm and walking in.

"We have left barns long behind," Dr. Scott said.

"And who is your ingenue?"

"You shall see, my dear. Although she shall never rise to your genius, she does a journeyman's service."

Glancing back as we entered, bowing politely to indicate that the Sage Hen should proceed before me and Nicky, I caught a look of pure spite on the older woman's face, staring daggers at Bronwyn. Perhaps this visit had been ill-advised after all. Why would the creature lie about being at Hunter's Camp? And did she not truly love Bronwyn?

Dr. Scott handed us off to the gangly youth, who conducted us to a box, stage right. A screen hid us from the other audience members, who stood restless before the raised and curtained proscenium stage.

The hollow Indian drumbeat began.

"Cast your minds into the blank and trackless emptiness of the Sierra wilderness," Dr. Scott proclaimed. "Savage, wild, forsaken by God and man. Thronged with ferocious packs of bloodthirsty beasts!"

Of the show itself, one need only imagine a pale imitation of the spectacle presented in Virginia City. It resembled Bowery Shakespeare after one's having seen the Royal Company perform in the West End. The exact same lines, but a more impoverished effect.

I contented myself with watching Bronwyn watch the show. She covered Nicky's eyes at the naughty bits. I detected her occasionally mouthing some of the passages in the script. The stick-figure child playing Savage Girl went mechanically through the routine.

The bath was, as before, the true raison d'être of the whole affair. The water level a little lower this time, the steam a little thinner, the breasts more paltry but on more prominent display.

Scott had completely reengineered his third act, quickly sketching out Bronwyn's rise to the top of New York society. Stick-Figure Girl emerged from the wings to trumpets, dressed in a ludicrous costume, a red satin creation that would have had an enraged Bev Willets rushing the stage in protest. Bronwyn merely laughed.

She sobered again, though, at the reenactment of the Fince shooting, displayed to dramatic effect, with a gilt-painted cardboard-cutout carriage standing in for Caroline Hood's Cinderella coach.

The audience enjoyed the shooting, Tu-Li's killing of Fince, the miraculous Lady Lazarus resurrection of the Wild Child. But what the spectators really wanted was to see the girl go back into the bath.

Afterward Scott introduced us briefly to his actress, a dull-eyed, wet-haired waif in a robe. "Hullo," she said without expression, shaking Bronwyn's hand. It was a moment *Harper's Bazar* or *Leslie's Illustrated* would dearly have loved to document, the real Savage Girl and the manquée, meeting there unheralded in the darkness backstage.

The Sage Hen was not present. Leading us out of the tent, Scott again took Bronwyn's arm, intent on claiming his place, it seemed, among the serial parade of her fathers. How many were there? Dan Bowen and Hugh Brace and Sun-Eagle and Dr. Calef Scott and Freddy. Too many.

"May we call on you at Sandobar?" Dr. Scott said to me. "Or perhaps the Fifth Avenue place. You're with your grandmother now, next door to the old mansion, aren't you?"

He seemed to know every detail about us. He was negotiating to bring the show to New York City, he said.

I drew Nicky aside as Bronwyn and Scott said their farewells. It had been decided—I decided—that Colm and I would stay at the exposition while my brother and Bronwyn would return to the train.

"Listen, old man," I said to Nicky. "Keep an eye on the girl for me tonight, will you?"

"Why?" he said suspiciously. "Where are you going?"

"Keep her close on the way to Sandobar and see that she stays in."

"The coochie tents, that's where you're headed," he said.

"Just do as I say, will you?"

"Bronwyn is Becky Thatcher," he said.

Since I hadn't read Mr. Twain's children's book, I didn't know what that meant. Nicky said, "Bronwyn is the kind of girl if you had a genie giving you three wishes, like in the *Thousand and One Nights,* you'd spend all three of them on her."

Bronwyn joined us and, as if overhearing, gave Nicky a reward kiss on the cheek. They immediately marched off together arm in arm, leaving me behind, feeling superfluous.

"Bye," she said, turning around and flashing me a smile.

"He needs to go to the coochie tents," I heard Nicky say to her as they were swallowed up by the crowds surging through the mucky Street of Wonders.

I arrived at the big sycamore at Lansdowne Camp at ten o'clock sharp.

Earlier in the evening, I did in fact visit the coochie tents. Merely as a psychological experiment. I wondered if my newfound status as an in-love person would affect my appreciation of a flesh show, the kind of spectacle that had repeatedly held my attention in the Tenderloin of New York City. As I surmised, I now took only distracted enjoyment from it.

No Colm at the sycamore. The cowboys and mountain men gathered around a campfire in front of the cabin, the fellow with the banjo leading them in a mournful prairie song, a rejiggered version of "The Unfortunate Rake" set on the western plains.

> *Muffle your drums, play your pipes merrily,*
> *Play the death march as you go along.*
> *And fire your guns right over my coffin,*
> *There goes a cowboy lad to his home.*

I was not a long time waiting. In the darkness at the back of Lansdowne Ravine, a muted shout. I became disoriented, blundering around in the underbrush behind the camp. Finally I broke out into a small clearing.

Someone was there. Quietly I drew my blade.

Time went funny, my mind playing tricks. How many minutes passed?

"Colm?" I called out softly. No moon. All was black.

Moving forward, I almost tripped across the supine body of a man. Still warm, but quite dead. Lying on his back, blank eyes pointed at the stars.

Not Colm. I put my hand down to feel the body at the leg. Sopping wet with blood, though the arterial pulsing had ceased.

The dead body, ripped open from the throat to the groin. Viscera trailed out into the blood-mucked dirt. The man's hands rested delicately atop the mess, as if he had been vainly trying to shove his guts back inside his body. He lay almost bisected, his fundamental male attribute missing.

The fury had escalated, victim by victim. This here was on a whole other level.

A gust of emotion took me, and suddenly I was sobbing. "I did not do this," I said, a hoarse whisper to God. "I could not, would not, did not."

Saying those words aloud, I felt suddenly fearful, exposed.

"Colm?" I said again to the darkness. Far off, the tinny campfire song continued.

Over my coffin put handsful of lavender,
Handsful of lavender on every side,
Bunches of roses all over my coffin,
Saying there goes a young cowboy cut down in his prime.

A figure moved against the far cliffside of the ravine. I stumbled forward, my hands wet with blood, hoping it was Colm and knowing, if it was not, that I had the murderer blocked off. There was no way through but past me. I would discover her. It would come to a head here in Lansdowne Ravine.

I wanted to confront her, even if in so doing I would become that man, the one on the ground with his innards pulled out.

The figure danced through the bushes ahead of me like a ghost.

Full night. The darkness felt tangible, a thick woolen blanket that had fallen over the whole landscape. Bracken, brambles and thickets of sumac rose in the back of the cabin, whipping my whole body as I ventured forward, and I held out my arms to shield my face.

Then nothing. Breathing hard, I stopped.

Dead quiet. I had lost her. A long beat of silence.

With an earsplitting female shriek, a figure tackled me from behind, leaping on my back with surprising weight. I fumbled with my own blade and saw a flash of steel, silver-black in the total dark, as the triple razors sang past my face.

I blocked that blow, then another. She stabbed at me, stabbed at me and stabbed at me again, aiming for my leg, and I realized that sooner or later one of the thrusts would get through. I couldn't hold her at bay forever.

Yelling like a madman, Colm Cullen emerged from the darkness, peeling my attacker off. The triple blades sang once again. The figure jabbed at Colm, hitting him hard in the chest. I lunged recklessly with my knife and connected with something, I didn't know what.

Colm fell. Struck by my hand or by the attacker's? The figure turned and fled.

Slipping in the blood coursing from the body of my friend, I collapsed. Colm lay in a groaning heap beside me.

As his lifeblood poured out, he tried to tell me something. "Bron . . . Bron . . ." The word didn't come.

"I'll get help," I said. But I was too late.

ᶓ 29 ᶔ

The sunlit waves of the Atlantic belied my mood. The coastal steamer *Phillip Wheeler* churned its way northward from Philadelphia toward Boston, its deck filled with fun-stunned fairgoers returning from their Centennial Exposition visits. I stayed in the hold with Colm Cullen's casket.

Miraculously, Colm's death had not yet become connected up to the expanding family scandal. TWO DEAD AT FAIR: MURDER IN LANS-DOWNE RAVINE was bad enough as a headline. Adding "Delegate Man Stabbed to Death" as the subhead would bring the press wolves howling.

The other man killed was the bandy-legged cowboy who danced so merrily with Bronwyn, who put his arms around her to scrape the wolf pelt of its bits of flesh. I recalled the stab of jealousy I felt at the time, watching them.

Yellow light slanted into the compartment through twin portholes. But a coffin manages to make gloomy even a pretty day in May. This was my duty, bringing Colm Cullen's body home to his family in Roxbury. I felt like a brother to Colm, a pesky younger brother who had just happened to get him killed.

Fulsome disaster struck my family, but we continued with our lives as if by momentum. Deadbeat poor, we acted as if we were still rich. During the chaotic aftermath of that night in the ravine, when I saw a police official give deference to Freddy, I wanted to shout, "Don't you realize? He's nothing now!"

Everything disordered, everything confused. Anna Maria hurriedly packing for departure, Bronwyn nowhere in evidence. I tried questioning Nicky as to the girl's whereabouts that night but failed to get a straight answer. My parents deserted the field, leaving me to the disposition of Colm's remains.

The waves lapped against the hull. Somewhere to the east, Nicky, Anna Maria and Freddy were on the same ocean aboard a transatlantic steamer, having taken passage to Southampton, England, in a first-class cabin that we could scarcely afford.

Our unhappy family scattered to the winds. We were like Sando-bar's consist—decoupled, shunted aside, parceled off. When we left Philadelphia, we left the proud train behind, to be gutted and sold. I felt more relieved than saddened by the loss. "Every increased posses-sion," says Ruskin, "loads us with new weariness."

Anna Maria had managed to secure a five-thousand-dollar letter of credit from her family in Boston. The Delegates' annual spring so-journ to Europe would be a lot different from, say, the fifty-thousand-dollar tours my parents were accustomed to take.

Fleeing to London would lift them out of the maelstrom of bad publicity in New York. Hunted by the gentlemen of the press—what bitter irony lay couched in that phrase, I had never realized—Anna Maria, Freddy and Nicky slipped out of the country at night like a trio of thieves.

Bronwyn journeyed home on her own, by public commercial rail-road, back to Fifth Avenue and Swoony and her dying mother. I finally concluded that the girl had a deadness around her heart. The chaos of her childhood, the breaking of family ties early on, had left Bronwyn emo-tionally maimed. She reacted with chilling coldness to all developments, including our leave-takings, Delia's tragedy and even Colm's death.

Could that coldness be interspersed with violent, even murderous, outbursts? A terrifying prospect.

I thought about the other examples of feral upbringing. A certain lack of affect was another attribute of the wild child Victor of Avey-ron's tortured existence. The doctors who examined him considered him so mentally damaged from his abandonment in the forest that they judged him unable to feel affection or attachment to others.

As the coffin-carrying coastal steamed north, I went over and over the events of that night in the ravine. All had been darkness and jolt-ing, fragmented, disordered images. I was badly frightened. I hadn't been able to think straight.

A figure in a blousy, shapeless dress, wild black hair. I felt her body upon mine. I even smelled her. I had denied that specific memory at the time, but it was true. Lost amid the chaos, a scent of oranges, fleet-ing but nonetheless there.

And if that were so, then Bronwyn resembled what I had lately feared myself to be, an unhinged individual, two personages stuffed into a single body, one capable of at least acting sane, the other quite mad. Perhaps we had made her so with all our meddling. Dr. Franken-stein and his monster, the creator and the created, two faces in the same mirror.

A girl in halves. It would be an unsurprising result of her tumultu-ous life if she was indeed like that. I ached, mawkish with the tragedy of my love. I had developed deep feelings of attachment for a person unworthy of it. After all that, I wasn't able to give her up. Once more I just felt sorry for myself. And still I loved her.

I couldn't force myself to bring her to justice. The only other choice was to condemn myself. It was I who was the creature in halves. I again went over the events in my mind.

The ravine completely black. I felt the heft of the knife in my hand. A man lay dead. I didn't know what made him dead. Then I myself was attacked. By something with long claws.

I thought of the bear chained at the Mountain Man camp. For a brief moment, I fixed on this possibility. The bear had gotten loose and rampaged through the darkness. First attacking the man on the ground, then me, then Colm.

Of course.

But the explanation did not hold water for long. A bear wearing a dress?

Equally unlikely, Bronwyn, a slight girl, embarked upon a murder-ous rampage.

So it had to be me. I was the killer. The beast on my back was my own insanity, riding me in the guise of Savage Girl. Spurred by some insane fit of mental instability, I had lashed out, first at the cowboy, then at my poor friend. It all sounded pretty unlikely. Even crazy. But I felt that I was, in fact, out of my mind.

The Cullens of Dudley Square in Roxbury summoned up a good hundred mourners for their favorite son's wake. They behaved with surprising kindness to me, the unintentional author of Colm's death. I never detected a hint of blame or anger.

At least I was bringing him back with his manhood intact.

"Shouldn't've never crossed the Muddy," said Colm's grand-uncle, old Pap Mahoney. The Muddy River being the demarcation line of the neighborhood in which Pap Mahoney Cullen himself had passed all his days. Quite a few members of the family demonstrated the same rootedness, professing uncaring ignorance of all aspects of life outside their self-imposed boundaries. They had everything they needed right where they were. Whiskey could be brought in.

As the night progressed, the wake settled into an endurance trial. The songs, the stories, the drunk. Colm Cullen had been a peach, a stalwart, the best man ever to walk the earth. Do you remember the time . . . ? Yeah, Jay-sus, and how about . . . ? The phrase "fookin' died at a fookin' fair" got a thorough airing-out, accompanied by head-shaking wonder at the sad ironies of life.

In the front parlor, the man himself, tight-lipped on ironies, sad or otherwise. Laid out, asleep. He had somehow maintained a stubborn sunburn in the clouded-over East, his sensitive Irish skin, pink-red even in death.

I should have left him where I found him, in the hoist at the Brilliant Mining and Milling Company of Virginia City, Nevada. His example had taught me to speak up, speak straight, but don't speak too much. He saved my life at the end.

My friend Colm really was, really had been, what they said. The best man ever to walk the earth.

While in Boston I again visited with Professor James and his dear sister, Alice, in Cambridge, strolled the brick-accented Yard again, cut

Teddy Roosevelt once more. I thought James might be able to shine a light on what mental disturbances could prompt a girl to murder.

At first I couldn't bring myself to ask. Here I had before me one of the world's most sensitive observers of human psychology, and I held back. Some instinct arose that made me want to shield her secrets.

Instead we spoke about nature versus nurture. When I asked James for his opinion, he said, "My first act of free will is to believe in free will." We are stamped ineradicably by nature, in other words, but after that we are free to make our own way however we can.

Slowly, though, after more conversational sallies and more avoidance, I divulged the outlines of a "special case" that I thought might interest him.

I didn't mention Bronwyn. Rather I spoke again about myself, as a disturbed individual unsure if he had performed unspeakable acts or not. Until suddenly the light broke through and his burden was lifted. Parsing out the circumstances of the latest killing, I suggested it proved at least that I was no longer a suspect in the series of crimes.

"I wouldn't be entirely sure," James said.

"But why?" I asked. "I experienced that attack myself, I felt the real murderer actually leap upon my back."

"I have encountered patients who are certain beyond doubt that they have physically wrestled with a demon of some sorts," James said. "They can even demonstrate bruises, abrasions. So this latest incident might simply be another symptom of an unsettled mind."

Ah, thank you, Professor, for demolishing what small hope I had.

"Consider the act of mutilation, of postmortem castration," James said, ruminating.

"Wouldn't that indicate a female was the assailant?" I said.

"A female, yes," he said. "Or an insanely jealous male."

Looking at me, it seemed, with an accusatory air.

Leaving James much more ill at ease than when I'd arrived, I hesitated over what to do next. Freddy had wired me from London, instructing that I should present myself, while in Boston, at Uncle Ezekiel Saltonstall's countinghouse. For a job.

Like Bartleby, I preferred not to.

Instead I went home to Bronwyn.

It actually felt a shade dangerous, taking up residence with her in Swoony's house. Not because of any physical threat, though there was that. But rather because I caught myself thinking of us as newlyweds, starting out married life together with our aged matriarchs in tow, a mastiff before the hearth and a green-plumed African parrot squawking on its perch.

We could have done anything with ourselves—with each other! There were a dozen empty bedrooms, their canvas-draped mattresses waiting to be uncovered. Swoony and Mallt Bowen were certainly unfit chaperones. One of them dotty and the other immolating before our eyes like a stalled Congreve rocket.

Bronwyn's mother customarily sat in the comfortable corner club chair, handkerchief always in hand. She would often go for hours doing nothing but staring into the distance. She rarely spoke. Occasionally she spit.

Incredible what she looked like. The wasting disease made her increasingly thin, which paradoxically rendered her younger-looking, until she came to resemble her daughter's invalid doppelgänger. She burned up like a candle. We could all see the flame get weaker and weaker.

Swoony persisted in calling Bronwyn "Virginia," Mallt "Anna Maria" and me "Friedrich." Random phrases dominated her conversation. "Never washed in his life" was one. "The floor has a door" was another.

Adjacent to us, a constant reminder of our demise, The Citadel had been taken by the bank as a prelude to sale. Passing through a hall in Swoony's South Wing one afternoon, I noticed Bronwyn standing in front of the now-locked communicating passageway between the two houses.

She motioned me forward. I put my ear to the door next to hers. A woman humming, the whisper of a broom against the floorboards. We never saw anyone enter or leave the next-door château. We avoided it. Now this. Renters? Caretakers?

"I suppose we should go over and introduce ourselves to whoever is in there," Bronwyn said. "Be neighborly, take them a fruitcake or something."

"I don't feel like it," I said.

"Neither do I," Bronwyn said.

Bronwyn and I existed in a suspended, timeless realm. She felt it, I think, as I did. We waited for what was to happen. Two clock springs coiled tight side by side deep within the escapement, anticipating release by the turning of some unknown gear. I could not help but wish she would take up the pastime of kissing me again. But I felt myself caught, unable to get unstuck.

Bronwyn cared for Mallt and Swoony. The butler Mike served us, Swoony's lady Sally dressed her, the cook Nancy prepared our meals, a nurse came in some days, there were two other housemaids besides. We weren't so badly off. Except for everything.

Occasionally, on afternoons when the weather was pleasant, Bronwyn and I went out with the two older women, pushing two wheelchairs around the Zoo. If the day was especially fine, we proceeded on to the Dene, that beautiful landscaped valley running near to the open, sunlit Sheep Meadow. Bronwyn loved the Dene the best, she told me, of all the places in Manhattan.

"If ever you lose me, find me here in the Dene," she said, holding out her arms as though embracing the sunshine.

At the Zoo Bronwyn would do a trick, getting Charlemagne the tigon to follow her back and forth in his run, back and forth. Swoony laughed and clapped. Mallt coughed. It seemed the big cat would do whatever the girl bade him to do. He'd jump out of the enclosure and do a pirouette if she asked.

After a few days of this life, I'd had enough. I wanted somehow to smash the ice between us but could not settle on how to do it.

I tried out various lines. *See here, let's just get married. . . . You and I really ought to be wed, don't you think? . . . What do you say, chuck it all, no ceremony, a quick trip to City Hall and we're man and wife.*

No, no, none of it would do. Earlier she told me to come to her as a man. In the train hadn't I done that? Why couldn't she make a reciprocal move now? As time went on, I felt a slow eroding of my nerve. My faults and weaknesses grew in my imagination until they blotted out the sun. I was inept, lily-livered, a milksop. I stood skinless before her. She could pour herself into me and I would have no defense.

What served to break the impasse appeared in Swoony's wicker call basket on May 19, 1876. A Friday. Of course I will always remember the date well. I had closed myself in my room that afternoon, rehearsing the question I felt sure I would finally be able to pose to Bronwyn.

When I emerged and went downstairs for tea at four, I found the usual tableau of Bronwyn, Mallt and Swoony arranged in the sitting room, my grandmother with her ever-present teacup potion. Three feline females, two aged cats and one more kittenish, lounging on a sleepy afternoon, waiting for their saucers of milk.

The western sun had started to flood in through the parkside windows. For once, Fifth Avenue was still.

"Friedrich, dear," Swoony said. "I want to follow you around." She made no move to rise from her chair to do so.

Idly I examined the cards in Swoony's call basket. Among four others, all impudent climbers, a carte de visite from Bev Willets.

Back in town.

His card had always annoyed me. It was a striking one, well celebrated among the Circle. Bev had pictured himself as an English gentleman about to embark upon a hunt, blunderbuss in hand, eyes fixed on some far-off prey. The costume managed to be fashionable and significant at the same time, as though indicating a questing character in search of truth and honor.

What infuriated me about it was that I knew Bev's hunt to be surely more ignoble than the image. Truth and honor could be well damned. The man limited his quest strictly to the human female. Case in point, Delia Showalter's tragic death.

I wanted to say, *I think I'll just pop downtown and murder Bev Willets.* What I said instead: "Was Bev here today?"

"Yes, he was," Bronwyn said.

"Why wasn't I told?"

"He wanted me," Bronwyn said.

The atmosphere became instantly fraught, Swoony and Mallt both oblivious. I wanted to scream at Bronwyn as I'm sure she wanted to scream at me.

You foul creature!

You're the foul one!

I know you want to go to him!

Maybe I will!

Instead Bronwyn said coolly, "I'm to see him tonight."

"Don't do it," I managed, choking myself off. *I'd rather see you dead!*

I couldn't believe that after everything we knew of Bev's perfidy, she would want to have any truck with him at all. She truly was cold.

"Don't do it," I repeated. "Don't go to him. You don't know what could happen."

She merely gave me a look. Was it pitying? I felt it so. For as long as she and I lived in this world, Bronwyn Delegate—was she Bronwyn Bowen now?—could always stare me down.

When she left Swoony's that evening—not bothering to dress in her usual male guise, a single woman in a dark brown dress, unaccompanied at night, like a common Tenderloin prostitute—I didn't have to follow right on her heels. I knew where she was going.

Before leaving the house, I slipped into Bronwyn's room. I located her sacred childhood bag and checked its contents. The books yes, and the doll and mirror, but the hand-razor rig was gone.

I returned to my study and hurriedly retrieved a Number 20 lancet, sheathing it in a leather case. Dressed informally, I went down to the sitting room and kissed a dozing Swoony good night, nodding good-bye also to the animated skull in the corner, Bronwyn's mother, peering out at me from the furnace within.

Gusts of early-evening rain had previously darkened the streets, but the night was gentle. What had I planned? I didn't know. She would kill him or I would. I was she. She was I. Somehow it would happen. How, I could not predict.

Its being quite possible to walk the length and breadth of Manhattan, I disdained a cab and headed south on foot, crossing over to Lexington from Fifth.

Past the Grand Central Depot. Should I drop all this and board a train? Flee? It was, as Hamlet had it, "a consummation devoutly to be wished." But I declined the option.

Down the island on Lexington, through cluttered, unfashionable neighborhoods, tradesman tenements, the precincts of the poor. Gaslights only at the major intersections, otherwise a spring dark. A drunk staggered across my path, shouted and faded into shadows behind me.

Finally Gramercy Park. There my nerve failed. I made several circuits, stopping each time across the street from the Willets town house. Bronwyn was inside, of that I felt certain. Silhouettes showed on a second-floor window shade.

But I could not force myself to confront her. I even walked down Irving once, to pass by the Lotos Club. Shuttered this time of night but closed to me whatever o'clock it was. I had been blackballed at my club since the scandal hit.

Then I returned to the park, lingering on the bluestone sidewalk beside the spiked iron fence. Waiting to kill a man.

Part Four

The Dene in the Central Park

❧ 30 ❧

I talk to Howe and Hummel through Sunday night. In the Tombs dawn is blocked by the limestone hulk of City Hall to the east, and the prison remains gloomy long after sunrise. They keep placing tea with lemon and honey in front of me. Talk, sip tea, walk over to pee into a chamber pot in the corner, come back, talk some more.

What is the precise disposition of a spider watching a fly struggle in its web? The two lawyers stare at me dolefully.

I want to say, *I have finished my story, for pity's sake. I'm at Bev's the night of May 19. This is where we came in.*

Monday morning. Silence from a chatterbox such as Bill Howe can be supremely unnerving.

So? Is what I finally say. I put my arms out as if for shackles. A joke. Sort of.

No response. Howe uncharacteristically mute.

Then not Howe but Hummel begins to talk, with words that might be more frightening than the other's silence.

That was all just a lie, Hummel says. Rising slowly to stand over me.

I say, You know, sometimes I think I'm telling a tale like Scheherazade. When I stop, I'm dead.

Hummel insists, But you haven't told the truth, have you?

None of this can be used in court, I say. You two just want to hear all the sordid details. People get carried away by the story.

Three hours from now, Hummel says, we will be standing before a judge for your arraignment. You can't bring your lies in there.

We want to help you, Hugo, Bill Howe says, but Hummel shushes him.

You lie when you tell us you killed Bev Willets, Hummel says. We know the girl did it.

You know nothing of the sort, I say.

This whole madness business, Hummel says, being unsure of your own mind, that's just some sort of cheap story.

A tale told by an idiot, I say, signifying nothing.

She did it all, Hummel says, hammering at me. Didn't she, now? Didn't she? Your confession is a ruse. Your knives? A fabrication.

I feel myself already on the witness stand. I told you, I say, the blood, the claws, the severed artery. All my doing.

Liar! Hummel shouts. He is trying to unman me. But even knowing that is what he is trying to do, I still feel a bit unmanned. This is harder than I thought it would be.

Hummel puts his face right into mine. You've been a nasty little boy, haven't you?

I blink.

Haven't you?

All right! Bill Howe says.

Hummel is about to dig at me more, but Howe stops him, calling off his partner, the firm's ghostly attack dog. The corpulent lawyer crosses to look out the window at the enormous sign advertising Howe & Hummel's services. We shall soon enough have to give the prison director back his office, he says.

Howe orders breakfast from one of the scurrying beck-and-call lackeys surrounding him, and for the next hour we speak of nothing except for the food that arrives posthaste in enormous quantities.

I surprise myself to discover a healthy appetite. Howe, of course, tucks in. Hummel sips hot water.

No matter what they may believe, no matter what untruths I have told, I feel as though I have put my case convincingly forward.

Sopping up the last bit of gravy with the last bit of corn bread, Howe says, When I am presented with a case, I never ask, What are the charges? I always ask, Who is the judge? Sitting on the bench this morning will be Bowman Harkington, a Democrat. He is a man whom the newspapers will characterize as one ill disposed to look kindly upon a wealthy scion such as yourself.

Formerly wealthy, I say.

Howe looks pained. It is the wrong thing to bring up, inadvertently reminding him that my father's long purse had recently been rendered considerably shorter. He whispers to one of the lackeys, who runs out of the room as if on fire. Off to loot what remains of the Delegate bank accounts, no doubt.

There are certain aspects of Harkington's background, Howe says, that make him preferable to us as the presiding judge over your arraignment, and especially over the hearing for bail. He is a man with whom we have worked in the past and will work again this morning.

Bribable, in other words.

Hummel nods and coughs into his hand. While in the courtroom, Howe continues, you will not speak. You will stand up and sit down as commanded. You are a mere poor player on the stage, but you do neither strut nor fret. You may not understand the proceedings. That doesn't matter.

I recall the last I saw of Bronwyn, the Friday night of Bev's death, three days ago now. I am still determined to save her. At present she could be anywhere in Manhattan. Or riding the transcontinental back to Virginia City. I hope, at least, that she remains safe.

I'm not at all innocent, I say.

Which one of us is? Howe says. You labor under a common misperception of the law. The law does not find you innocent, it merely judges you not guilty. And though you may not believe in your own innocence, in the unlikely event this case comes to trial, you will be proved not guilty. But first we will bail you out from this jail.

Two hours later I am led by a bailiff through the mazelike Tombs and into a courtroom on a lower floor. William Howe's grand prediction of a controlled and tidy judicial process goes off the rails almost at once.

.   .   .   .   .

Nothing demonstrates the awesome power of the firm of Howe & Hummel like the emptiness of Courtroom Four. By some method devious or masterful, they have been able to head off the press from covering the next installment of the Humiliations of the Delegates.

The empty chamber hosts only a few warm bodies. Apart from myself, there are two clerks, a bailiff, a tipstaff, my two lawyers and Judge Harkington, a man who appears to me to be comically unlike a jurist. With hair sprouting in all directions, he seems a hobbledehoy character out of Shakespeare, swallowed by his robes.

I am about to say, *Where did they exhume him?* when the words die in my mouth, as a second bailiff leads another defendant into court.

Bronwyn. In shackles. I had no idea she had been taken.

Her presence momentarily stuns me. Then, leaping to my feet like a stage actor, I call out, We're betrayed! Unthinking, I react, moving to strike the person nearest at hand, Bill Howe. The bailiff behind me wrestles me back into my chair.

Bronwyn is led across the room to take her place at a defendant's table a few feet away, wearing her now-somewhat-tatty brown dress, blood smears visible upon it, her black hair uncombed but that immensely frustrating unruffled expression on her face.

No more the lady, no more the fresh-faced debutante of the last few months.

The return of Savage Girl.

I readily grasp what her presence means, the depth of the lies Howe and Hummel have told me. They let me sit there talking for forty-eight hours straight, spilling all our secrets, but never once in that entire time did they divulge that the law had her in cuffs, too.

At the women's prison on Blackwell's Island, I find out later.

I realize instantly that while I am going to be freed on bond, Bronwyn is to be made a scapegoat.

Freddy. It is my father's doing. The transatlantic telegraph cables must have been buzzing the whole weekend.

Let the girl swing, but save my son.

I still have my suspicions about Bronwyn's activities. But when I see her standing there surrounded by burly jailers, alone and cast out, my fears melt away.

Though all men will set themselves against you, I take your side.

Your Honor, I call out, I wish to discharge these gentlemen and act as my own counsel.

Sit there and be silent, Mr. Delegate, Harkington says.

I insist, I say. My plea is guilty.

Silence! the hairy little judge cries. Shall I have you removed?

Excellence, Bill Howe says, rumbling to his feet, you see a defendant come before you unsettled in mind.

I cast a desperate look over at Bronwyn, who raises her shackled hands and puts a finger to her lips. Something I had not realized before, for all my reading in Spenser and Sir Walter Scott: Distress is exactly what renders the damsel-in-distress beautiful.

With Bronwyn's presence I understand even less how it is that Howe and Hummel have managed to keep a lid on the proceedings. The Wild Child of the Washoe appearing in court on a murder charge? Fresh meat for the jackals of the fourth estate.

I refuse to be silenced. I call out, Why is she shackled and I am not? Why am I represented and she is not?

Remove the defendant, remove the defendant, Harkington says. Straggly white hairs shoot out of his ears like flames.

Your Honor, Your Honor, Bill Howe says.

Hummel leans over, seizes my neck and twists me back into my seat. One more outburst, he hisses, and all your tawdry little secrets will be spilled.

This will take but a moment, Your Honor, Howe says to the judge, your forbearance, please. Harkington sinks back into his robes, momentarily placated.

Plea? Harkington says.

Not guilty, Howe says.

Bail?

A ten-thousand-dollar surety upon the Fifth Avenue mansion of his grandmawmaw, Howe says.

Mr. Newark?

A man rises to speak, a person so colorless I had not noticed him before. The prosecutor.

The state accepts the terms of bail, he says.

Stand, Mr. Delegate, Harkington says.

Howe hauls me to my feet. You may discharge your counsel, as you wish, the judge says. In which case the bond arrangement proposed by Mr. Howe and Mr. Hummel and accepted by the state prosecutor will be voided and you will be thrown into the lowest cell of this prison that I can find for you.

May I speak to my codefendant? I ask.

No, you may not, Judge Harkington says.

I lean toward Bronwyn. If I'm out, I can get you out, I say. If they keep me in, I won't be able to do anything.

Bronwyn gazes back at me, her face a mask.

Harkington erupts, banging his gavel, slapping me with a hundred-dollar contempt-of-court fine.

I'm wrenched back facing forward by the bailiff.

What about her? I say.

As if my words have unleashed the Furies, the courtroom explodes. Dozens upon dozens of reporters, news hacks and magazine writers invade the place at once, shouting, feverish, jockeying for seats. I have never seen a single room so transformed so quickly.

Wild Child, they call. Savage Girl!

Harkington's last few words are lost amid the general disorder. The bailiff leads Bronwyn away, the frantic journalists leaping at her like a pack of pink-skinned dogs. Deprived of their primary prey, they turn on me.

The Point is quiet on a Monday forenoon, though various bottles lie scattered across the sidewalk, dead soldiers left over from the campaigns of the weekend. Leaving the Tombs proved less difficult than losing the trailing newsmen. Bailed out of the prison, I only barely

extract myself from their clutches through means of sequential hansom cabs, by the end of which subterfuge I am out of ready coin.

I proceed to the Tenderloin nightclub, where I suspect that Tu-Li
and the berdache are holed up.

Penniless, hounded and betrayed, feeling bitter and weary, such is
my present status. I am cored out. If someone would bother to ask,
What are you feeling? I would say, I feel hollow. But no one bothers to
ask. Neither do other questions plaguing my mind receive much in
the way of answers.

Why did Howe and Hummel conceal Bronwyn's arrest from
me? For the entire time of my weekend interrogation, she was
lodged in a cell on Blackwell's Island. Yet they failed to mention this
salient fact.

They have shown their true colors. They represent not my interests but Freddy's. I can look for no more help from that quarter. It was
only my own naïveté that made me trust them in the first place.

And Freddy and Anna Maria? They, too, have proved themselves
unworthy. They fled the country, abandoning their children in need.
Then they callously directed their minions to allow Bronwyn to rot in
jail.

Was this really all my father's doing? Did my mother actively aid
and abet or merely stand by? Either way I judge her culpable. Why
would she turn on the former object of her maternal affection?

Save the son, sacrifice the daughter. Adults, I have noticed, often
behave like cowards.

Then again, Howe and Hummel did manage to roll away the stone
from the Tombs. I have risen again. Not many men emerge clean
from the Halls of Justice. To that degree my lawyers have served my
ends, since I believe that only in freedom can I work to understand the
series of killings that have followed me and Bronwyn step for step, like
trailing hellhounds.

But that thought only leads to another. Why have I thrown my lot
in with Bronwyn? Everything indicates she actually belongs in jail.
She is some sort of madwoman. I still feel the weight of her attack that

night in the ravine. I still blame her for the death of Colm. If she is a murderer, why would I want to free her?

Yet upon gaining liberty I go directly from the Tombs to The Point, seeking out her two truest partisans.

I think about my conclusion early on that Bronwyn is never a prisoner and always is where she is only by choice. Could she have allowed herself to be captured and prosecuted for Bev's murder out of some perverse strategy that is beyond my comprehension? Is she playing some high-level game?

Yes, I am penniless, hounded and betrayed, searching for allies among two former friends who now ostracize me. I climb the purple-painted stairs of the Tenderloin brownstone and push open the door of The Point.

In the harsh reality of morning, saloons and dance halls so gay just hours before display themselves shorn of ersatz nocturnal glamour, cold, bled out, a faint odor of excess left hanging over their interiors.

Thus it is with The Point. Its lurid paintings and exotic furnishings by the light of day appear merely silly. The tonsured apothecary behind the bar, tending to his bottles and potions, is stripped of his nighttime authority.

We're closed, the barkeep says, not turning around. He adds mysteriously, Deliveries go through the hole.

I'm trying to find Tahktoo, I say.

He does look at me then, and I see the light of recognition in his eyes. Young Mr. Delegate, he says. This is a clear violation of the sacred anonymity of the Tenderloin, but I let it pass.

Tahktoo? I say. Do you know where he is?

The Zuni Queen of the Night resides in an apartment upstairs, he says. But she doesn't want to see you. And like I say, we're closed.

Normally I would extract a bill from my pocket, wave it under the good man's nose and obtain entry. But I have no bill to wave.

Please, I say. I am penniless, the news hacks hound me, I am betrayed by my lawyers. I need to speak with my friend.

Ho! he says. Speaking only for myself, it is good to see a high-and-mighty Delegate brought low. Say that word again.

Which?

That first word.

Please, I say, wondering what I have done to make this man hate me.

Please, what?

Please, sir.

He stomps his foot heavily behind the bar. A creature emerges, popping up from the basement below, some sort of subterranean midget employee. One of Swoony's nonce phrases occurs to me: The floor has a door. The barkeep whispers to the midget, who looks over at me and scampers up the flight of stairs at the rear of the establishment.

I wait.

How do you like it? the barkeep asks.

What?

Disgrace.

Bitter as salt, I say.

Welcome to our world, he says.

The midget—through bleary eyes I realize it is merely an extremely dirty young boy—appears at the top of the stairs, beckons and leads me up four flights to the garret. At the top of a steep, narrow staircase stand the berdache and Tu-Li.

Wait, Tahktoo calls down to me.

We only want to see you if you have given up your wrongheaded ideas, Tu-Li says.

Is she guiltless? the berdache asks.

Colm Cullen is dead, I say.

Do you believe her guiltless? Tahktoo repeats, insistent.

Just this morning, I say, not two hours ago, I saw the blood of Beverly Willets on her dress.

They do not respond, staring down at me like the gods from Olympus. Tu-Li makes a motion with her hand, and the midget boy pulls on my sleeve, trying to lead me away.

All right, I say.

Say it, Tahktoo says.

She is innocent, I say, suddenly realizing that I actually accept it as true, despite the night in the ravine, despite what my own eyes have seen, despite all the evidence to the contrary. I am as though a believer, witnessing the blood flow from the relic, the tears on the cheeks of the statue.

Come up, you fool, Tahktoo says, and Tu-Li laughs.

As I start to climb the steep little stairway, my head goes dizzy and I fall backward onto the midget child. Although I almost immediately recover my senses, Tu-Li and the berdache put me to bed on a pallet in their tiny garret chambers, where I sleep like the dead for six hours.

Someone plays a tinkly piano downstairs when I wake in the garret of The Point, a strange bouncy tune of a type I have never heard before. I am alone. The room is thick with afternoon heat. The scent of opium seems to emanate directly from the walls.

The faint click-click of gambling tiles. I find Tu-Li and the berdache right outside my door, in a cramped sitting room, a made-over stair landing, really, that barely affords them space to play their game.

How do you feel? Tu-Li asks.

Rocky, I say.

Come and sit, Tahktoo says. We'll speak of things that matter.

Everything I know is wrong, they tell me. We talk over strong coffee, and I come to understand how my suspicions of Bronwyn are viewed by the two of them as a deep betrayal that renders me unfit for association.

It was either Bronwyn or the Delegates, Tu-Li says. We made our choice.

The blood I saw on Bronwyn's dress, they say, could have gotten there when she grappled with Bev's real killer. Which real killer? They neglect to say. But I suddenly recall that I also had bloodstains on my clothes that night.

If Tu-Li and the berdache saw the girl standing with red-smeared hand claws over a dead body, they would still believe her innocent. Such is their unconditional love for their darling.

I do my best to convince them of my allegiance to Bronwyn. I feel as though I am being accepted into some obscure religious sect.

We air it out, all of it, analyzing every event starting at the Comstock and through to the Philadelphia fair, always with the proviso that Savage Girl is somehow, in some invisible, unimaginable way, wholly blameless.

It is difficult to do. Logic suffers. I feel myself being bent into a pretzel. I go along, but I still harbor doubts.

She acts uncomfortable around me, I say.

You did something to her, Tu-Li says. You know how she has only a few memories from childhood?

Before the Comanches, the berdache says.

Yes? I say.

Well, you walked into one of them, Tu-Li says. She remembers, back when she was three or four, her mother talking about a little fleck she has in her left eye. Her mama says to her, "The first man who notices that spot, him you shall marry."

I can't quite believe it. But thinking back, I can precisely date the start of her increased skittishness around me, the time when I, blabbering like an idiot, mentioned the maculation in her eye.

This is a revelation.

So it's fate. We are meant for each other.

Tu-Li says, We can't believe after all this time that we know her better than you do.

But she loves no one except herself, I say.

The berdache erupts with a deep, snorting guffaw, and Tu-Li and I both look at him.

You know very well the one she loves, he says.

Bad luck to tell it out loud, Tu-Li says quickly.

Who understands both sides of the human heart better than me? the berdache says.

I don't wholly grasp what they're talking about until much later. It's like I won't let myself know. But something makes the blood run to my face.

As upset as the two of them are that I could ever have suspected their dear Bronwyn capable of violence, we are still able to make a deal. We begin to scheme and plot. We are three now.

Three against the world, I say.

Four, the berdache says.

Nicky is out of commission, I say. A prisoner of war. In England.

Then it will have to be three, says Tahktoo.

Briefly I consider hiding out with Tu-Li and the berdache at The Point but decide I'll just have to brave the press gauntlet at Swoony's.

So I head home.

Tu-Li has refreshed my pockets with a little cash, but I choose to walk, even though I still feel the old wound in my foot from the night of the debut. The pain I find pleasurable. It is a fine spring evening.

North and east, a crinkum-crankum route out of the Tenderloin, then passing by the Showalter brownstone, dropping a card to pay my respects. Up Fifth Avenue to the northern edge of town, a half-rural realm where only a few lonely outposts exist. Madam Restell's mansion, mired in shadow.

In the Fifties, as I approach the park, I pick up a ragtag gang of street children, who somehow recognize me.

Delegate-smell-a-rat! they shout. One of them has a kid goat on a dirty string tether. Such is my escort home.

A different sort of welcoming committee camps out in front of Swoony's. With torches. I am buffeted and blocked on my way into the place, fearing for my life and saved only by Mike the butler, who opens the front door to pull me inside. He must shove newspapermen aside to reclose it.

Mr. Hugo, the man says, as if I have just stepped in from a walk around the park. You will find Mrs. Delegate and Mrs. Bowen in the downstairs sitting room.

I want to say, *Where else would they be?* But don't.

I enter to Swoony and Mallt. Friedrich! Swoony calls out cheerily. Bronwyn's mother has sunk deeper into herself even in the space of the three days I have been gone. Her white handkerchief has turned a rust red.

I neglect to tell the two crones of my weekend adventures. A mutilation murder, a trip to the Tombs, a court appearance, bail. Why bother them with that? They have their own mortality in mind.

Instead I join Swoony for a cup, or two, of brandy. The scene resolves itself into an unreal domestic tableau. Rags makes herself a hassock beneath my feet. From the walls glower the succession of Delegate ancestors, gilt-framed chiaroscuro portraits that follow Swoony to Newport or New York City, wherever she happens to reside. I cannot imagine that any of the august personages who have stared sternly down at me since I was a child ever found themselves in worse straits than I do now.

Virginia is here, Swoony says.

Ah, I say.

I don't say, *She is in jail on Blackwell's.* I don't say, *She is imprisoned because of the fecklessness of your blackguard son, my coward father, Freddy.* I don't say, *Your addled mind mistakes even her proper name.*

Virginia has been taking care of us, hasn't she, Anna Maria? says Swoony.

Mallt doesn't respond. Evidently she can't handle even the simplest question. Her red-lidded eyes no longer burn, only smolder. I wonder if she has in fact expired.

Grandmother prattles on. She comes at night, Swoony says. You know I have trouble sleeping. The floor has a door.

Yes, I think. Yes, it does. Whenever you believe you have reached bottom, the floor has a door that will drop you lower.

I think I will go up, I say. Good night, Grandmother. Good night, Mrs. Bowen.

Tell Virginia to come down and talk to us, Swoony says.

Good night, says Bronwyn's mother, a whisper from the grave. I head to my room with the sound of her cough trailing me.

I make my way up the darkened stairs to the second floor, thinking to take out my sketchbook, my usual refuge in times of trouble. I pace along the gloomy corridor, and see . . . something.

In the skein of dark that hangs over the hallway, I catch a quick glimpse of a disappearing figure. A girl with long dark hair. But Bronwyn can't be here.

I blink back my fatigue and enter my room. Swoony's fantasies have invaded my mind. Attempting to draw, I doze over my sketchbook. But Bronwyn pries herself into my dreams, too, a bare-breasted Amazon who walks alongside a tigon.

❧ 31 ❧

The next morning, Tuesday, I venture to the front door, Mike beside me wielding a cosh.

Ready? I say. He nods. I step out onto the front stoop.

This early the newsman scrum has thinned. A preacher stands across the avenue, Bible open, ranting volubly. He somehow resembles a sober version of the Stone-Thrower. Then I realize it *is* the Stone-Thrower, Kleinschmidt, who has evidently found his true calling.

I think about crossing the street to greet the man, perhaps to suggest a text for a homily, something about not casting the first stone. But instead I motion over one of the newsmen, a tall, skinny, bespectacled fellow by the name of Wick Zinder. A leading light of James Gordon Bennett's *New York Herald*, he reports on the "serious" scandals, meaning the ones involving a lot of money.

It turns out I didn't need to summon him—he was heading my way on his own, along with several straggling reporters.

Can you give me a few words? Wick Zinder says. Like a lot of tall guys, he slouches.

Sure, I say. Come along inside.

Really?

Just you, I say. Come up, you fool, and make it fast.

The journalists begin to crowd in front of the door. Mike the butler brandishes his blackjack.

My photographer? Zinder says.

The two of them squeeze in, Zinder's unintroduced confederate hauling an immense wooden box camera. Mike beats back the rest of the rabble and slams shut the door.

I ask the two newsmen into the parlor. It has the smell of a sick-
room. The nurse is there with Mrs. Bowen and Swoony, still in her
pre-first-teacup funk.

This is my grandmother, Mrs. August Delegate, I say. This is Bronwyn's mother, Mrs. Dan Bowen.

Zinder has the stunned look of someone who cannot believe his
good luck. He already brandishes his little palm-size notebook and is
inhaling the room, scribbling furiously.

Have a seat, I say.

What . . . what . . . what . . . ? Wick Zinder stutters. I have a feeling he's not a man often at a loss for words.

Why me? he finally manages.

I like your work, I say. The man inflates like a swamp bullfrog,
and—I can't believe it—he actually writes this down.

I feel as though the true story is not getting out to the public, I say.
And I have an announcement.

His man sets up the camera in front of Mrs. Bowen. No need to
caution her to sit still for the exposure. Mike the butler enters with tea
and, to the delight of his mistress, teacups.

Your announcement? Wick Zinder says, prompting me.

Bronwyn Bowen will once again become Bronwyn Delegate, I say.
We will be married as soon as she is released from Blackwell's. Truth
be told, we are already married in our souls. The ceremony will just
be a formality.

Mrs. Bowen jerks awake, ruining the exposure.

I give Zinder a good half hour, the pages of his notebook flipping
like leaves in the wind. I tell him "everything." What my family thinks
of the match. Our deep feelings for each other. I am she and she is I.
How our marriage is step one in the rehabilitation of the Wild Child
of the Washoe. That the murder charges against her will be resolved.
A starry fabrication about our first kiss.

She is mine forever, I say. We will marry, even if the ceremony has
to happen in the Tombs.

I lay it on thick.

What I don't say, because Tu-Li and the berdache would have ex-

communicated me if I had, is that somewhere deep inside I still suspect that Bronwyn is a killer. If not her, who?

That afternoon a *Herald* special edition, headlined DELEGATE
SPEAKS. On page three a nice engraving of Bronwyn's mother, taken
from the photograph, and one of Swoony and myself, posed in front of
an oil portrait of my great-grandfather Stephen.

That night strange sounds in the household, the patter of footsteps
upstairs.

I am occupied in the front parlor, assisting Mallt Bowen in her efforts to shuffle off the mortal coil. She finally does so at the stroke of
midnight, in the presence of Swoony, the nurse and a minister from
Grace Church. Her portrait in the *Herald* that day acts as her last and
only one, the process of taking it probably helping her death along.

The next morning, the undertaker lays the old woman out, the
shroud-draped dining-room table serving for a bier. An exclusive set of
mourners, my grandmother's last few household servants, pass in be-
reavement. Swoony, under the mistaken belief that her daughter-in-
law, Anna Maria, has died, spends the day in a haze of tears and brandy.

I make sure the press knows about the burial service, scheduled for
Green-Wood Cemetery in Brooklyn. For the rest of the day, I immerse
myself in furious consultations with Tu-Li and the berdache. We send
a black dress of mourning over to Blackwell's Island prison. Tu-Li
stands in for Bronwyn during the fitting at Richardson's, since the two
of them happen to be of the same stature.

On credit we purchase an identical gown for Tu-Li and, to prevent
sulking, one for the berdache, too. All in silk crepe, full widow's
weeds, plain collar, nine-inch weepers cuffs made of white lawn, a
bombazine mantle, a cloak of Henrietta cloth, the bonnet's veil made
of gummed, tightly wound silk threads. Supple kidskin gloves and a
cambric handkerchief.

I am conscious, during the process, of making fashion choices that
would have done Bev Willets proud.

Tu-Li and the berdache have returned to live with us. By evening

Swoony has cheered up, working her teacup and playing the Chinese tile game with them. She has welcomed the two into her home primarily as gambling partners. The old woman has curious gaps in her senility. She can't remember the day of the week but is still a demon at cards and tiles.

By messenger boy from Blackwell's Island (I recognize the dirty midget child of The Point), we confirm our expectation. Bronwyn is to be allowed to attend her mother's burial in the custody of a special contingent of matrons and guards. I think of the girl's cold heart. Does she mourn her mother's passing? Is she weeping, alone in her cell?

Helped along by a thin slice of Tu-Li's opium, I pass out at midnight, troubled only briefly by swirling images of Bronwyn, jaguars, veins of gleaming silver deep within their beds of blue muck. The late Mallt Bowen appears to me also, floating in midair, then slowly crumbling into ash.

At ten o'clock the next morning, Thursday, the hearse, drawn by two immense plumed Belgians, pulls up in front of Swoony's. At the same moment, a cable arrives from Nova Scotia. Freddy, Anna Maria and Nicky, a day out from New York. I'm not sure what reception I will give, at least to my parents, when they arrive. At any rate they will miss the funeral.

We make a motley company, Swoony, Tu-Li, the berdache and myself in one black carriage, following along after the hearse, with about fifty newsmen, gawkers and fire-and-brimstone preachers tagging behind. The procession swells in number on the long trip downtown, some of the late-joining mourners treating the event more in the way of a festival. Through a teeming neighborhood of gasworks, tenements, rendering yards, warehouses, the city's viscera, to the Brooklyn ferry.

Green-Wood Cemetery, behind only Niagara Falls, is the greatest tourist destination in all of America. People come for carriage rides, for picnics, to view the statuary. Memento mori falls far down on the list as a reason to visit. Please do not refer to Green-Wood as a graveyard, say the docents. It is a Realm of Rest.

On this day, an overcast afternoon by the time we finally get there, all the spectators are eager to have a look at the Wild Child of the Washoe, fully five times famous (for her million-dollar wardrobe, her spectacular debut, her shooting, her bizarre background in the Comstock, her arrest for murder).

The cemetery grounds host a huge, craning crowd of avid spectators. Green-Wood visitors wholly ignorant of the event get swept up in the throng. The gentlemen of the press are relentless, the constabulary overwhelmed. It is perfect chaos.

I see Bronwyn arrive on the wrong side of the open grave, out of position, a matron and two guards escorting her. She takes her place, standing in her dull black dress by her mother's coffin, a weeping veil of crepe covering her face. She could have been anybody. The push and jostle of the mob force the graveside mourners to align and re-align themselves constantly.

A shout rises: Take off your veil! Other voices agree: Remove the veil!

The Grace Church pastor calls out for dignity, in vain. Repeatedly bumped, he almost stumbles into the grave.

Ashes to ashes, yes, yes, let's hurry this along before we have a riot on our hands. The Gospel reading, Matthew 11: "Come unto me, all ye that labor and are heavy laden, and I will give you rest."

Not by choice but by process of elimination, neither Bronwyn nor Swoony being up for it, I present the eulogy. I want to celebrate Mallt Bowen's life, I say, tracing her journey from Wales, to Pennsylvania, to the Comstock, to South America, always on the trail of "the color," as gold is named among its acolytes. I cite her love for her late husband, Dan, for her second husband, Hugh Brace, and for her children, only one of whom survives.

The hymn is taken up by the whole gathering, now over a thousand strong, the voices floating out over the spring-green hills of Brooklyn's city of the dead:

> *A mighty fortress is our God,*
> *A bulwark never failing;*
> *Our helper he, amid the flood*
> *Of mortal ills prevailing.*

Benediction, and out.

Oh, dear, oh, dear, moans Swoony, breaking her tear-streaked silence. Poor Anna Maria.

I get my grandmother away before the crush and before the minor riot that does in fact ensue. Those assembled, newsmen and onlookers alike, verge on panic.

At graveside, bedlam. The police are unprepared.

Two ladies in mourning pass each other, come together, fall apart.

A trample of spectators.

Afterward it is unclear exactly when the switch was made. The news ripples through the crowd, causing a second riot.

The Wild Child of the Washoe has been misplaced.

In her stead, wearing a dress so similar as to be easily mistaken, the prison matrons have erroneously taken charge of a Chinese woman named Tu-Li, also known as, in the popular press of the day, the Dragon Lady.

Bronwyn Bowen, Bronwyn Delegate—whatever is her name, she is nowhere to be found.

She is free and abroad in this city.

The police visit Swoony and me several times that evening. Officers root through the whole house, looking for Bronwyn, several uniformed goons led by a head goon, a detective who cannot detect.

The floor has a door, Swoony informs them.

What does she mean by that? Detective Billy Brevoort asks me. I need my men to examine this door she's always talking about.

It's nothing, I say. The family motto. *Solum fores constegit.* The floor has a door. It has been my experience that a bit of Latin satisfies even the most vigilant curiosity.

The mustachioed copper does indeed back off, although later I see him peering at the floorboards and lifting the corner of a rug or two.

After the police leave, it is just my grandmother, her teacup and me, alone together in the parlor with the evening shadows swelling.

I wonder about the next day, when my parents and brother are expected to arrive back from their aborted European sojourn. To Swoony's surprise, Anna Maria will walk into her mother-in-law's house resurrected in the flesh. I think about gently preparing the way but have no faith that Swoony will remember today's burial, who Anna Maria is or that Mallt has left the scene.

Everything is for Virginia, she says out of nowhere.

All right, I say.

I wonder where Savage Girl might be, right at the moment. The plan was for her to be smuggled into The Point by the berdache and stashed in his garret quarters. The place is accustomed to keeping secrets.

But with Bronwyn you never know. Man makes plans and Bronwyn laughs. She could be on the moon.

Not for the first time, I wish Nicky were around. My brother always knows where the girl is, even if she's not at home, in fact even during that period when she had moved out. It's as if he has some sort of network of adolescent irregulars keeping track of all movements of interest occurring anywhere within the shores of Manhattan Island. He always knows when the circus is in town.

Hey, sprat, where's your sister? I would say on some random afternoon.

She's with Edna Croker at the police stables on the other side of the park, he would say. Or with Anna Maria, at a dress shop. Wherever she might be, he knows it.

His certainty, if not his grasp of the truth, is uncanny.

Restlessness seizes me. I'm newly conscious of the vise that has been pressing in on my brain for a long time now, love and hope on one side, suspicion and dread on the other.

If ever you lose me, find me here. What she said that day in the Dene, the little valley in the Central Park she loves so much.

Impulsively, leaving Swoony to be put to bed by the nurse, I head upstairs to ready myself for a quick excursion into the park. I have to plan carefully. There remains a dogged coterie of newsmen keeping vigil outside Swoony's house even now, lying in wait all night, determined to be first with the story, whatever the story might be.

If I choose simply to walk out the front door, enter the park and head for the Dene, a few of these press sentries will inevitably follow me. In the unlikely event that Bronwyn is there, I will have led them right to her. They will slaughter us.

In The Citadel I could slip out through the stables at the back. Or do as Bronwyn had, scale the back wall of the South Wing. But because I am at Swoony's, I will have to risk a frontal assault, dashing out the Fifth Avenue entrance and hopping into a series of hansom cabs. Shake them off my tail and enter the park by another approach.

I dress in blackest black for the occasion. Then I flop down on my bed and decide it's all for naught. She won't be in the Dene, and I don't necessarily want to meet her there. Not in the dark. It might be not wonderful Bronwyn I encounter but terrifying Savage Girl.

Then, lying there in darkness, listening for the clock chime, I am troubled by the same sort of random sounds I have heard upstairs recently, ratlike scurries, footfalls, a whispery sweeping.

If she wishes, Bronwyn is certainly capable of entering Swoony's house surreptitiously. But I doubt if she would risk a visit. Unless she were compelled by urges too strong to be resisted.

They are hunting her down even now. She needs an enclave, a sanctum, a refuge. I suddenly am certain she has come. I venture out into the darkened hallway.

Light footsteps indeed.

Bronwyn?

What happens next is hard for me to feature. I see a white ghost pass through a locked door. Impossible. Groping my way, I arrive at the wall where the ghost vanished—the closed-off passage that leads from Swoony's residence into The Citadel.

I search by touch in the dark and find that the portal is open a crack. I swing it wide, and it gives way soundlessly.

Everything becomes clear to me then—the late-night sounds, the visits of "Virginia" to Swoony and Mallt, my own visions of a spectral girl in the upstairs hall. Bronwyn has taken up residence next door in The Citadel. Blackwell's is a sieve. She must come and go from the prison like an escape artist.

My eyes acclimate to the dark. A glow in the vicinity of the stairs where The Citadel's North and South wings meet. Poised at the landing, eerie in the downstairs light, a form in a shapeless dress that sweeps the floor, long hair down her back.

Bronwyn! I call out quietly, not wanting to startle her.

She disappears into the rooms of the South Wing.

I follow, quickly and quietly. On the way I pass doors left ajar, scattered possessions, evidence of residence. Has the place been rented? Have squatters moved in?

Who could it be? I try to think. In a flash of understanding, I surmise that Victoria Woodhull and her sister have somehow contrived to lease the place, have installed Bronwyn there and have been working all along to seduce her into their nefarious lives.

Well, no.

A thin layer of dust on the floor of the hall, patterned over with footprints. I venture into Bronwyn's old room. Cobwebs, more dust. But more footprints, too.

In the armoire against the far wall, its doors flung open, I see one of my immense five-gallon glass anatomical specimen jars. Stolen from me somewhere along the way. I cannot quite discern what's inside.

Then I realize.

Male members, swimming in a sea of foul-smelling formaldehyde. A half dozen at least. In a multiplicity of sizes and shapes.

Her trophy case.

Who could witness such a ghoulish collection without physically reacting? I don't faint. But I do feel my scrotum retract protectively into my abdomen.

At the sound of her footsteps, my whole body convulses with fear. Whirling around, I follow the sound through the deserted, dusty house. A ruined, abandoned Citadel. Room after empty room. Finally, at the end of the hallway, I see her pass quickly to the landing at the top of the stairs and descend.

As I follow Bronwyn down the steps to the stairhall, I notice several things at once.

The front door to Fifth Avenue is flung open.

A lamp in the stairhall is lit. It throws a gleam over a figure sitting in a straight-backed chair, knitting.

The Sage Hen wears a startled look on her face as I pass, heading out the front door on the trail of Savage Girl.

No doubt my own face exhibits a matching look of surprise. I force myself to revise my understanding once again. Not the Wood-hulls at all. I have underestimated the depth of Bronwyn's relationship with the Sage Hen. She might be the one she considers her true mother—not Mallt, not Anna Maria, not the Comanche woman Nautda.

Obviously the Sage Hen and Bronwyn have colluded all along, ever since Virginia City. I have always felt a nagging sense of someone watching, lurking, skirting at the edges of our lives. It was no doubt the Sage Hen, monitoring her prize pupil.

I poke my head outside. The newsmen collect themselves around a carriage half a block to the north, parked at the curb across the avenue from Swoony's. Freddy, back already? I can't stop to find out. Bronwyn is already across the street.

I follow her. I am still somewhat hobbled by my wounded foot, sore if I use it too much.

As soon as we enter the park, we leave behind gas jets, light, civilization. A half-moon dances behind the clouds, peeks out, dances back, but we are in Dante's *selva oscura,* the dark, dark forest. Black-headed trees stare down at me.

Midway through our life's journey, I found myself in a dark wood, for the straight way was lost.

How I know for sure it is her: Instead of skirting the Zoo, as any sane pedestrian might do at night, the figure ahead of me plunges directly in among its cages and walkways. A flash of her dress, disappearing next to the pen where the elephant sleeps standing up.

When I emerge onto the gentle southern slopes of the Dene, she is nowhere in sight.

Bronwyn? I call out. Softly, since I don't want the reporters out on the avenue to hear.

For a second, as the moon clears, I see her, twenty yards away, framed against the Willowdell Arch.

Yes, indeed it is Bronwyn, her that I love.

At the end of her right hand gleams the triple-bladed razor claw.

Yes, beauty and terror often bump up against each other. I have dwelled upon that before, in theory anyway. At the moment I have not a moment to dwell.

I turn and hobble away.

She knows the lay of the land better than I do, I think, desperately trying to figure an escape.

I limp west, across the loop drive, out onto the flat pan of the Sheep Meadow. White smudges in the darkness, spring lambs crying out for their mothers. The whole flock is there, settled for the night. My arrival disturbs them to their feet. I back away as though I have violated some peaceful scene.

As I do so, a figure rushes quickly out of the darkness and crashes into me.

I fall, hard.

Through wincing pain I look up to see looming over me not the Bronwyn I know, not a human being even, but some strange raging creature.

Savage Girl transformed. Not she but it.

Straddling me in Bronwyn's loose artist's gown, the beast pummels my face. I try to block the blows, but with astonishing strength it restrains me.

She is mine forever, it sneers. We are going to marry.

In a high-pitched voice, parroting my exact words, from the interview I gave to Wick Zinder.

So it worked, my strategy. The *Herald* story I had planted lured out the beast to attack me. I try and fail to reach into my pocket for my own blade.

Now we will have some fun, Mr. Anatomist. The same sneering tone. What leg do you prefer? Right or left?

My ability to speak has wholly deserted me.

No answer? Then I'll choose.

A wealth of black hair drapes over its face. It fixes the claw more snugly onto its hand and draws a deep slicing incision through the fabric of my trousers, deep into the groin-side flesh of my right leg.

Stop, I plead, childish and unconvincing.

I fall silent because it has made the mortal cut and all I can do is press my hands over the wound to stanch the blood. Woozily, I am aware that I have only a few minutes until my six quarts of red flow out of my body.

The creature rears upright, gloating over me.

I drag myself into a sitting position, reach my forefinger and thumb into the wound and with a strangled shout pull the artery from my leg, stretching it out like a night crawler.

The beast watches me, fascinated in spite of itself. Idiot, it hisses.

I scrabble inside the wound again, feeling myself fading into shock, desperate as the seconds tick away. Again I wrap the other end of the severed femoral around my finger and pull. Spurting like a fountain, it slips from my grip. I grab it again.

Pulling at the two ends of the artery, I attempt to pinch them shut. My hands fumble. My fingers are thumbs.

The beast laughs harshly. The surgeon! it cries.

But I manage, I manage. I tie the two ends off. The arterial gush stops for the moment.

Now the creature raises the claw hand, ready to drive the blades into my chest. I wave it feebly away.

A deep-thunder roar sounds in the darkness. Screaming meadow sheep scatter in all directions.

This beast, this apparition, bloody claw in hand, about to end my life, halts, peering off into the black.

The moon clears again. Across the greensward of the meadow walks a figure from my dream, Bronwyn as Savage Girl, not bare-breasted, all right, but Amazonian, striding purposefully directly toward us. Carrying the diamond-encrusted bow that Nicky had given her.

Beside her walks the black-striped tigon Charlemagne, muscles rippling with a lazy, stretched gait, tail erect and twitching.

Meaning the cat is on the kill.

The Central Park Zoo tigon, uncaged, unleashed by Savage Girl. She commands it as though it were a circus lion.

But if she is there with the animal, then who is my mysterious assailant? Who stands above me with raised claws?

I am petrified, watching the big cat come loping across the lawn.

Will it be drawn by the scent of my blood?

Faster and faster, then blazingly quick, finally leaping through the air, the tigon slams my attacker athwart the chest. I feel the heat of the big mutant cat as it flies past me. I smell its thick musk.

Knocked five feet away by the force of the blow, my attacker sprawls, its cheap wig goes askew, its artist's gown rides up, and I get a good look at its face. A strange twisted creature with slits for eyes and a lipless mouth.

The Toad.

R. T. Flenniken. Bronwyn's keeper in Scott's barn. Clutching his black wig, scrabbling backward to get away, his face a mask of panic.

Ignoring me entirely, the tigon delicately picks up the shrieking little man and carries him off in its jaws, bounding into the woods at the north end of the meadow.

Did he get you? Bronwyn says, running up to me. Meaning the Toad.

It's all right, I say. I tied it off.

She extracts a length of bowstring from her quiver and tourniquets my leg expertly, tightening it until I yell. And faint. I am always fainting.

I wake after what feels like only seconds later. But something is wrong. It is not Bronwyn standing over me but the Sage Hen. She attempts to untie the tourniquet around my leg. Pain overwhelms my whole body.

Stop it, I say. Although the words never make it out of my mouth, dying weakly in my throat.

Where is he? the Sage Hen shouts into my face. Where is my son?

Her son. That would be . . . R. T. Flenniken.

My mind isn't working right. I attempt to address her politely as

Mrs. Flenniken, to ask her to please stop jerking my wounded leg around.

Where's that witch of a wild girl? she says.

She has gone off and left me, I don't have strength to say. She's running with the tigon. Helping it punish your son.

You little shit, the Sage Hen says. We knew you were trouble the first time we laid eyes on you.

Please, Mrs. Flenniken, Mrs. Flenniken, please. Again no words actually see the light of day, or the dark of night, or whatever it is right now.

Far off, the roar of the tigon. The Sage Hen looks up just as her son did, fearful and paralyzed.

An arrow wings in through the night (it is night, yes, I remember now), barely grazing the Sage Hen's scalp. Another, whistling inches past her face, thuds solidly into a tree trunk at the edge of the meadow.

The Sage Hen staggers back and begins to run, to the south, away from the roaring sound, away from the flick of arrows.

The last thing I see is Savage Girl, jogging off lazily in pursuit, wielding her bow like Diana, diamonds sparkling in the moonlight, inflicting cut after near-miss cut on the Sage Hen's tublike body, surgical in her Comanche precision. The two of them disappear into the green meadow dark, pursuer and pursued, getting farther and farther away as my sight dims.

I am left alone. I sure as hell hope Charlie doesn't return.

A cloud obscures the moon.

I faint.

✍ Epilogue ✍

What happens a month later, at the end of June, finally pushes the Wild Child of the Washoe off the front pages of the newspapers. Three hundred U.S. Cavalry soldiers riding under George Armstrong Custer fail in their attempt to fight off a force of eighteen hundred Lakota, Arapahoe and Cheyenne led by Sitting Bull and Crazy Horse.

The hungry public can't get enough details from the Battle of the Little Big Horn. They are tired of Bronwyn Delegate. We are, finally, yesterday's news.

Which is just how we like it.

Mrs. Hugo Delegate sits astride my lap, facing me, wielding a straight razor, giving me a good, close shave.

We are at Sandobar. The house, not the train.

Nothing is more beautiful than summer on Long Island. Blue ocean, white-yellow beach, air so fresh it's like God's own breath on the first day of creation.

Swoony has died, and her death shook a lot of things out. Grandmother left me Sandobar House in her will.

Scritch, scritch, scritch. The razor hugs my jawline.

I like a man with a clean face, Bronwyn says.

When I think about it, I say, Comanche men don't grow beards, do they?

Who am I, Hugo? she asks me, a fierce expression on her face. This is our own private catechism.

I laugh nervously, aware of the blade. Not my sister, I say.

Who?

A Comanche girl.

Yes.

During our honeymoon sojourn on Long Island, she has certainly taken on the look of an Indian girl more than ever. She goes barefoot. Her black braids fall over her shoulders. I have never before seen a woman above the age of sixteen wear braids unless she has them pinned up elaborately in back.

Duende, most definitely duende.

Then again, Bronwyn the Comanche also resembles a bright, fresh young woman in the new style, wearing a flouncy, blue-and-white-striped seaside dress. And bloomers. Yes, I have accepted bloomers into my life. No more crinolines, no more bustle.

As she shaves me, we talk, not for the first time, of the fateful night in the Central Park. We speak of things that matter, as Tahktoo might say.

I ask her, How about the mother? The Sage Hen? The coroner's report didn't mention death by a thousand cuts, via bow and arrow.

She stumbled and fell, Bronwyn says. She ran to the top of the biggest rock outcropping in the park. It was a long drop, but she died fast.

Uh-huh, I say. You didn't give her a little push?

Hold still, she says, wielding the razor, don't talk, this is sharp. Applying the blade to my Adam's apple.

I say, How'd you know Charlie wouldn't go for the sheep in the Sheep Meadow, you know, instead of the Toad?

Man-killer, prefers human meat, she says. Ripped apart some farmers in India.

Then how did you know Charlie wouldn't go for me?

She sits back to appraise her work. Well, that I didn't know, she says. But I figured at least one of you two would survive, Delegate or Flenniken, so either way I'd have a husband.

Missed some, she adds, putting the razor to my throat again.

I'm surprised, I say.

I'm not surprised that you're surprised, she says.

When you went down to Bev's that night, you knew what would happen, didn't you? Flenniken would come and kill Bev.

Flenniken didn't like any competing suitors. Insanely jealous, in fact.

And when, dear Bronwyn, did you realize that?

She turned, picked up a hot towel soaking in the sink behind her and slapped it on my face. He deserved it, didn't he?

Bev, I say, my words muffled.

Yes, Bev, she says. He deserved it if anyone did.

Well, I think, we both have Bev's blood on our hands, don't we? Literally and figuratively.

The events of that dreadful night at the dead man's town house play themselves over in my mind. Greeted at the door by a bland, oblivious Margolis, climbing the stairs in a sort of suspended dream state, knowing where I was going and suspecting what I would find when I got there, entering the blood-soaked study. The killer gone.

I had smeared the red stain on myself, to convince detectives that I was the murderer. Bronwyn got spattered with it, grappling with Flenniken—not in an attempt to stop him from killing Bev but because she knew I was coming and that the Toad would try to kill me.

And the others? I say, taking the hot towel away from my face to look at her.

The others, she says. I didn't even know about some of them. Poor Graham, the groom at The Ditches. I was never sure what was happening until the very end. Until Percy. Everyone I smiled at died.

I used to feel hurt that you never seemed to smile at me.

That was me saving your life. Just like you telling that crazy story about killing people without remembering doing it. What was that?

Preposterous, I know. But it was the only way I could think of to save you.

Silly boy.

So you used Flenniken to kill Bev.

And used Bev to catch Flenniken, she says.

Part of the issue with R. T. Flenniken, it turns out, is that he and his mother, the Sage Hen (real name, Arthuretta Flenniken), were both convinced that Bronwyn had married the son.

It was a bit of stage business that Cal Scott tried out, Bronwyn explains to me. A wedding ceremony. We were going to put it in the show. Ever afterward the Sage Hen and R.T. seriously believed it to be real.

Madness, I say.

Well, yes, Bronwyn says. They were both unwell in the mind. I believe it ran in the family. Like mother, like son. He used to enjoy wearing my dresses.

Did he ever . . . ? I say, letting the thought trail off.

Did he consummate? she says, laughing gaily. What do you think? There was none of that. He couldn't do it. That is why he collected them from those who could.

Good Lord, I say. Lord, Lord.

Bronwyn loves Sandobar House, a cedar-shake beach mansion with generous porches, the whole estate half torn apart by the recurrent hurricanes that hit Long Island. The evening of the first day she spends there, she says, I think this is my favorite place in all the world. You grew up with this?

By a surprising bit of good fortune, we can live anywhere we want. A scrawled codicil to Swoony's will left the contents of her personal safe to one "Virginia Delegate," which was crossed out and rewritten as "Bronwyn Delegate," which was crossed out and rewritten as "Bronwyn Bowen."

Freddy and Anna Maria hired Howe and Hummel to break the will, to no avail. Judge Harkington, who became very fond of Bronwyn during her time inside Blackwell's prison, found for us.

The problem was, though, there was no safe to be found. Grandmother's bank, Guaranty Trust, knew nothing about it. Neither did Mike the butler. No one did. Swoony's house, which Freddy had mortgaged out from under her, was taken away. We looked and looked but couldn't discover a safe anywhere.

During our last week in residence at Swoony's, the furniture largely sold off, the empty shell of a town house nearly barren, Nicky managed to save the day.

Well, I'll miss her, the old bird, I said.

Our parrot? Nicky said.

Swoony, I said.

She willed me her teacup, Nicky said.

He never washed a day in his life, I said, imitating Swoony's nonce phrases. The floor has a door.

The floor does have a door, Nicky said.

Right, I said. I'm sure it does.

Want to see it?

What?

Nicky leads us into Swoony's old ballroom, lifts up a tattered Persian rug and points downward.

A brass-handled door set into the wooden floorboards. Locked.

I wonder if we have an ax left in the house, I say.

Clean-shaven at last (Bronwyn takes her time with her ministrations), I sprawl with her on the dunes above the shore, a warm Atlantic breeze washing over us.

We should ask them to come out and visit, she says.

Who? I say.

She digs me in the ribs. I'm serious, she says. Nicky at least.

Anna Maria and Freddy have moved to one of the new "modern" apartments on Fifty-seventh Street. Omitted in Swoony's will, Freddy has great hopes for a push into refining liquid petroleum, falling in with the Rockefeller cabal. Anna Maria involves herself with children's education. She still keeps a cockatoo.

Swoony's safe contained six hundred thirty gold ingots, worth six million dollars, give or a take a few thousand, figured at the current market price of twenty-five dollars an ounce. The loot was secretly cached beneath the door in the floor, not by Freddy, not by Sonny, but by Grandfather himself, August, the first Delegate to strike it rich.

Well, Bronwyn had said at the time of the discovery, at least it's not silver. I'm sick of silver.

We almost missed it. We could very well have given the house back to the bank with its hidden gold intact. If not for my brother knowing every nook and cranny of the house, the block, the island, the city and I'm sure, eventually, the world.

Nicky himself might now in fact be wealthier than my parents, not from the gold, which passed to Bronwyn, but because he invested some of his childhood inheritance in Bessemer furnace technology, as well as an Irish sweepstakes winner, a horse named Fat Dancer. I know I don't have to worry about my brother. He'll be the first king of America someday.

All right, I say, I'll invite Nicky out in August.

Our best man, Bronwyn says. The least we can do.

Also that fellow Edna's engaged to, I say.

Viscount Boris, Bronwyn says. He'll be entertaining. And I'd like to see Edna with her toes in the waves.

Later still, we ride together along the shore. Two dappled grays, shaggy and unshod, beach horses. I realize all over again that the girl never truly feels herself unless she's on horseback.

The last of the Long Island sunlight drenches the whole scene, with a quality of clarity I recall from my childhood, the numberless waves marching all the way across the sea from Europe, bowing themselves to us, humbly displaying their whitecaps as they reach our shore.

Shall I tell you a story? I ask her.

I've never figured out a way to stop you, she says. We're side by side on the grays, at a slow walk.

When I was young, when this was still Grandfather's estate—

Freddy's father, who died of grief over Sonny.

The one who died of grief. I nod. We would assemble here every Fourth of July holiday, the whole family, and one of our traditions was to provide ourselves with a huge lobster boil. Each year we would do this, until when I was eight or nine—

Hooo, she says, laughing, a nine-year-old Hugo.

—one of my crazy old aunts, Luisa, went in for radical vegetarianism, the whole antivivisectionist movement, further and further every year until she went a little too far.

She objected to the lobsters, Bronwyn guesses.

Exactly, I say.

Well, the poor bugs are boiled alive after all, she says.

Aunt Luisa declared no more Independence Day lobster feasts.

Independence for lobsters, Bronwyn says.

And more than that, I say, she insisted on marshaling the children together, and we went into town and scooped up all the lobsters at the local fishmongers, bought them out—

She was a crazy old *wealthy* aunt.

—and with us hauling the two or three dozen lobsters she managed to buy, Aunt Lou would march us down to the beach, to the stream, right over there, where the rivulet would debouche into the ocean at low tide—

Debouche, Bronwyn says, trying out the word.

—and there, I say, we would release the lobsters into the wild, free them with a little ceremony. Aunt Luisa would make a speech, and the boys, my cousins and I, would collect the pegs from the claws, and my aunt lectured us that a creature caged is an affront to God.

Amen, Bronwyn says.

Only one year, one early morning, the morning after the Fourth, one of those times when we had released the lobsters the evening before, I and Cousin Willie and Tommy Bliss, I don't remember who all, but a few of us were out at dawn to fish the surf.

I have a feeling, Bronwyn says, this isn't going to end well.

Daylight was coming up, I say, and we crossed the little stream down there, where we had given the lobsters their glorious freedom. We found them all dead, torn apart by gulls.

Liberty has its perils, Bronwyn says.

We had been freeing them, year after year, and that stream is freshwater, not salt, so it made them a little sluggish, and easy prey for the gulls. We weren't striking a blow for freedom after all. We'd just been feeding carrion birds that whole time.

Your stories are always so sad, she says.

I lean over and kiss her, tasting the salt and stray grains of sand on her lips, delicious.

We spirit the grays into the surf. Then walk them again, side by side.

She says, Do you think out of all the lobsters that you freed, dozens of them—

Over the years, I say, probably more than a hundred.

—don't you think at least one of them might have made it out to saltwater? Maybe managed to fight off a seagull on the way?

They do have pretty woesome hand claws, I say.

It'd be an old lobster by this time.

A wise old man of the sea, I say.

Could be a female lobster, Bronwyn says.

Could be, I say, laughing. A Comanche she-lobster!

She's out there right now, Bronwyn says, grown into some sort of monster, twenty or thirty pounds. Lobsters live a long time, don't they?

Yes, I say. Yes, I believe they do.

Author's Note

Though this book may have its head in the clouds of fantasy it has its feet planted firmly in fact. Stories of feral children, private transcontinental train travel and a tigon in the Central Park Zoo all are grounded in historical research, as are details of confectionary Fifth Avenue mansions and outlandish French ballgowns. The Hunter's Camp in Lansdowne Ravine was a real attraction at Philadelphia's 1876 Centennial Exposition. The law firm of William Howe and Abraham Hummel deserves a much more thorough airing than is offered here, and luckily two books treat the exploits of these interesting figures in depth: *Scoundrels at Law* by Cait N. Murphy, and an earlier study by Richard H. Rovere. Mark Twain chronicled the brawling atmosphere of silver-rush Virginia City in *Roughing It*. Fans of Alice James will be glad to read further in her diary, from which I drew some pithy Alice-isms.

I would like to extend my thanks to Dr. David J. Jackowe for his help, and recommend his superb *Atlas of Cross Sectional Anatomy and Radiological Imaging* as the real-life model for Hugo Delegate's anatomical drawings. Christy Pennoyer also merits special appreciation for lending me a crucial piece of the narrative puzzle. My wonderful editor, Paul Slovak, has always understood where I am coming from and helped me to get where I am going.

Heartfelt gratitude to those who are always there for me: Peter Zimmerman, Andy Zimmerman, Suzanne Levine, Josefa Mulaire, Bill Tester, Lisa Senauke, Gary Jacobson, Sandra Robishaw, John Bowman, Barbara Feinberg, Bethany Pray, John Donatich, Wendy Owen, Henry Dunow, Medith Phillips, Thomas Phillips. As always, Betty and Steve Zimmerman gave generously of their support and were avid first readers. Maud Reavill—a bit of a wild girl herself—supplied the enthusiasm, ideas and critiques that made *Savage Girl* a better book. And without Gil Reavill there would be no book at all.

Finally, no writer could ever have a better ally than Betsy Lerner. It is to her that this book is dedicated, not only as a sage professional, but also as a long-time friend who has challenged me to live fully and write well.